LAWYERS IN HELL

Perseid Publishing
Paradise Productions LLC
P.O. Box 312, West Hyannisport MA 02672

Lawyers In Hell

May, 2011
This is a work of fiction. All the characters and events portrayed in this book are fictional, and any resemblance to real people or incidents is purely coincidental.

Book Design by Ellie Herring; Cover Design by Sonja Aghabekian
Cover Art: Sebastiano Ricci, Sturz der rebellischen Engel, 1720

ISBN-13: 978-0615490199
ISBN-10: 0615490190

Published in the United States of America

Acknowledgements

Interview with the Devil by Janet Morris and Chris Morris
Tribe of Hell by Janet Morris
The Rapture Elevator by Michael Armstrong
Out of Court Settlement by C. J. Cherryh
Revolutionary Justice by Leo Champion
Tale of a Tail by Nancy Asire
And Injustice For All by Jason Cordova
Measure of a Man by Deborah Koren
The Adjudication of Hetty Green by Allan F. Gilbreath
Plains of Hell by Bruce Durham
The Register by Michael H. Hanson
Island Out of Time by Richard Groller
Appellate Angel by Edward McKeown
With Enemies Like These by David L. Burkhead
The Dark Arts by Kimberly Richardson
Heads You Lose by Michael Z. Williamson
Check and Mate by Bradley H. Sinor
Disclaimer by John Manning
Orientation Day by Sarah Hulcy
Remember, Remember, Hell in November by Larry Atchley, Jr.
Theo Khthonios by Scott Oden
Erra and the Seven by Chris Morris

Related Works:

Heroes in Hell
The Gates of Hell
Rebels in Hell
Kings in Hell
Crusaders in Hell
Legions in Hell
Angels in Hell
Masters in Hell
The Little Helliad
War in Hell
Prophets in Hell
Explorers in Hell

HEROES IN HELL: THE GREATEST SHARED UNIVERSE OF ALL

created by JANET MORRIS *edited by* Janet Morris, Chris Morris

with the diabolical assistance of the damnedest writers in perdition:

Janet Morris • Richard Groller • Nancy Asire • CJ Cherryh • Edward McKeown
Bruce Durham • Michael Armstrong • Allan Gilbreath • Michael H. Hanson
Kimberly Richardson • Deborah Koren • Larry Atchley, Jr. • Sarah Hulcy
David L. Burkhead • Chris Morris • Scott Oden • John Manning
Michael Z. Williamson • Jason Cordova • Leo Champion • Bradley H. Sinor

Table of Contents

LAWYERS IN HELL

Interview with *the* Devil

by

Janet Morris and Chris Morris

Go to Heaven for the climate, Hell for the company.
– Mark Twain

Satan was fuming, literally, when I was escorted into his office on the top floor of New Hell's Hall of Injustice by Marilyn Monroe in a tight red knit dress. Aside from the devil and his desk, the huge place was empty from corbeled, cobwebby rafters to filthy marble floor. The whole office reeked of smoke. Wisps of gray smoke curled upward from his big black leathery wings, his wide maw, and leaked between his glittering fangs. His yellow eyes burned into whatever soul I have left, and hurt.

"Sire, this is William Safire, from the New Hell Times Sinday Magazine," Marilyn breathed throatily. "For your interview." She teetered on red patent leather heels with six-inch spikes toward the son of the morning. "Here is the list of pre-approved questions, YSM."

"That will be all, Marilyn," said Satan in a cultured voice, taking the list between his diamond claws. The list ignited as he held it, crumbling to char in his hand.

Marilyn brushed past me and swished her way out of the office as if I didn't exist. There was no chair for me. I had to stand. On my belt was my mini audio/video recorder; I tapped it. Now we were recording video, against all the rules. How few among the damned souls sent to hell had ever seen the notorious devil, up close and personal? What I did, I did as a public service.

Mephistopheles sat on his desk, not behind it – looking at my crotch, it seemed. His tail lashed. He crossed powerful arms and said, "Safire. I do like the name. Just who were you, again? Before you came here to my domain?"

"I was Richard Nixon's speechwriter. He was an American president, you might recall. 'Nattering nabobs of negativism': that was my work. I wrote that line, sir – for Nixon's vice president.

Later, of course, I was a columnist for the New York Times. And now, for the New Hell Times...."

"'Sire', not 'sir,'" said the devil.

"What does YSM stand for ... Sire?" It was difficult to call anyone 'sire,' but I have interviewed my share of kings and queens and self-styled tyrants. And now, the most dastardly overlord of them all.

"'Your Satanic Majesty.' Can we get to your questions? We have windows to replace in here today."

HSM was using either the editorial 'we,' or the royal 'we,' I didn't quite dare ask which one: I might be the most famous etymologist of the twentieth century, but my interlocutor is *the* devil (from the Middle English *devel,* from Old English *dēofol*, an early Germanic borrowing from the Latin *diabolus*, in turn borrowed from Ancient Greek *diábolos).* "Sire, I've heard those windows always need replacing.... Howard Hughes built this building from Frank Lloyd Wright's design, correct? My readers want to know details like that: what your ... life ... is like."

"Immaterial. No unapproved questions. Get on with it, Safire, or I'll call in some demons to string you from my flagpole and eat your liver for a few hundred years." The devil stretched out his arms and unfurled his black wings. His form suddenly shimmered and shifted and a handsome, steely-eyed man with brush-cut gray hair in a pinstriped suit sat before me. The smell of smoke abated.

"Yes, all right. Well, this interview will be available on Gurgle and every other browser, so your subjects can read it on their phones and PDAs. But no video or audio, as your staff stipulated: just print. I'm required to tell you that. And that I'm recording this conversation – only for accuracy, of course."

"Read it on their what?"

"On their hellphones and Pernicious Demonic Avatars, Sire."

The devil reached behind him and pulled something out of his nether regions: a black-furred winged thing, part cat, part bat, with shiny white fangs. It yowled, swiped at the Father of Lies, sprang to the floor and launched itself straight at me.

Satan lifted a finger and pointed at the leaping bat/cat/leather-winged thing. It burst into a ball of flames in midair and disappeared, leaving only a few ashes drifting to the floor.

"Michael doesn't like you. One wonders why." Steely eyes

looked me up and down once more. "Your questions, Safire. I have a hell of a lot to do."

"Yes, well. Ah ... Prince of Darkness, will you please tell me what it means to the citizens of New Hell that you and all the other lords of hell are being audited by emissaries from on high, coming here to determine whether or not injustice is being fairly dispensed…?"

"'Administered.' Not 'dispensed,'" Satan corrected me. "It means that some in the manifold hells of creation have existences far too cushy. That some of my Devil's Children and my Insecurity Service have been lax. That Nero and Caligula and Sartre and Saddam Hussein and bin Laden and the rest of those perverts will get what's coming to them. That all the hells are about to become more hellish."

"I see. And is there any truth to the rumors that there will be new appeals possible, hearings for those damned who feel they're in hell unjustly?"

"Un*just*ly? You jest." The devil waved a hand toward me and my mini-recorder pinged insistently and began to overheat. I turned it off, foiled in my clever plan to podcast video of Satan in the flesh.

"Sire, what about the story that there's a 'Get Out of Hell Free Card' here somewhere, if one can just find it?"

"It's up my bum," said the Devil. "Do you want to have a look? Come right over here…."

"No, no; that's fine, Sire," I soothed. "Next question: What about the relics: the shrouds and chalices and spears and vials of holy water? Are they real? Can they save a soul? And if they're not, what is your administration going to do about those perpetrating theses hoaxes on so many gullible souls? We've heard the money made on those supposed relics goes straight into your administration's coffers."

"I am not a crook," said the devil, standing abruptly and shimmering again.

I'd heard those words before. I'd written those words before. "Yes, Sire, but I'm certain our readers are anxious to learn how your government proposes to deal with these supposed relics and with the auditors coming from on high. Can you tell us about the auditors? And what, if any, charges have been lodged against you or your various departments? Who will be the counsels defending your administration from accusations of incompetence?"

"'De*fend*ing?' 'In*com*petence?'" Now the devil changed his shape: gone was the handsome bureaucrat. In its place came no winged demonic form: Satan was now a spinning whirlwind of inky blackness that tugged at me as if it would suck me within itself. If you die in hell, you revive in the Mortuary, on the Undertaker's table, usually worse off than you'd been before. "*I* need no defense," came HSM's voice, ringing like hell's bells. "*I* am lord of the greatest hell in human history."

"Yes, of course you don't, YSM," I said hurriedly. "But we have heard that punishments will be meted out to the guilty and innocent alike by these auditors from the higher heavens."

From the lightless void came Satan's voice again: "In hell, Safire, all punishments fit the sins."

"You mean punishments such as George Washington having endless dental implants that don't heal and infect his whole system?"

"Never mind Washington. He got off easy. Cow's teeth and hippopotamus-ivory dentures should have been good enough for him." The spinning black vortex was expanding, the voice ringing excruciatingly in my ears. "I know who you are now, what you're trying to do. You have your interview. And you shall have a new punishment, more appropriate to your crimes. Your life here has been far too easy: you and your subscribers need to learn a thing or two about penance."

The black maw whirled around me and sucked me up and put me down far from the devil's office, far from New Hell itself, among the cactus and the tumbleweeds, in this tattoo parlor from which I'm logging my report. I'll be here quite some time, the Hell's Angels tell me, strapped to this table until the entire Constitution of the United States, including all amendments, is inked into my skin.

Tribe of Hell

by

Janet Morris

Be not too hard for my wits and all the tribe of hell
– William Shakespeare, *Othello*

Kur had been in hell long before the first cast-down gods and their damned worshippers took the fall; he would be here long after the last of them were gone. Kur was born here in Ki-gal, home of the indigenous tribe of hell. Golden-green sulphur tickles his nostrils, billowing down sweet and warm from the mountaintop. He breathes deeper, expanding his mighty chest, rippling the surface of the dark pool where he floats, content. Beneath his backside, tar bubbles pop, massaging his wide-spread wings, his long spiky tail. His red skin is gleaming, dusted with quills, warning all comers of his poisonous bite and his rank, highest among the tribe.

A sudden flurry of motion sets the tar sloshing: little black Eshi has arrived.

"Almighty Kur, I need to know something!" Young Eshi splashed toward him, tail flailing (black tail, black wings, black skin; crimson tongue and sharp white teeth); then clambered atop him, nearly sinking them both.

"You will need to know more than one thing, Eshi, to grow up red and strong. Which particular thing do you most need to know now?" Eshi was his *eromenos*: his protégé, his beloved, his passion and his joy. "Look what you've done, boy: I don't need a tarry front today. Lick me clean – every quill, every hair." Kur stretched his wings wider and the pool's surface calmed.

The black Kigali boy bent his head and began licking Kur's red skin. If Eshi lived to mature, his black skin would turn red as he sprouted quills. Yesterday, that fate had seemed certain. Today, little was certain. Trouble was coming, falling from the heavens.

Young wings, dripping tar, rustled and folded tight. "I need to know who Erra is and why he's coming, and about the Seven, and who they are and why they're coming, and why the tribe is afraid of mere men and gods from the heavens."

"And this is what you most need to know now?"

"I need to know, great Kur, if the others are right. Should I be afraid? You're not afraid…." Eshi shifted, slid, and nuzzled Kur's groin. "See? You're not."

Kur reached for Eshi and brought the boy up into the curve of his strong right arm and the hammock of his wing. "Never listen to rumors, Eshi. Erra … deserves my attention. I always host his kind when they come. No one has come to Ki-gal who wields such power in a very long time. Erra is an ancient god of plague and mayhem, who lays low the mighty and makes politicians weep. And he brings with him the Seven – the *Sibitti* – peerless champions, personified weapons, pitiless and terrifying: sons of heaven and earth. Hell is under audit from on high, and Erra and the Seven shall deliver punishment summarily, as they see fit, where injustice has been unfairly distributed. The Seven destroy guilty and innocent alike when they roam the earth, but in hell there are few innocents – only those of us in the tribe. So the tribe is worried."

Eshi squirmed and kicked his feet, making tarry spume, scrambling for purchase. "So they're right, the tribe, to worry? There is destruction coming? Havoc? Requital? But I'm innocent…. Aren't I?" Glowing eyes implored him.

"Perhaps the tribe is right; perhaps wrong. The future is unknowable. You are with me. You are without quills, having yet to stir your blood with a kill: in that way, you are innocent. It is my honor to succor Erra and the Seven and guide them through hell. I always do so, whenever great powers need lodging and meals and local wisdom. You will meet Erra, and you will help me in my tasks. Now, a little more licking, please, just a bit to the left…. We must look our best when we greet Erra and his Seven on the Downward Road."

*

In the dung pit, two men met with Lysicles to decide the fate of his soul: Draco, lawgiver of Athens, tall and lean with a wooden triangle in his lap and a linen robe belted round him that was gray and long and dirty like his hair and beard; Hammurabi, his inky Babylonian coif oiled and jeweled and his beard resting on his ample paunch, with a pile of stone tablets beside him on which his two hundred and eighty-two laws were inscribed. Facing them sat Lysicles, the supplicant: still the same muscular, war-braided Athenian commander who'd been executed for rashness after his infantry was routed by Philip and Alexander's Macedonians.

Begging tastes bitter. Lysicles was desperate but dared not show it. These two 'old dead' might be his only hope: Draco had set the precedent for Lysicles' downfall long before the soldier was born; Hammurabi had set humanity on the path to endless slaughter with a code of laws that made one man right, another man wrong, and allowed punishments to be inflicted by third parties and levied by a state. These two were the most influential lawmakers in hell: they had made laws that later, lesser men reinterpreted and misapplied. Lysicles had done terrible things to secure this meeting: worse things than had sent him to hell in the first place. While alive, during battle, he had been as innocent as a general could be: those he had killed with his own hand, or with his armies, deserved death with honor and got it. Now he was no longer so innocent. But no one was asking him what he'd done since he'd gotten to hell: only why he thought he deserved to get out of here.

"Eye for eye; tooth for tooth," Hammurabi reminded the other two. "No presumption of innocence is possible when a thousand died following your orders, Lysicles."

"Let Lysicles finish making his case," suggested Draco, who had created the law-code by which the Athenian assembly had duly ruled to execute the general.

"But my commanding officer, Chares, walked away, a free man – exonerated." Exasperated, Lysicles stared at Draco until the other soul lowered his gaze.

"And was he innocent, by the law, this Chares?" Hammurabi asked, twirling an oiled curl of beard in stubby fingers.

"Innocence has little to do with this. Chares had better orators in his pay, making his case," Lysicles said. "I followed my orders to the letter: if I hadn't, I would have deserved to be put to death. And if I was guilty, Chares should have died by my side. If I'm in hell, he should be too. One commander cannot have been wrong and the other right, when the result to our forces was the same."

"How do you know this Chares is not in Hades? In Tartaros? Alexandros has raised a new army: they war as they always have, against other Greeks and Asiatics, until the ground runs red with blood and shades of fighters long dead decide the winner of the day.... Go fight it out again: find your fellows, and go you back to the battlefield." Draco was haughty, cold, and always harshly logical.

"That's not what he wants, you Athenian imbecile. If justice has miscarried here, it is because your laws were too strict, with no humanity applicable. He wants a new trial. The auditors from Above are coming, so it's said. He wants to talk his way into those much-vaunted Elysian Fields of yours, see his lovers again, his wives, his sons.... How many *eromenoi* did you have, Lysicles? That alone, according to *my* law code, could bring you here for infidelity or sexual misconduct." The Babylonian's eyes were sharp in their nests of fat; they pierced Lysicles to the heart.

"Irrelevant," he said, head high. "I did what men do in my culture. Are we judging all souls by all standards? In that case, none would be in heaven, neither men nor gods. All the gods had eromenoi, and wives as well: take a man's son for your lover, send him a fast horse or two; sleep with a man's wife and beget a bastard demigod, give the child immortality in exchange for the human parents' forbearance. And goddesses played the same game with mortal heroes. I –"

"We'll take your case," Draco interrupted, looking past Lysicles and up, where three men were peering at them over the dung pit's rim.

"Crap," said Hammurabi under his breath. "Not them." And, louder: "Yes, Draco and I will appeal your sentence. It is decided: we are the best in hell; we shall win your release if the Seven have souls."

The three newcomers above elbowed each other. The tall, bony-nosed one said, "You don't say? 'The best in hell?'" He wore khakis, motorcycle boots, and had bound a scarf around his head. He looked to be in his late thirties. He assessed Lysicles with a warrior's precision ... and something more.

The short, even prettier one in flashy Macedonian armor put

one hand on his hip and said, "O wise Aristotle, let's help them. At the least we can be character witnesses.... I fought against Lysicles. I know his rage, fierce; his bravery, unquestionable. And my word still means something."

Then Lysicles stiffened where he sat, realizing the identity of this handsome youth. *Bastard. Liar. Fool. Alexander, you little fop, you know no such thing. You fought on the Macedonian left that day, on horseback, behind daddy's crack hoplites, surrounded by daddy's best generals, and never risked a hair of your beautiful head.*

The balding old man in robes said, "Alexandros, you mustn't mix in where you're not wanted." But Aristotle slipped and slithered his sandaled way down into the dung pit and the other two followed. "Shit," said Aristotle when they reached the bottom, hiking up his skirts.

"Best place to meet, if it's something like this," said the tall, pale-eyed man from the legions of the 'new dead.' "Offal's just food and water."

"We know, T.E. Gentlemen, as you heard, I am Aristotle, and I fancy myself a bit of a tutor. This is my student, Alexandros – he tells the truth: he fought in that battle against Chares and Lysicles."

"So ... who's the soldier?" Lysicles asked, pointedly ignoring Alexander and looking past him to the man in khaki.

Alexander frowned. "I'm Alexandros Philippou Macedon, called 'Alexander the Great' by history."

"Not you, Alexandros," Draco said, tapping his wooden triangle on which the laws of Athens were written. "You, tall one – who are you?"

"Thomas Edward Lawrence ... I fought in the desert for queen and country."

"Queen?" Hammurabi wanted to know.

"Queen of England." The newcomers squatted down in the muck, extolling their *curricula vitae*, until Lawrence asked, "Lysicles, do you believe in the Card? Wouldn't it make sense to send out operatives to try to find it, if you want out of hell so much? Although I could show you some places and people that might make you decide this place isn't so bad." Lawrence smirked suggestively.

"Ssh," said Hammurabi with a shake of his curls. "This place is bad enough. Don't tempt the gods."

"Card?" Lysicles asked.

Before the new-dead officer could answer, Draco told Lysicles: "It is said there is a Get Out of Hell Free Card somewhere and whoever finds it … gets out of hell free." Draco snorted. "I wouldn't waste time trying to find it. No one knows what it looks like, so how could you know if you have the real one? It's a cottage industry, buying and selling these so-called cards, along with relics from every age – holy water, shrouds, grails, what have you. Let's get back to the matter at hand: if Lysicles can be saved by anyone, then we're the men to do it."

*

Whenever Erra goes to battle, the world is turned upside down: righteous and unrighteous alike are slaughtered by his terrifying Seven, his Sibitti, the personified weapons of heaven and earth who do his bidding. Everyonc knows this. The strong and the weak are equally afraid. Always.

So why, on the Downward Road to hell, are these damned not cowering? Erra cannot fathom it. All around him are fools staggering toward their just deserts, bleary and wan. New dead and old dead, sinners from every epoch crowd the wide road with disbelieving souls. Some cry and bewail their fate. Some snarl, full of hate. But none make way for Erra and the Seven, on their way to Ki-gal, bumping and jostling through the forlorn and irate.

Then up comes Almighty Kur, red as blood, with a black Kigali boy. Now the crowd parts. Souls make way and skitter back like leaves in a gale.

Seeing this sign of respect for the Kigali but not for them, the Seven are incensed. Slighted. Shimmering in their dusty cowls, promising fury barely under wraps, they wax impatient to unleash their plagues and blades and flames, their torrents and storms and ice, their chasms underfoot. But the Sibitti will wait for his command. He is Erra. He is the wrath of eternity, ready to visit annihilation on gods and men alike.

"Kur, time to begin. We shall cleanse this place, for a start." Behind Erra, his Seven spread out silently across the road, hands on hilts, cowls tossed back: dividing up their targets, each facing a compass point among the throng of victims.

"Erra, well met," Kur says, regarding him narrowly. "I see you have changed out of your divinity and made yourself like a man, ready for battle. These damned are not yet at the gates of hell, but still trekking toward their fate."

"Think you that I care where they are? Or who they are? They need to know their fate is nigh. Fear me, and mine. *Now.*" Above Erra's head, the sky goes dusky and stars, the soldiers of the gods, deploy amid the distant heavens.

Unknowing or uncaring, a knot of newly dead begin a brawl nearby, kicking and screaming and pulling one another's hair. Their curses rend the air.

And the wind picks up those curses and brings them home to each and all.

The first of the Seven draws his shining sword and stabs its tip into the ground: the ground falls away, into a chasm that spreads and cracks the earth under foot until the brawlers tumble into the abyss, screaming and clawing as dirt and sand and rock fall on their heads. The ground closes over them as another chasm opens, chasing after more damned souls, hungry until it catches them and sucks them down. And from that chasm, yet another crack in the earth pursues fleeing souls like a serpent hunting mice. And another. The Seven sidestep the chasms as if they were puddles in the grass.

The Kigali boy spreads his wings and flutters them anxiously, then reaches for Kur's long-nailed hand. "Almighty Kur," says the youngster, "look at them: the Seven. So big, so strong, so fast."

The second of the Sibitti peers over his shoulder, turning his molten gaze on the Kigali youth.

"No," Erra tells his weapon. "Not the boy. Only the damned today."

Then the second of the Seven drops his eyes, frees his sword and lightning splits the air, surrounding men and women, swathed in tight clothing, who clutch at one other. The lightning dances over them, over their faces, over little boxes in their hands, over their belts and shoes and over the clips on their ears. They scream and dance and fall, flaring, blackened into ash, while those around them push and stampede, trampling one another, trying to escape.

"Be very still, Eshi," advises the Almighty Kur, and grips the

Kigali boy's hand tightly. "Move no wing, take no step."

The third of the Seven has a sword of ice and this he waves before his eyes, and breathes upon it. One mighty breath sends the cold into a clutch of folk who turn pale, then white, then blue, then fall crashing to the ground and smash into sparkling shards.

The fourth of the Seven doesn't unsheathe his sword. He points a finger toward three women in the crowd, whose skins turn purple. Boils sprout and break and spout pestilence onto all those around. Wailing folk drop to the ground, retching yellow bile.

The fifth of the Seven points his blade to heaven and his cowl falls away entirely. He is all edges: sharp points and glittering blades sprout from his limbs until he is a juggernaut, a man-high ball of death that rolls and undulates and smites and shreds and slices through the souls who are pushing and shoving at one another, frantic to get away. When that ball of bright death is dripping blood, it stops. A tall man in a dusty cowl emerges from its center, holding just one sword in his hand. All around his legs, piled high, are bodies dead and bodies dying, limbs askew, blood in pools, heads piled upon buttocks, eyes sightless and mouths spewing gore. The fifth steps over the carnage and resumes his position behind Erra.

The sixth moves not one step, but stabs at the dusky vault above. A torrent comes rushing, swirling into a river abruptly roaring along the Downward Road, washing away the blood and the dead and the dying, and those too weak or small to withstand a tide that knows their names and overwhelms them with no regard to whether a flood should be able to reach so high or be so bold … or so selective.

Now the last of the Seven bares his head completely: an heroic form, all muscle, glowing eyes ablaze. Like a cat, he swipes his weapon across the vista: fire breaks out in once-mortal flesh wherever his sword points. Damned bodies, engulfed, hiss and snap like kindling. Howls of agony come from incandescent folk who run hither and yon and set all nearby flesh alight.

The cacophony of the damned is deafening. Those souls remaining upright before Erra on the Downward Road are bleeding or pestilential or charred. Yet they stagger toward one another, away from the chasms and the Sibitti and the gory mud.

Almighty Kur says something to his boy that Erra cannot hear over the din. The wailing of the damned becomes a symphony. Erra throws back his own cowl and makes a sign. The Seven resume their formation behind him, each wrapped once again in dusty raiment: on the faces of his warriors, Erra sees the pride of weapons well deployed.

Beyond Erra and his Seven and the two Kigali, the would-be denizens of the netherworld crowd and push and run wildly (if they can) or limp slowly (if they can) or crawl sobbing (if they can) toward the gates of hell.

When the skirling and the yowling and the counterpoint groaning and praying have subsided, there are none around them on the Downward Road. A crowd waits silently, far behind them, afraid to approach. Before them, the terrorized damned disappear toward their new home.

The boy says, "If they die like this, not in hell yet, not anywhere yet … are they still reborn on the Undertaker's table? Are they resurrected?"

"What do you care, child, about the evil damned?" asks the second of the Seven, the most beautiful of the sons of heaven and earth, and cocks his head and stares again through those molten eyes at the young black Kigali.

"He does not care," Kur says before the boy can answer. "He is here to learn. The young question all. It is their nature."

"Let it be so, then," says Erra, raising his hand from his hip just enough to forefend any strike from his Sibitti against this boy. "Keep him with you, and he will learn what heaven and earth and hell are made of. It shall be our pleasure to show your protégé what the young should see."

"We are here to serve your purpose, Erra," Kur says. "You and the Seven are generous. This I knew. And your message now precedes you into hell. They shall fear your righteous wrath hereafter. They will know you whenever you come: all your plagues, your blades and flames, your floods and storms and ice, your chasms as deep as the underworld itself. Welcome, Erra and the Sibitti, to my realm. And now, perhaps a hot meal and some rest for the deserving…."

Erra saw the Almighty Kur smile down at his boy, who was

rubbing the back of one hand where black skin was pimpled and raw: the first quills of adolescence were beginning to sprout.

*

"Are they demons, these Seven?" Eshi demanded of Kur as they sat amid golden smoke billowing down from the mountaintop, awaiting the appointed time. Below, folk of the tribe strode back and forth until the feast-boards on the flat were bent low with delicacies being laid on by artful hands.

"The Sibitti? Not demons. They are sons of heaven and earth," Kur told him patiently. Eshi yet had the shimmer of the innocent: Kur could see it out of the corner of his eye in the light of heaven's vault burning overhead. But the carnage had awakened the adult in the child, and Eshi was beginning to change: he still rubbed the back of one hand absently with the other; quills, their needle-sharp points plainly visible, were poking their way through his velvety skin.

Seeing the slaughter had stirred Eshi's blood. All too soon, he would be full-grown, a mature Kigali. Then everything would change between them. Would they sit here together then – in a year, a dozen, a hundred, a thousand – as they did now, on the hillock where the sulphur springs bubbled, above the tribe's agora, enjoying the beauty of land and sky, smelling the piquant wind blow down the mountain's slope?

"You told me that before, Kur – that the Sibitti are sons of heaven and earth. But what does that mean?"

"That means they were born of unions between humans and gods; that they have the attributes of both, and allegiance to neither. They are the terrifying Seven, personified weapons in service only to Erra, lord of pestilence and destruction, here to visit retribution and havoc among the damned and their fallen gods."

"These Sibitti destroyed so wantonly. How can they be allowed to do that?"

"Who would stop them, Eshi?"

"You." Eshi looked at him imploringly. *"You* could. You *could."*

"Why would I – or anyone – try to stop them? The damned are not here on holiday, or to make new lives: they are here to suffer the fates they have earned. They live shadow lives here, and die shadow deaths, and are reborn into the torment they deserve – again and again. And keep it clear in your mind: the damned are already dead. You are not. Life is a precious gift to those who have it, and to those who have lost it. Gods and men, banished from heaven and earth, are no friends to the Kigali. The Kigali are no friends to the damned."

"But Erra and the Seven are so cruel…. Are we friends to them?"

"We are the Kigali. We live here. We lived here before any of them came; we will live here when they're gone. We tolerate the presence of the downcast gods and their damned among us. We cooperate with those who rule over them from Above. And we keep the tribe safe. I do. You will, in your turn, someday … when you take my place."

"My place is by your side – forever, Almighty Kur," said Eshi softly, and climbed into his lap.

Kur scratched Eshi's downy spine, comforting him, and felt the young body relax; Eshi began to hum contentedly. They sat that way until a rush of wings shadowed the ground, soaring on the updrafts and diving with the downdrafts: the tribe was gathering, turning the sky into a canopy of Kigali riding the wind, blotting out the smoldering vault above, fluttering to earth to honor Erra and the Seven at the feast.

Kur and Eshi went among their own, greeting and blessing the flock.

When the tribe was all gathered in a circle, wing to wing, before the laden feast-boards, Erra and the Seven came down the slope from Kur's cavern to join them. They were robed in splendor and beautiful to the eye, glowing with the sanctification of the heavens. Up to Kur they came, Erra in the lead, the first of the Seven on his right hand, the others by twos behind.

"Almighty Kur, we bring greetings from on high to you and yours. Our merciless vengeance will cleanse this land of evil and satisfy the heavens above."

This land? Among the gathered Kigali, every head turned suddenly, in unison, staring at Erra. Wings went up high. Silence dropped over all the tribe like sudden death.

Again all heads turned as one, looking to Kur. Kur must say

something. The tribe is waiting. Eshi is waiting. Eshi cranes his neck and fixes Kur with wide, luminous eyes. Beside and behind ancient Erra, the bloodthirsty Seven stare not at Erra, but at Kur. This breach of protocol is no accident. Erra challenges Kur and Kur must respond in kind, or more than face will be lost this day.

Restate the agreement. Make its limits clear. "This land on which you stand belongs to neither men nor gods, but to the Kigali. So it was agreed, long ago, when your betters first traveled here. This Kigali world of ours was made not by men or by you gods; its fires burned before you came, and will burn when you are gone: keep this clear in your mind and in the minds of your seven weapons, Erra. Satisfying elder gods is your task, not mine. But by the mountain that bears my name behind us, and by the tribe that shares my blood, we shall keep to our agreement and assist the will of heaven as we may, *if* it is consonant with Kigali ways." Kur's mouth was dry, but these words must be said to the arrogant Erra and his peerless emissaries of destruction. "We shall feast you and house you, assist you in your work among your believers. You shall be as guests of the blood in Ki-gal for howsoever long you do remain here, until you withdraw once more to your godly seat in Emeslam. And you shall behave as good guests should, on Ki-gal's beloved and honored ground. And now, pile your plates high and taste of Ki-gal's bounty, brought fresh here for your pleasure."

Eshi slides his young hand into Kur's. Kur squeezes it, feeling new quills scrape, but then must let it drop. Eye to eye, he faces Erra while not a wing rustles and the Seven barely breathe.

Too long they consider one another. Too hot is the blood of Erra and the Seven, brought to boiling with their day's labors. Too hot is Kur's own skin, blazing as if it might burst with rage: Eshi is not the only one stirred by the carnage on the Downward Road. If there was war between the heavens and Ki-gal, who would win? The skies would flame and rip with battle, if the Kigali ever went to war against gods who depended upon faithful for their strength….

Behind him and high above, the mountain that bore Kur's name growled, and grumbled, and brought forth smoke and flame and shook the ground underfoot: sometimes Kur slept in the mountain's bowels; sometimes the mountain slept in his; forever they were linked. All his Kigali waited, motionless, wings yet unfurled, to see what Erra and the Seven would do.

Erra drew himself up, aglow with righteousness; his Seven cocked their heads and spread their legs wider.

Eshi tugged on his hand again. Never looking away from Erra, Kur put his hand on the boy's head. A great cloud of sulphur rolled down the mountainside toward them; the ground trembled beneath his feet.

Finally Erra looked away, to his right, where the first of the Seven waited, attentive; and behind him, to the others of the Seven, ready for war. Then Erra looked back at Kur and said, "Your generosity overwhelms us, Almighty Kur. The friendship of the tribe of Ki-gal is highly prized by all of us from the heavens. We thank thee, and accept thine offered bounty."

Close enough to a battle to taste it, he and Erra both step back.

"Now, if it pleases you, godly Erra: get your plates before the food grows cold."

So they went to the feast-boards together and heaped their plates with Ki-gal's bounty of meat and grain and toothsome fruits and wine. And they ate together, as friends together, sitting amid the circle of Kigali together: two wary lords of inconsonant domains. Erra sat shoulder to shoulder with Kur, with the first of his Seven on his right. On Kur's left sat Eshi, staring about, eyes as wide as the sky, and on his left sat the second of the Seven.

"You haven't touched your food, Eshi," said the molten-eyed weapon. "Is it not pleasing?"

"I wanted the tail of one of those," Eshi said boldly, pointing to the sulphur cloud above in which a bevy of red-tailed flying lizards hovered, chirping loudly. "There were none left on the feast-boards. Kigali love the taste of red-tail best of all; but they know we want to eat them, so they're hard to catch."

"Are they? Hard to catch?" Those eyes like the inside of the mountain weighed the boy, then caught Kur's: "With your permission, Almighty Kur, we will get the boy his lizard treat."

"Go you, then, but be warned: red-tails are canny quarry, fast and tricky."

The second of the Seven and Eshi got up together, and left the circle together, while Kur watched uneasily as this most beautiful weapon led Kur's precious one away. Perhaps this was a good thing, he told himself. Kur knew why Eshi couldn't eat, and it wasn't because of any lack of food: Eshi was still full of the events of this day. Even Kur had lost his appetite, but ate because he must.

When Eshi and the second of the Seven stopped under the thickest billows of sulphur, the tall weapon spoke softly to him. Eshi stretched out his wings, and his arms, and pointed. Then the second of the Seven raised his sword. Lightning spat from its tip into the cloud and the bevy.

There was a snapping sound, then a squawk, then a screech, and Eshi nearly took wing. But before the boy could leave the ground, down plummeted two fat red-tails. The second of the Seven caught them both before they struck the earth, so fast was he.

Erra's molten-eyed destroyer bent down on one knee and, with teeth bared, solemnly presented Eshi with the two fresh kills. Eshi took them both, then made a gesture worthy of a lord: he gave one red-tail back to the weapon of the god. The pair of them squatted down there, Kigali boy and son of heaven and earth, and ate their lizard tails raw, together, tearing off the wings, cracking the spines, and letting the blood dribble down their chins.

At this Erra said, "Good. Your boy and my bringer of lightning will be allies."

"Good," Kur agreed, not sure that this was so, but proud of Eshi: there was a leader growing in this child of Ki-gal.

When the two returned to sit once more in the circle, Kur took the boy under his arm and told him so: "You are brave and you are clever, Eshi. You have made a friend."

Then Eshi and the second of the Seven presented Kur with both pairs of chewy wings in front of everyone, and the tribe began to call and chirp and sing, once the gift to their leader was bestowed.

*

In New Hell, there was but one Hall of Injustice, where the gravest cases were tried. Overnight the primordial sea, Tiamat, had flooded city streets knee-high; flotsam and jetsam bobbled on an ancient tide: Erra was in town. Or so Draco had told Lysicles.

Flanked by counsel on either side (with Alexander, Lawrence, and Aristotle bringing up the rear), Lysicles splashed through streets awash in brine until they reached the slippery stairs of the Hall of Injustice. Here and there, Hellions with rubber rafts and leaky dinghies floated, hawking their services. But few rode the rafts and boats: a plague was abroad, and no one in New Hell wanted to be close to anyone else. On stoops and from second-story windows, vendors offered prophylactic amulets of the god Anu and lesser charms guaranteed to keep the boils away.

Someone had written with paint or blood on the marble pediment of the Hall: "He who steals my words steals my soul." And someone else had crossed it out and scrawled: "We, the resentful, do the minimum for the incapable. We have done so little with so much for so long, we can now do nothing with everything." And a third scribe had scribbled under that: "The truth shall get you torment."

Lysicles took one greaved step after another, looking neither left nor right, climbing up the slick stairs toward his judgment. His senses were sharp: he could hear his five companions breathing; he could smell the garbage floating in the brine. Now, finally, confrontation with his accusers was upon him. He felt joy.

Battle is battle, and a battle about to be joined always calms him. No more interminable delays. No more unanswerable questions. He was and is a man of action. Today he would act: his gut thrilled with anticipation. In hell where food has no taste and drink no intoxication, where all is hopeless, he tastes hope. A second chance for glory might lie behind those tall bronze doors.

At the top of the stairs, they are stopped by two scaly green fiends, to whom Hammurabi announces: "We are on the docket."

The doors open, creaking and scraping across the muddy marble.

Then they are inside, in the dimness of futures unformed and chances to be taken. Almost, Lysicles thinks he sees the three Fates, Atropos and her sisters, unsnarling his life. But it is just a wall carving of the Fates. Beyond them, on the opposite wall, the dreadful *Erinyes,* personifications of the anger of the dead, are carved: dwelling here beneath the earth to punish those who swear false oaths, waiting for a taste of irredeemable flesh. Will they step out of the wall, shed their marble skins and flap overhead among the damned? Bite throats? Tear out hearts? They might: it's hell.

It is so quiet here, footsteps are too loud. They walk and walk in silence, turn and turn and turn again amid labyrinthine corridors, looking for their appointed judgment hall.

When they find it, there are hundreds waiting, and these are all murmuring at once. Row after row of benches against the walls have signs above them: gluttony; sloth; murder; theft; rape; betrayal … and on and on. The gluttons overflow their benches, their vast envelopes of flesh bulging, eating ceaselessly from stained sacks, complaining about the tasteless food. The slothful stink, sitting on the wet floor atop stains and mud and their own feces, tangled and disheveled. The smell is so bad even the murderers put their bloody hands over their noses and turn away. The thieves are nearly buried in their treasures, guarding all with promissory stares, hands too full to fend off one another: they curse and threaten anyone approaching. The rapists are skeletons in coffle: heavy chains keep their hands bound at their waists (below which no fleshy organs remain) and their feet together. Near at hand, the shifty-eyed betrayers promise anything for a price, if only you will forsake all others and place your trust in them alone….

Lysicles has seen it all before. He remains unmoved. With his champions beside him and his hangers-on behind, he leans against the marble wall and waits: he knows how to wait – he is a soldier yet.

Then they are called: the doors screech back like harpies; within, there is no one: empty benches; an empty dais.

Behind them, the doors screech shut again with no human or inhuman hand upon them. Every hair on Lysicles' body stands up straight. A chill pervades his soul. His mouth dries up. His hand wants a weapon; his belt holds no comfort for him: he has come unarmed, but for the truth.

The bailiff's voice from a gallery high above intones, "All rise to honor the godly Erra and his Seven, weapons of pitiless justice, auditors from Above."

Erra and the Seven arrive, dreadful in their raiment, their tread heavy and loud, glorious and proud as their power is announced. They wear cloaks of human skin, decorated with long-haired scalps like fringe. Teeth are their buttons; braided entrails hold their scabbards on their hips; pouches made of scrota dangle from their horrid belts.

Erra and the Seven climb the dais.

"Present the accused." Near the source of the bailiff's voice in the gallery, Lysicles sees two pairs of glowing eyes catch the light.

Lysicles and his counselors are already standing before the dais in plain sight.... He looks around: Aristotle, Lawrence, and Alexander have taken seats as if they were an audience at a play.

With Hammurabi on the left of him and Draco on the right, Lysicles takes two steps forward. His future hangs by this thread. He knows what he sees in the Seven: warriors from the home of the gods, mythic, heroic in form, bloodthirsty and full of rage under wraps: these are here to render judgment, exact punishment, carry out whatever sentence is pronounced. They are not the ones to reason with.

Hammurabi begins detailing the facts of the case, as the Seven flank their lord and master and Erra looks Lysicles up and down.

Hammurabi is saying, "And on the battlefield, our client was brave and true, fighting beside his soldiers, never quailing, until the enemy, with its oblique phalanx and its longer spears and its mercenary cavalry, broke through Athenian lines...."

"Enough," said Erra. "I know. I walked that battlefield. I saw that carnage. But this death was inflicted by senators, by orators, by the most civilized, upon the accused – for rashness causing death to a thousand. Is it so, damned soul? Were you rash?"

Draco attempted to intervene: "My lord Judge, he was merely following his orders. And his commander was tried on the same evidence and exonerated. This soul is innocent of all but doing his duty...."

"Quiet, fool," said the second of the Seven, whose eyes were hot like the deepest pit of hell. "Let him answer. It's his fate, not yours, at stake."

"But *my* laws were used to –"

"Silence or I will silence you myself," said the first of the Seven in a voice like chariots rumbling over carcasses. "One more outburst, and all here will share his fate. Who are those behind you, Lysicles? More of the damned? Here to gawk?"

Then Alexander popped up, his hands waving. "I am Alexander the Great, victor in the very battle under discussion, here to testify to the glory and heroism of this soul, unjustly condemned."

Old Aristotle pulled hard on Alexander's pteruges, jerking the skirt down to his buttocks.

But it was too late. The second of the Seven said, "Out, or the bailiff will eject you – all three of you – unless you wish to hold the accused while judgment is rendered. We are the auditors here. We know the facts. We come prepared. Will you hold him, or will we?"

Now Alexander took his seat, and huddled with Aristotle and Lawrence. Lysicles liked the sound of this not one bit: he looked first at Draco, then at Hammurabi. Hammurabi looked away. Draco shook his head and spread his hands.

Lawrence rose, speaking for all three character witnesses: "We will stay and perform whatever service is required of us." Then he sat down quickly, one hand on Alexander's shoulder.

Lysicles wished he'd never met those three. Something here was very wrong. This Erra was godlike; the Seven were executioners, terrifying even at rest; and the word 'audit' meant 'judicial hearing' in the most primitive meaning of the term, today. But he had asked for this and here it was. He squared his shoulders. He tried to see in his mind's eye his wife, his sons, his lovers, laughing and running through the green fields of Elysion to greet him. All he risked was his eternal soul, he presumed to think. Hell was forever if he did nothing to better his lot. And he had never been a man for standing by and doing nothing.

"Once more, Lysicles: do you say you were rash? Or were you just when you led your men to their death?"

"I was just. I believed we could win. And we could have won – if so many citizen-soldiers had not deserted; if Philip hadn't outsmarted us; if our allies could have held the line…."

"Were you just?" Erra's booming voice boxed his ears and caromed around the room, echoing: *"Just…ust…us…s."*

"I was just. I, Lysicles, say it so." Old formula, from wars gone by, from days standing straight and tall. Athenian generals were meant to die of old age, or at least in old age … not the way he had died. He blinked back tears that had never overcome him in all this time: he wished he had never brought that battle to the enemy, never gone along with Chares' plan, never had marched his men into that valley of doom….

Erra looked into him, past his eyes, into his heart, into his soul.

"Good," said the god of pestilence and mayhem, now auditor of Lysicles' fate. "You see the truth. You speak the truth. And here is my judgment…."

The Seven rose up on either side of Erra and strode down, off the dais, to form a semicircle in front of Lysicles, Hammurabi, and Draco. Hammurabi and Draco took two steps back, away from Lysicles.

And he was alone, facing his judgment.

"Character witnesses, approach and do your duty," said the molten-eyed weapon of the god, one hand upon his sword-hilt. "Take hold of this damned soul. Hold him tight."

Now the hands of Lawrence, Aristotle, and the hated Alexander were upon him. He almost fought: insult to injury, was Alexander's touch. But the irony was not lost on Lysicles, only unwelcome. He kept his head high and his eyes on Erra's awful visage as it changed from beautiful to horrible and back again.

Erra said: "Your audit is complete. My judgment is this: we shall cut out both your eyes, which have seen the truth; we shall cut out your tongue, which has said the truth; we shall cut out your heart, which knows the truth. Then we shall eat them and we shall know the truth. If the truth is as you say, you will be sent to Erebos, in the realm of Hades, and from there to Elysion, where you believe you belong. If you are lying, then you shall go from there to Tartaros, and suffer its tortures thereafter, never to leave again."

Lysicles nearly staggered, but held his ground. He said nothing. He had a soldier's pride. The three souls holding him from behind tightened their grip. *Alexander, I'll find a way to take you with me if this goes bad.* Hammurabi blustered and Draco began officiously to object.

Then the second of the Seven fixed Lysicles with that fiery stare from an impassive face and said only, "I am very skilled at this, have no doubt." He drew his glittering sword.

Lysicles reached around and grabbed Alexander in a death-grip. Then lightning exploded in his face, in his brain, in his heart and soul, and Lysicles knew nothing more.

*

Erra and his Seven eat the eyes and tongue and heart of Lysicles the Athenian, and of various other defendants of the day, until the auditors can eat no more. In the corridors of the Hall of Injustice, crowds thin as liars and nuisances and the guilty learn what sorts of verdicts are being handed down and what punishments meted out. Fools flee, but all petitioners and their counsels are apprehended and brought back to await their turn in the dock. Those who have come to bear false witness sneak away, only to be returned to their places in the lines that stretch to the street….

When darkness falls over New Hell, Erra is content with the day's labors: the wailing of the adjudged is like a paean to heaven. Out the back of the Hall of Injustice he goes with his Seven. Up in the air they rise, and Kur and Eshi take wing to lead their charges back to Ki-gal. The damned queued there will still be there in the morning: anticipation is its own special kind of torment. Lesser evildoers will be processed all night long, and the next day, and the next, to await Erra's pleasure whenever he and his Seven may return here. There are many cities in hell, and many sinners, and the work of Erra and the Seven has just begun. Fear must overtake so many wizened hearts. This audit of the underworld will be neither quick nor easy.

"Godly Erra, how do you fly on invisible wings?" the Kigali boy wanted to know when they reached the burning mountain of his ancestral home and wings were folded. "And what will happen to that first man, Lysicles, who was so brave? And to the others: so many blinded and made dumb, with no hearts in their chests to beat."

"Do you question my judgment, son of Ki-gal? Why do you care about the fate of one damned soldier out of millions? Like my wings, my judgments come from on high, perfect and without peer, whenever I need them. Like my wings and my Seven, my judgment is unerring, every time, for every crime – past and future." *Go carefully with this Kigali and all the children of Ki-gal under Kur's protection.* It has been long since Erra felt need to tread softly; so long, he'd nearly forgotten how. But war with Ki-gal was not his mandate right now, and this Kur had shown his fangs and a rage bright as the stars in heaven when Erra tested him.

"But I want to know what will happen to him. He was so brave –" said Eshi.

Kur put a hand on his eromenos's shoulder: "Eshi, Erra is

fatigued. It is time to rest."

"No, Almighty Kur, let him ask his questions. As you say: the young question everything. It is their nature. I have not been young for eons. But you are right, as well, great Kur: the day's labors were strenuous. I will rest. The second of my Sibitti will answer all, to your boy's satisfaction. Take me to my cavern and let the boy stay here."

So Kur took Erra up the slope with six of his Seven, and the molten-eyed one stayed behind with Eshi. When Kur stopped at the mouth of the tunnel leading to the cavern where Erra and the Seven would sleep, Kur said to him, "Eshi will keep asking until he's satisfied, so tell me: What will happen to that first soul you judged: was he innocent? You ate his eyes, his tongue, his heart. What did they say to you?"

"Lysicles the Athenian? He thinks himself just." Erra shrugged. "But he is full of hate and regret. When he awakes in Hades, his heart will beat again; he will learn to see again; he will learn to speak again. Then he will begin a different journey, full of the pain he has earned. For a soul to make its way out of hell is not easy, but that one has a chance now. He will remake his own fate. It's what the best of humanity always does." Erra looked past Kur, at his six Sibitti waiting patiently in the blazing green and gold billows of the Kigali night. "I see why you cherish this place, Kur. But the night is short and we must rest. Be you well. And thank you and the tribe for sharing your joy in Ki-gal with us who see so little of joy."

The Kigali lord bowed his regal head and backed away with risen wings. So things were not healed between them, only controlled. Sometimes, control is enough.

So be it. Eternity was long and Erra could have great patience when it was warranted. He signaled his Sibitti and the six of his Seven surrounded him. Safe from all harm, even from the Kigali, in the arms of his peerless weapons, he made his way into the sulphurous cavern of this deepest underworld, and from there, to sleep. And Erra dreamed there, in the stench of hell: he dreamed of his bright, sweet-smelling home in Emeslam, where the sky was blue and the stars his protectors and the will of the gods ennobled heavens and earth.

*

"Eshi," said Kur. "Come to sleep. Your new friend will be here in the morning." *Come away. That warrior is not to be trusted.*

Eshi left the molten-eyed weapon of heaven and came running to him, all aflutter, then jumped into his waiting arms. "Almighty Kur, that one says the soldier, Lysicles, will have a new chance, that Erra is always fair and his judgments are the will of the gods."

"Eshi, I must ask you: why do you care? Is that soldier Kigali? Is he even alive? No. He had his life. He pays for it in his death."

"But he loves his family, as I love you. I understand him. He is lonely."

"Eshi, he is dead. You are alive." His boy squirmed in his arms. Eshi wrapped both legs around Kur's waist, both arms around Kur's neck, and held on tight. Not until then did Kur realize that the boy was shivering.

"Time for bed, Eshi. Long past time for bed. We will sleep in my cavern tonight, close to the heart of the mountain, as you love to do." The mountain would soothe him, bring the boy warmth and comfort with its thrumming. Sometimes, in the bowels of the mountain that bore his name, in the darkest night, Kur could hear the heartbeat of creation. Someday, Eshi would hear it too.

"What happens when Kigali die, Almighty Kur?" came a small voice from the boy in his arms. "Where do we go? We won't be tortured like these human damned, reborn into torment – will we?"

"What happens to the snow when it falls and melts, Eshi? What happens to the wind when it doesn't blow? We are Kigali: we are part of Nature. We go back to Nature and become one again with the sea and land and sky. We live on in the tribe of Ki-gal who remember us and share our blood. We are the wind; we are the earth; we are the fire in the mountain. Don't worry, Eshi: you will have your fill of life before you leave it. Kigali live a very long time. And when we die, we are still part of the world we love. We sleep content. Do you understand?"

"Yes, great Kur."

As Eshi trembled against his chest, Kur carried the boy up the slope and into the cavern, while the boy asked him questions no one could answer about the cruelty that men and gods visited upon one another – cruelty Eshi had seen repeatedly since Erra and the Seven had come.

Kur did his best to answer every question, knowing full well that these moments were critical now that Eshi's innocence was besieged from within and without. And Eshi's innocence was more important to Kur than the fate of every soul in hell.

When Eshi's body relaxed, and not before, Kur put him down and lay down by his side, stroking his downy skin until the boy began to cry softly. When at last Eshi started humming even more softly, Kur promised him that all would be well with them and with the tribe in Ki-gal, forever and ever.

Kur had expected Eshi's questions. Kur had told Erra the truth: the young question all. He had not expected Eshi's tears, but he was glad for them.

Eshi would be everything Kur had hoped, someday, if Kur could keep him safe until he was red and strong.

The Rapture Elevator

by

Michael Armstrong

What is there that a man will not dare?
– Scott of Buccleuch, to Queen Elizabeth I, when asked how he had broken into Carlisle Castle in the Raid of Kinmont Willie

In the center of New Hell, in the misgovernment district, a tall marble building stood out among the squat concrete buildings, walls pocked with shell holes. Some said Stalin's architects had designed the buildings, but Kinmont Willie did not know this Stalin, did not know or really give a Sassenach's fart about anything beyond the 17th century, not that he ever worried about English emissions

The marble building might once have been a splendor, clean and shiny in another world, but not this one. Nothing could be clean or shiny in hell, as Kinmont Willie had learned long ago. Still, compared to the rest of New Hell, the building almost glowed – almost. Things could never be pure, but they could be less dirty. You took what you could get.

Willie sat on his horse, Jamey, a squat Border breed, a hobbler, low and stout but not light, its hair shaggy, its hooves heavy and thick, all the better for riding over mossy fields, rough roads, and the good-intentioned streets of hell. On a hill overlooking the rebuilt, destroyed, and being rebuilt again, capital, Willie watched the marble building.

A golden beam rose from it, a column no wider than a knight in full armor. The beam soared into oblivion above, ending as a prick of light in the charcoal-gray ceiling of hell. Nay, not a ceiling, thought Willie, but a barrier, like rising into a thick cloud that could be entered but never broken through. He'd known a pilot, that's what they were called, a rider of an airship, who had flown to that awful height and seen it, that's what he'd said.

But that golden beam broke through, went beyond, because its essence was of the Divine. The truly evil could not look upon that beam, those cursed by Satan for the most heinous crimes. Lesser evil like Willie could gaze upon it and feel that grace, because in seeing it they would be tormented – they would be reminded of their sins and why they could see that grace but not be with it.

They would know that on that beam some came into hell and some left hell, the impossible made true, although no one had ever actually seen this. Some said if a damned could enter that beam, he could get out of hell. Board the Rapture Elevator, they said, and you would go straight to Paradise.

Back in his life, one fine spring day in 1596, when he'd been a struggling reiver trying to feed his family the best way he knew how – pillaging and robbing, but only English – Willie had been taken by a zealous English deputy, Salkeld, may his soul rot in hell, as he probably did. Minding his own business on the Scottish side of the Liddel Water, Willie had been shocked to see Salkeld and two hundred Sassenach scum cross the stream and give chase.

Aye, he gave them a good chase, Willie thought, and had he a hobbler as fine as Jamey and five hundred lances at his back, they never would have caught him. But they did, hauling him to Carlisle Castle and the hospitality of the queen. Through stratagem and subterfuge, not to mention a bit of bribery and bravery, Scott, the Bold Buccleuch, and eighty good reivers against England's might broke Willie from Carlisle Castle.

Ah, that had been a great escape, Willie thought as he looked at the rapture elevator. He had done the impossible once, with a little help from his friends. Could he do it again? Down below from the Hall of Injustice some essence rode the beam of the elevator up, the column collapsing below it, until the beam shut off. A shaft of clean sky, cleansed by god's grace, remained behind until bats and dust and wasps filled the shaft with their corruption.

*

Jamey picked his way down from the hills above New Hell into the harbor district. Willie had wondered what a horse could possibly have done to land in Hell. Betrayed its rider? Not marched unto death? Not taken a command? Thrown a king? Did horses even have souls? Perhaps it wasn't even a horse, but a soul in a horse's body.

In matters of theology Willie didn't know the truth of anything, the why and because. He only knew that he was there, Jamey was there, and they had met. He'd rescued the poor thing as a foal, dirty and stinking and caked with mud, halfway to another death – or another transformation on the Undertaker's table. Willie had saved the thing, if saving could be done at all, but even Satan in his cruelty now and then allowed small acts of kindness – at least toward animals. If it was an animal. Willie had raised the horse, broken it and trained it. He felt guilty for naming it after King James, the bastard, but couldn't resist always being on the back – if only in name – of that wretched monarch who had condemned the clans to Ulster.

Willie rode Jamey down the North Road from the mountains and toward the three-story dark gray cube that was the Oasis. Boats burned in the harbor and the Titanic had its sundown sinking. Ships came and went, offloading cargo, taking on passengers, heading out to the far flung corners of hell. Wait long enough at the Oasis, some said, and you could see every damned soul in hell, because sooner or later everyone came to the Oasis. Might be a long wait, Willie thought, for the damned were so many and eternity endless.

A gate on the harbor side of the Oasis led into a small courtyard at the entryway. Willie got off Jamey, led the horse to a stable. The hay only somewhat stank, the mud didn't rise more than a few inches, and the grain had not yet gone to rot. A stable hand took the horse into a stall.

"Feed and water him, aye, my lad," Willie said, flipping a diablo at the boy. A Scotsman might be cheap with many things, but never with his horse's care.

A long dark hallway led into the Oasis, demons and hellions lining the way. Willie kept a hand on the hilt of his dirk, staring straight ahead and not at anyone lest a wrong glance lead to a fight. On any other day he would challenge all who dared glance at him, but not this night.

A squat Neandertal blocked the entryway, good ol' Shanidar. Dumb but smarter than an Englishman – not that this was hard – no one dared pass without his blessing. Willie held out his arms, spread his legs. Once he'd dared to wear a Highlander's kilt, not that a horseman would ride in such shite, just to mess with Shanidar. The brute had smiled and ran his big hands up Willie's legs, under the kilt, and squeezed his balls. Willie got the message. Trews, me lad, always trousers in the Oasis.

Shanidar patted Willie down. He'd seen the dirk, of course, but any who entered the Oasis was allowed one weapon. Shanidar ran a finger around the top of Willie's boot, pulled out a small knife with a red deer handle. He glared at Willie.

"Ye call that a knife, Shanidar?" Willie asked. "Tis nothin' but a *sgian dhu* – a little bone picker, that's all."

Shanidar shook his head, palmed the *sgian dhu,* and waved Willie in.

It didn't seem fair, Willie thought. A dirk and a *sgian dhu* were no possible match against the rifles and handguns and other modern weapons some wore in the Oasis, but rules were rules. One weapon, that was it. Not that he came into the Oasis looking for battle, but still, violence had a way of finding you on its own, and it didn't hurt to have a knife in your boot, just in case.

Across the bar, on the opposite wall, Ringan's Tam waved at him.

"Willie," he said as Kinmont came up to him.

"Tam, me boy." Willie slid next to him on the booth, their backs against the wall, looking out at the Oasis. You always sat with your back against the wall at the Oasis.

"So how'd it go at the trial?" Willie asked Tam.

"Convicted," Tam said. "Poor Johnny lost his case. He's gone back to the Undertaker. The hanging was quick, though."

"And the angel?" Willie asked.

"It sighed, shook its head, stepped back into the elevator, and was gone."

"How many seconds?" Willie asked. "How long before the door shut?"

"Fifteen," Tam said. "It was a long sigh."

"Long enough," Willie said. "Long enough."

A bar-maid came up to them, a tall brunette in desert cammo fatigues, wearing an olive drab undershirt stretched tight across her breasts. She wore her hair cut in short bangs and a bob, the ends just touching her lips, bright green streaks framing her face.

"Gentlemen, a drink?"

"Bellhaven's Best," Tam said, his own little joke. You could ask for any beer you wanted and you got Oasis's Own, a foamy bottle of piss that tasted like it had been brewed in sulfur water.

"A tall glass of iced water for me," Willie said, also a joke. It would be water, and tall, but not iced. And it would taste like sulfur, too.

"No beer for ye, Willie?" Tam asked.

Willie shook his head. "Why torment meself? No beer, no wine, no whiskey." You could get drunk in the Oasis if you tried, but you paid for it. Once, just once, that's all he asked, he would like a sip of real whiskey.

"I set it up for you," Tam said. "The appointment with the Ombudsman. Got you a lawyer, too, a mighty fine one."

"A lawyer?" Willie asked.

"The best. He comes highly recommended. A Liddesdale man, too… Ah, here he is."

Willie turned as a stout man came down the aisle toward them. He had the long face of a Borderer, with a hawk nose, dark black hair swept back from his forehead and curling at his shoulders. He kept his beard trimmed short, long enough to count as a beard and not an unshaven mess, short enough a fighter couldn't get a grip on it. A boil the size of a dime oozed pus on his forehead, and another seemed ready to explode on the tip of his nose.

The Liddesdale man wore a leather jack, aye, but unlike the gaily quilted affair of Willie's, his jack had little pieces of metal that seemed to ripple around the man's chest. As he came closer, Willie could see names and numbers stamped in them.

"Kinmont Willie?" the man asked. "Dick of the Side. Nixon, that is."

"A Nixon?" Willie stood. "Ye're no Nixon I know."

"He's of a different era," Tam said. "Centuries past us. This Nixon led a nation, led great armies."

"Well, not that great," Dick said. "May I?"

Dick took Willie's glass of water and poured it on his jack. The metal steamed and, for a moment, quit flowing.

"Aye, that's better," Dick said.

"Your jack," Willie said. "That metal – what is it?"

"Dog tags," Dick said. "Soldier's identification of my era. They're the names of the dead killed on my watch. Killed without cause; it's supposed to be my sin."

"All of them?" Willie asked.

"Most of them." Dick shrugged. "You get used to it after a while." He winced as the dog tags heated up again, as if to show the lie of his statement.

Watching Dick of the Side, Willie felt his own torment – not that the pain ever went away, but sometimes you could push it back. Satan liked to make hellions suffer with every breath, and had devised an entire cruel couture. Sharp bones in Willie's jack poked through the quilted leather, scratching his skin, exotic staph infecting every cut. Like Nixon's face, his skin oozed pus.

The bar-maid came to them again, took their orders, and came back moments later with new drinks. Willie pulled his glass of tepid water toward him. Dick sipped at a yellow brew that looked like horse piss – was horse piss, Willie realized, smelling it from across the table.

"Well," Dick said, putting his hands flat on the table, "I hear you need a lawyer."

"Want, more exactly."

"On what crime?"

"All of them," Willie said. "Well, one in particular. On February 19, 1596, I am alleged to have burned down a peel tower near Annandale with the widow Bell inside."

"Well, did you?" Dick asked.

"Aye, I burned the peel tower, from the top down after scaling it. But my men held back to allow escape."

"Was the widow Bell inside?"

"There was a body, true, and some said it was her. But the bones had cuts in them, including her skull. Someone killed her, a son or daughter-in-law. She was known as being especially vicious to her daughter-in-law, Darcy. A Musgrave, I think."

"Did you answer for justice?" Dick asked. "Mortal justice?"

"Aye, at Kershopefoot, at a Border meeting. Salkeld, the English deputy brought it up, but he had such a pathetic case even his own men laughed. Ye can't take blame for burning a body found hacked to death. If it's a crime, that would be, what, tampering with evidence?"

"Well, that's all well and good, but Divine justice has its own rules. Are you held accountable for it here?"

"Aye," Willie said, and he pointed to his own jack. A spot of blood oozed through the fabric, hellion blood, sickly yellow and bubbling.

"But I seek Evil justice here, by our own laws," Willie said. "If I can be relieved of such an injustice, my torment will be lessened a bit, you see?"

"I see," Dick said, looking down at his own jack, and perhaps hoping that one of those dead could be taken away – a death laid not at his hand but to a wretched general.

"So are you up for it?" Willie asked.

"Do you have witnesses?"

"Aye. Tam and I, my men, we have prowled the plains of hell seeking them out. If you serve subpoenas backed by the court, they will be compelled to appear."

"And has the court agreed to take on your case?"

"Aye," Willie said, turning toward a man coming toward them. "The Ombudsman himself has agreed."

A thin, stooped middle-aged man came toward them, a robe turned pale gray after many washings hanging on his body. He'd pushed the hood of his robe back, showing his dark eyes, dark hair speckled with gray, his gray beard. Small white scars pocked his darker skin, but his face was otherwise unblemished.

"A Moor?" Willie asked.

"Nay, a Jew," Dick said. He pointed at a gold Star of David on a necklace around the man's neck.

Willie looked at the Ombudsman's clean features, his washed robe, his body burdened by age but apparently not by sin. "He is not tormented? Not evil?"

"I am human," the Ombudsman said, coming up to their table and sitting across from Willie, his back to the rest of the bar. "A human soul, anyway," he said, waving his hands at the wretched in the Oasis. "My name is Job."

"Job? As in the Bible?" Willie asked.

"That Job, yes," the Ombudsman said. "But I am not

tormented … not tormented as you are, anyway."

"The Ombudsman has chosen to serve in hell," Tam said.

"You could be in Paradise but choose to be here?" Willie asked.

Job shrugged. "It's complicated." The bar-maid set down a glass before him, pure and clean, little drops of condensation dripping off it. "Now as to your case…."

"You got my petition?" Willie asked.

"Yes. It has passed the usual … review," Job said.

Willie nodded at Job's implication, motioned at Tam. Tam slid a bag of diablos at Job.

"Then your case is scheduled. I inquired at the Hall of Injustice. There happened to be a cancellation in Lord Scrope's schedule. He will see you in court on the morrow," Job said.

"Lord Scrope?" Willie asked, amazed at the coincidence, but also knowing in hell nothing was coincidental. Scrope, the man who had unjustly imprisoned him at Carlisle Castle, the man embarrassed by the Bold Buccleuch's raid that had freed him.

"Scrope," Job said. "It's just a coincidence, but it seemed fitting, don't you think?"

"Aye," Willie said. "But who are we to question the machinations of Satan?"

Job stood, and Willie, Tam, and Dick stood with him. As Job left, Dick remained standing.

"I'll take my leave then, too," Dick said, holding out his hand. "I have an opening argument to prepare."

Willie nodded, and Tam put another bag of diablos in his hand. If this kept up, Willie would have to sell his horse to pay for his trial, he thought.

"There's just one thing," Willie said to Nixon. "This trial might lead to … to Borders justice. Are you prepared to defend me in that manner, too?"

Dick glared at Willie, put a hand on the hilt of his dirk. "I may have been born far away from the Liddesdale, but I am of Borders blood, true and proud," he said. "If it comes to Borders justice, then aye, I am there for you, too."

*

Willie and Tam came early to court. Money almost gone, they'd slept in the stable with Jamey, curled up on the damp straw next to the horse. They'd risen early, went to court not so much to be on time as to find someplace warmer. In hell, Willie thought, in hell you were always too damn hot or too damn cold. The closer you got to true evil, the colder it got. The Hall of Injustice had been built on evil – literally, its walls writhing with those imprisoned within. Walk too close to the walls and grimy hands would grab at your coat.

Benches lined the hallways outside the courtroom, benches running between every door, only in one of those cruel jokes Willie had never gotten used to, the interior designers had cemented broken bottles and sharp rocks into the benches. Why build something to sit down on if you didn't want someone to sit down on it? Willie wondered. It was the least of hell's paradoxes, and yet as good an example as any.

Tam kicked at a section of bench, breaking away the bottles and rocks, and sat down. Willie joined him, the sharp points digging into his butt anyway. Another theory had it that like a penitent saint if you took on pain not necessary to your hellish existence, somehow that would take away meaner torments. This didn't make a lick of sense to Willie, though. Wasn't every torment in hell, intentional or not, part of Satan's grand misdesign?

The minutes ticked by as Willie and Tam sat in silence, staring down at the cracked floors. Willie kept shifting his foot as a face in the floor moved beneath his boot, teeth trying to bite the leather.

"Willie me lad!" a voice boomed from down the hallway. "Focking Kinmont Willie! Cain't escape judgment here!"

Willie looked up, saw Salkeld himself, the English deputy who had betrayed the truce there at Kershopefoot in the spring of '96. He rose, Ringan's Tam at his side and Nixon mere seconds later, all of them ready to draw their swords.

"I escaped your justice," Willie said. "Your injustice."

"Peace, Willie," Salkeld said, holding out his hands. "I did not come here to fight ye – not with swords, anyway." Salkeld held out a tattered scroll, its edges smoking. "I'm here to prosecute you, called forth by Scrope himself as to the crimes you should answer to."

"Ah, there's a conspiracy of injustice," Willie said, spitting, his phlegm steaming on the pocked floor.

"What else did you expect, Strang?" Salkeld said, calling him by his family name. He strode by them, pushing forth the thick ironwood doors of the courtroom.

Willie, Tam, and Nixon followed. Thick candles made of rancid fat burned in sconces along the wall, their wretched scent almost perfume compared to the reek of hell. A large dais occupied one wall of the room, more ironwood and steel plates protecting the judge behind it. Rough made benches, but smooth unlike those in the hallway, spread out before the judge's throne, an aisle between them. The defense sat on the left, the prosecution on the right, and no wall between them and the gallery. A clean circle of marble – cleaner than the gray stone, anyway – was on the far corner of the room.

Salkeld sat on his side; Willie, Nixon, and Tam on the other. A grizzled old man in rusty armor entered the room, stamped his pike and, in a voice barely audible, the bailiff said, rasping, "All rise for his Lord Scrope."

Willie and Nixon stood, and when Tam stayed seated, Willie nudged him.

"Go along with it, cousin," he said, and Tam rose reluctantly.

Scrope strode in, robes swishing, but as they twirled Willie heard the clank of chains. Boils pocked Scrope's face, and blood oozed from his shirt. Weights burdened Scrope's robe, and barbed wire poked through the hems of the robe. The chains pulled the wire into Scrope's flesh, the weight of all the men and women he'd unjustly tried. We all have our pentagrams to bear, thought Willie.

Scrope settled in his grand chair, settling his robe around him with more clanks of chain. Both sides sat.

"In the case of the Damned versus Kinmont Willie, William of Morton Rig, also known as –" The bailiff said.

At Willie's name, a great light descended into the courtroom. Willie turned toward it, looking at it as close as he dared, one hand shielding his eyes and peeking through faint cracks between his fingers.

The Rapture Elevator, the Divine, a manifestation of the Lord G'd Himself. Behind its glow Willie thought he saw a great winged figure, a patch of white in the golden beam. The angel did not have to announce its presence or why it had come. They all knew. It had come to bear witness and if a hellion through justice, mercy, and good deeds had redeemed himself, herself, the damned might, just might, be lifted up into Paradise.

Or so that grace suggested.

Scrope turned away from the grace, stared down at Willie and his supporters.

"Kinmont Willie, you have petitioned this court to relieve your torment, to judge again a crime already charged to you. How do you plead?"

"Innocent," Willie said, "at least of said crime against the Widow Bell."

"We shall see." Scrope banged his gavel.

In filing his petition with the Ombudsman, Willie had been warned that injustice would be swift. It had seemed peculiar that petition would even be possible. How could an all knowing, all merciful, all powerful G'd have been wrong? How could a mistake have been made? How could the damned be wrongly convicted of a crime already known? That challenged the very nature of hell and of The One True Justice.

And yet, Job had said so himself days ago when Willie had approached him.

"And yet here am I, a just and worthy man, a good man, punished unfairly for my sins," Job had said. "Punished for no other reason than a bet between Satan and G'd, if only to prove man's faith. Y'h'w'h himself cannot see, does not see his own darkness, his own shadow. If he cannot see that, what else does he not know?"

Willie did not understand such subtle theology. All he understood was that his torment could be lessened, and in the process, he might escape.

The trial went quickly. No tedious selection of jury, no long orations, no opening and closing statements. Nixon presented their petition, Salkeld countered with his own. They laid forth their summonses, their evidence, scrolls and documents slapped down on the floor. Hellions came forth in a burst of light, their testimony presented as a blast of screeching sound, and faster than it took

Scrope to shuffle from his office to the bench, the trial was done.

"Shall I pronounce judgment?" Scrope asked.

Willie looked up at Scrope, over at Salkeld. If Scrope judged him unfairly, it would be another chain added to his robes. So deeply had Willie offended Scrope, though, he did not dare risk Scrope judging him wrongly. What would be another spot on a leopard, another pound on an already unbearable weight?

"I demand Borders justice," Willie said.

"Borders justice?" Scrope said, sneering. "You have already gotten that."

"Not yet," Willie said, and he drew his sword.

Tam sprang to his left, Nixon to his right, faster than before, Willie was glad to see. They flanked him, swords ready, as Scrope leapt down, his own sword drawn. Salkeld drew his own sword then, the two prosecutors against their three.

But then the bailiff joined in, his pike sweeping before them. Out of the walls Englishmen came forth, dozens of them. Willie, Tam, and Nixon had their backs to the angel, to the Rapture Elevator.

The Sassenach circled, closer and closer. Nixon parried their crude thrusts, meeting blade to blade. Scrope pushed down the center, massive in his robe, the armor of his robe fending off sword cuts. He winced at the weight of his judgments, but pressed on nonetheless.

"I would have acquitted you!" Scrope shouted, but Willie knew it was a lie.

"As you acquitted me before!" Willie yelled back.

Tam took out two fighters with one blow, and Nixon a third. For every one they killed, two emerged from the wall. Soon a mob pushed them back to the elevator. Willie jumped up on a bench, knocking another down in front of him, and Salkeld stumbled. Willie swung his sword down, blade slashing Salkeld's throat.

"That's for Kershopefoot!" Willie yelled as Salkeld's body shimmered and went toward the Undertaker.

Scrope pushed the three of them up against the Rapture Elevator. They could not enter it, but the grace cooled them, supported them like soft summer moss. Willie looked to Ringan's Tam, to Nixon, and nodded.

"Take your leave, my friends," he whispered.

Tam, then Nixon, reached for tabs sewn into their jacks, yanking the ripcords and disappearing off into the mist. An easy death on the Undertaker's slab, an easy resurrection, perhaps. He hoped.

Scrope stepped back at the explosion of air rushing in to where their bodies had been, and then he smiled at Willie standing there alone. Willie slashed down at Scrope's shoulder, the force sundering the barbed wire, his cut slicing through Scrope's chest. For a moment Scrope grinned in ecstasy as his burden was relieved, and then he, too, went to the Undertaker.

The bailiff stood stunned, pike at his side, then raised it, glancing at the wraith army to push their advantage. Willie whirled, spun, and came around to the bailiff's left side, his open side, and cut his head off. The head spun away squirting dark green mud. Willie laid down his sword, and the wraiths fell back into the wall.

"*Innocent*," the angel said, its voice booming, blowing out the candles and shaking loose dust from the stone walls.

A door opened in the elevator, a bare crack as the angel spoke. Willie rolled backwards, through the door into the elevator and at the angel's feet.

The bones in his jack rolled back under the leather, their sharp points no longer piercing him. His skin felt light, his joints like honey, and all the pain he had endured rolled away. Willie felt pure, blessed, out of his hellish body. The angel rose up in the elevator and Willie with it. Willie watched Hell race away below him, its smoke, its filth, its damned fading to a small dot.

And he smiled. He had done it, had grabbed a ride out of hell. It took but another moment to rise up to Paradise. The angel held Willie's body, its soft hands cradling him like a mother. The elevator slowed, a golden trumpet blared, one pure note singing through Willie's skin. The angel held a cup to Willie's lips, and he had taken but a sip of smooth whiskey before the angel shoved Willie down.

"But not innocent enough, my child," the angel said, its voice sweet with sorrow. "Not innocent enough."

Willie fell back down through that golden column, the motes of hell already filling it up, and he hit the ground so fast he did not even feel his bones shatter.

When he woke up, he stared into the bloodshot eyes of the Undertaker, smelled his foul breath.

And smiled.

Out of Court Settlement

by

C.J. Cherryh

Snip. Snip-snip. Snip.

Partly overcast in hell, a few spots of rain – but the job had to be done, and when jobs of a less elevated nature had to be done in Augustus' villa, there *was* a question of rank involved. Augustus wasn't going to do it. Neither was Caesar or Cleopatra, nor Sargon of Akkad; nor was Hatshepsut. The villa had Roman rulers and Egyptian pharaohs, but no gardener, and *that* elected the two Renaissance refugees who'd found the villa a comfortable berth in hell.

Dante was dithering around in the basement about some research project.

That left one Niccolo Machiavelli to be dragooned into the job, when Augustus came out of his office in a dither – *not* about the flood downtown, *not* about the Audit of Injustice proceeding in the Law Court, but about two young fools, both Julius' sons, who'd decided to burgle Tiberius' villa, over across the greenspace and a good hike beyond.

The lecherous old goat, the Emperor Tiberius, had them dead to rights. And was suing Augustus for instigating the permanently young fools in the invasion of his premises.

It was *not* a good time to have a lawsuit questioning the peculiar status of *any* Roman in hell, not that one could explain that to the syphilitic old fool, Tiberius, who'd died insane and who'd not improved in the process.

That was why Machiavelli was out there trimming roses into shape … in a light rain. With an extensive flood spreading over the greenspace. Cardinal Richelieu's place had half the lawn underwater. Tiberius had a regular canal behind his mansion. It was a lawn-rimmed grey sheet beyond the gate and the hedge, and it might get beyond the gate tomorrow, but for now, the garden had to look its best, old roses, Roman roses, cuttings from Paestum, Augustus swore, a little bit of earthly paradise, around the beautiful statue of weeping Niobe, mourning her lost children, symbolic of the rain, and more than appropriate today.

Bailing the boys out was the mission.

Getting that old sybarite, Tiberius to settle.

And with every high-level Roman being, in essence, a lawyer, representing his house, his clients, his sympathizers, voters, and connections, in whatever court – there was still a time to call in the experts.

Tiberius had, on his side, the law firm of Stalenus, Dolabella & Crassus, the most unprincipled law firm in hell.

That was a bit of a problem.

So … up against scoundrels, potentially pleading in front of antiquity, go for the headliner. The Dershowitz of his day, Marcus Tullius Cicero.

And getting Cicero to come in, was a dicey sort of request to have to make. Julius and Cicero had history. Augustus and Cicero had history. Oh, did they have history.

Snip. Snip-snip.

Cicero had died rather messily, head and hands tacked up in the Forum (shocking beyond belief, and a clear indication of the barbarity of Antony's revenge).

But then, Marcus Antonius had always lacked class. Even Cleo said so.

"What choice did I have?" was Cleo's statement on the situation – quietly not mentioning the other choice, Augustus. But marrying your father's wife was beyond déclassé … a little fact the historians since had neglected to add to *their* reasons why Cleo had taken the liaison she had.

"Good in bed," she'd remarked of Antonius, "when he was sober."

The drinking problem hadn't improved, so the rumor was. Antonius hung out sometimes at Tiberius' villa, sometimes at Claudius', in close company with Caracalla and Caligula, and *Antonius* was one of their current most serious problems – a loud mouth, a loose habit, and a rarely sober judgment.

Bad judgment in the two teens, who'd ended up in Tiberius' basement.

And the biggest inducement to Cicero to take their side might, amazingly enough, be the fact that *Antonius* was over on Tiberius' side, currently resident with the old goat.

Snip. Snip-snip.

Boom! Boom-boom-boom....

Which wasn't thunder. Or hell's occasional indigestion in the lower levels.

It was coming from the front of the villa, out on the street.

Or across the street, where Decentral Park's graceful trees concealed a multitude of hell's own problems.

It was worth wondering. Especially when it came again.

Artillery.

Damn it, it sounded for all the world...

Damn, damn, damn. He heard the yelling as a misshapen thing the size of a six-year-old child bounded over the yard's back fence, from beside the driveway and raced past him to the sound of howling pursuit.

Imp. Niccolo had only seen a few in all his stint in hell, and this one was fast ... encumbered as he was with a greasy paper bag from Hellzacre BarBQ.

A noisy black-pants mass was coming down the drive, across the gravel, and didn't bother with the gate: they came over the fence, waving AK-47's and Tokarevs and screaming at the top of their lungs. Niccolo backed up, dropping the shears – and the basket of rose clippings, which rolled across the rose garden aisle, scattering thorny bits across the path of first the barefoot imp and then the barefoot Cong.

Coals of fire rained down, the imp's doing, a veritable hail as the imp vaulted the back gate and splashed off across the flooded lawn. Howls of indignation went up from the Cong, and a volley of shots rang out and stitched across the grey flood – no damage to the imp.

The Cong went right over the fence and splashed after him, firing and howling, and leaving behind a confetti of rose debris and curls of white from the smoldering coals, where falling raindrops hissed and sent up steam, commingled with burning lawn.

The roses obliged with an instant spurt of green leaves and soft sprigs.

Hell's roses were, if anything, tenacious, especially if abused. Sprigs grew from every angle, pale green and vigorous.

"Dannazione!" Niccolo cried. And it was a good bet when the Cong gave up tracking the imp they'd be back, right across the same route to Decentral Park. *"Dannazione!"* He snatched up the shears and the empty basket, and began gathering up the clippings that now were scattered all the way to the back gate.

It thundered overhead. A spate of rain followed. And a third *"Dannazione!"* from Niccolo, whose fingers were bleeding from the thorns, and whose shirt and doublet were getting damp. A particularly chill gust sent him back toward the portico, with the intention of heading for the basement and rousting Dante Alighieri out of his library hunt, with threats of murder.

A car pulled up in the drive. Caesar and Cleopatra were back from a very essential quest, and that, momentarily, outranked thoughts of revenge. Niccolo set the basket and shears on a plinth and wiped his bleeding hands, standing by for a courteous little bow as the two came hurrying in out of the rain – Cleo in a smart cloche hat with a feather that was showing drops of rain, a trim little black skirt and smartly-seamed black nylons, Julius in a MacArthur jacket and a Red Sox cap.

"Where's Augustus?" Julius asked.

"In his office, I believe, signore – anxious for news. Which one hopes is good."

"Moderately," Julius said. A Viet Cong shell boomed out, flew overhead, and burst somewhere beyond the garden gate. "Is the Cardinal at odds with the Cong?"

"An imp came through, signore. One believes it came from the Park."

"There's some sort of a tower in the Park, that wasn't there this morning. A metal tower, straight up, like an antenna."

"One has no idea," Niccolo said. He hadn't. He'd been working in the garden since breakfast. "I have not seen it."

"Taller than any obelisk!" Cleo said. "A metal eyesore! And an imp! In *this* neighborhood!"

"One has no idea, signora. One has been preparing the garden. Or one was –" Niccolo cast a reluctant eye to the roses, lush and undisciplined, and sprouting shoots from every knot and branch of the tree roses. "– until the imp." Another shell went over. Another explosion. "May we hope for Cicero, signori?"

"Hope is the word for it," Julius said and headed off, Cleo close beside, snugging her purse under her arm. "I have to talk to Augustus. The wretch is wanting an apology."

*

"Pro di immortales!" was Augustus' predictable reaction, on the other side of the desk. *"I* didn't kill him!"

"He is what he is," Julius said with a shrug. "He is what he always was. *I* got along with him. Mostly. He's an old Republican, he's a vain old man … death didn't youthen him a bit. We want something from him. He's named a price. He wants an apology in the Hell's Tribune, and he'll take it once the case is settled. You just have to put out a little press release, 'Old Feud Settled, Augustus Denounces Former Ally,' that sort of thing. He's willing to wait."

"Contingent," Cleo said demurely, from the corner chair by the potted palm. "Contingent on settling."

Augustus glowered. He'd died old, of a dish Livia had served him, but lately he'd gotten younger, lost the chins, and now his ears stuck out. Maybe, Julius reflected, it was the combination of young Marcus Brutus and Cleopatra's boy Caesarion in the household, that had Augustus, First Citizen of Rome, suddenly looking thirtyish, with a prominent Adam's apple: Augustus, his nephew, was a posthumous adoption of his – born simply Octavius, a two-name man, a commoner; adoption by a patrician Julian had made him Caius Iulius Caesar Octavianus, and the Senate, doing all it could to bolster the man who'd steadied the ship of state on course, had tacked on the Augustus bit.

Good administrator, his namesake. Good kid. Thank the gods he'd stuck that adoption in his will, even if it upset Cleopatra, whose Caesarion had not been Roman enough, and Marcus Brutus, who hadn't been legitimate enough.

It had *really* disappointed Marcus Antonius, *magister equitum,* who in the way of Roman adoptions, had had every right to think his old mentor might have adopted *him.* Do Antonius credit – he had had his hands on the will, had gotten that nasty surprise, and still, in the haze of an honest grief and in fear for his own life, had added two and two and figured first, Octavius could cast legitimacy on the government and second, that a boy like Octavius could be handled.

Right, on the first count.

Wrong, on the second. Octavius, once turned Octavianus, couldn't be handled.

Cleo had gotten clear of Rome before she caught hell. Antonius had stayed and tried to take Octavian's share of power. Really wrong.

Antonius had had his enemies' list. He'd had Cicero killed. And cousin Lucius. Among others. And he'd tried the old gambit of establishing an authority outside Rome, off in the east. That never had worked. Neither had alcohol.

In the end – he'd killed Brutus and he'd gotten on the bad side of Caesarion. Neither of the boys had liked him. And truth be known, he'd fallen on Julius' bad side long before the Ides of March business ... so much so Julius just wasn't damned sure he hadn't been involved.

He couldn't ask Brutus. Who didn't remember the event. And Caesarion hadn't been there.

But, damn, he wondered. Ask him which he felt better about, Cicero or Antonius, and the unlikely answer was Cicero.

He'd said as much, talking the old warhorse into taking the boys' part against Tiberius.

"I'll give him his statement," Augustus said, a muscle jumping in his jaw. And in English. "Damn him."

"Damn Tiberius," Julius muttered, "first."

"When is he coming?" Augustus asked, and looked ceilingward as something screamed overhead. "What are they *doing* out there?"

"The Cong are out of the Park. On Richelieu's lawn."

"With the Audit going on," Augustus muttered. "We do not need the attention, uncle. We do not need it."

"He should be here within the hour. He refused the car. One believes, however, he is actually taking a taxi."

"Marvelous," Augustus said. "Talk sense to the boys. They'll listen to you."

*

That was an optimistic estimate.

"Let *me* talk to him," Julius said, delivering a kiss to Cleopatra's cheek.

"Don't hit him," Cleo said.

"I won't hit him," Julius said, took a deep breath, and resolved not to, no matter the provocation.

There was a science to handling the boys – it relied mostly on talking to Brutus and letting Brutus talk to Caesarion. Long hair, grease, and leather jackets had become the vogue … since Caesarion had turned up. Rabbit's-foot key chains, and the plaint that they *needed* a car.

Not *this* decade, they didn't.

Especially not with Erra and the Seven downtown.

Loud rock-and-roll resounded from the pool room – had been a part of the library. Had been. Now it housed two teen rebels who had a round-the-clock guard on their whereabouts – quietly, politely, but there.

Julius passed the legionary guard – on loan from a lower tier of hell – and quietly nudged the door open. Inside it sounded like the Gauls in head-on attack. The teens who lived in this lower hell called it music … and played it at full volume.

Julius walked past the infernal device and switched it off.

Stunning silence. And two teenagers going on twenty and too damned old for stunts like Caesarion had pulled.

"I've got you a lawyer," he said. "We're going to try to settle with the old goat."

"Doesn't matter to me," Caesarion said, pool cue in hand. He turned and made his shot. His half-brother just glowered.

"Nothing's our fault," Brutus said.

"I wouldn't care if you drowned the old sod," Julius said. "What I do care about – isn't for you to know. Figure it out. Let me explain, however, that if you get sued, and if you have to testify downtown – they'll slice off parts of you until they're satisfied. Ask Niccolo how it is to wind up on Slab One. He'll give you a description. But then – downtown – they might not kill you. They might just leave you in viable pieces. Will I be sorry? Probably. But you'll be a lot sorrier."

Caesarion had stopped the pool shots, and looked at him about as level-on as Caesarion ever had. Thinking. That was an improvement.

"Dying's a bitch," Julius said. "But there's far worse. You *don't* want to attract attention until these prehistoric types are out of town. So stay here – And," he added, since he had the undivided attention of both of them, almost unprecedented, "Cicero was born a prig, he practiced at it, and he died one. But he *is* good with the establishment. And it's my earnest hope he'll come up with a way to avoid your going to court, which you really don't need right now – because if the old goat doesn't settle, you'll be arrested, you'll be presumed guilty until proven innocent, and we haven't got a way to prove you're innocent. So let us get you out of this, and then you can go back to being whatever you like."

He flipped the switch on the music again, and walked out.

*

"He's bluffing," Caesarion said.

Brutus shook his head. "I don't think so."

"Come on. We're supposed to shake in our boots. Big deal."

"I don't want to go downtown," Brutus said. "I really don't want that kind of trouble. They don't care, brother. They beyond don't care, downtown."

Caesarion didn't say anything for a few beats. Then he shrugged, parked the pool cue against his hip, flipped a comb out of his pocket and swiped it through his hair. "Let the old man sweat it," Caesarion said. "Not our problem."

Brutus cast a look at the door, thinking that it *was* their problem. Julius would bluff. Julius was good at it. But there was no percentage in thinking he was doing it right now. In point of fact, Julius had told him how it was – how *soft* it was being a Roman in hell, compared, for instance, to the types with more specific afterlives. And how they had all the freedom they wanted, so long as they didn't rock the status quo … and get the whole lot of them assigned to one of the nether levels.

Hell did have other levels. Sargon swore to them. Hatshepsut said this was the best place, and told him about space and planets and how he could have tech if he could believe in it. Julius stopped with World War II, but he was working on Korea. Sargon was taking advice from Hatshepsut, who was the best of all of them at believing.

Himself, he believed in *here,* real hard. He had fallen off a horse on his way back from the south of Italy, and he was *here,* and Julius treated him like a son, which was what he had wanted.

Until Caesarion showed up, who was Cleopatra's and Caesar's son, and who blamed Augustus for his being dead, and his mother for just about everything. Augustus said he'd been a fool to come back to Egypt, that he'd listened to bad advice, and Caesarion had said that he had had a safe conduct, and there it went: Caesarion ended up stalking out and refusing to listen and now Caesarion was having a private war against the rest of the house, *including* Julius.

Which was how they'd ended up in Tiberius' villa, and in trouble.

He didn't want get into a lawsuit and go downtown. And he didn't want to come near Tiberius' villa again. 'The old goat,' Julius called him.

Old goat didn't begin to cover what the old man was. Every *inch* of the place done up in erotica. Even the door handles. And at the heart of it, like a spider, a fat-bellied, spindly-limbed, decaying and syphilitic old man with designs on anything, male or female, that came within his reach.

Hell no, he wasn't getting into a lawsuit with that old lecher.

Question was – how good was this lawyer Julius had gotten and what in hell could they buy the old lecher off with if they could get him to drop the lawsuit?

Caesarion nudged him with a pool cue.

"Your shot."

*

Band-aids. Sticking plasters. Rose scratches. And this time a determination to get Dante out of the library, hand him a basket and a pair of shears and get the job done. Machiavelli was in no mood to temporize. If the roses didn't get trimmed, Augustus was going to be upset, and an upset Augustus was not going to deal well with Cicero, who was already on the outs with practically everybody.

He headed down the stairs to the library – and met Dante coming up, with an armload of books of various ages.

"Dante, my friend. I need help."

"No time, no time."

"What, no time! You left me with the rose garden, we had a damned imp, and now the roses are twice the mess."

"One regrets, Niccolo, one regrets it entirely, but I have a chance – I have a *chance*, my friend. You know it's a mistake that I'm here, a complete confusion of records. I have my justification – I have to file a petition!"

"Downtown? A petition with the Injustice Department? Dante, Dante, you are mad! You will not be filing petitions!"

"I have to tell them! I have to make them understand!" Dante began to push past him. He caught Dante's sleeve, and books fell, thumping down the stairs.

"*Dannazione,* Niccolo!"

"You are *not* presenting any petition to the Audit! Not from this house!"

"You cannot stop me! No one has the right to stop me! I do not belong here! It's a simple, stupid clerical error, and the Audit will fix it! Let go of me!"

They had acquired onlookers, at the top of the stairs. Hatshepsut, resplendent in a skin-tight catsuit, and stocky, bearded, barrel-chested Sargon, in a kilt.

"What's the trouble?" Hatshepsut asked.

"This fool wants to file a petition with the Audit," Niccolo shouted up, and took a firmer grip on Dante's arm, propelling him up a step. "He wants a review of his case!"

"A review!" Hatshepsut said.

"These are heaven's agents. They are my chance! It is all a mistake, a terrible mistake that assigned me here! You have no right to stop me!"

"They are not your heaven's agents," Sargon said. "They are from deep, deep places. They bring the Tiamat. They bring the Scorpions. You cannot deal with them, brother!"

"I have a right of appeal!"

Niccolo shoved him up the stairs and Dante fought him, batting at him and trying to set his feet: poor Dante, who had turned up in the villa with a computer and an obsessive belief that if he could reconstruct his great *Commedia Divina* from memory he could be forgiven, and reassigned to heaven, with his beloved Beatrice forever.

"If you appeal," Hatshepsut said, "you can lose everything. Worse, you can draw attention to this entire household. Augustus will never permit you to go to the court."

"He cannot stop me!" Dante cried, and shoved him, hard. Niccolo's heel slipped off the step, backward. He fell against the wall and rail, and kept his grip on Dante, which brought Dante down, flailing and shouting, "No one can stop me! It's my right, my right!"

Dante had led cavalry once. But muscle had gone, with age, with bookish pursuits, with obsession. There was nothing of that in the man, now, just a sense of injustice and betrayal.

"I can manage him," Sargon declared, thumped downstairs with bandy-legged force, reached out and seized a fistful of Dante's doublet, Dante flailing and cursing the while.

"He is hell's iconic poet," Hatshepsut said from above, "and if you are reassigned, son of the ibis, it will very likely be to the domicile of that Crowley person downtown, never to see your good friends again, let alone your Beatrice. If you go there, you will *live* in your hell, Dante Alighieri!"

"He should be so lucky," Sargon said, as Niccolo unwound himself from Dante's legs and hauled himself up against the banister. Sargon hauled Dante up, too, now that he was free of the tangle, seized him by the front of his collar and brought his own tanned, aquiline, curly-bearded face all but nose to nose with Dante's pale, mince-mouthed, large-eyed countenance.

"Let me tell you, scribe, the thing you court. The Auditor is Plague. He is Injustice Incarnate. He kills the just and the unjust. He *deals* injustice. His helpers slay whoever they cast eyes on. He brings turmoil and pestilence. Go to him with your plaints about a lost love and he will track down that love and slay her before you. Where his eye falls, there follow boils and blindness. Where his breath goes, is fever. Where his steps fall, scorpions spring up. He brings the Tiamat, the great ocean dragon. He is here to audit *hell,* Dante Alighieri, to see if he can find fault in its misery! His handiwork is Overthrow, and if he can find the least chink in hell, he will rip its guts out and cast down every soul into older, deeper elements. The good Augustus, who is far too merciful, and a lover of the arts and of fine things, has given us place among the secrets under his roof, in a paradise which the Romans have made. The Romans have given you sacred hospitality, scribbler, have admitted you to their Elysian Fields, which they have managed to make exist – they have protected you, they have housed and fed you, and shielded you from such things as you have not imagined! This is a good place, Dante Alighieri, and you are a fool if you think we will allow your besotted dream of this chit in heaven to bring Overthrow into it!"

"You will not speak of Beatrice in such disrespect!"

"You will not deal with our eternity in such disrespect!" Hatshepsut said, descending a step also to lean very close to Dante. "The asp of the earth and the vulture of the sky are mine, the crook that rescues and the flail that beats out the grain in judgment! I am the Osiris and the Ra Ascended! I am Isis and Sekhmet, and I rule on the spiritual Nile. Yet I have preferred this house to the Fields of the Blessed – for its knowledge, its seeking after new things, its gathering of minds and its vantage on eternity. I have gained things here that I will not give up, not for all the honors that would be mine if I were *willing* to go to the Eternal Fields. Oh, you want *hell,* son of Thoth – try an afterlife of no change, never change, not a day different than any other, for all eternity! I *refuse* to go back to it – but that is what you threaten! If you bring the eyes of Erra on this place, he will know it is a hotbed of things out of place, and *enjoyment,* and *anticipation,* which are not a part of hell outside these walls! Appreciate what you *have,* scribe! And respect the house of our host! We have enough trouble with Tiberius, who is mad enough to think he can win in this court! But you, you, poet, I have thought you were wiser than that. What use is a poet if he is not wise?"

Dante had begun to wilt, in Sargon's grip. And now he began to shake his head. "Beatrice," he moaned. "Beatrice. Beatrice!"

"Hopeless," Sargon said. "We cannot let the scribbler loose until this is resolved. We cannot have him wandering about with his *'Beatrice'* and his petitions."

"We have the basement," Niccolo said. "He will be happy with the library and the books."

"You cannot lock me up!" Dante cried. "I shall never forgive you! Never!"

"For his own good," Hatshepsut said, and bent and picked up a book, as Sargon picked up Dante and marched him downstairs.

Niccolo arranged his cuffs and raked a hand through his hair and tried to compose himself, trying not to think what could happen if Sargon's hell descended on the villa.

He picked up a couple of books himself, and heard Dante still shouting about Beatrice as a door shut, below.

Dante was going to be very upset with them, but not half as upset as he would be if he got what he wanted to petition for.

Boom! From outside.

The Cong might be coming back through. Or might take another route. He hoped so.

Dante was still screaming, distantly. A door thumped shut. Niccolo looked up, about to go back to the main floor.

And looked up at a scowling Augustus.

"Signore," Niccolo said, dismayed.

"What is that?" Augustus asked.

"Dante, *signore."* Deep breath. "He thinks to petition the court for a new hearing...."

"Di immortales," Augustus breathed, gone a shade paler. "And the garden? The garden, Niccolo?"

The booming was still going on outside. The shouting from inside.

"I shall go see," Niccolo said, and added: "If the German Guard could be set to guard the stairs, *signore..."*

"A good idea," Augustus agreed.

"Auguste!" One of the servants came running up. "A car. A taxi in the driveway."

"Damn!" Augustus said. "Damn!" And left.

It was by no means certain there would *be* any of the German Guard showing up. And it was too late for the rose garden. A car in the driveway?

It likely was the great man himself. And Niccolo was not about to leave the stairs unguarded, even with Hatshepsut and Sargon attending arrangements below. He *liked* his arrangement with the Romans. He *liked* being here and not in Cesare Borgia's basement. He had come here after his initial trip back to Slab One, had reincarnated and gotten shipped *here,* and he existed in mortal terror on every trip back – every time he died in hell – that some clerk in Infernal Records would realize that someone had gotten Cesare crossed with Caesar and dropped him into the Roman paradise.

Oh, he did not want that mistake reviewed. And the Audit that might send the Roman paradise to a nether hell was terrifying. Personally terrifying.

Hell if he was going to let a love-besotted poet end his residency here.

*

There was nothing for it. Julius had that figured. The old man was Republican, give or take his penchant for honors, public acclaim, and being important, and staying decently in the house and letting servants bring the visitor to him and Augustus just wasn't going to set the right tone.

The personal touch. There was a lot of water under the bridge with them – from pristine and sweet to not-so-good water under the bridge. But he'd done the man favors. He'd saved his damned *life*. Never mind the likelihood the conspirators that had assassinated him had probably approached Cicero and Cicero hadn't warned him. He'd forgiven Brutus. For Brutus' sake – and Caesarion's – and the safety of the household, he could damned well forgive Cicero.

The old man, toga-clad, meticulously coiffed, in the spitting rain, was paying off the taxi – and arranging a stand-wait, apparently, since the cabby nodded several times.

Damn! There was that tower in Decentral Park, big metal thing, like a girder, straight up.

But it was closer now. Right across the street. *Hell* of an eyesore. And gods knew what it did.

Phone public works and ask? They weren't phoning *anybody* official until the Audit was out of here.

"Cicero, my old friend," he called across the drive, as Cicero *still* admonished the unfortunate cabbie. "I'm sure he understands." Best classical form. "Please, come inside!"

"Here!" Cicero said, stabbing a finger at the driveway. "Do not budge! *Intelligisne?"*

"Si, signore," the driver said, and Cicero edged away with a second *stay* gesture.

"Please," Julius said with an inviting sweep of his arm.

"You seem well-adapted to this place," Cicero said, casting a jaundiced look at Julius. "I suppose that Octavianus is the same."

"Well, well," Julius said, waving the old man inside the foyer. "We do get along, but mentally, sir, mentally, we keep the old ways. Please. Come out to the back. We have everything arranged." The old man didn't hold with electric lights, didn't accept this or that invention, and the taxi was a major concession. The Republicans could be like that.

And if it was daylight, the place for reading and paperwork was, yes, the portico overlooking the rose garden – whence there was a fair view of the back gate, and Tiberius' villa, or at least its back boundaries.

Augustus was on his way – note that Cicero used his adopted name, Octavianus, *not* the Senate-awarded title Augustus preferred.

And they had maybe a quarter of an hour to set the tone, deliver the old senatorial warhorse enough wine to mellow his mood, and talk him into handling the case.

Keep the boys out of sight.

And *try* not to talk about old times.

Augustus had arrived there, in toga. Cleopatra hadn't. Cicero would *not* approve, and she had discreetly headed off to find Hatshepsut. Decius was standing by, looking Republican, likewise in toga, instead of the usual fatigues. And one of Augustus' household was there to play servant, in simple tunic and sandals – jeans and a tee-shirt was Galba's usual. They were so good.

"Delighted you came," Augustus said. "So glad. Thank you."

Augustus offered a handshake, perfect old-fashioned manners, and Cicero stood a moment and surveyed the grounds, the beautiful nude Niobe in the middle of the rose garden – which was shaggy as hell with new growth.

"Amazing vigor," Cicero remarked. "Quite. No buds however. What are you feeding them?"

"It's not the food," Julius said, "it's the variety. I'm sure we'd be happy to send you one – they're rather crowding the bed. They're red, mostly."

"Very kind of you," Cicero said, taking his seat. Galba hastened to pour wine all around.

"Your health," Julius said.

"Indeed," Augustus said.

They drank. They sipped for a moment in silence. "So," Cicero said, with a gesture to the modest stack of paper. "I understand you're in receipt of a letter from the man."

This was the best part. Caesar quietly slipped the letter in question from the stack and handed the scroll over – parchment, with red wax, no simple tabula for this official creation. They were keeping records in Tiberius' establishment.

Cicero read it. Or started to. "Stalenus!"

"Caius Stalenus," Augustus said quietly. "Law firm of Stalenus, Dolabella, and *Marcus* Licinius Crassus – not to be confused with the esteemed jurist of that cognomen. You and I have had our difficulties. Fate assigned me an ally I repented at leisure, my dear sir – you know who I mean. An ally once dear to Julius, and estranged, even before the plot. When *you* opposed Julius, you had the grace to do so absolutely, publically and on the most honorable of terms; and would that I had had you at my side, sir, rather than Lepidus and Antonius – who *hired* that infamous law firm in Tiberius' name. The flood yonder – as good as the Mediterranean, which once divided me from Antonius – separates us from that vile house, and would that it would wash out the corruption. Hell has spared your domicile, and spares this house, honorable gentleman, but hell has full sway across that flood, and if you are so brave as to take this commission, I do not envy you the task of negotiating with that collection of scoundrels. You see what we are up against!"

Cicero took in a breath. "Allow me to read this."

Julius took a sip of wine. Augustus did. There was a moment of profound silence, just the crinkling of parchment, the unrolling of a fairly short scroll.

Then Cicero laid it down and brushed his hands off as if brushing off dirt. His chins, immaculately shaven, acquired more wrinkles, with an expression of distaste.

"These are venal men. You need no lawyer. You need a full purse!"

"One might conclude so," Julius said, "but we need a release. A definitive statement. You know what's going on downtown. The old lecher, Tiberius, wants to file a lawsuit. Look at it this way. First of all, the boys are innocent."

"You say."

"On my honor, Tullius Cicero! On *clan Julia's* honor, which I take fully seriously. I've bent my own a few times. But not in this. Not in this, Tullius Cicero. These boys made a foolish, youthful mistake. They ended up in Tiberius' villa, scared out of their minds, and were lucky to get out with their innocence intact, if you take my meaning. The man is notorious."

"My wife's son," Augustus said glumly. "Livia. She spoiled those boys. But syphilis and an old age of debauchery hasn't improved the old goat's intellect. He's a polluted, bloated thing with a taste for things one had rather not name. His house guests are no better – one of whom you well know. The *other* great orator of our age."

"I do not admit he is great."

"He certainly isn't now," Julius said, "which is *why* he's hired Stalenus, Dolabella and Crassus to represent Tiberius. He's rarely sober. You won't have to deal with *him,* Marcus Tullius. But in his sober interludes he'll know you won."

"I haven't agreed to this!"

"There's no one better to deal with it. *You're* more than a lawyer. You're a legal scholar. Centuries have not dimmed your reputation." Flattery, absolute, disgusting flattery. But the old man loved it. He always had.

"The question is a binding legal agreement. An agreement to hold these young men harmless. Are they?"

"One is Marcus Brutus. You know he's honest."

Cicero frowned. "And the other, the Egyptian woman's boy."

"Caesarion. Yes. Likely he got Brutus into it. But they're both far out of their depth. And the household, Tullius. The household! A drunk and a syphilitic madman have decided now is the time to launch a lawsuit. Now, of all times! If *we* go to court, the inquiry may well ask – not why is Tiberius' house a cesspool of iniquity and misery? But rather, why are Romans in hell enjoying their villas and their comforts, their rose gardens and their traditional ways? You are an astute man. You know *exactly* what will happen if an inquiry shines a light on this villa. The inquiry will leap from us to your tranquil establishment, to the Elysian meadows, to all the Roman souls that now have the reward of just lives and honorable dealing. You are more than a lawyer, Marcus Tullius. You are the exemplar of an honest lawyer – who fought corruption and challenged wrongdoing in high places. You do not *deserve* to spend eternity as a courtier in Tiberius' villa – and that is what is at stake here."

"That is entirely what is at stake," Augustus said. "We cannot deal with Tiberius. But we must stop this lawsuit going forward."

"An out of court settlement," Cicero said.

"Exactly."

"Both boys."

"Yes," Julius said. "They're *both* my sons."

"There are three positions, one to settle, one to defer – to countersue, which I gather is not desirable."

"Not desirable," Augustus said. "Even after the Audit departs, the court may be unsettled."

"In the remaining options, cost may be an issue."

*

"No," Augustus said. "It is not. This is *family.*"

Well-played, Julius thought. Cicero, besides being an odd combination of puritan and peacock, *was* an honest man, and Roman to the core. Family. Clan loyalty.

And Cicero was thinking now, fingering the scroll. "And the payment?"

Trick question. A test. A traditionalist did not *take* pay for legal representation.

"You would never ask payment," Augustus said.

Bright lad, Caesar thought, and eyes did not meet, while discussing that nasty word *money* between clans. Cicero was clan Tullia. They were Julia. And *should* represent themselves. Asking another clan to do it – was a little dicey.

"We want the best," Julius said. "And you *are* the best. You are absolutely impossible for Tiberius to hire – but we hope, not out of reach for us to engage on *honorable* grounds."

"There is the matter of Antonius."

"Of whom clan Julia has washed our hands. Entirely. On

many grounds. *You* opposed me openly, siding with Pompeius – but did I hold that against you, when that side went down? You used that eloquence against me. Yet I respected you. I did *not* heed the advisors who wanted you dead. I was handed a list of my political enemies. I burned it."

"After reading it?" Cicero asked pointedly, and Julius laughed, honestly.

"I knew the source, the self-seeking bastards. But *your* name crossed my desk repeatedly, yes, from Antonius. And I trusted Antonius less and less."

"Would that *you* had not listened to him," Cicero said to Augustus.

"What can I say? I was in a situation. I didn't have the power to stop him. Not on that. Power – came at Actium. After that – I could have. But it was much too late."

Cicero arched an eyebrow. "You are glib, Octavianus."

"I was twenty years old, Marcus Tullius. I was a *boy* allied to Marcus Antonius. I was a boy dragged into public life by Julius' *will*, with a handful of advisors and a copy of Aristotle's *Rhetoric*. I did what I could on the side of justice – but I could not stop him, where his mind was made up. It gave me nightmares, what he did."

"It gave *you* nightmares, First Citizen! It was more than a little inconvenient to me."

"Yet – may we talk of *favors,* Marcus Tullius? Of clan Julia's protecting you, as long as it could…"

"You *did* support the law," Cicero said. "I give you that, Octavianus."

"We are all in this together, now," Julius said. "If that lawsuit goes forward, not only clan Julia will find the attention of the Audit directed on it – we may find those lunatics downtown assigning damages that will ruin us. That may set *Tiberius* in charge of the Roman establishment. And that brings Marcus Antonius, as his chief officer, and Stalenus, Dolabella and Crassus as his legal office. To an administration interested in increasing the misery of hell, that should do it."

"Appalling," Cicero said.

"And of course," Augustus said, "there is no tit for tat, no recompense, and of course no shameful offer of money, but if the undying friendship of clan Julia weighs anything with clan Tullia, we shall be very glad to do this on a handshake."

Cicero stood up and proffered his hand. Augustus stood up and took it. Julius extended a hand.

"I shall need," Cicero said, "a letter of apology from the boys individually. And a letter from the head of clan Julia. Is that yourself, Julius, or has the burden passed –"

"– to my heir, indeed. Augustus will see to it and we shall courier all the letters to you."

"Make it good," Cicero said. And winced as, with a screaming passage overhead, a boom and a huge splash amid the flood – a horde of black-clad Viet Cong poured toward the garden gate, on their way back.

Galba moved fast, reached the driveway gate and opened it, allowing a yelling tide of Cong to go through and down the driveway, past the garage.

"Does this happen often?"

"Usually they keep to the other side of the park," Julius said, and from the front of the house there was the sound of a motor revving and tires squealing. "One fears that will be your cab."

"Damn the man," Cicero said.

"By no means concern yourself," Augustus said. "Shall we let a friend of the clan take a cab from our door? Perish the thought. Galba, tell Mus we shall need the limo. And we shall be couriering letters back and forth."

Smoke was still going up, despite the rain. "They'll do well not to make a habit of that," Julius said. "But again – we're being quiet for a little while. If the Cong want to get audited, let them. I believe that last one landed quite close to Tiberius's villa." He gestured toward the door. "Please. Let me walk you to the drive."

*

Pool had proved boring. Television was a *Mr. Ed* marathon on the only steady channel. It was grim, and their lives were threatened if they tried to leave the house. Besides, the weather was still rotten.

So they played dice. While an English-speaking talking horse ruled the airwaves. Some miracles palled quickly.

But Julius came in – without knocking – and said, quietly, "Son. Brutus. Please come outside."

Brutus cast a look at Caesarion, got up and left the table, out into the hall with Julius.

"We've met with Cicero," Julius said. "He's going to do it. An affair of honor, understand. To enable him to do it, and to deal with these people you're involved with –"

"I'm not involved with that place!"

"Technically, involved, since you're in danger of being sued by them. And bringing the whole house down, taking the Greeks and the Egyptians with us ... we're a major irregularity in hell's accounting, and, yes, you are involved. So a dutiful and pious son will write an apology to the house of Tiberius, and I shall, and your cousin Augustus will – make it good. *Anything* to get us out of the likelihood of the Audit on our doorstep. Count this a defense of the house. In that light, *anything* is honorable. Understood. Make it short. But make it very sincere."

It was hard to say *I will.* But he knew that look. He had no choice. Absolutely none, or he was going to be talked to by everybody in the house, in succession, until he said he would.

"I will, Father."

"Good. Good lad. Send your brother out."

"I'll try," he said, and went in and said, "Brother. Father asks for you."

"So let him ask."

He went over to the table, pulled back his chair and was quiet a moment. "I think Father is respecting your privacy. He'd like to talk to you. And it's important. We're in a lot of trouble, Caesarion."

"Screw 'em. Screw 'em all."

"Look. It's not bad here."

"What's not bad? We're stuck in a damned room with a talking horse."

"Had you rather be hiding in an alley somewhere? We're in a room with a roof and good food and there's all sorts of reasons we could be in jail downtown. And you know that. So just go with it. Isn't that what you say? Settle it so we don't have to be stuck in a room anywhere. Father's got a lawyer. A good one. He's going to get us out of this."

"Screw 'em, I say."

"Well, I don't! I don't want to get locked up downtown, and you don't either! So let's talk sense!"

"Been there," Caesarion said with a shrug, not looking at him.

"You want to go back?"

No answer.

"Look, brother. I'm asking you. Me. I was with you. I've stood by you. I'm on your side. Just – just do it."

"What's he want?"

"A letter."

"A letter."

"Caesarion, I'll write it. You don't even have to look at it. Just sign it. And it'll all be cool. Just go out there and tell him you'll do it and you don't even have to turn a hand. It'll happen. It'll get dealt with."

"He hasn't called my mother into this, has he?"

Brutus shook his head. "No. Just him."

Caesarion set his jaw. "What kind of letter?"

"You don't need to know. Just shut up, go out there, tell him you'll do it, and I'll write it. Go on. You don't want him to call your mother in."

Caesarion shoved back from the table and slouched his way to the door. Attitude. A lot of it. But he was fragile. Brutus had that pegged.

It didn't take too long.

Caesarion came back in, scowling. "So," he said, shoved his hands in his pockets and went over and stared out the window.

Brutus didn't say a thing, just went over to the desk and got paper. Didn't want to know what Julius had said, what Julius had offered, but he didn't want to tip the balance, whatever it was. Julius could be damned scary. Usually he wasn't.

But you didn't want to be his son and tell him you weren't going to do something.

*

The house sent papers to Cicero. Back came back more papers.

Decius Mus took more papers to Cicero. A considerable sum

of money. A case of wine. And a potted rosebush. Mus was gone more than he was present that day, ferrying this and that here and there.

The very next day Cicero announced he was coming to the villa *with* papers to sign.

*

"He wants *what?"* Augustus cried, reading same.

They sat in the portico, overlooking the rose garden. Galba served, Mus stood by, his Republican-era armor all polished and oiled. Julius and Augustus were in togas, and everybody else – *everybody* else – was told to keep to the house.

On the other side of the garden gate, the flood had reached the very shadow of the gate. It stretched past the several estates, and glowed hellfire red as the sky in the distance, next to the skyscrapers of downtown hell.

"It could be further negotiated," Cicero said. "But it is very likely the position will harden on some matters. Right now we have a settlement that costs nothing in personal favors, one statue, a dozen rosebushes, and one truckload of Chian wine."

"A Praxiteles," Augustus lamented, looking toward the Niobe, who stood amid the rose garden, appropriately spattered in rain and framed by floodwaters.

"I'll scour up another one," Julius said. "We'll get something. That fool Memmius lost a raft of them into the bay. They come on the market."

"It took a century to get her!" Augustus said.

"And our alternatives?" Julius said ... and noticed, oddly enough, that Dante Alighieri had come out of the house, ahead of two Scorpion Guards in hot pursuit.

The scholarly little Italian was no athlete. They had him before he reached the gate. And Cicero didn't even notice. The two Mesopotamian bruisers got to the gate first, snagged the little poet up, each by an arm, and carried him off, screaming ... which *did* get Cicero's attention. The genteel old man cast a look that way, raised an eyebrow, and looked at Julius.

"One of the houseguests," Julius said. "Late. You wouldn't know him. A poet. Quite fond of Vergilius. Based a lot on him."

"Ah," Cicero said. "Does he give recitals?"

"For a select few," Julius said. "Of course – our friends are invited. We can ask Vergilius himself. If you'd be interested."

"A traditional fellow? None of this Beat poetry."

"Oh, absolutely traditional," Julius said. "Best of the new Old School. Cheer up, nephew. We'll find another Praxiteles. 'Prometheus and his Vulture,' maybe."

"Not funny," Augustus said. "I love that statue. The old goat is aiming this straight at me. And where did I deserve it?"

"Your adopted brothers owe you one," Julius said. "Let's get this thing signed, get ink dry on the line and get that statue moved, the roses dug, and the whole transaction done today, before something worse happens. Galba."

"Master."

"Tell Niccolo. The bushes could stand thinning as is. Tell him we can't wait for the weather."

The house door shut, on Dante and his problems.

"All right, all right," Augustus said, downcast. "I'll sign it. Damn him."

*

It was a damned downpour. Niccolo was soaked to the skin and had *no* help. Dante, damn him to a nether circle of hell, was sitting warm and dry in the basement and they daren't let him out until it all had blown over. So Niccolo Machiavelli got the job of pruning, wrapping, then digging up ten prickly, man-high rose trees, shaping and wrapping their rootballs – the damned roots *moved* when insulted, and stabbed you if you hung on. Then, solo, in the rain and cursing Dante all the way, he turned the ten thorny, muddy, burlapped bundles over to the armored, uniformed bevy of regulation legion engineers, who showed up with a noisy truck and a small flatbed load of timbers, regular legionaries, and chain.

Niccolo wrapped himself in spare burlap and slogged over to the shelter of the portico, ordering a passing servant to fetch him a mocha latte. "Grandissimo. And very hot."

Then he tucked up in a chair, unwilling to hose off twice. He'd have work to do when the engineers had their go. If something was going to go wrong, if somehow they ended up missing a rosebush and in technical violation of the agreement, giving the old lecher a way to wiggle – well, Niccolo Machiavelli wasn't going to let that happen. They didn't *have* mocha lattes in the nether circles of hell. They didn't have a lot of things, and Niccolo, who'd had his personal dose of dungeon life, didn't intend to let anybody screw up.

Besides, they'd gotten a rumor of what one of Erra's Seven had *done* to a complainant in court.

No. Niccolo wasn't going to go there. Niccolo wasn't going to make a mistake.

Boards thumped and boomed down off the truck. The legion engineers, likewise dripping wet, supervising a handful of legionaries, poor sods, who hammered down the disturbed earth and laid planks. Then while Machiavelli shivered under the portico, and huddled in dry burlap, being muddy from head to foot, the serious work started.

Up went beams in an A frame. Pulleys. The engineers set up a pentaspastos on the bed of planks and sent the soldiers swarming up to gird poor weeping, naked Niobe in belts and rope.

One so hoped they didn't drop the old girl and doom them all. Niobe rose, rose, rose from her pedestal, and set down again beside the rear of the truck.

Then the pedestal moved, by the same expedient, while legionaries, with sly grins and roving hands, steadied la signora Niobe.

The engineers gave orders, and quite smartly those who weren't mauling the statue disassembled the pentaspastos and reassembled it on the truck bed, fast as fast. It *wasn't* as if the age of the truck didn't manage hoists somewhat more complicated, Niccolo thought. *His* age had had them.

But the engineers, stubborn fellows, clearly didn't believe in powered winches and hoists, and it was amazing how very fast that ancient machine reformed and got into operation. The legionaries on the ground attached the robes, the legionaries on the flatbed, three of them, hauled, and Niobe rose, rose, rose to the truck bed.

The legionaries scrambled up then to put the lady into her web of braces and ropes, which would hold her steady on the short drive down past the park. They'd turn at West 96th, round the corner and turn again – easy drive. They'd manage it.

The engineers gave orders. The pedestal joined the weeping lady.

Did a romantic imagine a look of panicked distress on the marble face? Rain glistened on her skin. Her outstretched hand, so delicate, appealed to brute men for salvation, to the thoughtless heavens for a rescue.

None such was coming. *You play chess with gods, signora, you just do not expect to win. You were a vain bitch.*

Now you get a new admirer. Doubtless you'll grace his bedroom. Lucky signora. You're marble. He's – shall we say – less than pure.

"He-us!" the senior engineer shouted, and the legionaries scrambled to grab rose bushes and to get them aboard. And Julius had probably been watching the progress, since he came out, looked the situation over, counted rosebushes – little nods of his head – and walked grandly back indoors, into the dry.

Well.

Dannazione. Not a shred of notice, his direction. Julius was thinking about those two boys of his. He was thinking about Augustus, or Cleopatra, or any of a dozen others.

Who did *he* have? Dante Alighieri. Who believed heaven and Beatrice awaited him – if he could ever reconstitute his great epic.

Ha.

Well, he had the garden to keep his mind off his problems. He had to move some rosebushes to cover the scars the trucks had made – and the missing ten bushes. Eleven, counting Cicero's.

Couldn't have made it an even, easy-to-apportion number, could they?

Maybe *he* should send a gift of his own to Cicero … just paving the way for future favors. One never had too many favors of the inbound sort.

He thought that, gathering up his garden spade from its place, leaning against a pillar of the portico.

And saw, through the gate, three things.

First, there was a great metal tower in the far distance – right next to the edge of the flood, right on the edge of Tiberius' lawn.

Second, on Richelieu's lawn, there was a small band of the Cardinal's men, armed with swords, determinedly facing something, short and singular, splashing its way across the flood at an angle.

Thirdly, and equally determined, there was one of the

Cardinal's men in galoshes, headed for the villa's back gate, sword in hand, and fire in his eye.

"Toi!" the man shouted at him.

That did it. "Don't you *toi* me, *vous!*" He flung down the shovel. "You are addressing Niccolo di Bernardo dei Machiavelli, Secretary to the Second Chancery de la Repubblica di Fierenze, lately Secretary to Caius Julius Caesar Octavianus Augustus, master of this villa. Whom do you think you are addressing?"

"A most peculiar occupation for a gentleman, sir! You are head to foot in mud, and *that – "*

It was an imp, emanated from the tower on Tiberius' green rolling lawn, and the Cardinal's men were having at it, with poor effect.

"Don't look at us! We had one cross our grounds with the Viet Cong in hot pursuit! If you let it get to the Park you'll have that horde coming back after it! Tiberius is not under my lord's jurisdiction! He's *your* neighbor!" There was a horrendous scream. Niccolo winced. "My lord views *this* as his property line, and kindly respect it. I am sure my lord wishes your lord well, and hopes you will succeed in driving that creature back to Tiberius' premises, where it will be aptly situated. I shall report it immediately, and you may rest assured *we* will not let it pass."

"You may rest assured His Eminence will seek damages!" the Cardinal's man cried.

"You may rest assured His Eminence understands exactly the situation downtown. If you cannot deal with this yourselves, then appeal to my lord, and we will take over your defense – in a neighborly way. But *I* think His Eminence has a very clear reason why we will *not* be seeking anything in the law courts at this precise moment!"

"Vous," the Cardinal's man said – the respectful pronoun, this time, then at a renewed scream from his men, spun around and started to run. "Idiotes! Chut! Tenez! Tenez-vous!"

Damn the roses. Niccolo turned and ran for the house, but Julius was already on his way out into a sudden spate of rain, armed with a pistol, with Mus, Scaevola and Sargon's two Scorpion Guards – that was two M-16's and a pair of tall spears; and behind them came Augustus' German Guard, howling like wolves, invoking one-eyed Wotan and waving their Gewehr 98's at the lightning above.

Niccolo simply wiped the mud off his hands and nicely opened the garden gate, as the French rallied and began to chase the imp back in Tiberius' direction.

Rifle fire stitched the water. The Germans and Sargon's Scorpion Guards waded out after the retreating imp.

Julius and his bodyguards stopped at water's edge, watched for a moment, then walked back through the villa gate.

"I think that's handled," Julius said. "Was he appropriately polite, the Cardinal's man, Niccolo? I noticed a little waving of hands."

"He had to have things explained, m'lord."

"You might write the incident up," Julius said. "In case."

Niccolo bowed. Smiled at Julius, despite a raindrop making a slow path down the side of his nose, and another down his opposite temple.

He so appreciated little chances like that, to advance himself in the household, to become – perhaps – essential. Essential was good.

Essential was always good, where it came to princes.

Revolutionary Justice

by

Leo Champion

"You're a damn failure, Guevara," said the man who'd kicked open the door to the shanty where the rebel leaders slept. "You failed as a doctor, you've failed as a revolutionary and you couldn't even die well."

Slowly, Guevara looked up. "Who in hell are you?" Che Guevera took a final swig from his beer and threw the empty at the pile on the floor, where it hit a full bottle. The full bottle exploded with a punctuating bang, showering the shack with foam and glass.

"William Walker." Walker ignored the bang and the spray. "Get your ass up and listen for three seconds."

A hairy man in a filthy tie-dyed shirt sat upright on his cot, pawing shards of glass from his beard. None of his snoring compatriots so much as moved. "Who does pint-size, here, think he is, boss?"

"Yeah," echoed Guevara. "Who do you think you are, Walker?"

"Ask the Hondurans. Ask the Nicaraguans." Walker's eyes scorned the shanty, jabbing disgust at empty bottles and empty souls passed out on furniture or on the floor. Rusty, half-assembled, hell-made AK-47s were nearly buried under rum-stained leaflets on a coffee table. "Ask the Sonorans or ask a Vanderbilt. Who I was, and who I am, doesn't matter. What matters is that you're no longer in charge of the revolution, you over-the-hill sot."

"Wha' the?" the hairy man asked. "You tryin' to take us over?"

"This bunch of losers?" Walker gave a harsh laugh. "Who'd want you? What I said is that you're no longer in charge of this so-called revolution. Now I've said what I came for." Walker turned on his booted heel and left.

The man in the tie-dyed shirt turned slowly to Guevara.

"Wha's *that* all about?"

"I don't know," said Guevara. "But I guess it means we got a problem. Americans. Again." Guevara spat a phlegmy chunk so heavy it landed on his steel-toed boot.

*

Why can't we ever meet somewhere classy? Walker wondered, clattering down the rickety stairs into the basement of a factory built to be abandoned.

Tiny. Mid-thirtyish. Slicked-sideways hair and a hummingbird's intensity. With a flickering pen-light, he picked his way through broken girders and pooled filth.

"Yo, who that?" someone asked from shadows.

"Walker."

"Yeah, come on." Something rustled. Something thunked. "Yo, it's Walker!"

He was escorted into a dim room. Around a table covered in maps and notepads, several damned souls craned their necks, making sure he was who he claimed. A red-tinged lantern swung slightly on its ceiling chain: back and forth, back and forth.

"How'd Che react?" asked Saul Alinsky, darling of American leftist reform in the third quarter of the twentieth century.

"Does our committee really care?" Walker retorted.

"Give him a little respect," said Alinsky. "He was something in his time, you know."

"Was he, much?" asked Eric Blair, also known as George Orwell, who didn't think anybody was 'much.'

"He did kill a lot of people," Maximilian Robespierre said.

"He was a melodramatic failure in life," said Walker. "He's equally pathetic in afterlife. Didn't understand what was happening."

Noise from the outside. In came a crew-cut black man with a billy-goat tuft on his chin, carefully shutting the door behind him.

"Ah, Patrice. What did Bolivar say?"

Lumumba shrugged. "Wasn't interested. Didn't even hear me out. Said he was sick of being badgered by people wanting him to lead them to freedom."

"Who said anything about leadership?" asked Walker.

"Who said anything about freedom?" asked Blair.

*

"What went wrong?" Guevara asked, blinking, outside his shack. The baleful glow of Paradise above couldn't dispel the miasma over the camp's rusted vehicles, half-built shanties and listing tents. Guevara's head hurt and, he badly wanted a drink already. When he couldn't manage to be a wet drunk, he was a dry drunk. Alcohol was unpredictable in perdition and it tasted like … hell. But he kept trying to get drunk enough not to care….

"You fucked up. *Good.* You deserve it," said Giuseppe Garibaldi, fair-haired boy of the Italian revolutionary Carbonari in life.

"It? You mean I deserve him? Walker? Gringo swaggers in and says – screw you; we, the whitest – the best and the brightest – will take it from here?"

"I *said*, you damn well deserve it," his old friend interrupted. "In life we were *expected* to drink, get morose, go all poetic. But this is afterlife and drunks in hell get drunk on water, or can't get drunk at all. You're an old dog and the ones who want revolution are right to want new tricks. Not because of that 'effectiveness' drivel – define 'winning,' in *hell!* – but because nobody in their right mind is going to die for a self-pitying ass."

Defensively: "I haven't been asking them to die."

"And you don't see anything wrong with that? The revolution hasn't drifted away from you: *you've* abandoned *it*. You've been in a stupor over that bitch, Tania, for *how* long now? Get over it all: the whore; being doomed to hell where the booze is full of glass and sand and shit – or *I'm* going to find new associates."

"You say – you think *I've* abandoned the revolution?" Guevara said.

"Done anything revolutionary lately? *Tried* to do anything besides slouching between irrelevant camps in the middle of netherworld nowhere?"

"Don't make this about me. I was your compadre yesterday, and a thousand days before that, and you weren't complaining. Now this little *cabrone* walks right in and says his gang's taking over. So *I'm* to blame –?"

Garibaldi bitch-slapped him, open-handed, back and forth. "I."

Slap. "Did." *Slap.* "Tell." *Slap.* "You."

Hard enough that Guevara staggered, his face blazing, stinging, going numb while his eyes teared.

"You *didn't,"* Guevara snarled.

Garibaldi raised his hand for another round of blows. "Che, you wouldn't listen, didn't care. *Now* you want this revolution back, because someone else wants it? Fine. You want to lead? Fine. If you're serious. But I need to know: do you want to be just another unshaven loser in a beret, or do you really want justice and glory?"

Guevara nodded once. "Justice. Revolutionary justice. Above all else. You?"

"All the fucking time. Let's start by doing something about these upstarts. This isn't going up against Satan and his Fallen Angels, or even the Devil's Children. Walker's guys are only power-hungry pussies. No better than us. Take this."

Tentatively, Guevara accepted the fragmentation grenade that Garibaldi held out. It felt cold and unfamiliar, heavier than he remembered. How long since he'd lobbed one? Too long.

Since forever. Time was the enemy in hell: eternal penance wore you out, tore you up, filed you down to a quivering nub: fucking up was the way of the afterlife.

"Now throw that grenade in there, fearless leader." Garibaldi pointed to an open trailer nearby. *"Do* some damned thing, so you know you're alive and we know you've got your *cojones* back." Garibaldi waved again at Guevara's personal supply trailer: pocked aluminum; its tires sunk into waterlogged ground.

"Man – but *every*thing's in there. All the best rum in hell's in there."

Guevera caressed the grenade's pineapple-curves. The right weapon. For destruction. For power and anger and conflict and *significance.*

"That's the *point,* Che. Ready?"

Followers were gathering; whispers rattled on the still, fetid air. Garibaldi's men, neat in mottled green jungle fatigues, with their feathered hats and clean bolt-action rifles, kept the crowd respectful.

I used to have troops like that, he thought. *Before* –

He fingered the ring around the pin, then – in a wave of anger –

yanked it off and hurled the grenade into the trailer, hard. The grenade hit the mildewed carpet and bounced, then rolled out of sight.

One of Garibaldi's men swung the door closed. The grenade exploded inside, the trailer's aluminum walls bulging and prickling with its shrapnel. Guevara thought he could hear glass breaking.

"Viva Guevara!" Garibaldi shouted, raising both fists.

"Up the Revolution!" Garibaldi's troops shouted. "Viva Guevara!"

"We'll stick this revolution right up Satan's ass," Guevara thundered in a voice he hadn't used since he'd had motorcycles. Maybe he'd get another motorcycle, roar across hell's blasted wastes....

Guevara grinned at Garibaldi, looked across the crowd, and raised his own fists.

"Viva Guevara!"

*

Walker picked his way down a cobbled street, through a dockside neighborhood where it always seemed to be night. There'd been flooding in New Hell recently, and thick puddles of foul water still blocked the road in places. Something with gleaming eyes and sharp teeth scurried away and glared at him from a clogged drain.

Here and there came noise from taverns; not as much as there'd been before the floods and the plague. People were scared; the rumors, always thick, were at high tide now.

Walker didn't believe the rumors, himself. He hadn't been here too long – a certain firing squad in Trujillo was still a painful memory – but he'd learned that Satan was the undisputed ruler of the modern hells.

So, why revolution? Why bother? Everyone here had already lost the most important battle – for ownership of their eternal souls. Rumor said hell was changing for the worse. Could hell get worse?

Perhaps hell would change, perhaps it wouldn't. But ... revolution. Struggle. Overthrow. For the joy of it: to fight a good fight; something a man like Walker could battle and try to win. Even if Mithridates had failed and men like Caesar were afraid to risk....

A foursome of tipsy medievals came by, singing a war song in Occitan: 'old dead,' the moderns called them. Walker gave them extra room as they passed but one of them glared at him anyway. Likely, from Walker's suit and gun-belt, they mistook him for Authority.

He wasn't. Yet.

Walker turned onto a street along the docks. Things splashed and hissed in furious, dark water. A grey-haired woman in robes and a tricorne leaned against one of the big steel bollards, absorbed in a deck of cards: dealing herself a hand, studying it, reshuffling the cards.

More diviners out, too.

He'd never believed in anything but his own ability. Brilliant – a lot of people thought they were, but he'd proven *he* was. *Summa cum laude* graduate of the University of Nashville at fourteen; medical doctor at nineteen. He'd co-owned a newspaper, practiced both medicine and law, and fought three duels by the time he was twenty-five.

The year 1848, though, had decided the course of his life. He'd been studying medicine in Europe during that year of revolutions – in Heidelberg where Germany's first parliament had been organized, and then in Paris as the Second Republic tottered into existence. The violence, the excitement, the *importance* of those events had given him a direction.

His first foray had led him into the Mexican state of Baja California. There, with forty-five men, he had captured the state capital of La Paz and created the Republic of Lower California. The Mexican Army had moved against him too fast, with too much force, and he'd eventually been driven back into California, where the Federal government had charged him with conducting an illegal war. That was the era of Manifest Destiny. His patriotic intentions had been clear: a jury had taken all of eight minutes to acquit him.

"Yo, Mister?" An emaciated, shirtless, one-eyed man lurched out of an alley, bare chest covered in slashes and half-healed scabs. "Cut your palm, Mister? Cut your palm and tell you 'bout the days to come?"

Walker's hand moved to his gun.

"No."

"Dark days coming, Mister. Dark days coming for all souls. You know your fortune through it, Mister?"

"I create my fortune," Walker told the freak, and increased his pace.

Something big howled or screamed, way out in the thrashing dark ocean. The scream reechoed from the waterfront buildings.

Two years after his Mexican adventure, he'd found another opportunity in a civil war between the two political parties of Nicaragua. Walker had set sail from San Francisco with fifty-eight men to join the Democratic side. More had joined him on arrival.

The American press had named his small army 'the Immortals.' They weren't, yet a quick series of battles led to his taking the national capital and, before long, setting himself up as president.

In six months, Walker's government was recognized as legitimate by the United States. In eight, double-crossing robber barons got that legitimacy withdrawn. Costa Rica declared war on him, repelling his invasion at Santa Rosa and eventually besieging his capital at Grenada. His men had burned that ancient capital to the ground during their retreat and evacuation, and once again he'd found himself Stateside.

Failure: if you survive failure, you learn from it and try again. Four times, Walker tried returning to Nicaragua. On his fourth attempt, the captain of a British warship handed him over to the Honduran government.

He'd really thought he'd meet his end – on a humid, overcast September day before a firing squad: *Listo* ... a blindfold sticky on his face … *Objetivo* ... ropes chafing his wrists as he desperately tried to think of *anything* to save himself … *Fuego*, and the crackle of musketry.

And you really *don't* feel it….

He woke, some timeless duration later, *here*. Here in hell, where chances and challenges seemed infinite; where he could test himself against history's greatest on a playing field laughably level. That Guevara, the legend, saw neither chance nor challenge disgusted and disappointed Walker.

More bars. Too many bars and restaurants, serving unpalatable food and acid drink that no man could stomach…. It was humanity's habit in life to congregate and fight and fornicate (or try to) and fabricate all manner of dirty dealing. So they did the same in afterlife, no better than they'd been before: no smarter, no more inventive, with eternity beckoning and Paradise shining its unattainable light.... Either they couldn't get drunk, or they were drunk all the time, these hellions, souls accursed with just deserts.

One of the damned lay in the gutter with his throat slashed, somehow still alive and moaning slightly. From another alley came grunts and moans. Walker scanned the cheap facades; worn brass, paint crackling over an infernity of rot; flickering neon here and there. Old dead, new dead: souls not quite either – here where the worst scum in all the hells came to meet and scheme and hate and kill and die, again and again.

Walker's hand was never far from his gun; every so often he settled the rapier on his left hip, making sure it was free in its scabbard. Too often in this place, guns failed. Steel could too, but less often.

His destination was a brick building, set slightly apart from the others, its facade pitted and corroded by the sea's salt spray. Shattered windows seeped fumes from the darkness within, and a thuggish bouncer with a spiked club stood outside.

"Some say the Gracchi brothers hang out here. They in tonight?" Walker asked.

The bouncer lazily looked up, then spat something green – something that moved and writhed when it hit the ground – before answering: "They're always in. Can't leave."

"You know where, in here?"

Contempt twisted the bouncer's thick lips. "Where they always are, fuck-head. Behind the bar, serving the poor."

*

Even in the semi-darkness, Walker could tell this place was filthier than the worst sailors' dive on the Barbary Coast. The floor's carpet of putrid spills, vomit, blood and shit sucked at his boots as he walked. Oil-lamps flickered and smoked, hung from the ceiling of the half-empty common room. Fewer people than he'd expected; not a problem. They clustered in knots, muttering or gambling or just quietly (out of lifelong habit and the hope that *this* time it might work) trying to get themselves wasted. Individuals lay here and there, dead or unconscious and always with their pockets turned inside-out.

A wide bar ran along the side of the room farthest from the door, a grimy surface punctuated by the occasional broken tap-handle. Behind it were two bartenders and rows of liquor bottles, many cracked and empty.

"There's broken glass in my beer," a big ponytailed man was growling at one of the two bartenders. He wore dirty, torn workman's overalls and there was blood in the gobbet that he spat on the floor.

"I'm *so* sorry, sir," said one of the bartenders in a tone that made you know he wasn't. The bartender was short, with a narrow aristocratic face and a spill-stained toga. "They come from the brewery with the broken glass already in the bottle – no extra charge."

"Bless you. You sold me shitty beer, and we got a problem."

Good, thought Walker, heading toward the bar. First impressions counted, and this was his chance to make an ideal one, if the disagreement escalated. His hand closed around his rapier's hilt.

"Ran out of the shitty beer last night," the bartender said. "All we have is the broken-glass beer and the dog-vomit beer. Selection's on that chalkboard – can't you read?"

"No," said the customer flatly. He glared at the bartender, who met his eyes and said nothing. After a moment, the customer threw down a coin. "Screw it, just gimme another one." The customer snatched his foul-smelling drink and stumbled back to his table.

Drat. Walker let the half-drawn sword slide back into its scabbard.

"Which do you want?" the bartender asked, as Walker reached the counter. "You look like *you* can read."

"Tiberius Gracchus?" asked Walker.

"I'm Gaius." He gestured at the other bartender, bearded and a few years older. "That's Tiberius. What can I get you, sir?"

"Do you have a minute to talk? You two have a reputation, you know. A famous name." *Romans. Nobles. Reformers.*

"Ssh. None of the damned who come in *here* know it, or need to," Gaius sighed. "But yes, we were something. Fought for the

downtrodden. Tried to do some good. If I'd known what some of them were actually *like* –" he gestured around the dive "– I'd have reconsidered."

"Maybe you weren't wrong. There *are* people who remember what you tried to do. Maybe we can pull strings to get you out of here. And maybe there's something you can do for us."

*

Across the room from Walker, a half-naked whore with a client atop her rolled her head sideways on the table and squinted at the little man just arrived, who was dressed like he actually had some money: new dead. Looked a lot like –

"Get off me," she said to her customer.

"Ain't done yet." He kept working at her, or trying to, buttocks straining.

"Ain't gonna be. Never." She reached for a derringer, pressed it to his throat.

"Not gonna pay you," the customer said, arching back as she cocked the gun.

"Someone else gonna pay me more'n you'll scratch in a year. Now sod off."

Muttering something, the customer got off her. She yanked up her dungarees. With another careful glance at Walker, still talking with the two bartenders, she made for the door.

*

Nouveau Paris, or at least this part of it, had degentrified rapidly since Guevara had last been here. Once-dignified terrace houses were papered with peeling, faded posters for shows, movies or disc releases; handbills stapled over them advertised lower-level shows or amateur releases. The street teemed with hippies, beatniks, goths, flappers and a hundred other types; their self-absorption was, after what Guevara had seen trekking here, almost refreshing in its honest naiveté. After all, what did any damned soul have left but its self? OK, so they should have been looking at *him,* not at themselves, but at least they weren't nervously looking up at the sky for signs of Erra and his pitiless Seven, sent from Above to punish guilty and innocent alike.

Guevara's trip had been productive, so far – valuable contacts made, and a *lot* of new recruits. But the traveling had been a nerve-racking stream of insults and humiliations. His dignity was deeply wounded. Though they'd passed through the Roman hells unharmed, at one point a centurion *(an officer, no less!)* looked straight at Guevara without recognizing his face, his beard, his beret … nothing. He'd wanted to shrug off his cloak, take the man by the shoulders and shake him into awareness, but Garibaldi and Kurt Cobain pulled him back at the last moment.

Here, things were no better: no one recognized him. Che Guevara's star, he admitted glumly to himself, had been eclipsed.

"Scum from the wharf district ruining everything," Cobain muttered, as the two passed a busker screeching his nails on a chalkboard. "Wasn't this bad when I was *last* here."

"It's been too long," Guevara agreed.

"Our most fertile ground." Kurt Cobain, heroin-addicted rock star in life, had died before thirty, but looked forty in hell, with his long blond hair, scruffy beard, and needle-scarred arms. He'd been one of Guevara's top lieutenants since arriving in the underworld. A couple of beatniks strolled by them, passing a joint back and forth; the smell was one-quarter marijuana, three-quarters pungent horse-shit. "Never should have abandoned it. It's where we find *our* people."

They turned down some surprisingly-clean stone steps into a basement club. A big venue: dark with a high ceiling and a real stage on the far side of the room. A band onstage was trying to be heard above deafening squeals of feedback and a bouncy tune coming from somewhere below counseled the listener what to do "if you're happy and you know it."

Feedback squealed above the drummer's attempted solo while the lead guitarist fumbled to replace a broken string.

Wincing, Cobain moved them in the direction of the bar.

"Broken glass or shit?" Guevara asked. "Or maybe some of that dog piss these people call whisky?"

"I used to work here, before you showed up. Maybe I can get us something better."

"Oh, *man,"* came voices in an awed tone Guevara hadn't heard for far too long. "Is it *him?"*

"It's really him!"

Guevara turned around, a gracious smile on his face. Two scraggly girls in flannel and jeans were approaching, excitement glowing on their faces. Bad beer, insulting inattention from Authority – the love of the masses could make up for *all* of that.

"I *killed* myself over you! And we *finally* found you!" the black-haired girl squealed.

"I told you we'd find him eventually!" came from the redhead. "I *told* you, bitch!"

"I'm back." Guevara extended his hand for them to shake.

"Seriously!" said the black-haired girl. "It's Kurt Cobain! Right? It *is* you! We *love* your music! Damned well lived for it!"

"Died for it!" said the redhead. "Blew ourselves away, just like you!"

Guevara gave his rock-star henchman a murderous glare.

"We've been waiting an eternity for you," the redhead said. "Shit. Hot demon shit. It *is* you!"

"It's good to be back," said Cobain. Noting Guevara's irritation, he added, "But screw music, unless it's about revolution, right?"

"Right," the girls said enthusiastically. "Screw society. Screw everything. All that crap. Die and screw everyone."

"We're making a *real* revolution," said Cobain. He inclined his head toward Guevara. "This is Che Guevara, our leader. We're back!"

The girls scrutinized Guevara.

"Devil up my ass," said the redhead. "You're *real?* I thought you were made up by some tee-shirt designer."

Guevara raised his chin and gave the girls his better profile, staring into the middle distance.

"He's leading a rebellion against Satan Himself," Cobain said. "You want to fight Authority? This is your chance. You want to stand up for freedom? He's your man."

"We were down for a while," added Guevara, "but we're back. We always come back. They can't fight the human spirit. Not even Satan can crush our dreams!"

"My dream was to meet Kurt Cobain," said one of the girls. "And it's come true!"

Guevara gave Cobain another warning glare.

"And now you can follow us in afterlife," Cobain said. "Just like you did in life!"

One of the girls turned, waving at a passing friend. "Hey, Tim! Come over here! It's Kurt Cobain and the guy from the tee-shirt!"

Tim had close-cut blond hair dyed purple in spots, thick black-rimmed glasses with no lenses, and a white-and-black striped tee-shirt. His wrists were bleeding from deep cuts. Blood ran down his forearms; every so often he wiped the blood on his crusty jeans.

"Awesome," he said, flat and sarcastic.

"You've got to excuse Tim," said the redhead. "He's still kind of pissed that he ended up here."

"We all are," said Guevara. "But when we overthrow Satan, we'll make hell a better place. Create our own heaven. A world of brotherly love and unlimited equality!"

Feedback screamed in a deafening burst. Guevara's hands twitched toward his ears, and then the 'If you're happy and you know it ...' song came back. One of the guitarists on stage played a few barely-audible notes before another string snapped.

"Yeah," said Tim, maybe sardonically. "That's even better."

"Tim's pissed not so much that he ended up here," the redhead said, "but *how.*"

"Suicide, right?" asked Guevara.

"Nah. Accident. I wasn't trying to die. I cut my wrists to get those cool scars," said Tim. "To show my friends how smart and desperate I was. I was supposed to look like a really cool nonconformist. Not *die.*"

"You want to be a nonconformist?" Guevara asked. "They call us the 'Dissidents.' We're organizing to challenge Authority. Again. And this time, we'll win."

"I don't know," said the redhead. "Really, actually fighting Satan would be *dangerous.* These guys aren't hall monitors. They're *mean.*"

"It's *real,*" said Tim. "A real fight. Not just this fake hipster bullshit." He adjusted the empty frames of his 'eyeglasses.' "I'm in, tee-shirt man."

"They can kill us," Guevara said to the girls, "but they can't kill our souls. They've killed me – how many times? Ten, twelve, fifty? I come back." Raising his voice, he looked soulfully into first the redhead's eyes, then the other girl's. "So what if they kill us? *Si,* it hurts! Who cares? You can live with pain or it kills you, but either way, who *cares?* So long as you're fighting. So long as you're challenging them, fighting them, showing them an alternative!" One by one, if he had to, he'd rebuild the revolution. Inspire them. Give purpose to those who had nothing with which to fill their emptiness. "This is *hell*, guys. This is real. *Fighting* repression is real!"

"He's right about it being real," Cobain put in quietly. "Nothing's more real than the struggle. Not the music, not nothing."

"We're going to challenge the overlords; fight for you. You want to stand up for yourselves? Join us." Guevara told them. "You want to show Satan and the Romans and the goose-steppers what you really are? Join us. You want to *be* something, to be part of something? Join us. Then when you die again, you'll die for something, not for nothing."

Movement nearby: someone in the corner of Guevara's eye; he was too focused on converting these youngsters to care. But Cobain touched Guevara's elbow. Then pulled on it.

"A moment," he said to the girls. Then snarled at Cobain: *"What?"*

"Sorry, boss. *Important.* Rosa found something – someone." Cobain gestured at Rosa Luxembourg, a youngish member of Guevara's cadre. She was trailed by a ragged woman with the look of a dockside whore and a broad, gap-toothed smile.

"Mister Guevara, boss?" asked the gap-toothed whore. "Rosa says you was pissed off by some little guy. Told me about him: he's trying to start his own revolution and fucked with you."

Walker, thought Guevara; merely the memory of that humiliation made him angry. "And?"

"He's off by himself. Talking to some guys. How much you gonna pay me to tell you where?"

Whatever you want, thought Guevara.

"No need. He's in the bar with the Gracchi brothers," Rosa told him. "Probably trying to recruit them. *I* know where –"

A screech of feedback interrupted her.

When it was over, Rosa took the whore by the elbow to hustle her away.

"Madame Rosa, you said you was going to make him pay me!" the whore complained.

"You have the thanks of Che Guevara and the rebellion," Guevara dismissed the whore. "Rosa, how far is this place?"

"Mile and a half from here," said Rosa as the whore shook free of her grasp.

"You guys gonna go shoot somebody?" Tim asked, finally engaged.

"We're going to go protect the revolution," said Guevara, "against treachery and usurpation."

Rosa reached under her long skirt and tossed Cobain a shotgun.

Cobain checked it over. Then he looked up. "By shooting somebody," he put in.

"By doing whatever is necessary to protect the dignity and integrity of our revolution," said Guevara. "Are you with us, or not?"

"Oh, *hell* yeah," said Tim.

"Let's go," said the red-haired girl. "You're right, tee-shirt man."

"She said you was gonna pay me," the whore repeated.

"With a higher currency than mere gold," Guevara said. "With the gratitude of the people."

"This Walker's not going to hang around there forever," warned Rosa. "I've got an arms stash in my apartment. Couple of blocks from here; on the way."

"Then," said Guevara, raising his voice and his fist, "follow me!"

*

"And so, Mister Walker," Tiberius Gracchus was asking, "what makes you think that your revolution and its committee would benefit the people? Assuming it succeeds. Assuming it *can* succeed."

Walker flicked his index finger along the top of the glass of beer he'd ordered a little while ago to pretend he had legitimate business in this bar. "The leadership committee is comprised of people. We're inviting you to join those people," he repeated.

"And the *other* people, these other revolutionaries?" Tiberius Gracchus wanted to know. In the 2nd century BCE, he and his brother Gaius had been the founding fathers of both socialism and populism.

But this wasn't Rome in the 2nd century BCE; this was a dockside bar in New Hell and the Gracchi brothers were getting tiresome. He didn't think Gaius and Tiberius were truly indifferent, or feigning indifference as a negotiating tactic, but they were asking too damned many questions.

"What about them? They'll continue as usual, I suppose. I don't wish them any particular harm. I don't think anyone else on my committee does, either."

"Hey, Roman," said one of the locals, a rat-faced man with ugly wounds on his bald scalp, wearing a ripped-up crew shirt and what once had been dress pants. "Two more beers, now."

Gaius moved to pour them. Walker turned, gave the room another of his periodic once-overs. He was turning back when someone kicked open the door.

Three men – no, five, six – trooped into the bar carrying an assortment of long guns and headed straight for Walker. The rat-faced little customer fled, and others seemed to melt into the bar's walls or their seats.

In the light of one flickering lamp, he made out a face – fiery-eyed and mustached and the only one without a gun in his hands: Che Guevara.

Oh, *shit*.

There were six of them: one woman; three trashy-looking kids; Guevara; and a blond man whom Walker recognized as one of the drunks in Guevara's shack. They headed to the front of the common room. The blond man held his shotgun with casual precision, aimed straight at Walker's chest. The woman and two kids moved across, to Walker's other side. The way they were handling their AKs made Walker flinch. And then there was that shotgun, and the woman's Uzi, pointing directly at him.

He said nothing. This was no time to go for your own gun; this was a time to talk your way out.

Slowly, almost casually, he placed his hands in clear sight, behind him against the bar.

If they kill you, you come back, he reminded himself.

What was Guevara doing here? Didn't the Argentine know that he was a spent force, a closed chapter, a nuisance who'd been pushed out of history's way?

"William Walker," Guevara finally said.

"Che Guevara." Walker responded as casually as he could: "I didn't know you drank here."

"My *friends* call me Che," said Guevara.

Walker kept his eyes on Guevara, or tried to. He and his shotgun-toting henchman were six or seven feet away, too far for a rush. The other kids were about the same distance on his other side, covering him.

Six to one were beatable odds under some circumstances. Not these.

Why the fuck *didn't I bring some backup with me? Approaching them alone to impress them? Damned stupid, in retrospect.*

"You're not a friend. You and your imposters' committee have been tried and found guilty of insult, sedition and usurpation. Of *my* revolution."

They say you come back. They say it hurts like hell and they don't always fix you up quite the same way.

"Very well," Walker said. Slowly. Breathing deeply. "I can pass that on to the Committee. I suppose you would like it – prefer it – for us to subordinate ourselves to you – as the revolutionary leader."

"We gonna waste this guy or not?" one of the kids – the boy – asked.

Ka-chack: The blond man cocked his shotgun, a solid sound in the bar. Walker tried to force himself to take a *(last?)* breath.

"No, Kurt," said Guevara, pushing the shotgun's muzzle slightly away. "We're going to do it the proper way."

Walker kept silent. Kept his eyes on Guevara. His palms were sweating, slick with grime from the bar counter. He forced himself to keep his hands still.

"A blindfold," said Guevara slowly. "A last cigarette."

Walker's wrists itched with the memory of rope chafing them … not so very long ago …

"Your final words. All very proper. If you had been a worthy opponent, Mister Walker, we might even have allowed you to give the firing commands yourself."

Listo. Objetivo. Fuego.

Oh, yes. Walker remembered *that*.

"But you're not a worthy opponent," Guevara went on. "You were nothing but a filibustering pirate in life, and a cheap usurper in death. Even a formal execution is more dignity than you deserve."

Tense. Very tense. Half in memory; this had happened before. This had happened before, and he was reliving it, and somehow his mouth said: "Very well. One more drink, before we go outside?"

"A final drink," said Guevara slowly, mulling it. "Yes. I am a generous man, even to my enemies. Even to pathetic, *tiny* little enemies like yourself. Rosa, tie his wrists afterwards."

The woman with the Uzi produced a length of cord.

Walker carefully reached for his tankard of beer. It slipped slightly in his sweat-slick fingers – his face, too, was sweating, and his wrists were tingling, and a part of his brain was thinking *this is Trujillo all over again,* the gloom of the bar replacing the blackness of the firing squad –

With his mind going numb, he slowly raised the tankard.

And then Walker whirled, hurling the beer (the kind filled with tiny glass shards) up into the face of the blond man with the shotgun.

Running. Gunshots.

The shotgun exploded upward as the blond man dropped it, his hands pawing at his eyes.

Then Walker was throwing himself past that blond man, between the blond and Guevara, because – a part of his mind told him – those kids wouldn't fire at their leader –

Stammering automatic fire, *loud* in the enclosed bar.

Walker wasn't sure if he'd been hit. But *any* death would be better than another cigarette, another blindfold, another firing squad, helpless, with his wrists bound.

Walker charged along the side of the room, bolting for the door. His boots pounded on the sticky floor. Leaping over a passed-out drunk, he aimed his shoulder at the door, kept his head down, and ran like hell.

More gunshots.

*"Ass*hole! *Asshole!"* one of the kids screamed.

An AK spat a long, ragged burst. Bullets smashed – exploded – one of the lamps a foot from Walker's head. More rounds blasted a table to splinters and ventilated the side of a booth…

…but they weren't hitting *him*, and he could still run –

Through the door, where the bouncer stood, and onto the docks, and *running*.

Running like hell for darkness to escape into, or at least into cover he could shoot back from, because somehow his gun was in his hand now and he *could* shoot back, and six to one odds were reasonable on *these* terms.

Guevara was the first out the door behind him, waving a revolver. Then came one of the kids, who pointed at Walker and shouted something.

More wild gunfire, not even remotely close.

Two of Guevara's bunch – then another, then two more – were in pursuit.

The docks were dark and bare, in the direction he was running. Dark shapes loomed, dull floodlights somewhere in the middle distance where a massive crane swung. Stacks of shipping containers towered not *too* far away, black hulks that at least would provide a moment's cover.

He turned for a moment, fired a shot over his shoulder. *Slow down pursuit* – they were taller than he, longer legs, he *had* to slow them – and then another shot, and the third time his gun did nothing but issue a faint and useless click. Jammed.

Fuck. Fuck, fuck, *fuck.*

No time to clear it, not now, not with those five in pursuit and gaining. If he had fifteen seconds…. Frantically he jacked the slide, pointing the barrel down: *nothing* – but, no, it *couldn't* be one of those easy ones, could it?

If I'd brought a squad of Minutemen or some Bolsheviks, or some of Quantrill's –

No. No time to think about that. Think about running. Cover. Somewhere he could get the time to clear his gun and shoot back.

Heavy automatic fire burped from behind him. Bullets clanged into the shipping crates, ricocheted hard against the metal, blowing chips off a cobblestone. The wind was moist and salty and pushed hard at his face as he threw himself into the cover of the crates and swung right.

His slick and sweaty hands worked at the gun as he ran through the darkness in the containers' shadow, one foot splashing into a thick puddle of filth. An alley…

…an alley and safety.

The first of Guevara's men appeared behind him, momentarily unsure where he'd gone. It took a moment for them to get their bearings.

By then, Walker was already through the alley; on a street again; in a doorway, and *finally* the gun was clear.

"Where'd he go?" One of the kids.

"Alley."

"He's got a gun."

Six to one. Five to one, perhaps, if the shotgun man was still down. He had a gun and a sword and cover, and *these* were circumstances where *those* odds were reasonable.

They knew it, too. They were hesitating.

You were a closed book, Guevara. You were no longer relevant. We'd moved on.

And suddenly it had been Trujillo again, the man taunting him…

"I'm here," Walker shouted. Leaned out of the doorway, gun up. Several figures, slowly moving along in the shadow of the containers about thirty feet away.

"Come out." Guevara's voice. "I'll even allow you to give the commands."

Instinctively, not rationally, Walker fired twice at the nearest of the dark figures. The response was a blazing stammer of automatic fire that came nowhere near him.

No. Get the hell out of here. There is *a time to run. You have resources….*

The hell with that.

He'd take them on personally – except that he'd had eight rounds, and he'd used at least four, and there were five of them.

The Committee must be told about this. He could deal with Guevara later.

Carefully, slowly, he moved back along the alley, keeping to the darkest shadows. Another burst of automatic fire, apparently aimed at the doorway where he'd just been, showed that Guevara's men were buying it.

At an intersecting alley, a three-foot-wide crack, darker than a cesspit, appeared to his right. Out of their line of sight. Good.

You bastard. You drunkard, has-been, son of a bitch, Guevara.

He slipped into the alley, his foot sliding on something dead and rotten. The alley stank like a cesspit, too, and invisible things scuttled away as he moved.

Guevara's voice: "Running imperialist dog! We showed him a thing or two!"

A half-hearted cheer.

"Viva Guevara!" came a female voice. Followed by a slightly stronger cheer.

Moving along the alley, ready to shoot (although it didn't *sound* like he was being pursued), Walker clenched his lips.

You were supposed to stay out of the way, Guevara. You'd been *a potential nuisance. You've now become a real problem.*

Trujillo. Guevara's gloating about blindfolds and cigarettes.

And it's just become very, very personal.

*

Eric Blair lit a new cigarette from his old, dropped the old one to grind it under his shoe-heel on the rough concrete floor. Coughed a couple of times. "Guevara's back," he repeated.

"And we need to do something," Walker growled. The Committee was gathered in the same under-factory basement, although the meeting had taken a day or so to arrange. So had doubling the guard: a company of Minutemen, uncomfortably cradling newly-issued M-16s, was stationed throughout the factory. "He almost killed me. He tried to kill me. He was going to put me up against a wall and shoot me."

"Don't worry," said Voltaire, the French Enlightenment writer. "You get used to the Undertaker's halitosis eventually."

"No, I agree," said Russian revolutionary leader Leon Trotsky.

"He *does* pose a certain threat."

"Damn right he does! Are we going to do something about it or not?"

Alinsky looked at Walker. "You propose killing him?"

"I propose we take these Minutemen, the Bolsheviks Leon has hanging around, everyone else we can gather up at short notice. Head downtown right now and blow him to hell," Walker snapped. "Oh."

"'Oh' is right," said Alinsky. "He's already *in* hell – New Hell, to be precise. Do you know *how many* times that man has been killed? He bounces back. He doesn't even seem to mind dying all that much. If you kill him, he's martyred. Again. All these young neo-hippies and whatnot who make up his following? They'll be dismayed for a few hours, and then all the more impressed when he returns."

"We can't let him live," said Walker, fighting to control himself. To convince himself that this *was* professional and operational, and not personal anger about having to retrace old steps and about how the son of a bitch had – knowingly or unknowingly – taunted him with flashbacks of Trujillo. "He's a problem. He's going to recruit cannon fodder that *we* could use. People are going to think *we're* him and our revolution is being mounted by Guevara's bunch of incompetents. He's going to get the credit for our successes and we're going to get the blame for – for pretty much everything he does."

"You're angry," said Trotsky. "But those are legitimate points. Guevara's return is more than trivial, and killing him won't solve the problem more than briefly."

Blair took another long drag of his cigarette and blew the smoke toward the room's high and dark ceiling. "Why should we care about killing Guevara?" he asked.

Walker glared at him. "Were you even *listening?"*

"If you want to hurt a man, you destroy what he most values," Blair went on calmly. "For Guevara, that's not his life – he knows he'll come back and the pain doesn't matter to him. If you want to make Guevara afraid to trouble us again, you need to hurt him where it *does* count."

"And where would that be? Don't shoot him in the head, kick

him in the crotch?" Walker asked sarcastically.

"Metaphorically, yes. Guevara is egotistical," said Blair. "I propose we continue Operation Primus as planned –"

"Ignoring him won't work," Trotsky cut him off. "He'll simply try harder to get our attention."

"– with one thing changed," Blair finished. "I don't propose we ignore him. Guevara's built his identity as a romantic legend. Heroically attacking only the most glamorous targets. He likes attention. He likes credit. I propose we credit him."

*

The rally had been at a different performance venue in the same degentrified neighborhood, and it had been packed to the walls with hundreds of Guevara's new recruits. Red banners and flashing lights, and somebody had blown up large photos of Guevara's face to focus the decor. An opportunist with a printing press had gone into business, and there'd been damned souls outside hawking badges and tee-shirts.

Much cheering and shouting of his name. This rally had been the best time Guevara had had in who knew *how* long. He was back!

Now, as things died down and the crowd left, Guevara stood smiling on the stage with his hands on his hips.

"We should have come here a *lot* sooner," he said.

Cobain touched a wet cloth to his eyes. He'd been doing that all day; the shards of glass in the beer Walker had thrown at him hadn't blinded him, but his eyes still *hurt.* He nodded. "Coming back here was a good idea. Now what does this joker want?"

The kid Cobain had indicated, coming up to the stage, was gaunt, spiky-haired and tattooed.

"Hey, Guevara, bossman. Great speech you gave. You ever given any thought to publicity? Like, getting the message out to the wider hells? Convey to them what we're all about?"

Guevara cocked his head.

"Yeah, I'm a communications guy, man. Name's Boz, and I'm totally volunteering. Real experienced writer, I am."

"What have you written? Manifestos?"

"Graffiti. My tag. More than five thousand times across the

greater Los Angeles area."

"Anything else?" *'Che,' five thousand times...*

"Sometimes I said 'rules' or 'lives' next to it. I can write yours the same way."

Oh yes. That's all we need and more.

Guevara extended his hand to the kid. "It's great to have you with us, Mister Boz. If you want pens, spray cans, anything else, just call on me."

"Viva Guevara," the kid said and headed off.

"Well," said Guevara to Cobain and Rosa, who'd been handling sound for the event. "We're back in charge. That jerk Walker and his committee fled like the Administration puppets they probably are."

Cobain wiped his eyes again. "I don't know," he said, shotgun in the crook of his arm. "That little bastard Walker was serious. Got away, too."

"Fled like a running dog," Guevara gestured dismissively. "To tell his friends that we're back in town, back in charge. The next rebel strike that happens –" his gesturing hand made a fist, pounding upward toward glory "– everyone will know is *ours.*"

*

'Totalitarian Club,' the sign said. 'Attendance Mandatory.'

Except, the olive-skinned man in the DeadEx uniform thought, *nobody seems to be here.* He rang the doorbell again, or at least pushed the button and hoped it was connected to an actual ringer. Around New Hell, you never knew.

Eventually, the big hardwood door opened.

"You interrupted a meeting," said a man in a business suit, beside a casually-dressed companion. "That's against the rules."

"You got a present for us?" asked the guy with him; short and balding, in shorts and a Hawaiian shirt. "From who? Nobody ever sends us presents!"

"From *whom,*" the man in the business suit corrected him.

The man in the DeadEx uniform shrugged.

"I just deliver 'em, boss. You want it or not? This thing's heavy."

The suited man took it. A two-by-two-foot box in festive

wrapping paper.

"Something for us to sign?" asked the man in the Hawaiian shirt. He'd been Administrative Secretary of the Ocawa Meadows Homeowners' Association, in southern Florida, and his name was Harry Innis.

"Nothing to sign that the company ever gives me," shrugged the deliveryman.

"They should," said Innis. "All deliveries should be signed for. The rules say so. I'm Third Associate Section Head for Traffic and Parking Enforcement, and I know. Rules are rules."

"Yessir," said the man in the DeadEx uniform. "I just follow mine, sir. Have a good afternoon."

The door closed. Free of the package, the delivery man walked down the stairs, past tight brownstones on a slope, along wide sidewalks several feet below the buildings' entrances, and onto the street. Quiet street, genteel neighborhood. A few cars were parked here and there, and a big tan van, right outside the club.

He stripped off the stolen jacket and cap and began jogging quickly away.

*

"They sent us a present!" Innis exulted, as the two brought the package into the front room. The suited man set it on a table.

"That is completely out of order," said the Deputy Associate Director of the Infernal Bureau of Sewage and Drinking Water Management, Fourth Division, New Hell Department. "A motion must be introduced, extenuating circumstances notwithstanding."

"I object," said Max Weber. He was a middle-aged man with a black suit and a bowler hat under his arm; in life he'd been a pioneer of modern social science. "These are *very* extenuating circumstances. This is the first present anyone's ever sent us, and I don't think Robert's Rules of Order cover it."

Brigadier-General Henry Martyn Robert, who'd written those rules, banged his gavel.

"No, they don't," he said.

"Very well," said Weber. "I motion that we open the present."

"I second that motion," said Innis.

"Improper," said Weber. "You're not seated appropriately."

"I'm *seconding your own motion,*" said Innis.

"Rules are rules," Weber said.

"You're right. Sorry."

Another man raised his hand. "I second Mister Weber's motion."

"Objections?" asked Robert.

There were none.

"Motion carried," said Robert. "As the presiding member of this recreational gathering, it is incumbent upon myself to open the present."

He went to the table, carefully undid the bow and stripped away the wrapping paper. A card was taped to the underside of the box's top flap. Robert opened it.

"'Dear Bureaucrats of New Hell,'" he read aloud. "'Enclosed is fifteen pounds of high explosives. Die, scum. Signed, Che Guevara.'"

There was a long, long moment of silence. A faint ticking could be heard from the package.

"No motion was put forth, let alone properly carried, that he read the card," somebody objected weakly.

Someone else raised their hand: "I motion to adjourn."

"Seconded," somebody added hurriedly, on the heels of that first person.

"Carried," said Robert. He ran for the door ahead of the crowd.

*

"I thought Guevara was out of it," Innis snapped at Weber, as the three-dozen club members formed lines in columns of threes, in accordance with the rules that had long ago been established for emergency evacuations. Not that that had ever happened: nobody had ever cared about Administration's middle-management enough to send mail bombs in the past.

At least, none that had ever arrived. No DeadEx executives hung out here, but Innis thought he would *definitely* have a word with Weber suggesting that he talk with Robert about going through appropriate channels of communication (as stipulated by the correct organizational charts) to reach the damned bureaucrats responsible for this kind of thing.

"Very well," Robert addressed the crowd. "Everybody is

accounted for. We just have to wait for the bomb disposal squad to arrive."

"And whine some more about their seventy-two virgins," an elderly man muttered darkly.

"Oh, stop bitching," snapped Weber. "Just because you were one of them. They're on their way, all right?"

*

Walker crouched on a rooftop, across the street and about a hundred yards away from the Totalitarian Club. He fingered the remote control and glanced at Lumumba.

Lumumba put down his scope.

"Forty-one. All of them outside, per proper procedure."

"Per proper procedure," Walker repeated. In the back of the van sat forty-five pounds of dynamite, set to blow a respectable fraction of New Hell's middle management back to the Undertaker. You couldn't get a sufficiently-large bomb into their clubhouse, but you could bring them out to where a proper bomb *could* get them....

"So?" Lumumba asked. "What are you waiting for? A motion to be carried?"

"Not particularly," said Walker, and hit the detonator.

*

Inside the van, a remotely-triggered spark flashed.

Nothing happened. In the half-hour since the van had been parked, the nitroglycerine had sweated completely out of the dynamite and leaked across the bed of the van, six inches below the level of the detonator.

*

"Something looks wrong about that van," said Innis. He headed toward it.

"You're just upset," said Robert. "Stay where you are."

Innis puffed himself up: "I am the Third Associate Section Head for Traffic and Parking Enforcement, thank you very much. I motion that I be permitted to step out of line for the cause of professional duties."

"Motion seconded, for the cause of professional duties," said Weber.

"Very well," said Robert. "You may inspect the van as you see fit. And we shall accompany you."

*

"Shit," said Walker. "Backup detonator. Now."

Lumumba passed it to him. The bureaucrats outside were getting agitated. Two were approaching the van, with the rest filing along behind.

Walker hit the second remote.

Nothing happened.

"We put *forty-five pounds of dynamite* into that van," Walker snarled. "What the hell is wrong with it?"

*

"I've figured out what's wrong with the van," Innis declared to Robert, triumphantly getting up off his knees. He folded his ruler neatly back into his chest pocket.

"And?" Robert asked. The other members of the Club were antsy, standing by. None of them much liked the fact that *one* of them had authority to act while they didn't.

Innis drew a blank ticket-form from his pocket, and a pen.

"It's improperly parked," he said. "Almost a *full half-inch* farther from the curb than is allowed."

*

"Failed bomb," said Lumumba. "You sure those detonators were right?"

"Triple-checked. And we had that backup for a reason."

Lumumba raised his scope again.

*

"Rules are rules," Innis said, finishing the ticket citation. He pulled up one of the van's wipers and placed the ticket – careful to align it at a perfect, ninety-degree angle against the base – on the windshield. "Damned rulebreakers. They commit murder or something to get here, and then they expect to continue their misbehavior? Jaywalking, inappropriate expense deductions –" he gestured at the van "– parking almost seven-sixteenths of an inch beyond regulation maximum distance...."

There was a chorus of sympathetic agreement from the others, still in their neat bomb-evacuation lines. Administration middle-management had no love for rulebreakers.

"We'll let these people know that rules are rules, and in hell there is justice," said Innis, emphatically slapping the wiper down on the ticket.

Boom.

*

Walker was turning away just as the van blew up. The explosion threw him and Lumumba forward and down onto the rooftop's wet tar only a moment before bits of shrapnel from the blast showered them.

Carefully, he got to his feet. The van and everything close by was a shredded inferno.

"You got that scope?" he asked Lumumba.

Lumumba checked. "Broken, man. But even from here, I can see there aren't any survivors."

"Original package and the card inside it should be intact, right?" That was important, Walker thought; critical to getting back at that son of a bitch, Guevara.

"Should be. Doesn't look like the club itself took much damage. Six feet of rock between the blast and the meeting room," said Lumumba.

"Good," Walker said. "The attack needs to be appropriately credited." He smirked. *"Viva Guevara."*

*

'Car Bomb Kills 41 Administration Staff,' read the headline of the next morning's New Hell Times. *'Guevara Claims Credit.'*

Guevara threw the newspaper hard against the café wall.

"I didn't *do* that!" he snarled.

Cobain, who'd heard the news on the radio a little earlier, squinted at him. "I know, boss. You don't have to convince *me.* But somebody did it. Left the card, and called Authority five minutes later. Our guys aren't happy."

Tim and a couple of goateed hipsters stormed in, Tim kicking at a chair as he marched angrily up to where Guevara and Cobain were sitting.

"I thought you were going to give us a heroic, *romantic* revolution," Tim hissed. "Not some cheap car-bombing of bureaucrats nobody *cares* about."

"I didn't do it," Guevara muttered. "It's a slander attempt."

Tim threw down a copy of a badly-mimeographed magazine.

"Reliable media says you did. And says that *you* said you did. Man, I thought you were cool. Not just some terrorist." He wiped his bloody wrists angrily on his jeans.

"You didn't even go in shooting," one of the hipsters agreed. "Just blew them up. Cowards."

"It's slander," Guevara muttered again. These people had been worshipping him last night. Hanging on his every word. And now they were saying *this* about him?

And they turned their backs and left – *deserting* him.

Rosa came in, agitated. "You want the bad news first, boss, or –?"

A moment of relief: "No, the good news. Thank you."

"I was going to say the bad news or the *worse* news. OK, the *relatively* good news is that the new kid, Boz, is out there writing your name, although he's writing 'sucks' after it."

What was *happening*? All these people – they'd loved him! They'd worshipped him!

Those Committee *bastards*. That little jerk, Walker.

If this was the relatively good news, then…?

"And what's the worse news?" Guevara asked, starting to get nervous. Something *worse?* What *could* be worse?

"Somebody ratted you out. Administration's coming. They didn't care before, but now they think you killed a bunch of *them. And* they know where you are."

Yes. Faint sirens in the distance. Getting closer.

"We better scram," Cobain said, starting to get up.

"Yeah. You, get out of here," said the beatnik behind the café's counter. *"Revolutionaries* are welcome in my place. Jerkwater terrorists can go hang."

Those sirens were getting louder.

"I didn't do it!" Guevara pleaded. "It was those Committee people!"

"You said something else in the note at the scene," the beatnik growled.

"Camp's still there," said Cobain. "And I've got some

connections out in Lost Angeles. But if we don't blow town *now*, we might not be able to."

On the street, agitation. A man in a pink Afro spat at Guevara, got his boot. You could feel the hostility. The woman who'd emceed his speech last night saw him coming and crossed the street. And those sirens were still getting louder.

Damn it. There had to be alcohol somewhere; he needed a drink. *Not even my fault! I didn't* do *anything!*

Battle was one thing. A fight to the last with his gun in his hand – but *this*: running; his supporters contemptuous; people writing shit about him when they'd *worshipped* him earlier?

"Yeah, run, cowardly bomber," sneered a goth who'd worn a red bandanna in his honor the night before.

Somebody in the crowd pressed something into Guevara's hand; his fingers instinctively closed around it. But Rosa and Kurt were urging him on, and it was only a couple of miles later, with sirens lower and fainter again, that he could stop to see what it was.

In the mouth of an alley, Kurt looking nervously at the street, Guevara found he'd been given a small radio detonator with a bit of notepaper wrapped around it.

'I told you the first time, you'd been fired,' the note said, in smooth nineteenth-century cursive which Guevara had to struggle for a moment to read. '*Saying things twice is unpleasant. — W. Walker.'*

Tale of a Tail

by

Nancy Asire

"What's Wellington doing now?" Marie asked Napoleon.

Napoleon glanced to his left toward Wellington's house. From his vantage point on his front porch, he could see over the top of the neatly trimmed hedge to what appeared to be a carefully manicured lawn. His neighbor was crouched down, apparently engrossed in minute examination of his grass. Napoleon lifted an eyebrow and turned to Countess Marie Walewska, his mistress in life and afterlife, who stood at his side.

"Who knows? Maybe he's found a new pest destroying his grass. Or, he's worried it will turn yellow from what's left of the flood in New Hell City." He looked across the street to Decentral Park. The Viet Cong had, for the moment, gone to ground. There hadn't been an artillery shelling from them for a while now, and that was without benefit of the periodic delivery of barbequed ribs, courtesy of Hellview Estates. The whole thing made him nervous. And farther across the Park, it was equally as quiet. He hadn't heard from the Romans in days ... well, more like a month. All in all, hell being hell, something was going on. Something with a capital "S."

And as for the French.... Installing his friend, Grand Marshal Duroc, as his surrogate in Louis XIV's overly opulent palace had been a stroke of genius – even if he had to admit so himself. Napoleon loathed the place. Oh, he was still in charge of the French in New Hell, but he preferred his house by Hellview Golf and Country Club above anything that could be found in that baroque mishmash Louis preferred. From the beginning of his sentence to hell, Napoleon had earnestly tried to stay invisible if possible. Pull a few strings here, pull a few strings there. Stay out of the way of those who could do real damage to the old timers and the newly arrived. Still in charge? Well, *that* might be open to debate, too. News was hard to come by these days. What little filtered to this side of Decentral Park bore the taint of rumor upon rumor. And one thing he had learned since he had arrived in the infernal regions was not to trust rumor. Unless, of course, the rumor was rumored from someone he *could* trust, or a rumor he himself had concocted.

"Why don't we go see for ourselves what Wellington's doing?" he asked.

Marie shrugged her shoulders and led the way down the drive and around the hedge. Wellington was now nearly flattened on his lawn, his posterior much higher than his head. So engrossed in whatever he was doing, he didn't seem to register he had company. Napoleon crossed his arms on his chest.

"Wellington, what the shit is going on?"

Wellington jumped nearly a foot, his head snapping around and a startled expression crossing his thin, long-nosed face.

"Damn, Napoleon!" he got out. "You really shouldn't sneak up on someone that way. Heart attack and all that."

"I wasn't sneaking. I walked here like any normal person would. What is it you're so focused on?"

"My grass!" Wellington stood, brushed stray green remnants of his lawn from the knees of his white British officer's breeches. "Look at it, will you! It's beyond belief!"

"What ... the grass or you, butt to the sky, examining it?"

Wellington drew his chin back and assumed a hurt expression. "You needn't act that way. I'm trying ... *really* trying to obey the rules. And it's impossible! Bloody impossible!"

Napoleon studied the grass. "Looks fine to me. You just cut it yesterday."

"Precisely my point." Wellington held out a ruler. "The Home Owner's Association says my grass can only be, at the very most, two inches tall. And, believe me, I measured the entire lawn. Every last part of it. There wasn't a place where the grass was taller than an inch and a half. And *now* look at it!"

"I'm looking and I still don't see the problem." Napoleon glanced sidelong at Marie, who was trying her absolute best to hide a smile. "I'm no horticulture specialist, but it can't be much over two inches tall."

"Then check it out yourself, since you've got the bloody eagle eye." Wellington offered the ruler, his face going red with frustration. It was obvious he only now realized Marie stood next to Napoleon. "Good day, my lady," he said, bowing slightly.

She smiled at him and nodded back.

"Eagle eye, is it? Let's see." Napoleon knelt, placed the ruler down to where it touched the ground. "*Merde!* What's happening here? Your grass is two and a half inches tall!"

"That's what I'm trying to tell you! It couldn't have grown an inch in a night!"

"Huhn." Napoleon rocked back on his heels and stared at the ruler. "Marie," he asked, "could you bring me the ruler I've got stashed in my desk? For comparison's sake," he finished, looking up at Wellington who was still red-faced and the picture of exasperation.

"Damned Home Owner's Association," Wellington grumped. "If it isn't one bloody thing, it's another. And that new HOA president ... he's, well –"

"Quiet." Napoleon hissed. "You don't know who's listening."

Wellington made a show of looking to the left, the right, behind his back and across the street. "No one, that I can see."

"How long have we been in New Hell, Wellington? Long enough that by now I'd think you'd know ears don't have to be attached to a body to hear."

"Oh, you're right. It's just so frustrating!"

"No argument there. We've been lucky so far that eternal frustration is one of our main sources of torment."

Marie came around the end of the hedge, Napoleon's ruler in her hand. "Found it," she announced. "But it wasn't where you left it last."

"Where now?" Napoleon asked with an exasperated sigh.

"In the kitchen."

"And *this* is new?" Napoleon took the ruler and shook his head. "I don't know about you, Wellington, but everything in my house grows legs in the dark and relocates." He knelt and duplicated the test he had made with Wellington's ruler. This time, the results were even worse.

"It seems you're in trouble, *mon ami*," he said, standing and fixing Wellington with a stare. "Three inches."

Wellington's shoulders slumped. "If I'm caught with grass

three inches long –"

"I know, I know. The fines."

"I suppose I'll have to mow again. Damn! At this stage, I'll run out of fuel before the week's out."

"Don't feel so bad," Napoleon said. "You've got grass that grows inches in hours. *I've* got the driveway that births weeds in the cracks when my back's turned. And they bloom, spreading their seeds to my yard! Which, I hope, is better behaved than your lawn. If I have to pull another weed today, I'll ... well, I'm not sure *what* I'll do."

"We'll pull weeds," Marie said. "I've already got a basket full."

"Do you think *he's* home?" Wellington asked, a slight nod of his head toward the residence of the president of the Home Owner's Association on the other side of his house.

"Who knows." Napoleon lowered his voice. "One more thing that's annoying about this HOA is that damned rule book for Hellview Estates. I've read the entire thing, but every time I open it, there's a brand new list of prohibitions. Remember? Last month, any wood on our houses had to be painted a tasteful shade of taupe. The month before, it was ecru. I don't know about you, but I got awfully tired of painting."

"Oh, well. I'm off to mow. And if you're smart, Napoleon, you'd better check your lawn, too. Whatever my grass has might be catching."

*

Dinner that evening was shared with Wellington who, keeping to past tradition, turned up at the precise time when Napoleon and Marie were fixing it.

"Mooch!" Napoleon groused. "Don't you have your own kitchen?"

"Oh, I do, but it's so much more pleasant here." Wellington spread his napkin across his lap. "Besides, I'm rather tired from mowing. If that grass is taller than two inches tomorrow –"

"Scalped it, did you?"

"To three-quarters of an inch. I measured twice."

"Here, Wellington," Marie said, extending a glass of wine. "There's nothing you can do until tomorrow anyway."

Wellington snorted something vile under his breath, but accepted the glass in good grace. He glanced around the kitchen. "Do you still have your security system up and running?"

"Of course. Attila provided me only the best. And don't ask me where he got it. I don't want to know."

"Well, I hope your house isn't bugged," Wellington said, glancing around. "I've been hearing rumors. Something *big* is supposedly going on."

Marie extended a plate to Wellington. "We're surrounded by rumors," she said. "It's hard to determine what we should listen to."

"Which one this time?" Napoleon asked.

"Someone overheard someone else saying we're being visited from Above."

"Oh, *that* one. And where did you hear this someone recounting someone else's rumor?"

"At the Club."

"And how much had they had to drink?"

Wellington managed to look offended. "I would hardly know. But that's not the only time I've run across something similar."

Napoleon exchanged a quick glance with Marie. "We've heard it, too. From what I gather, it's Erra and the Seven, and they're kicking ass throughout the hells."

The Iron Duke grimaced. "I understand they're here because some of us are being treated too leniently, considering we've been condemned to New Hell."

"This from a man whose grass needs mowing every day?"

"Would you be serious!" Wellington snapped. "This rumor has me worried."

"We might need to be worried," Napoleon acknowledged. "All in all, we *have* been treated much better than anyone would expect."

"But it's not our fault we're better treated!" Wellington protested. "We've served our time in Satan's armies. There should rightly be some reward for that."

"No choice in it, *mon ami*. Neither you nor I exactly volunteered."

"I should think not!"

A bewildered hurt surfaced in Wellington's eyes. This,

Napoleon could easily understand. They both continually suffered what could be termed "the death of a thousand cuts." Here he sat, across from his one-time enemy who'd been victorious over him at the battle of Waterloo, yet Wellington had proved a dependable friend. Their friendship was odd at first glance, but not all that surprising: they'd shared common experiences in life and afterlife; they'd even been born in the same year. Once the darling of Europe, Prime Minister of England, advisor and companion of kings and queens, Wellington the Iron Duke had fallen to the level of measuring the grass in his yard, bound by the petty rules of the HOA. No chance here for glory beyond the grave.

And himself? At the height of his power, he had ruled an empire. Europe had bowed to his will and armies had fought historic battles under this command. And now? Paint the house again, Napoleon. Pull the weeds in the driveway. Offer advice to people who asked for it, only to have them decide to go their own way, discounting what wisdom he had gained dwelling in New Hell. He and Wellington had possessed a degree of authority when serving as generals in Satan's armies, but it was often ignored by other commanders who, on their best day, couldn't out-think either of them.

Colossal figures from the same era of Europe's history, they had both become diminished, their ability to decide the direction of their existence for the most part destroyed. *Ah, yes, Wellington, we're in the same boat, you and I. And there's not a damned thing we can do about it. Suffer in relative silence, make the best of what we have, and hope we don't draw unwanted attention to ourselves.*

Wellington had been saying something. Napoleon blinked, abandoning his thoughts.

"Quoi?"

"I said, Have you heard anything regarding this rumor, my lady?" Wellington asked Marie again. He shot Napoleon a puzzled look, as if to question his inattention.

"Only once," she said, "down at the Unsafeway. I was buying ribs for the Cong –"

"And *that's* got to come to an end. Damned terrorists! We're going broke feeding the bloody lot of them!"

"Think of it as insurance," Napoleon said. "As long as we

keep them happy, they protect our side of the Park, *n'est-ce pas?"*

"In between killing each other off."

"Just like everyone else, they keep coming back. Discounting the heavenly audit, what precisely has you so upset?"

"I still can't figure out why I'm here. In hell, I mean, not your kitchen."

"According to the Bible, there are more than three hundred and fifty commandments, not just the original Ten." Napoleon leaned back in his chair. "Everyone alive has broken a goodly number of them."

"It's unfair!" Wellington seethed. "How can we break a commandment if we don't know what the commandment is?"

"Ignorance of the law is no excuse."

"Don't pull out that old saw again. And is it just us ... we who professed Christianity while we lived? What about all the other people in the world who never heard of the Ten Commandments?"

"To say nothing about the other three hundred or so," Marie inserted.

"I don't make the rules," Napoleon said. Then he grinned. "But if we all break most of those commandments, and are eternally punished for it, there must be plenty of room in heaven."

"What about Attila? He was anything *but* a Christian!"

"Huns have their own views. Demons. Ghosts. Terrors of the night."

"Maybe," Marie speculated, "as some of the old dead think, there are different heavens and hells for different religions or different epochs or cultures."

"Then why did Attila end up on our side of the Park? Who made that choice to place him among those of us who shared somewhat common beliefs?"

Marie reached across the table and patted Wellington's hand. "Satan. In league with his non-Christian equivalents. Devising tortures for the damned. You know that."

"I suppose I do. Rather stupid question, I must admit."

"Not to change the subject," Marie said, "has anyone seen our HOA president lately?"

"Damned lawyer," Wellington sniffed. "That rule book of his

is a veritable nightmare!"

"It *is* a tangle of legalese," Napoleon agreed, "I'll grant you that. But once you pick up on the rhythm of the thing, including all the new additions, you can get some sense as to where it's going."

"Well, you must come by it honestly. *Your* father was a lawyer."

"True. But what was legally written down in his time didn't change from day to day."

Wellington snorted and finished his meal.

"Coffee?" Marie asked.

"No thank you, my lady. I'm going home and attempt to get some rest."

"Good idea," Napoleon said, taking his cup from Marie. "But I don't want to wake up in the middle of the night to find you squatting in your yard, armed with a flashlight, watching your grass grow."

*

Napoleon locked the front door and joined Marie who waited by his car in the driveway, frowning at the new crop of dandelions and crabgrass that had sprung up over night. So far, it hadn't reached the stage where a fine would be incurred but, after their trip to the store, they would be back to pulling weeds. Chemicals didn't slow their growth that all. In fact, the invasive things likely thrived on poison.

"Where's Wellington? He knew we're going to the Unsafeway, though I can't figure out why he wants to come along. He's always sponging off us and probably has a grocery bill a tenth the size of ours."

"He'll be here." She looked across the front yard at the house to the right of Napoleon's. "Have you talked to our new neighbor yet?"

"No. He came in the middle of the night a few weeks ago. I've only caught glimpses of him in his backyard."

"Rather unfriendly, isn't he?"

Napoleon shrugged. "Getting the lay of the land is my guess. Who knows where he came from, what period in history, what crimes he committed to land him here in New Hell. We'll find out eventually."

"Here comes Wellington," Marie said. Her expression changed. "And what is he up to now?"

Wellington rounded the hedge and headed up the driveway. Today, instead of his red British general's coat, his snow-white breeches, and his spotless black boots, he came clad in a neat pair of slacks and an open collared shirt.

"Damn, Wellington." Napoleon couldn't help but smile. "I didn't know you owned civilian clothes."

"Oh, these." Wellington glanced down at his outfit. "I decided to go casual today. After all, we're only going to the mall."

"That's never slowed you down in the past. As I recollect, you were examining your grass yesterday all decked out in uniform. No, no. I'm not making fun of you. After all this time, I never thought I'd see you without your customary spit and polish. Now, come on. We're running late as it is."

*

The drive to where the Unsafeway lay at the far end of the strip mall proved a series of delays. The mobile potholes had moved since the last time Napoleon had driven this way, potholes large enough to swallow a fair-sized child. Napoleon was sure, if he looked close enough, he might find one of Attila's brats at the bottom of one. The HDOT had timed the stop lights, making the wait for them to turn green seem to last at least forever. Finally, after avoiding a driverless car left parked in the middle of the street, Napoleon pulled into the parking lot.

"Oh, bother. We'll have to hike again," Wellington complained. "Never a parking place near the front door."

Napoleon managed to find a spot relatively close to the Unsafeway. As he and Marie exited the car, Wellington headed off in another direction.

"Where are you going? I thought you wanted to grocery shop. Oh, I forgot. You don't need to buy food. You eat all of ours."

Wellington pulled a face. "I'm going to nose around. There might be something new in one of the stores."

And with that, he sauntered off in the direction of several shops that lined the mall. Napoleon watched him go.

"What now?"

"Oh, don't question," Marie said, taking his arm and steering him toward the Unsafeway. "At least we won't have to put up with his running review concerning the food, its quality, or the lack of it."

As grocery shopping went, this trip turned out to be less of a nuisance than usual, grounds for well-founded paranoia. Everything but two items on Marie's shopping list was available, the aisles were merely crowded rather than packed tight, and the checkout clerk less surly than normal. Leaving the store, pushing the cart that had only one wheel that wouldn't turn, Napoleon and Marie headed to his car.

Wellington was waiting for them, looking vastly pleased with himself.

"Where have you been?" Napoleon asked, helping Marie deposit the grocery bags in the car trunk.

"Oh, I nipped into the hellphone store." Wellington extended a new, shiny hellphone. Red for Britain, of course. "I thought it might come in handy since I'm not having any luck in getting through to the other side of the Park. My landline is always so full of static it's difficult to hear. Times being what they are, I really need to know how Queen Victoria is bearing up."

Napoleon briefly closed his eyes. "My Ma-hell landline seems to be operating as well as anything does hereabouts. It *is* New Hell's telecommunications monopoly after all. Do you realize what you're getting into? If our objective is to stay quiet and nearly invisible on our side of the Park, did it ever occur to you what activating a hellphone might entail? The downside to operating one?"

"Well, I've heard the hell towers can move around a bit."

"A *bit?* They jump from place to place, all without notice, and usually end up somewhere extremely annoying, leaving you in a dreaded dead zone if you're making a call. On top of that, the possessor of a hellphone can be tracked at all times, even when the phone isn't being used."

Wellington's expression was hard to read. "I think I've got that covered. If I run into trouble, I'll toss the bloody thing in the trash."

"You just bought it!" Napoleon growled. "You're on record for having it, and you're obligated for an entire two-year contract, unless you want to pay a stiff cancellation fee."

Wellington lifted one shoulder in a shrug. "I might have a solution to that. Do you honestly think anyone would recognize me, dressed as I am? I'm not even wearing a hat."

Napoleon glanced at Marie, who was shaking her head.

"Probably not," she said. "You do look, well, rather ordinary."

"All right, Wellington," Napoleon said, echoing Marie's earlier comment. "What are you up to now?"

"There are times," the Iron Duke said, assuming his best put-upon expression, "when I have the notion you don't think I have a brain. I wanted a hellphone and, by Jove, I've got one!"

"Let's assume you have a plan. What happens when the bill arrives?"

"I won't see it. I only want the phone for a month or so, and then I'll chuck it. Queen Victoria must be advised that I stand ready to assist her in any way I can."

"I know you and Victoria are close," Napoleon pointed out, "but do you really want to put yourself in potential danger simply to let her know you're thinking of her?"

"And consider this," Marie said. "I've heard the hellphone collection department is very thorough. They'll track you down if you let your payment slide."

"I've solved that," Wellington said, a smug expression flitting across his face.

"Oh?" Napoleon cocked his head. "Come on, Wellington. You can share. What have you done now? I smell something dishonest."

Wellington blushed slightly. "I gave them the wrong information as to who I am." He reached in his pocket, pulled out his wallet and fished out a New Hell I.D. card. "Here. Take a look."

Napoleon took the proffered I.D. card. Wellington's slightly altered photo was on it (a bit out of focus, as usual), but the name was different, as was other information pertinent to the possessor of the card.

"Vincent Saint-James? A solid British name, I'll grant you that. Where did you get this?"

"My cigar supplier, for a small fee, but he gets his hands on only the best."

"Congratulations, Wellington. You've really slipped into the seamier side of New Hell, haven't you? First the black market for cigars, and now counterfeit I.D. cards."

"One has to be inventive at times to maintain one's position."

Napoleon returned the card. "You never cease to amaze me. By hook or by crook, you get what you want, don't you?"

"Sometimes. At other times, I fail. After all, I *did* end up living next door to you."

"Touché!"

"Let's go home," Marie suggested, "before the frozen food defrosts."

"Now I know why you broke out your civilian clothes," Napoleon said, sliding in behind the wheel. "The Iron Duke, hero of Britain, would never be caught in public dressed as someone he wasn't. Get in, Wellington. And, for our sakes, try to keep out of trouble. We've got entirely too much as it is."

*

Several evenings later, after numerous mowings of Wellington's yard, never-ending weedings of Napoleon's driveway, and the rise in petty vandalism in the neighborhood which needed to be taken care of before the Home Owner's Association levied yet more fines, the time had come to partake of the one dinner at Hellview Golf and Country Club all members were required to purchase every month.

Wellington came clad in his usual British red uniform, resplendent in gold braid, spotless white breeches and boots so polished he could have probably seen his reflection in them. Marie had donned a simple light blue pantsuit, while Napoleon had changed into a neat pair of jeans, a newer denim shirt and thoroughly broken-in boots. As they climbed out of Wellington's Sedan de Ville, the last person they expected to see was Attila.

The king of the Huns stood at the edge of the polo grounds, his mount at his side.

"Hey, Napoleon! Wellington! Marie!" His voice carried across the short distance from the field to the parking lot. "Come see my new horse!"

"Oh, drat," Wellington muttered. "Knowing Huns and horses, this could go on forever."

"Humor him," Napoleon advised. "We'll get inside quicker if we do."

"Don't get too close." Attila tightened his grip on the reins. "He's a wonder on the polo field, but he'll take your hand off if you let him."

The beast that stood by Attila seemed, at first glance, to be an ordinary polo pony. Then, with a strange flicker of half-discernable light, its appearance changed. What stood by Attila now was a perversion of horseflesh: scaled, red eyes, snaky mane and tail, plus the very real threat of impending bodily harm to anyone who ventured too near. The illusion changed again and, to all outward observation, the "horse" looked much like a normal Hun mount.

"Where did you get this one?" Napoleon asked. "It doesn't look any friendlier than the last horse you bought."

"Oh, well. *This* one's a murderous fiend on the polo field. I'm fine, as long as I keep my hands and feet away from his teeth."

"Which," Wellington observed, "appear to be fangs rather than teeth."

"That's why I keep the chain attached to the industrial strength martingale. Keeps him from tossing and turning his head."

"Does he breathe fire, too?" Marie asked.

"No. Only farts it." Attila laughed at his own comment. "You here for the monthly dinner?"

"Yes, and we're going to be late for our reservation," Napoleon said. "I suppose you should be very proud of your new mount. I'll wager the other Huns and Mongols don't have anything quite so 'murderous.'"

"Damn right! Well, go on. I'll be seeing you soon." He turned, then grinned widely. "We won the game today. Beat the crap out of those Mongols! See you around!"

The Club was moderately crowded this evening. As Napoleon, Marie and Wellington stepped up to the hostess to be seated, Napoleon gave the bar a cursory glance. The usual assortment of people sat at their places at various tables, but he only saw a small group of Romans and didn't recognize a one. Something was definitely amiss on the other side of the Park. A quick call to Caesar might clear things up but, the way things were going, perhaps not.

Seated at their customary table, they ordered and sat back to wait for dinner.

"Incoming." Marie nodded at someone crossing the room toward them.

Napoleon and Wellington turned to watch the man approach their table. He was a person who would disappear in a moderately large crowd. Nothing about him was particularly memorable, except the arrogant way he carried himself.

"Oh, damn! It's the president of the HOA," Wellington said in a hushed voice. "What can *he* possibly want?"

"I suppose we'll find out." Napoleon gestured to the empty chair at their table. "And how are you this evening, Martin?" he asked in his best conversational tone.

"I've been better," the HOA president said, "and I need to talk to you."

"Me in particular, or Wellington and me?"

"You. It's about your new neighbor."

"What about him? All I know is that he moved in several weeks ago. Nobody ever sees him unless he's behind his house."

"Well, his yard is the main problem." Martin Chase Standish, Esquire, lawyer to the tips of his toes, shook his head in what could only be a combination of bewilderment and frustration. "I've sent him innumerable letters requesting a cleanup of that yard of his. And he's ignored every one."

"The ruddy nerve," Wellington commiserated.

"You've fined him?" Marie asked.

"Several times."

"Has he paid?"

"Late, of course. He's why I need to talk to you, Napoleon. Have you ever spoken to him?"

"No. He's not the friendliest sort. I don't even know his name."

"Then listen to what happened when I paid him a visit. I knocked on his door and, when he finally answered, I very politely began to explain what the Home Owner's Association expects of its members." An odd expression crossed Standish's face. "You know, I've never been one to be cowed by other people. After years and years in court, it takes a lot to unnerve me. But the cold menace that poured from that man ... let me tell you, I was on the verge of turning tail."

Napoleon glanced at Wellington and received an imperceptible shake of the Iron Duke's head. "I've not been close enough to him to notice. And you, Wellington?"

"Never met the chap, nor exchanged even one word with him."

"Marie?" Napoleon asked. "Have you ever talked to him?"

"No. I think I've seen less of him than you have."

"There's something wrong with this picture," Standish said, "and I don't like it. Not at all. We can't have something ... someone like *that* living in our neighborhood."

"And what do you expect *me* to do about it?" Napoleon asked.

"I'm not sure. Maybe you can ferret out a bit more about him. Where he came from. What his name is."

"So you sent your letters addressed to 'Occupant' when you notified him about the condition of his yard?"

"I've tried to get his name as a new homeowner from the New Hell Human and Urban Development database, but the damned HUD computers refuse to cooperate."

"Oh, *that's* something new and different," Wellington huffed. "Why, just the other day –"

"Down, Wellington, down." Napoleon met Standish's eyes. "I'll see what I can do, but I can't promise anything. If he keeps to his normal routine, I'll rarely see him."

"Well, try. Something has to be done, and I'm not sure what it is."

A waiter arrived with their three dinners on a glass and bronze cart. Standish rose.

"I won't keep you any longer." Again, a strange expression crossed the lawyer's face. "Be careful. He's not the kind of person you want to have frequent contact with. He even insulted me, calling me all kinds of vile things, mainly in reference to my profession."

Napoleon, Wellington and Marie watched the Home Owner's Association president walk away, across the dining room.

"Now, that's bizarre," Wellington said, leaning forward to sniff his food.

"Beef Wellington again?" Napoleon asked. "Only you would continually order something named after you."

"I happen to like it. Do you mind?"

"Oh, no. Not me. And don't start about the pastries."

"Have you reached Queen Victoria?" Marie asked, taking a sip of her wine.

"I got through several times, but the damned tower must have moved and my last call was dropped."

"Told you so." Napoleon grinned. "I don't trust those things. I don't even trust my Ma-hell landline. I wish we could get our hands on a good, old fashioned phone. One of Caesar's field phones would do the trick, too."

"Maybe Attila can get us one," Wellington suggested.

"Or your Cuban, in between cigars and fake I.D.s."

Wellington looked pensive. "I'll see what I can do."

"And meanwhile, we have to figure out what to do about my neighbor. I'm not overjoyed with the prospect of talking to the man. And if he's totally unsettled Standish, that's saying something. After all, Standish *does* practice law at the Hall of Injustice."

"Well, he's a lawyer," Marie said. "That's where some of them earn their keep."

"He ought to sue your neighbor." Wellington waved a hand. "If he was called all kinds of scurrilous names, he could go for defamation of character."

"A lawyer? A hell-certified lawyer?" Napoleon laughed. "That would be hard to prove, especially with no witnesses and given the professional company he keeps."

*

Grass growing inches in hours was annoying; weeds springing up in every available crack in the driveway made matters worse, but now, adding insult to injury, the petty vandalism that had recently plagued the neighborhood had escalated. Napoleon stood in his front yard and glared at the remnants of his living room picture window. The repair people were on the way, but the cost to replace the window was something he didn't look forward to.

He'd found the large rock that had done the damage in the

center of his living room after being awakened from a sound sleep. He and Marie had nearly levitated out of bed at the sound of shattered glass and the piercing alarm from the security system. Try as he might, he couldn't imagine who would have taken aim at his window in the dead of night.

Perhaps uncharitably, his thoughts turned to Attila. Well, rather, to Attila's brats.

Marie joined him in the front yard, bringing him a cup of coffee, and contemplated the broken window.

"Who could have done this?" she asked. "Surely it wasn't the Cong."

"Oh, no. *They* would have shelled the house, or at least the driveway. This isn't up to their standards."

"At least we've got all the glass up from the carpet. Who's coming to fix it?"

"Windows4U." Napoleon reached into his shirt pocket and extended a business card.

Marie stared at the card. "Windows4U? What kind of a name is that?"

"They're newly arrived," Napoleon explained, "and technology happy. It probably comes from their texting back and forth."

"Oh. Can Wellington do that with his phone?"

"If he can, I'm not going to tell him."

"Where did you find them?

"I got their name from Standish."

"Speaking of whom," she said, a twinkle in her eyes, "I wonder if he gets a kickback."

"Hush. We don't need to be on his bad side."

"I'd think since he's been after you to talk to our reclusive neighbor, he'd want to stay on your *good* side."

"Possibly." Napoleon finished his coffee and handed off his cup. "Do me a favor, Marie. When the repair crew gets here, hover close enough to make sure they're doing what they're paid to do, but far enough away so they can't accuse you of meddling."

"Where are you going?"

"I think it's time I paid a visit to Attila."

*

Attila's house appeared unscathed, his front yard neatly mowed, and all seemed quiet. Napoleon rang the bell and waited, now and then glancing at Decentral Park. It was about time to deliver another round of ribs but, with the expense of replacing his window, things were going to be a bit tight. Fortunately, he still received his generous pension as a retired general in Satan's armies, as well as the fee he collected when he taught strategy at headquarters. Nevertheless, another outflow of cash was unwelcome.

He rang the bell again. As far as he knew, Attila was off-duty from the Infernal National Guard and should be home. It was late enough so that any hangover from one of Attila's frequent drinking bouts should have worn off by now. Finally, the door opened and one of Attila's wives, Ildilco, stood there, her beautiful face puffy from sleep.

"Sorry to bother you," Napoleon said. "I need to talk to Attila. Is he home?"

"That low-down bastard! Got in at who knows what time, drunk beyond drunk, singing off-key ... yes, he's here. Staying out of my sight, mostly. He'd better."

Napoleon patiently waited for her venom to dissipate. Ildilco's tirades were nothing new and were to be weathered like any passing storm.

"Where is he?"

"In the backyard." She glared at nothing in particular and slammed the door.

Napoleon smothered a grin. It must have been some party Attila had attended for Ildilco to be so out of sorts. Out in back, he found the king of the Huns standing in the midst of three longhaired goats. Or what, at first sight, he took to be goats. Whatever one assumed to be normal usually wasn't. Attila seemed none the worse for wear and the goats were contentedly grazing in his yard.

"Why you sly old fox," Napoleon said, watching the goats make short shrift of the lawn. "Now I know why your yard always looks so neat."

"Don't get too close," Attila cautioned. "They bite."

"I'll bet they do. Much like your new polo pony, I'm thinking."

"True. But I don't have to mow and that's worth it."

"Don't let Wellington in on your secret. Mowing his lawn keeps him occupied."

Attila stepped aside as the goats began to move to an uncropped portion of grass. "What do you want?" A suspicious expression crossed his heavy face. "Not another favor for Caesar, I trust."

"No. I haven't heard from him in a month or so. I'm here to ask you about your children."

"By the Vault Above! What have the little monsters done now?"

"Besides drawing scandalous things in chalk on the sidewalks, nothing I know about. But last night someone threw a rock through my picture window, and I was wondering if you did a nose count when you got home."

"They were all asleep. I checked. Not that I wouldn't put it past them, but this time I think they're innocent."

"It was just a thought. Have you been targeted lately?"

"The usual small stuff." Attila gestured Napoleon back. The goats were coming closer. "Soap on the screen doors, shit in burning paper bags on the doorstep. Nothing bad as a broken window. Do you have any suspects?"

"No." Napoleon followed Attila to a safer corner of the yard. "Here's the latest. Wellington bought a hellphone using a false I.D. He's concerned about Queen Victoria and has to talk to her at least three times a week."

"Why doesn't he just go see her?"

"Can't say for sure. You've heard the rumor?"

Attila's eyes narrowed. "Which one?"

"The big one. The hells are being visited by some kind of heavenly auditors, a Babylonian god and his seven weapons. They're here on instructions from Above to make sure everyone receives injustice justly. Or something like that."

Attila nodded slowly. "I've heard the same thing." Then he grinned. "All the lawyers must be shaking in their boots or salivating over their opportunities."

"And you haven't even mentioned Satan."

"Hoo boy!" Attila's grin disappeared. "I hadn't thought about that. Slipping up on his duty of tormenting us, hey?"

"I don't know. Wellington's upset because of the rumor, and I'll admit I'm none too pleased. I think that's why he doesn't drive to see Queen Victoria, why he bought the hellphone, and why he used a fake I.D."

"Huhn. Makes sense. It's got me worried, too." Attila pulled on his mustaches, his usual bluster dampened. "It's ... what's the word? Arb ... arbi –"

"It's arbitrary," Napoleon supplied, "Erra's comings and goings. I agree. No one knows where or when he'll show up next. And there's not a damned thing we can do about it if he comes to this side of the Park. You heard what happened in New Hell City: the flood and the plague? I don't know about you, but I don't want to end up on the Undertaker's table. Our only hope is we get some kind of protection from Satan."

"By my ancestors' ghosts! *That's* a first, hoping Satan keeps us safe."

"I would imagine His Infernal Majesty is in a towering rage over this heavenly visit. Defending his turf, I think the term is. And as for our protection, Wellington and I served him for years and years, though we didn't have a choice in the matter. You still serve. It's obvious times are changing and we're powerless to do much about it."

For a long moment, he shared an uncomfortable silence with the king of the Huns.

Attila straightened, drew a deep breath, then gestured to the other side of his backyard. "You'd better move, Napoleon. The goats are coming." Physically shaking off his somber mood with a shrug, he rubbed his chin thoughtfully. "So, what *else* has got you troubled?"

"Two things. I'd like to talk to Caesar; however, the Romans have, for all practical purposed, disappeared. I used to get periodic calls from him but, lately, nothing. I can't trust my Ma-hell landline for anything save boring everyday conversations. Wellington's hellphone can be traced no matter if it's in use or not. Can you get me a vintage phone or a field phone, or something that's secure?"

Attila shook his head. "I can try, but it won't be easy. What's the other thing?"

"My neighbor. The one who moved in next door more than three weeks ago. There's something about him that has our HOA president spooked."

"Standish? I didn't think anything could bother him. He thrives at the Hall of Injustice and that takes guts."

"Well, he wants me to try to find out more about this new neighbor. And I'm not particularly eager to do so."

"I can't do anything about that," Attila admitted. "I've never seen him, even close as I live to you. Now the field phone ... maybe. But I've heard another rumor."

"What a surprise. Is this one legitimate?"

"Sounds like it. Has to do with leeches."

"Leeches?"

"That's what I've heard." Attila spread his hands and took unusual care with his words. "There are supposedly different types of leeches that inhabit several pools somewhere beyond the outskirts of New Hell. Now the interesting thing about these leeches is that some of them can communicate among themselves. If someone attaches one of those leeches to a part of his body, he can communicate with another person wearing a leech from the same pool. Totally undetectable by any means."

"You're a fount of information. I suppose while you're talking, or whatever it is you do to communicate, the slimy things are feasting on your blood."

"I guess you have to give a little to get a lot," Attila said. For a moment, he looked surprised to have made such a profound statement.

"Well, if you can't get a field phone, bag phone, or whatever, keep me in mind. I don't trust the technology in New Hell right now. Too much can go wrong."

"If that's all you want me to do. I was afraid you might suggest I go fishing for leeches."

"No, and I wouldn't ask you to go alone. There *has* to be somewhere else to acquire them. New Hell City seethes with dishonesty."

"Hah! And I'd place a safe bet that's why Satan likes to live there."

Napoleon felt something brush against his leg and looked

down. One of the goats was nibbling on the grass by his foot. "Damn! Warn me the next time your four-footed lawnmowers are getting too close!"

Attila laughed. "They're pretty tame now that they're not so hungry. Look at the yard, will you, it's neat as a pin!" He slapped Napoleon on the shoulder. "Good luck with your weird neighbor. And I'll see what I can do about the field phone."

*

The repair crew from Windows4U had done an excellent job. Marie had followed Napoleon's instructions and watched carefully without appearing to do so. Payment made, she decided to walk around to the backyard. A small stream ran along the row of houses next to Hellview Golf and Country Club, separating the 18th green and club house from the residential neighborhood. There were times when the flowing water sounded soothing and she enjoyed a brief respite from the continual trials of dwelling in hell. Oh, she'd chosen her lot, refusing to leave New Hell and ascend back to Purgatory, because she couldn't imagine leaving Napoleon. As she had told him time and again, love was something the devil couldn't understand and had difficulty dealing with.

She didn't dare go too close to the stream. Though it seemed innocent enough, nasty things periodically surfaced from beneath the water, and viewing them was something she scrupulously avoided. Today, she stood in the middle of the yard and tried to enjoy a few moments of solitude.

A slight noise and a very faint scent of something noxious roused her from her thoughts. She turned and was surprised to see the new neighbor standing by his back door. Not wanting to appear nosy, she didn't look directly at him, only slightly to one side. And nearly let out a cry of surprise.

The few times she had seen the reclusive neighbor, he appeared to be a very tall, thin fellow, dark-haired, and with no memorable features. But what she saw now was not human. Scales covered his body and (oh, no!) he had a long, barbed tail that was slowly swaying back and forth. Heart in her throat, she glanced away, hoping he had not noticed her looking in his direction. Drawing a calming breath, she let her gaze focus squarely on him, then looked to the side so she could still see him with her peripheral vision. The tail was there again, as were the scales.

Slowly, so as not to draw attention to herself, she turned and walked around the side of the house to the front yard. Only then did fear consume her. Napoleon! He had to know! And he had gone to Attila's. She rushed down the driveway and had just rounded the hedge when she saw Napoleon returning from his visit to the king of the Huns.

"Napoleon!" she gasped, grasping his hand. "You've *got* to listen to me! It's important!"

"What's wrong?" he asked, concerned softness touching his grey-blue eyes.

"It's the new neighbor," she explained, catching her breath. "He ... it ... He's a demon!"

*

Napoleon stiffened in surprise. "A demon? Are you sure? How can you tell?"

She quickly explained how the neighbor's true form had been revealed by viewing him with her peripheral vision. He watched her closely as she talked, knowing full well it took a lot to intimidate her. She'd witnessed too much in New Hell to be easily frightened, but what she had seen today had truly disturbed her.

"I'm going to see if he's still out there."

Napoleon let loose of her hand and hurried to the back yard. Assuming a casual demeanor, he inspected the hedge that separated his yard from Wellington's, ostensibly examining the growth of the bushes. He glanced over his shoulder. Yes, the neighbor was still standing by his door, seemingly unaware he was being spied upon. Napoleon looked directly at him, then let his gaze move slightly to one side.

Marie had been correct. Scales *and* a tail.

As if nothing had happened, he rejoined Marie.

"You're right," he said. "Some kind of demon, I'm not sure of the genus. You'd better warn Wellington, Attila and the rest of the neighborhood." He frowned. "I'd like to know what's going on here that we rate our own resident demon."

Marie shook her head, to his eyes, she was still upset by what she'd seen.

"Let's go." He took her arm and they set off around the hedge.

*

Wellington sat in a lawn chair on his front porch, his legs stretched out in front of him, apparently taking a nap.

"Wellington! Wake up, will you!"

The Iron Duke lifted his head, blinking several times. "Can't you let a man rest for a moment?" he grumbled. "I've just finished mowing."

"This is more important that your yard right now. We've got a demon living next to me. You can't tell by looking at him, but if you glance to one side, you can see his true form."

That got Wellington's attention. "Damn! You're certain?"

"Marie pointed it out to me and, yes, I saw the same thing."

"Oh, Damnation! What are we going to do about –"

At that very moment, Martin Chase Standish, Esquire arrived unannounced at Wellington's porch. "Napoleon," he said, without so much as a how-do-you-do, "have you had any luck yet with your new neighbor?"

"You might say so," Napoleon replied, interested in Standish's reaction. "He's a demon. That's why you were so disturbed when you talked to him."

"What? A demon? Posing as a human? That's totally irregular! Unless they're on some mission from their superiors, they're supposed to retain their infernal form."

"Thanks so much for the reassurance," Wellington sniffed.

"What do we do about him?" Napoleon asked. "You work at the Hall of Injustice. I would guess you'd find a few demons there."

"You'd be right. But ..." Standish's voice trailed off and he assumed a thoughtful expression. "I don't think he's supposed to be here. This neighborhood is pretty much off limits to them."

"You would know," Wellington said.

Standish glared in Wellington's direction. "And what's that supposed to mean?"

"He *means,"* Napoleon quickly inserted, "you're more familiar with demons, because of your profession, than we are. No offense meant, I'm sure."

Wellington lifted both hands. "Of course, I wouldn't dream of insulting you."

And how do you know this neighborhood is "pretty much off limits"? What else haven't you shared with us? "You're the Home Owner's Association president," Napoleon said. "What are you going to do about the fact we have a demon living next to me? And I thought Goebbels was bad enough."

"Whatever happened to him?" Wellington asked. "Do we even know?"

"Here one day and gone the next. Forget Goebbels. We've got a bigger problem now."

"Hmmm." Standish rubbed his nose. "I'd be willing to bet that demon's gone AWOL."

"AWOL? A demon? Absent without leave?"

"Yes. There have been instances when a demon of lower rank has tried to escape torment by his superiors. They attempt to disappear into the population of the damned, keeping as low a profile as possible. That's probably why no one ever sees him except in his backyard."

"Thanks for the history lesson. That still doesn't solve our problem. As far as I know, it's not easy to kill a demon."

"Well ... in certain circumstances...."

"Don't let Attila know," Marie inserted, much calmer by now. "He'd try."

"Mostly for the fun, sport and amusement of it, I'm sure." Napoleon locked eyes with Standish. "Maybe there's a legal way to get rid of him."

"What?"

"You're the lawyer. Certainly you have something in your bag of tricks that can help us."

Standish's face lit up. "There's a good possibility of that, especially if he *has* gone AWOL."

Wellington drew himself up to his full aristocratic height. "And?"

"I'll have to do some research. I'll get on Gurgle and check the list of local demons to ascertain their locations. I *do* have access to such things. A highly restricted password, you know."

"And then?" Napoleon asked, allowing just a bit of impatience to tinge his voice.

"If it *is* true, I'll file an emergency petition." He lifted his chin and assumed his best trial lawyer's stance. "Hellview Estates Home Owner's Association versus Demon of Unknown Origin, Emergency Petition Alleging Fraud Against the Infernal Government." His voice deepened and smoothed, as if he addressed a jury. "Hellview Estates Home Owner's Association (hereinafter referred to as 'Petitioner') alleges –"

"Save it for your brief," Napoleon said. "We've got to get busy."

Standish grinned, the first time anyone had seen such an expression cross his face in months. "I'll get points for this, of course. Can't hurt my standing. Leave it to me. I'll let you know what happens."

With that, Standish turned and set off toward the sidewalk and his house.

"I thought mowing my grass every day was a bloody pain," Wellington complained, watching Standish go.

"Welcome to New Hell," Napoleon said.

*

Several days passed without so much as a peep from Standish. The demon neighbor still kept to his backyard and totally ignored anything happening around him. The vandalism that had escalated in the neighborhood had died down, leaving Attila's children as the likely culprits. No one had mentioned the neighbor's true identity to Attila for fear the Hun would try to solve the problem in his usual bloodthirsty way. In fact, Attila had been called up for maneuvers with the Infernal National Guard in response to mounting unrest in the region. That left the goat herding up to his wives who, as usual, were not overly fond of such duty.

This day, Napoleon and Marie were busy trimming the hedge. The bushes had grown bushier during the night and, along with fighting the ever-present weeds in his driveway and grass, Napoleon was certain he would reach master gardener status before long.

"I wonder why we haven't heard from Standish," Marie said, dumping a handful of hedge into the basket that had become her ever-present accessory.

"Who knows?" Napoleon took another swipe at the hedge with his clippers. "I'm familiar with how events unfold at the Hall of Injustice and it's as they say: the wheels of justice grind slowly."

He lifted an eyebrow. "If there's anything that might bring New Hell to a stop, it would be bureaucracy run amok."

"Where's Wellington been? He didn't even join us for dinner last night, and I haven't seen him all day."

"I think the fact a demon lives two doors away has rattled him; not that it hasn't rattled us. I also think he's beginning to regret the purchase of his hellphone."

Marie laughed. "Did you see the hellphone tower in the middle of Decentral Park yesterday? I happened to look up and there it was. Not five minutes later, it had disappeared."

"Huhn. Let's hope one of them doesn't end up in our living room."

"I imagine the Cong weren't thrilled with the intrusion."

"Probably not." Napoleon straightened and surveyed his handiwork. "Speaking of the Cong, we're going to have to deliver ribs soon now, or they'll go back to shelling the neighborhood."

A mischievous expression crossed Marie's face. "Maybe we can get them to target our neighbor's house. In exchange for an extra large delivery of ribs," she amended.

Napoleon shook his head. "I wouldn't want to be a party to that. We have enough trouble as it is." He winced inwardly. He had to stop saying that. Not that it wasn't true, but it verged on the repetitious.

Marie half-turned toward the stream. "Don't look now; our neighbor is in his backyard again."

"Scales and tail and all?"

"Hullo!" Wellington came through the side yard. "Your hedge looks smashing. Nearly as neatly trimmed as my side."

"Where have you been?" Napoleon asked. "Have you managed to 'lose' your hellphone yet?"

"Not yet. I'm working on it." Wellington studiously avoided looking in the direction of Napoleon's new neighbor. "I think you and I need to have a talk."

"Oh?"

"It's about the goats. Attila's goats. The goats you never bothered to tell me about."

"Oh, *those* goats. I didn't think you'd be interested."

"And how would you –"

Suddenly, the air temperature felt like it dropped at least twenty degrees, and the afternoon light dimmed slightly. Marie stepped closer to Napoleon, and Wellington's face turned pale. Napoleon couldn't resist the temptation to look at the demon neighbor's yard. And fervently wished he hadn't.

Things that could only have been conjured from a nightmare had crawled up out of the stream running behind the neighborhood. Not the usual nastiness that sometimes rose up above the water, these things were straight out of one of the lower planes of the hells. And from the front of the neighbor's yard stalked four large demons, each uglier and more vicious looking than the next.

Napoleon's neighbor let out a shriek that probably curdled the blood of anyone within a half mile radius. The things from the stream advanced quickly, as did the newcomers. The demon neighbor stood transfixed, frozen still as stone.

Napoleon put his arms around Marie, unable to look away from what transpired next. Wellington had turned to watch as well, his face gone paler still.

The four demons surrounded the demon neighbor, as the things from the stream drew closer, and a cloying scent of coppery decomposition wafted on a slight breeze.

"Whatever you do, Marie," Napoleon said in a hushed voice, "don't look."

The demon neighbor shrieked. The other demons growled and howled.

With deliberate slowness, the attacking demons began to systematically dismember Napoleon's neighbor, throwing chunks and strips of him toward the things from the stream. Drops of thick, gelatinous fluid flew in all directions. The aquatic newcomers snarled and hissed as they fought for the dripping pieces thrown to them. The screams grew in intensity. All semblance of humanity had vanished from the demon neighbor, now revealed in his true form.

It seemed to go on forever, with demonic screams and agonizing howls rising in pitch, then dying slowly away. Soon, there was nothing left of him but a slowly twitching tail on the gore-drenched grass.

Sated, the things from the stream turned and oozed back to their domain, as the four large demons slowly turned toward Napoleon, Marie and Wellington.

Napoleon swallowed heavily, hearing Wellington murmur something that might have been a prayer if offered anywhere but here. And then, amazingly, the demons nodded once and slowly evaporated into the late afternoon light.

"Oh, my benighted soul," Wellington breathed. "What was *that* all about?"

Napoleon lifted Marie's head from his shoulder. "I think," he said, amazed his voice was steady, "we've been acknowledged for revealing our former neighbor's whereabouts."

Wellington drew a deep breath. "If that's all –"

"Ah ha!" Standish walked into the backyard. "I assume you've witnessed the fallout from my emergency petition. Not bad, was it?"

"It all depends on whether you saw it or not," Napoleon replied. "Maybe you're used to such things downtown, but we're not. I haven't seen the like in years, and I'd rather not witness something similar for a long time."

"Well, it's over now." Standish smirked, pleased with himself. "And, if you happen to look in front of your ex-neighbor's house, you'll see a large sign posted that says 'For Sale.'" He looked at the basket full of hedge clippings. "Glad to see you're keeping up your property."

And with that, he turned and made his way back toward the sidewalk.

"That ... that bastard," Wellington said in a tight voice. "Not that I'm sorry about what happened, but I bloody well wouldn't be so damned jovial about it."

Napoleon glanced at the empty yard next door. The tail was still twitching, but its movements had become feebler. Finally, it faded from view, leaving only stained grass to give evidence of what had happened.

"Remember what Standish said. He gets extra points for this."

"And *we* get thanks from a pack of demons. What a privilege."

"Don't look a gift horse in the mouth," Napoleon said. "If it means being ignored for a while, that's a good thing."

Marie still refused to look at the neighbor's now empty yard. Napoleon could see she was struggling to overcome her disgust.

"All right, Wellington," he said. Anything to change the subject. "You came here for a reason. Something about goats?"

"Oh, right. The goats. Why didn't you tell me Attila used goats to keep his grass under control?"

"I just found out myself," Napoleon replied, relieved to be on safer ground. "As I said, I didn't think you'd be interested."

"Well, I am. I'm bloody tried of mowing, so I borrowed the goats today."

"Really? And how did that go?"

"Nasty beasts, I'd say. Ildilco told me not to get too close to them because –"

"They bite. Attila told me."

Wellington grumbled something, his pallor fading. "And why would you think I'd not be interested?"

Napoleon didn't even try to hide his smile. "Take a look at your boots."

The Iron Duke snapped his mouth shut on another comment and dropped his eyes to his always perfectly shined boots. "Oh, for the love of –"

"I said I didn't *think* you'd be interested. You know what happens. What goes in one end usually comes out the other. And I see you've been walking in it."

"Damn! Now I'll have to thoroughly clean my boots. I hope it's not caustic." Wellington looked up from his feet. "I'll wager it doesn't bother Attila."

Napoleon shrugged. "Have you been downwind of him lately? Between horse sweat and goat shit, the man's a walking stench factory."

"Hmmpf!" Wellington was trying to scrape goat dropping from the bottoms of his boots. "There *does* seem to be a lot of it."

"The taller your grass is, the more –"

"I'm getting the picture." Wellington shook his head. "I might have to rethink the whole enterprise. Those damned goats ... I swear they have fangs. At least my mower behaves itself without trying to take a chunk out of my legs."

"So far. Tell Attila you're not interested. I'm sure he won't mind."

Wellington snorted. "Don't worry. Events around here have turned strange enough without having to wade through goat manure, too!"

Marie laughed quietly, her voice now sounding close to normal. Napoleon squeezed her hand, but wondered if he and Wellington would get a good night's sleep after seeing the ever-present, but thankfully mostly-hidden, side of New Hell erupt next door.

He exhaled softly. Hell was hell and, no matter what happened, the residents of the neighborhood had no choice but to make the best of it.

Ancient gods, demons and goats notwithstanding.

And Injustice For All

By

Jason Cordova

"I've had it!" Marie Antoinette screeched, entering the dilapidated apartment. The former Queen of France pointed one manicured finger at the shrunken head perched on her dining table. "You! You did this to us! You *lied* to me!" She stamped a petite foot on the ruined carpet and glared at the bearded head.

"That could be construed as slanderous, you know," the head of Rasputin the seer replied. His normally warm brown eyes were cold. "If I didn't know better, I'd say you were accusing me of not fulfilling my duties."

"You haven't fulfilled a single thing, you egotist!" Marie stomped over to the table and grabbed the shrunken head, hoisting it up by its beard, letting it sway dangerously, upside down. "I did exactly what you told me to do. And now I'm going to have to move out of this *dump –"* she spat the word emphatically, "– and into Unwelfare housing!"

"We're going to do what, now?" a familiar voice called from the other room. Henrietta Maria, once consort of England's Charles the First, poked her head around the corner, concern etched upon her face: "We must move again?"

"Oui," Marie snarled, glaring at the swaying shrunken head. "Our dear prophet has lied again!"

"I did not lie," the shrunken head stated simply. "I only did as you asked."

"I asked for a prophecy about how to move into a place befitting my status!" Marie shrieked. "And your 'advice' got us evicted from this dump and into Unwelfare housing, like common trash!"

"Then obviously my prophecy was correct…." Rasputin's head muttered, exasperation lacing his tone.

"Oh, this is horrible!" Henrietta whined, looking back into her bedroom. "I only now *just* unpacked the final box! Dear Rasputin, please tell me this is a mistake!"

"Look lady, I don't know how you survived in the real world, but here in hell you … well, you just aren't cut out for this," the shrunken head replied. "But Marie here demanded a prophecy and I gave her one, fulfilling my contract. Prophecy Dolls, LLC, takes no responsibility for actions taken by a customer based on that customer's interpretation of a prophecy. It says so in our liability waiver, which you automatically signed when you placed an order for one of the many thousands of miniature heads we offer."

"Every single prophecy you have given me has ended up bringing me misery!" Marie complained and tossed the head back onto the table, where it rolled to a stop against the wooden perch whereon it normally resided. Marie began to pace, thinking of all the misfortune that had befallen her since her purchase of the shrunken head from the Perdition Broadcasting System. "First I asked how to move in a higher circle of company, and by following your prophecy I somehow ended up in the fifth circle of hell…"

"I'm rather proud of that one," Rasputin smirked.

"Then I said I wanted to know the touch of a man, and I was changed into a doll for a weekend," Marie moaned, shuddering at the memory. "I could not move an inch and the Undertaker's breath was *horrid.*"

"Yeah, that was funny," Rasputin agreed, before hastily adding "– and prophetic."

"Oh, don't forget about the cake incident," Henrietta called from her bedroom.

"The cake," Marie hissed dangerously, her eyes narrowing as she glared at the shrunken head. "I had to ask around, but I finally understand your 'let them eat cake' comment. I'm still digging cake out of every crevice of my … person. And none of those new dead will return any of my calls!"

"Hey, that was very pertinent to your prophecy request," Rasputin protested, trying to roll so he could see Marie. After a few abortive attempts, he managed to roll onto one ear. He sighed and looked up at his owner. "You wanted to know how you could become popular. I prophesied how: 'let them eat cake.'"

"I'm going to sue your makers," Marie announced suddenly.

She rubbed her hands together, a gleeful expression on her face. "I'm going to sue them for false advertisement and breach of contract!"

"Look lady, I know we don't always see eye-to-eye on this whole 'prophecy' thingy," Rasputin said with a chuckle.

"You're a vile little head," Marie growled, hands clenched tightly at her sides.

"Marie," Rasputin sighed. "I know you may not have benefitted from my prophecies, but I can almost guarantee you that you will not win any lawsuit against Prophecy Dolls, LLC. The contracts are iron-clad and designed to be litigation-proof. Any claim will be summarily tossed out of court if the plaintiff cannot present clear, convincing evidence of intentional fraud."

"Henrietta!" Marie called out in the direction of Henrietta's bedroom. "Do you know any lawyers?"

"In hell?" Henrietta asked, peeking through the crack in her door. "Yes, one. But he's a stinking rat."

"Call him."

"But, Marie…" Henrietta protested, opening her door and stepping into the dingy living area, "…what if the head is correct? What if we cannot win in the uncivil court? You know how corrupt the circuit court of the Hall of Injustice can be."

"We must win," Marie stated firmly. "We must be given what we're owed."

"To retain what you are given, great sacrifice comes with great reward," Rasputin intoned from the dining table. "Without sacrifice, nothing comes."

"Shut it, you," Marie ordered, glaring at the shrunken head. "No more prophecies. Henrietta, call your friend."

"I dislike John Pym very much," Henrietta muttered as she went back to her bedroom, searching for her hellphone. "He was always so rude to my little King Charlie. Pym and that ghastly 'Lord Protector' Cromwell…"

Marie picked up the head from the table and set it back on its perch. She looked around the cluttered apartment before she found a box the right size to hold the shrunken head. She brought it to the dining table and looked down at Rasputin. "And as for you, I'm returning you to sender." Marie grabbed Rasputin by his disheveled hair, hoisting him into the air.

"Oh no, *not* 'return to sender,'" Rasputin mocked and rolled his eyes. "Well, could be worse. At least this time *I* won't be the one blamed for a screw up…."

"Shut up." Marie shoved the head back into the box. Rasputin glared up at her as she closed the box flaps. "Don't look at me like that. You're the one at fault – better, you're the faulty one."

"That argument might hold up in court," the seer's muffled voice called out from inside the box. "Assuming, of course, I could be proved faulty, that is."

"Henrietta? Can this lawyer meet us?" Marie called out, ignoring the miniature head. Henrietta poked her head out of her bedroom, frowning. "He said yes, but he said there would be certain 'stipulations' if he took the case," Henrietta warned, a very royal pout on her face.

Marie, doubtful, pursed her lips. "What are they, these 'stipulations'?" She smacked the box. A muffled "Hey!" angrily sounded from inside it. Ignoring Rasputin's protests, Marie carried the box to the doorway and tossed it into the hallway. Someone would be along eventually to collect the trash, she hoped. Or not. She was done with Rasputin.

"About the stipulations … I don't want to tell you what he's demanding from me, but I've agreed," Henrietta admitted after Marie returned. "He's asked us to come by now, since he is between appointments at the moment. At least, that's what I think he said."

"Well, let's go then." Marie led the way out the door, through the apartment building's halls, and into the street.

The air outside their building was scorching hot and filled with soot – another constant reminder they lived in hell. Hell was far hotter than her beloved Austria (what she was able to remember of it). Events before she arrived in hell were blurred memories.

Marie avoided the random couples and groups groping each other out in the open as she led Henrietta toward Gremlins Chinese Theater, crossing the Hellywood Walk of Shame. She ignored the screams of horror and pain which emanated from Gremlins and turned toward the rundown building which stood in the shadows of the massive theater. Covered in grime and encircled with broken pavement, the dilapidated building fit perfectly with the underbelly of Hellywood.

She ignored the pitying looks from the souls who were succeeding in hell; women with disdainful faces and elaborate furs adorning slender shoulders; men, fattened and well-fed, smirking at Marie and Henrietta as they passed. Marie bit her tongue and refused to acknowledge any of them, holding tight to her temper. Henrietta kept silent as well.

"This, all this humiliation," Marie said: "This is what the prophecy doll was supposed to prevent." Being snubbed by passersby enjoying a more luxurious existence further enflamed her. After all, she was the former Queen of France.

With Henrietta hot on her heels, Marie pushed open the front door of the small building and stepped into the lobby. The hellevator bore a crudely drawn sign informing all that it was out of order.

"Typical," Marie growled angrily as she looked for the stairwell. She turned her basilisk stare on Henrietta, who cringed. "Your *friend* is on the top floor."

"You should not have worn heels, then," Henrietta murmured, her gaze averted. Marie scowled for a moment longer before she turned and marched to the stairs.

"Is he a good lawyer, at least?" Marie huffed as they ascended the stairs, their worn and faded skirts snagging on the angular edges of the steps.

"He was a fairly good one, from what I recall," Henrietta admitted reluctantly as she struggled to keep pace with the faster and younger Marie. Her ample waistline hindered her much more than the dress she wore. "But still, a disgusting traitor and a rat."

After a few pauses to rest, the two women climbed to the very top floor of the building. There the stairway ended in a long hallway with a single door. A cracked window and a broken doorknob were the door's only features. A pale blue carpet, stained and threadbare, covered the floor. The plaster walls were ancient and cracking. A single, flickering fluorescent illuminated the hallway.

Marie and Henrietta cautiously made their way to the lone door with the cracked glass pane; aside from their muffled footsteps, they heard no other sound.

Just outside the lawyer's door, Marie and Henrietta stopped. Marie raised her hand to knock on the glass pane but before she could do so, the door swung open.

Just within the doorway a stooped, elderly man awaited them.

Marie blinked and stepped back, startled.

His face was twisted in an unpleasant frown, and unevenly shaven. A thin scar ran along the side of one cheek; his hair was in complete disarray; his eyes were bloodshot, with dark circles beneath them.

"Counselor John Pym," said Henrietta. "This is my friend, former Queen of France and of Navarre, Marie Antoinette. Marie, Counselor Pym was leader of England's Long Parliament."

Nothing she'd seen in New Hell had prepared Marie for the hooks that now replaced John Pym's hands. A menacing hook ended in a sharp point below each wrist. Barbs angled from the bases of each rusted and ancient-looking prosthesis.

Unable to help herself, Marie stared.

"Go ahead. Take a good look. Get it out of your system," Pym said bluntly.

Still mesmerized, Marie blushed.

Pym grunted. "Don't worry. You're safe with me. They frown on regicide here. Yet despite my minor part in Cromwell's execution of England's King Charles the First, I've fared better in hell than Henri Sanson, the man who guillotined you. My apartment even has a bidet. Granted, the water is usually either icy cold or scalding hot but it's hell, is it not?"

"I s-s-s-see," Marie stammered, confused. She dimly recalled the name Sanson, though not from where. She looked past Pym and into the attorney's office. "May we enter?"

"Certainly," he said and waved them inside with one rusty hook. He raised an eyebrow and leered at Henrietta: "Charlie the Martyr was always the fool in the old days, wasn't he, my dear queen? Letting a handsome piece like you near the likes of me."

"You traitorous rat!" Henrietta hissed through clenched teeth, squinting in the dim light as she shoved her way past the lawyer. "You were lucky to avoid arrest when Charlie's guard came calling for you."

"That was a long time ago, Henrietta Maria," Pym reminded her calmly, his leer disappearing. "Anyway, what is the old martyr up to these days?"

"I don't know," Henrietta replied primly. She folded her arms across her chest and looked down her nose at him. "The king's affairs are none of your business."

"Oh, so that's how it is!" Pym exclaimed, slapping Henrietta on the backside with the curved side of one hook. "Love beyond the grave? Or did he get his fill of little Catholic French princesses while he yet lived? You were always good for a laugh, Henrietta."

"We are not here to reminisce, Mr. Pym," Marie interrupted. "Henrietta told me you could help us."

"Yes," Pym nodded, closing his office door with his shoulder. He kicked aside one of many stray manila folders scattered on the floor, motioning the two ladies to seat themselves on his couch before he pulled a chair out from behind his desk and sat heavily. "So you want to sue Prophecy Dolls, eh?"

"They lied in their advertisement on PBS – you know, we should be able to trust Perdition Broadcasting System … PBS, funded by us, the damned…." Henrietta played nervously with a loose strand of hair. "The broadcast said the prophecy doll would help improve our fortunes. So far, it has led to misery."

"I bought one of those dolls myself, actually," Pym nodded, smiling at the memory. "I picked up the Nostradamus one. Swell gag gift, if you ask me. He predicted that the two 'dames of air' shall head into my office. Classic prophecy…"

"Your Nostradamus doll dared to call *me* an *airhead?* Oh, never mind, I'm not asking about *your* doll," Marie reminded him sternly. "The Prophecy Dolls company is in breach of contract for saying that their dolls work. Maybe PBS is, too, for offering the dolls to contributors. Henrietta said that you could possibly sue them … Prophecy Dolls, I mean, not PBS." Her voice trailed off.

Pym was leaning back in his chair, his eyes half closed. "We could, possibly," he allowed after a moment of silent contemplation. "Someone else brought something like this up a few weeks ago and has a court date scheduled. We could piggyback on it and join them for a classless action lawsuit, though the defense may scream for a continuance while going over the new evidence. If memory serves, the burden of proof is on the defendant to demonstrate lack of culpability in these cases. Hell is strange with rules and laws. Contracts are especially important."

"How fast can this lawsuit happen?" Henrietta asked. "Do you think we could win?"

Pym leaned forward in his chair and frowned. "Usually something like this can take an eternity." Ignoring cries of outrage from both women, he pressed on: "However, someone over at the Lost Angeles Circuit Court owes me a blood favor. I think we can be in there next week, at the latest."

"That soon? Really?" Marie gasped.

Pym nodded. "Despite my appearance, I'm still at the top of my game," he reminded them self-deprecatingly. "Uncouth I may be, and just a relic of hell now, but I practice law as badly as possible and try not to end up in the Mortuary. I am forever damned to suffer for using my religion to usurp and overthrow your Charlie."

"As well you should be!" Henrietta's voice shrilled. Her pale cheeks flushed an angry pink. "May you suffer more!"

"I assure you, I will. Is there anything else I can do for you ladies today?" Pym asked Marie, ignoring Henrietta's outburst.

"Guarantee us a victory," Marie sniffed as she stood; Henrietta followed her example.

Pym said nothing more. He stood and ushered the two former queens from his office. In the doorway, he paused.

"Henrietta?" His eyes caught those of Charles the First's queen.

"Yes?" Henrietta replied carefully.

"My stipulations?" he reminded her.

Henrietta sighed. "Does it have to be now?" she asked.

Pym shrugged his shoulder and idly scratched the top of his head with a hook.

Henrietta gave Marie a resigned look. "I'll be home later," she muttered, her voice low. "Don't wait up."

"Wait up? What?" asked Marie, confusion in her voice. "What are you talking about?"

"She's going with me to the Gremlins Chinese Theater this afternoon," Pym said, tapping the door with a rusted hook. He grinned wolfishly. "I've got us prime tickets to *Bad William Slaying*. I've heard the seats are simply *torturous!"*

"Torturous, yes," Henrietta acknowledged miserably. Marie suddenly realized what Pym's 'stipulations' had been and felt a momentary pang of pity for her roommate.

"Merde. I'll see you later tonight," Marie said and, deserting Henrietta, left the attorney's office with a jaunty bounce in her step.

Nothing in hell could stop Marie now.

*

For their court appearance, Marie wore the best dress she could find in Beasterly Hells. Madame Toadstool's Finery had a gown she was able to buy for only a pittance in blood; the blood-letting itself was something Marie no longer minded. And the blood-red dress was reminiscent of the coronation gown she had worn in life, but with tiny demonic symbols embroidered at the folds of the material. She'd pulled up her hair in a french twist; for once, it was not frizzy from the oppressive heat.

Beside her, her fellow plaintiff, Henrietta, wore a demure black dress, her hair swept back from her face. Marie shifted to see the lawyer across the aisle, representing their opponents.

A nondescript man in a brown suit stood alone at a large table, a small folder before him on the polished wood. His expression was noncommittal. In fact, everything about him was innocuous. His hair, face and features were forgettable. His suit was neither fashionable nor out of date.

Marie studied the opposing counsel carefully, then shook her head. The other lawyer was wearing black shoes.

"Incroyable," she whispered to Henrietta. "Black shoes and a brown belt? *Mode erreur!"* Henrietta tittered nervously.

Marie turned and leaned closer to Pym, waiting impatiently on her left. "Who is he?" Marie asked, jerking a thumb in the direction of the opposing counsel.

"Someone named Smith," Pym said with a shrug. "Nobody of great consequence, really. I was afraid we'd be up against a bloody genius like Stephen Douglas. That man can orate, I'll tell you. Arguing against him would be a nightmare."

"So if Prophecy Dolls only sent a single lawyer who is a

nobody…" Marie's voice trailed off hopefully. Pym was already nodding, a slight smile on his stubbled face.

"Then that means they really don't have much faith in their defense argument and are conceding," Pym finished for her. He waved a hook nonchalantly toward the judicial bench. "Depending upon our judge, we could be looking at a very hefty prize for our victory."

"Yes," Marie breathed, her eyes bright and shining. Hope filled her heart. "I'm finally going to get what I deserve."

The bailiff, who had been sitting quietly near the judicial bench, stood up and looked at both tables. He cleared his throat noisily.

"All rise," he intoned, his eyes flickering to his right. Marie turned her head and watched as a tall, statuesque figure strode purposefully into the courtroom. His robes were blood red, matching Marie's gown perfectly. Two large horns protruded from his forehead. His pale skin shone in the dim light of the courtroom. His black hair was slicked back from his face and swirled around his majestic horns. His face was clean-shaven, and his lips betrayed a soft smile. The bailiff continued: "The court is now in session; the Dishonorable Raum, Great Earl of Hell and Demonic Lord of the Lost Angeles Uncivil Circuit Court of the Hall of Injustice, presiding."

"Oh, shit," Pym hissed through clenched teeth, eyes wide and terrified.

Marie stared fearfully at the lawyer. Pym was visibly shaking where he stood before the demon judge. Marie felt her hopes jump into her throat and violently escape, leaving her soul bereft. Her knees felt weak.

"Be seated," Raum muttered, reaching into his robes to pull out a small pair of reading glasses. Once the glasses were settled upon his nose, the judge glanced over at the bailiff. "Barney, what's on the docket for today?"

"First case, Your Demonic Lordship, is case number Two Eight Four Three," the bailiff recited from memory, adjusting an obscenely large revolver against his bony frame. "Marie Antoinette and Henrietta Maria versus Prophecy Dolls, Limited Liability Corporation."

"I love those little heads," Raum murmured as he flipped documents, eyes quickly scanning the pages.

Marie watched him, sweat forming over every inch of her as she realized just how far up a creek they might be. She'd been expecting a judge who was a damned soul, not a demon.

"I've got two of those little Rasputins and a Madame Blavatsky at my house," said Raum. "Hilarious to hear them argue with one another about a prophecy. Better than advertised. Do the plaintiffs have their argument prepared for the issue at hand?"

"Uh, yes Your Demonic Lordship," Pym said, nearly choking on his tongue at Raum's admission. "Um, would Your Dishonor like to recuse himself from this case, per the potential conflict of interest resulting from your ownership of said Prophecy Dolls?"

Raum looked at Pym. The lawyer squirmed as the demon judge regarded him with barely-controlled rage.

Seconds dragged by. Marie waited anxiously. Just how much power could an enraged demon wield?

"Uh, very well then: plaintiffs withdraw the request for recusal. We're happy to have Your Demonic Lordship hear our plea for injustice," Pym stammered.

"You may begin when ready, counselors," the judge rumbled. Leaning back in his chair, he nodded at Pym to begin.

"My clients claim they are victims of breach of contract and were led astray by Prophecy Dolls, LLC's, false advertising campaign," Pym began, his voice tight and constrained. "My clients followed the instructions advertised on the Perdition Broadcasting System exactly. After purchasing their Rasputin-model prophecy doll, my clients asked their Rasputin doll how they could obtain a better existence.

"Wrongly advised by the Rasputin model, my clients proceeded into misfortune, time and again. Prophecy Dolls, LLC, therefore breached their contract to deliver viable prophecies and profited from the suffering of my unfortunate clients. My clients believe that Prophecy Dolls, LLC, made false claims of performance to entice them to purchase a doll. We seek only restitution and injustice, Your Dishonor."

"Defendant? You may now answer these charges," said the demon judge.

Marie felt a tiny flicker of hope as the judge's eyes bored into the defense attorney.

"May we approach the bench, Your Lordship?" asked Smith, the opposing counsel, suddenly, surprising everyone at the plaintiff's table.

Raum grunted and motioned for both attorneys to step forward.

With only one sheet of paper in hand, the defense attorney walked calmly to the bench and was met there by Pym. Smith handed the piece of paper to the judge, who read it.

After a moment, Raum nodded his horned head. "I'll allow it," the demon stated and looked at his bailiff. "Barney, fetch the witness."

"Witness?" Henrietta asked in surprise. "What witness?"

Pym ignored her and waited as the bailiff returned, carrying a small black box with both hands. Gingerly the bailiff set the box down on the witness stand, angling one side of the box toward a small microphone. With a satisfied grunt the bailiff moved away, leaving the mysterious box perched atop the small wooden stand.

"To protect the identity of our witness, we ask that the person inside the box *remain* inside the box during questioning and cross-examination, Your Demonic Lordship," Smith intoned as he walked slowly back to the defense table.

"That's fine with me," Raum stated. Anticipating an outburst, he held up a big hand before Pym had risen fully to his feet. "My courtroom, my rules, counselor."

"Yes, Your Dishonor." Pym sank into his chair, defeated.

"I'd like to introduce witness 'R,' an assumed name to protect the witness from recrimination or reprisal," Smith proclaimed with a satisfied smile. "Mister 'R,' will you tell us what you saw that last, fateful day of your association with plaintiffs?"

"Objection!" Pym brayed. "Defense counsel is leading the witness."

"Overruled!" Raum growled. "Shut up, Pym. Witness will answer the question."

"Well, Marie came into the front room of her apartment in a snit and accused me of lying to her," the voice in the box said. "She began ranting about how my prophecies had ruined her life and I had failed in my duty as a prophecy doll."

"Rasputin?" Henrietta squeaked.

"In your capacity as a prophecy doll, Mister 'R,' what do you do for a living?" Smith asked, ignoring Henrietta's outburst.

"I provide prophecies," the box stated.

"Witness, please tell the court how you define a prophecy."

"Objection!" Pym interrupted, rising to his feet. "I see no dictionary here."

"Overruled," Raum rumbled deep in his chest. Pulling a thick dictionary from beneath his desk, he thumped his clenched fist down onto the book. "Got one right here. Please continue, witness."

"Yes, O Wise One," the voice in the box responded. "Marie Antoinette and Henrietta Maria did not want prophecies in the traditional sense, Your Dishonor, yet that is precisely what I was created to do: prophesy. Marie and Henrietta wanted career and social counseling, which is not my function. Yet, knowing this, they continually asked me for prophecies. As I told them repeatedly, a prophecy reveals the future; knowing the future may allow the owner of a prophecy doll to act accordingly, and seek advantage. I performed to the best of my capabilities for my owners. It is not my fault that my owners are unable to distinguish a prophecy from a career path."

"Thank you. Witness may be excused. Barney?"

Barney the bailiff walked over to the box and carefully lifted it from the stand. The bailiff and the box disappeared into the courtroom's side chamber. A long moment passed before the skinny bailiff returned and took his place next to Raum's bench.

The judge glanced over at Marie and shook his horned head.

"Marie Antoinette," Raum intoned, his deep voice filling the cavernous courtroom. "You asked for 'housing befitting your status,' is that correct?"

"Yes, Your Dishonor," Marie acknowledged slowly.

"And the Department of Unwelfare Housing is moving you into one of their apartments?" Raum continued, his glasses nearly falling off his thin nose.

"Yes?" Marie answered, confused.

"I fail to see the problem there," Raum said. "You are a damned soul who can barely hold a job. You received exactly what you deserved and, quite frankly, what you could manage." Looking back at his notes he continued, "Let's see … then you requested a prophecy on how to be popular?"

"Yes, Lordship," Marie nodded, still confused.

"Surely you admit you were popular when you had *tres leche* cake emanating from certain regions of your body," Raum informed her with a delicate shrug. "This document attests to the fact that gentlemen came flocking to you. I will, however, sanction Prophecy Dolls, LLC, for their use of the 'let them eat cake' portion of the prophecy. That phrase could be construed as slander against the plaintiff, Marie Antoinette, since it has been proven that she never uttered those words before the arrival of said prophecy head."

"My clients, Prophecy Dolls, LLC, deeply apologize, Your Lordship," Smith piped up quickly, remaining in his seat. He folded his hands on the table before him and smiled at Marie and Henrietta. "We shall issue a public apology to Madame Antoinette forthwith."

"Sounds fair to me," Raum muttered as he scanned the page. "You told your Prophecy Doll 'I want to be in a higher circle of friends.' That's a classic. I'm surprised you didn't end up somewhere worse than the fifth circle of hell."

"Your Lordship, I most strongly object!" Pym protested loudly.

"Shut up, Pym."

"Yes, Your Dishonor."

Raum raised his eyes from the notes before him. "Are both parties ready to receive my ruling?"

"Yes, Lordship," Smith said, rising.

Marie, Henrietta and Pym followed suit. "Yes, Demonic Lordship," Pym acknowledged.

"On the first charge of the complaint, regarding breach of contract," Raum began, steadying his spectacles on his long nose, "I find in favor of the defendant. The plaintiffs did not demonstrate that the *caveat cadaver emptor* disclaimer had been sufficiently insufficient to constitute a breach of said contract."

"Caveat cadaver emptor?" Marie whispered to Pym, completely confused. While she understood some Latin, legalese was beyond her.

"Let the deceased buyer beware," Pym translated for her in a low, defeated tone.

"On the second count of the allegation…" Raum continued "…regarding false advertisement, I also find in favor of the defendant. False advertisement applies only when the purchaser is purposely misled, not when the purchaser is inarticulate or imprecise when utilizing the product. The advertisement clearly states that prophesies are interpreted by their individual owners and the *results* of that interpretation are not the responsibility of Prophecy Dolls, LLC."

"On the subject of this frivolous lawsuit filed in my uncivil court, however…" Raum scowled at Marie and Henrietta. "…I find both plaintiffs in contempt of my court and sentence you as follows: you *will* learn the difference between prophecy and career advice. I sentence you both to be remanded into custody, where you will be taught the difference by a court-appointed advocate of this court's choosing."

"No*ooooo….*" Marie moaned, her eyes closing to keep her roiling stomach under control. After a moment, she turned to Pym, who slunk away.

"My legions are awaiting my command to fight against *them*, that damned Erra and his Seven peerless champions, and His Infernal Majesty is *not* one to forgive an earl for being late to war with enemies of the realm. Here in my courtroom *I* provide injustice, and injustice is what you two deserve. Court's adjourned," the demon snapped, slamming his gavel onto the bench. "I've got a battle to lead."

"All rise!" the bailiff called out needlessly.

*

Marie blinked and looked around at the large dusty room, where indeterminate shapes hugged the walls and clumped in ragged rows. Dim light from narrow windows revealed dust swirling on the air amongst the shadows. Not a sound could be heard as she sat in the hard wooden chair. So far as she could tell, they were alone. Beside her, Henrietta shifted listlessly.

"This is worse than Unwelfare Housing," Henrietta carped under her breath.

"I wish I could find a way out of this mess," Marie complained. Ignoring her friend, she closed her eyes and tilted her head back until it was resting against the wall. "Or find someone who can."

"You already have," a voice said, right in front of her. Her eyes snapped open and she found herself face to face with a wizened old man, a folder in his gnarled and arthritic hand. She looked at the man with the folder in confusion: a grayish man with a gray folder in a cavernously long gray room wrapped in dust and shadow.

"What? Who? Where?" she asked, baffled.

"You asked for a copy of the floor plan for the Mortuary, didn't you? 'Help me save myself; I must find a way to escape from the dreaded Undertaker's clutches,' you said." The man wheezed tiredly, his grayish skin blending perfectly with their surroundings. He pushed the folder forward. "The note you gave my assistant said you'd be sitting in this very chair. This shows everything, including the new ventilation system the Undertaker recently installed."

"Wait, what...?" Marie's voice trailed off as she looked around and realized that the indeterminate clumps and shapes scattered about the room were wraithlike, dust-covered people.

A trail of footprints marred the dirty floor. She followed it with her eyes and saw that the strange man had moved through the room without disturbing anyone else there. Marie looked back at the old man. "Where am I?"

"Decapitol Records Eternal Waiting Room," the old man informed her patiently. "We call it the Lobby. Here." His hands were gray too, and skeletally thin. He held out the folder.

Marie took the folder. "I don't understand...." But maybe she did: she'd wished for a way to save herself from the punishment that the demon judge had decreed for her and Henrietta. Hadn't she?

"Who does?" the man shrugged as he tugged on his gray shirt. He rubbed his thin hands. "Anything else?"

"How do I get out of here?" Marie asked him, looking around the shadowy Lobby through the thick air. None of the others waiting in the room had so much as twitched since she arrived. Some of the people sitting in the Lobby appeared to be sleeping, their shoulders leaning against their neighbors as they slumbered. She clutched the gray envelope tight to her breast. "Tell me how, tell me *now.*"

"Well now, that's the rub," the old man smirked, his teeth

blackened and worn down to nubs. "You must wait your turn."

His breath is almost as bad as the Undertaker's. A sudden urge to vomit overwhelmed her. "Wait my … turn?" Marie swallowed nervously. Nobody else in the room was moving. How long would she wait here? A month? A year? A decade. She sighed. "And my turn won't come for a long time, is that it?"

"Ayup," the old man nodded, grinning. "It's hell, babe. What'd you expect?" And he was gone in a puff of dust.

Henrietta hadn't moved all this long while.

"Someone's going to miss this folder eventually," Marie muttered as she closed her eyes. "Come for it. And when they come to get it, the only way I'll give it up is if they show me how to get out of here."

"Sssh," Henrietta whispered to her, her own eyes still shut. "I'm trying to sleep while *I* wait my turn. Time will pass more quickly if we sleep."

The two women waited quietly in the Lobby. Someone would want the envelope, Marie was convinced. Some important person would eventually come to get it. She had the plans to the Mortuary – a bargaining chip. When someone came for the plans, she would convince that person to take her and Henrietta to freedom.

Until then, she would wait. Patiently, if she must. She looked down at the gray envelope clutched to her chest: her ticket to freedom. And Henrietta's, too. Marie squirmed in her seat, trying to find a more comfortable position.

Would she give up the plans to the Mortuary, when the time came? Items of power came rarely to anybody in hell. Even if it was a mistake, she now had her hands on one of those rare items. The gray envelope held the power to someday set her and Henrietta free. It was hope for her, and hope for Henrietta. The wait would be but a small price to pay for freedom.

A little wait. She could stand it. Henrietta could. However long the wait might be, waiting in this room was but a small price to pay. Satisfied, Marie closed her eyes and leaned against Henrietta, using her larger friend as a pillow.

A very small price to pay, indeed.

Or so she thought, until something bumped her right foot,

jittering on the dusty floor. It was a cardboard box.

From that box, a muffled voice she well remembered said, “So, we meet again, Queen of France and dimwitted friend Henrietta.” Rasputin’s voice was unmistakable, even through the cardboard. “Let me prophesy for you, Marie and Henrietta, just how long we’ll be waiting here together ... *until retribution finds you both!”*

Rasputin’s voice screeched through the quiet waiting room like fingernails on a blackboard.

Measure of a Man

by

Deborah Koren

Lose your temper and you lose a friend; lie and you lose yourself.
– Hopi

Gunshots shattered the quiet, glass broke, and a man screamed. Alan Bensinger jolted awake at the noise. The lumpy mattress creaked on unsteady springs beneath him, and he gripped the edges of the unfamiliar bed in alarm. He did not recognize where he was. He sucked in air to calm himself and touched his chest, face, and arms. He was in one piece; he was all right.

"Good morning," a voice said.

Alan jumped.

In a chair a few feet away sat a short, broad-chested man, with blue-grey eyes in a face boyish despite the thick moustache. Dark hair curled under the brim of a worn cowboy hat.

"Who are you?" Alan knew his stare was rude, but he was unable to make sense of the man's unusual outfit. He wore black trousers held up with suspenders. A partially unbuttoned blue shirt showed the pink of a well-washed union suit beneath. The rolled-up sleeves exposed muscular forearms. Alan's gaze dropped to the man's waist where a gun-belt was buckled, the silver handle of a pistol in obvious sight. Alan swallowed.

"I hear you're an attorney," the man said and pushed his hat back on his head with his thumb.

"I … where am I?"

The man gestured to the window.

Alan got cautiously to his bare feet. He was wearing long johns himself, he found. He brushed the material with one hand, self-consciously, then looked around. The small room seemed old-fashioned somehow. Maybe it was the floral wallpaper, or the lack of carpeting on the floorboards. A low chest of drawers held a pitcher, water basin, and a folded white towel. He saw no adjoining bathroom, nor any modern accessories, not even a light switch. The window seemed cloudy, and he scrubbed at the glass with his fist before realizing it wasn't a film of dust, but the imperfections in the glass itself that marred his view. He glanced over his shoulder at the visitor, then thumbed open the latch and pushed the casement wide.

The second floor window faced onto a dirty street. The buildings across the way – a general store, a saloon, and a stable – looked old. Not built old, but time-period old. He'd never seen a street like it in New Hell. It was crowded too, and the people bustling past looked *old* too, cowboys and farmers and women in head-to-toe dresses. It was like peering onto a movie set for a Hollywood Western. Two cowboys cantered by on what he took to be horses until he looked closer and recoiled in horror. They were shaped like horses, they moved like horses, but their ropy sinews appeared spun of human body parts. Arms and legs twisted, re-shaped – and, on the hell-horse's wither, a gape-mawed face stared outward with one eye.

He spun back toward his guest. "Is this a joke?"

The man smiled. "Welcome to New Bodie."

Alan managed to keep his mouth shut and not echo the town's name like some idiot just off the bus. Or stagecoach. "Look, Mister…?"

"Masterson. William Barclay."

"Look, Mister Masterson," Alan automatically dropped into his soothing lawyer voice, "there's been some mistake. I am an attorney, you're right. I was just on my way to a courtroom in the Hall of Injustice, but this place … wait a minute." He cocked his head, puzzled. "Masterson? Why do I know that name?" He studied the man. No, he didn't seem familiar, but he never had been as good at placing faces with names as he should have been. "Did I win a case against you back … before we died?"

The man laughed, an easy laugh, but it did nothing to put Alan at ease. "What's the last thing you remember?"

Did the man never answer a direct question? "Now look here –"

Masterson got to his feet, and Alan backed into the window

unconsciously. Something about the man's manner – the easy physical grace, the smooth voice, the pale eyes – intimidated Alan. He tried not to look at the gun-belt strapped around the man's hips. "What do you remember?" Masterson asked again, and Alan understood he had just enjoyed a sort of rare luxury. Masterson did not look like a man who repeated himself.

Alan gnawed his lip and tried to recall. "I was walking through the Hall of Injustice. I was late for an appointment – there was so much tension – nobody knew where Erra and the Seven would appear next. There was an enraged demon racing through the halls… Then I remember … the Undertaker's table. It was horrible, God, it was horrible." He blanched. "Does that mean…?"

"Yep, you died. You were reassigned here."

"But my apartment, my cases, my –" He started to say *my life*, but realized the pointlessness of those words. This was hell. The concept of having a life was not the same as it once had been.

"Well," Masterson said, "all that's gone. You can't leave here, and I have a job for you, if you'll come along with me." He started for the door, but Alan balked as the sound of rifle shots blasted away outside.

"Where is this New Bodie I've been brought to?"

"Out in the boonies of hell somewhere. What does it matter?"

"What do you mean I can't leave?"

"Well you can, but you'd have to die again, and I don't think you're looking to reacquaint with the Undertaker quite so soon." His lips quirked sympathetically at Alan's hasty headshake. "Now, hurry up, get dressed."

The pants and shirt laid out for him were similar to Masterson's outfit, but clean and pressed. Alan tugged the clothes on, cursing under his breath, dreading how hot he was going to be, wearing long underwear. The boots pinched uncomfortably. He left the vest and jacket draped over the metal bed frame, and ignored the hat Masterson offered him. "If this New Bodie is so isolated, how do you know who I am?" he asked.

"Oh, I've seen you in New Hell." Masterson winked and grinned at him again. "Now come along, I have a client for you. And a good thing too. 'Cause that's ten you owe me for the clothes."

Reluctantly, Alan followed him out of the room, unwilling to be left in this new hellhole by himself. He'd learned the hard way that traversing any city, town, even a building, was best done first with someone who could show you the ropes.

The lobby of the Unlucky Strike Hotel seemed luxuriously appointed, with chairs upholstered in deep green velvet, and a fancy rug spread in the lobby. Then Alan saw the bullet holes spattering the walls, the half-shattered and canted chandelier, the broken pulley fan; a closer look at the velvet revealed just how threadbare it was. But it was the bullet holes that worried him. Not more than ten minutes at a time had passed without at least a couple shots fired.

When he hesitated inside the lobby doors, Masterson's hand snaked back, caught the front of his shirt, and yanked him out onto the boardwalk. "What's the matter?" Masterson demanded.

"Am I going to be shot at?"

Masterson shrugged. "Probably. That's life in New Bodie. Stop fretting. No one's going harm you as long as you're with me."

"Why?" Alan asked. "Who are you?"

"I told you who I was, now come along. You bellyache more than a penniless drunk."

William Masterson.... Alan rolled the name around in his head, realizing he needed to stop thinking about his own lifetime and start thinking more broadly. Two hell-horses were tethered at the hitching post outside the Unlucky Strike Hotel. They watched him with small, evil eyes and bared fangs. Alan shuddered and edged by as close to the wall and as far from the beasts as he could. A charnel-house stench rolled off their sweaty amalgamated bodies, and Alan covered his nose and looked away.

"What's that?" He squinted at the horizon, shielding his gaze with an up-thrown hand. "Looks like a dust storm?" He knew he sounded more worried than he meant to, but any kind of storm in hell was dreadful. Or worse, it wasn't a storm at all, but the approach of something bigger and more dangerous. Like Erra and the Seven. There was nowhere in hell so isolated they couldn't visit whenever they chose.

Masterson didn't even bother glancing the direction Alan pointed. "That's the boundary of New Bodie, you might say."

"A dust storm?"

Masterson snorted. "It's not the dust storm you have to worry about, son, it's what's causing it."

"All right," Alan said. "I'll bite. What's causing it?"

"A stampede of the biggest, orneriest, fire-breathing, man-eating hell-cattle you ever did see. They roam the desert out there waiting for some dumb-as-shoe-leather tenderfoot to try to leave here that way."

"But, you said *you* leave here," Alan objected.

"Regularly. But I told you, I'm special. And I don't go that route."

A large stagecoach clattered by, pulled by six hell-horses, and Alan jumped back from the proximity of it. Masterson walked on, and Alan had to hurry to catch up. A bunch of miners pushed out of a noisy saloon as he passed, the batwing doors slapping to and fro behind them. Alan stumbled through their midst, trying to ignore the glares and the insults flung at him. Boot heels stomped on the boardwalk around him.

"I'm sorry," Alan apologized as he smacked into one large, bearded man.

Meaty fingers shot out, knotted in Alan's shirt front, and hauled him close. Alan gagged on the man's rancid breath. "Sorry?" the man wheezed. "Who asked you for an apology?" His other hand drew back in a fist, and Alan flung his arms up in front of his face.

"I thought you liked free things," Masterson's voice said calmly from over Alan's shoulder. "Don't make that apology he gave you pick up a price tag."

Porcine eyes squinted malevolently at Masterson, clearly weighing options. The big miner growled behind twisted lips and hurled Alan sideways. Alan slammed hard into the saloon wall and barely caught himself. He gasped at the pain in his shoulder.

The miner ignored Alan entirely, gave Masterson one last glare, spat at his feet, then strode into the street with his unsavory companions. Alan tried to smooth out his shirt front.

"Dead Hat Joe. Mean one. Not much on brains though." Masterson glanced curiously at Alan. "Just how'd you survive in New Hell?"

"I didn't," Alan reminded him curtly, then he shrugged. "Not very well. I stayed in the Hall of Injustice as much as I could."

"You're not going to enjoy that luxury here, I'm afraid. You want to strap on a gun?"

The idea shot a tremor of fear through Alan's gut. He pointed one finger at Dead Hat Joe's retreating back. "That was the closest I've ever been to a fight in my life, and you want me to carry a gun?"

Hands on hips, Masterson frowned. "What kind of privileged life did you lead anyway?"

"Not privileged. Just … civilized."

Masterson snorted. "Bet you a pretty pine coffin you're begging for shooting lessons by the end of the week. Come on, Mister Civilized."

Ahead, a red awning overhung the alcoved entrance to a theater called simply the Ungrand Opera House. Posters proclaimed an ongoing performance of *The Girl of the Golden West*, directed by the composer himself, Giacomo Puccini. The open front doors beckoned, and Alan paused to peek inside. The small theater offered an intimate setting. Only a few rows of wooden benches stood in front of the orchestra pit and stage, backed by an open floor area for the rest of the patrons to stand. He could just make out a balcony of more opulent box seats that ringed the stage, but the red velvet seats and curtains appeared a hundred years old: ragged and faded, instead of lush and elegant. His glance jumped to the splintered gold-painted wood of the balcony and the rents in the walls, and his eyes widened as he realized they were evidence of more bullet holes. A lot of them.

The onstage set featured the interior of a saloon. A baritone was singing to a woman, the lone woman in a crowd of men. At least, that's what Alan thought he was *supposed* to be doing, but it was the worst, most out-of-tune singing he'd ever heard, and he cringed, shrinking back until the horrible noise ended abruptly as a man ran out on stage.

"No no no no no no!" the man cried. Dark-haired, mustachioed, his curly hair frazzled, he proceeded to rant at the singer in rapid-fire Italian. The baritone quailed under the tirade, but the woman stomped her booted foot and crossed her arms.

Young, blonde, petite and curvaceous, in some sort of a cowgirl costume designed to make her fit in with the boys, he supposed, but it just made her look cute. Like a college co-ed dressing up for Halloween. She looked down the opera house main aisle, straight out at Alan. Their gaze met. She smiled, apple cheeks dimpling, and Alan smiled back. He had the urge to wave at her, but he stopped himself.

A tap on the shoulder made Alan jump. Masterson nodded toward the angry man on stage. "That's the composer himself. Poor guy. He's gone off his nut, and I can't say I blame him. He's stuck directing the same opera over and over, cursed with the worst soprano, an awful tenor, an over-the-hill baritone, and an orchestra cursed with instruments that can't stay in tune. They've never finished a performance. The cowboys keep coming back, hoping for something better. By the middle of the first act, they know that's as good as it gets, and they shoot up the place. Puccini and the gang fix the place up and start in again the next day. You notice the empty buildings?" He gestured around the street. The buildings within a block radius seemed to be boarded up or abandoned. "Even residents in New Bodie have standards," Masterson said. "No one wants to live or work within earshot of the rehearsals."

"Who's that blonde woman in there?"

"Minnie?"

Alan found himself smiling. "Minnie."

"No, that's the character she's playing. The soprano is Sally Lockett."

"Oh," Alan muttered. Then he smiled again and tried out her name. "Sally."

Masterson rolled his eyes and caught Alan by the sleeve, hauled him along. "Come along, son. You haven't heard her sing and, trust me, you don't want to."

*

Their destination bore a simple legend: Josie's. The first thing Alan noticed was that the interior seemed to be decorated with fewer bullet holes than either the opera house or the hotel. The second thing he noticed was the man playing solitaire at a far table: a tall, lean, sandy-haired man, sporting a broom of a moustache over thin lips. He was dressed neatly compared to the other residents in

New Bodie. Even Masterson's garb looked shabby next to this man's white shirt, red brocade vest, black coat, and string tie.

"This him?" the man asked.

"Yep," Masterson said.

The man raised his eyes from his cards, and Alan felt like he needed to take a step back. It was a casually appraising glance that couldn't have lasted more than a couple seconds, but Alan knew the man had sized him up in that brief moment, and it unnerved him. He wasn't used to having his measure taken so completely in a bare whisper of time. The man turned up a couple cards, shifted another across the exposed piles, then looked up again. Pale blue eyes fixed on Alan, and he said, "I hear you're an attorney."

"Yes, sir." Alan winced. He hadn't meant to throw the "sir" on there, but it had just slipped out.

"Looking to hire an attorney," the man said. "Harry Piper's lost one too many times, and he claims my faro tables are rigged."

"Are they?"

The man gave a short bark of laughter. "In hell? Don't be ridiculous. Trying to cheat here is an exercise in futility. Hell itself cheats whenever it feels the inclination. You don't act like you been down here long, but you had to have noticed things don't work the way you expect them to."

"Well, yeah," Alan said, remembering his office in New Hell. "I learned fast not to take the elevators in the Hall of Injustice, and there was this coffee maker … worst coffee you ever tasted when it did work, which was only part of the time, the rest of the time it …"

Masterson and the other man were starring expressionlessly at him. Alan shut up. He swallowed and got back to business. "My name's Alan Bensinger."

"Wyatt Earp."

"Wyatt…" Alan gaped. "Wyatt Earp? *The* Wyatt Earp?"

Earp scowled at Masterson. "You didn't tell him?"

Masterson grinned innocently and spread his hands.

"You were really at the O.K. Corral and all that? With Doc Holliday and –" Alan broke off. "You don't look like Wyatt Earp."

The man raised an eyebrow. "Is that so?"

"Yeah, well, I've seen the movies, you know, Burt Lancaster and Kurt Russell, Henry Fonda…."

Masterson cleared his throat.

Alan shut up. "Sorry," he said. "I guess that's kind of silly, isn't it? I mean they're just actors, you're the real thing." He spun toward Masterson. "That's why I know your name. You're Bat Masterson!"

"Yeah, and I know," he held up a hand to forestall any comments, "I don't look like Gene Barry either. Or Joel McCrea for that matter. Rather wish I did."

"How do you know what they looked like? Never mind, never mind," Alan said quickly. Excitement ran though him. Now this he could do. He'd never been offered the chance to defend anyone famous back in New Hell. New Bodie was looking up. "So you want me to represent you? Well, you've come to the right man, Mister Earp. You see, I can win any case." Alan grinned. "I got this deal, see, as part of my torment, as long as I lie in court, it's a cinch. A done deal. We can make up whatever story you want, and if I tell it, it'll stick...."

The blue-eyed man paused mid-deal and gazed at him coldly, and Alan trailed off. He'd been in a lot of hostile courtrooms, but that icy stare not only disapproved, it completely dismissed him. The same glance flicked toward Masterson, and Earp said, "Throw him out."

Alan's mouth dropped open.

"Now, Wyatt," Masterson said, "give the kid a chance –"

"You heard me."

Masterson sighed and grasped Alan's sleeve again without further ado and tugged him bodily toward the exit. The man at the table kept playing solitaire without watching them go.

"Now wait a minute, wait!" Alan's objections went unheeded until they were outside in the stifling heat. "What the hell was that about? Man needs a lawyer, I tell him I can't lose, that his case is a sure thing, and he *fires me*?"

"Gotta be hired to be fired, son," Masterson said. He spread his hands. "You didn't make it that far. Sorry. But trust me, around New Bodie, you won't lack for work. Plenty of mining claim disputes, murder charges, robbery, assault and battery, rustling... Just set yourself up, put up a shingle, and the clients will be pouring in."

"But –" Alan deflated. "I don't know anything about mining law."

"You have something against learning?"

"No, I ..." Alan glanced back into Josie's. "What'd I do wrong, Mister Masterson?"

Masterson's expression grew serious, and he said simply, "Wyatt don't take to lying, that's all."

"I don't either, that's what got me sent here, I'm sure of it, but...." He heard the old bitterness coming out in his voice and cut himself off. Masterson wouldn't want to hear about his past, and he sure as hell didn't want to tell it. It was too depressing. "So, now what?"

"You can't throw a stone around here without hitting a saloon or a cantina. Go get yourself a drink."

"Anything like the drinks in New Hell?"

"Worse."

"No thanks, then." He recalled how, once upon a time, shortly after he had arrived in hell, he had thought he might be able to drink himself into oblivion. That hope had died fast. Alcohol had been no relief whatsoever. He couldn't get properly drunk, and all it had done was turn his gut into a sea of churning snakes and make him even more miserable. If that was possible.

"Go take in a show then."

Alan remembered the blonde singer and smiled to himself.

Masterson groaned and shook a finger at him. "Just remember I told you so."

"What?" Alan said.

"You haven't heard her sing."

*

She wasn't singing when Alan returned to the opera house. Another argument was in progress, this time between Sally Lockett and the composer of the opera, Giacomo Puccini. In Italian. Alan couldn't understand a word they were saying, but he thought she was marvelous. Fiery, passionate, beautiful – and she seemed to be winning whatever dispute they were having, as Puccini grew redder and redder. Alan liked a woman who knew how to use words.

Then, almost as if she sensed his presence, she looked his way.

And that dimpled smile crossed her face again, in clearly surprised pleasure. She'd remembered him! At least he thought so for a moment, until she summarily ended the discussion by slapping Puccini hard and storming past him backstage. Alan's shoulders slumped.

Puccini held his cheek and stared after her. The members of the chorus and the large rotund tenor slunk off the other way while he was distracted, but the movement caught the composer's eye, and he cried out in a heavily accented voice, "No! We must rehearse again! *Andiamo!*"

No one noticed Alan at all, and, as the conductor raised his hands to the small rag-tag orchestra at the composer's command, Alan solemnly left the theater. Maybe she smiled at all strangers, anything to break the monotony of rehearsals.

He walked right into her outside the theater doors. "I'm so sorry!" he began, but she shushed him with a finger across her lips, grabbed him familiarly by the hand, and pulled him away from the theater entrance.

She'd changed clothes somehow, he noticed. She wore a dress now, a blue and white checkered affair that seemed to cling to all the right places. Her blonde hair had been swirled on top of her head where it seemed to stay as if by magic.

"You're new here, ain't cha?" she said. "Ain't seen you 'round before."

He stared at her a moment, trying to reconcile the image of an opera singer talking like that. Then he remembered Masterson wincing at the thought of her singing. Alan shrugged it off. "Yes," he said.

She smiled again, batting her eyelashes at him. "Well, why don'tcha buy a girl a drink?"

By the time she'd had two drinks (and he hadn't touched the one he'd felt compelled to buy out of old-fashioned courtesy), he'd learned that, growing up, she'd wanted to be just like Jenny Lind. "You know, the Swedish Nightingale?" she had said, and Alan had nodded as if he had the slightest clue who she was talking about. She'd studied to be a singer, but the War Between the States had broken out, and her teacher had gone off to fight. She'd died herself of typhus that same year.

"I guess it was enough training though, 'cause here I am, stuck singin' that cursed opera for that cursed composer." She downed the rest of her glass as if it were water, and Alan grimaced.

"How can you drink that stuff, doesn't it…?"

"Curdle in my belly?"

"That's not exactly what I was going to say, but…"

"Well, sure it does, honey. I haven't been able to get good and soused since I arrived down here, and let me tell you, that is hell. You try singin' to an audience full of riled up cowboys who wanna hear something good and get stuck with me and that damned opera. Think we can do *Lucia di Lammermoor* or *La Traviata*? Oh no, just *La Fanciulla* over and over and over. And after they boo and shoot the place up, I can't even drown my sorrows in a good whiskey." She shrugged, a lithe raising of her petite shoulders. "But I keep figuring, maybe one of these days, one good drink will somehow slip in among the bad, you know? Keeps me hoping." Her smile turned shy, and she looked up at him from under those big lashes. "Sort of like meeting a man like you. Keeps me hoping."

Alan blushed and found himself speechless.

*

Alan stared in the mirror and rubbed a palm over his scruffy jaw. He hoped Sally liked beards because he did not know how to use the straight-edge razor that lay beside the wash basin. Even the smallest paper cuts tended to turn septic in hell; he dreaded the nicks and outright cuts he could give himself if he attempted shaving with that sharp blade. There were bound to be barbershops around, but he wasn't sure he trusted them either. That old adage about being paranoid … it applied in spades to hell – everything *was* out to get him. Or at least make sure he was as miserable as possible.

But then, there was Sally. Meeting her wasn't miserable. Quite the contrary. It was the best thing that had happened to him since arriving in hell. They'd had dinner together last night in the Unlucky Strike Hotel's restaurant, a relatively safe place to be when unruly drunks started their nightly fighting. New Bodie's streets, bursting with gunshots as rapid as firecrackers, sounded like a Chinese New Year celebration. He dreaded the thought of venturing out there. Anything that moved outside seemed fair game. Sally blithely ignored the whole thing, her attention fixed solely on him. And, he found himself increasingly charmed by her.

They had talked about inconsequentials, just two people discovering each other. It felt almost normal. More than that, he'd been *happy*, and that worried Alan immensely. Hell liked to wait until you relaxed before it smacked you down again. Nothing that felt good could last down here.

Could it?

His mind chewed over the possible consequences of his newfound happiness as he left himself unshaven and hurried downstairs to meet Sally in the hotel lobby.

"I found the perfect place for you to set up shop," she said, arms snaking through his to lead him outside. The heat sucked all the energy right out of him, but she bounced along at his side unfazed. She was wearing a deep green dress today, that made her blonde hair seem even blonder. "It's right beside the opera house," she said. "A lovely building with real windows. Furnished even! With a room upstairs, so you can live there too and get out of this hotel."

He didn't tell her he liked the hotel. Even in hell, there was something comforting about having your bed made up for you and meals available right downstairs. So the bedbugs bit and the towels reeked of mildew. But it was expensive, and the cash Masterson had loaned him would barely cover a week's lodgings there. He was going to have to find work fast, and a cheaper place might let him stretch that money a bit longer. And he had Sally to wine and dine, too.

They sauntered down the boardwalk, and Alan jumped every time a gun went off or a hell-horse cantered down the middle of the dusty street. Sally paid no attention, but he found himself distracted by everything, both by the newness of it and the worry that something was going to shoot him or run him down. Somehow, crossing through rush-hour traffic in New Hell seemed less threatening than simply walking among the snorting, revolting hell mounts.

Alan drew up abruptly. "Oh, no."

"What is it?" Sally asked.

Dead Hat Joe was coming straight for him, his gorilla-like gait standing out amid his posse of flunkies.

"Quick!" Alan steered Sally down the nearest alley.

"Alan –"

"Don't argue!"

Decaying brick and mortar walls rose on either side, funneling them through smelly, dark shadows toward the brightness of the next street. They came out, and Alan glanced over his shoulder. No one had followed, and he sighed.

"There he is," Dead Hat Joe's wheezy voice called out.

Alan turned to see the miner swing around the corner of the building, retinue in tow. He closed his eyes for a moment, contemplated running, and discarded the notion. Joe and his boys were armed. Alan wasn't that eager to find out what getting shot felt like. He tightened his arm around Sally, wondering how he could protect her.

The big man stopped a few feet away, his henchmen a fan of ugly support behind him. "You sure do scurry like a broken-tailed rat."

"The only rat around here is you," Alan said.

"Oooh!" Dead Hat Joe flailed his arms in mock terror. "Lookee here, boys, he can talk for hisself!"

"That's right, and if you dare lay a hand on me, I'll file charges against you with the marshal."

Dead Hat Joe laughed and spat into the street. "When I'm done with you, there won't be anything left for the Undertaker to put back together, let alone to 'file charges.'"

Alan licked dry lips, then steeled himself. "Masterson was right, you haven't got any brains."

Dead Hat Joe's eyes narrowed and he moved forward, fists clenching.

"Dead Hat Joe," Sally interrupted crossly, and Alan couldn't prevent her from stomping forward to get in Joe's face. He watched her nervously, but she didn't seem afraid at all. "You go take your fun somewheres else. I'm a-courtin'!"

Joe's guffaw was incredulous. "With this mail-order cowboy?"

"Stop it!"

"Or what? You'll sing?"

Her mouth dropped open in outrage.

He leered at her. "I once heard me a screech owl sing prettier," he said, "when I shot it."

"Caterwauling banshee!" one of his minions added.

"Why you –" Sally lunged forward, snatching for Joe's own gun.

Appalled, Alan jumped forward and grabbed her around the waist just as the miner shoved her away from him.

She yelled, "You let me go! I'm gonna kill that loud-mouthed, claim-jumping, lying son of a bitch –"

"Sally!" Alan said, shocked.

Dead Hat Joe laughed, with a wet coughing sound. "Why don'tcha just get behind the little songbird and let her do your fighting for you, saphead?"

"I'm an attorney," Alan said stiffly. *What did this guy know anyway? How hard would it be to scare him off? Besides, what did he have to lose?* "Do you know what that means?"

"I know law ain't got no place here."

Alan forced a confident laugh. "That's what you think, buddy. Why do you think I'm here, in this bloody town of yours? Do I look like I belong here? Oh no, I've been sent down here specifically. The status quo here is being challenged. And with you caught in *flagrante delicto* like this, with witnesses no less –" Alan gestured dramatically to Sally and Joe's own men as he threw out any old phrase he could think of "– the *onus probandi* is on you, and if you think any judge is going to think twice about sentencing you to hang, well, the new *modus operandi* is going to be swift and speedy, *res ipsa loquitur!"*

"You make less sense 'n a drunk Indian," Dead Hat Joe muttered, but his brow had furrowed in what Alan took to be some semblance of caution.

"I suggest," Alan said stiffly, "you let us pass because the legal consequences to you would be dire."

"This law stuff ain't got no bearing –"

"Surely, you've heard of Thomas Frank?" Alan didn't wait for an answer, just plunged on with his fiction. "He was a colonel in the U.S. Army. He won the Battle of Sandy Bottom, by infiltrating the enemy's side so skillfully they never knew he was there. Well, he's been in New Bodie for two months already, checking the lay of the land for me, and let me tell you, his reports …" Alan trailed off as he realized Dead Hat Joe had taken two steps back and drawn himself up into a more respectful stance. But Joe wasn't looking at him. He was looking over Alan's shoulder.

Alan spun and found himself face to face with Wyatt Earp.

"That true?" Earp asked him, one eyebrow raised slightly as he waited for an answer.

Alan opened his mouth to say yes, but he flinched under the implacable blue gaze and shut his mouth again without saying a word. Wyatt's expression changed to a grimace of distaste. "Haven't learned, have you?"

Alan's shoulders sagged.

Wyatt shook his head, tipped his hat ever so slightly to Dead Hat Joe, and walked on.

As soon as the former lawman rounded the corner, Joe's sneer returned, and he swaggered forward. "So, you was *lying* to me, Mister Attorney? Is that what I'm hearing? You made all that up?" His fingers balled, and he raised one brawny fist. Sally squeaked and hopped sideways out of the way.

Alan threw up his arms to shield himself, but it made no difference.

*

Alan groaned and tried to sit up. A firm grip pushed him down just as bruised stomach muscles screamed in protest. "Sally?" His jaw was stiff and ached so fiercely he thought it might never move properly again. He ran his tongue gently over his teeth, but there were no gaps.

"About that gun," Masterson's voice said. "Change your mind?"

Alan groaned again and opened his eyes. No Sally. He was back in his hotel room. Masterson sat on the bed beside him. The ruddy glow of an oil lamp cast somber shadows in the corners of the dark room. He'd been unconscious for a few hours then.

"Shoot first and never miss. It was true when I was alive, and it's even more true down here," Masterson said.

"That bastard did nothing – nothing! – to stop that bully from trying to kill me!"

Mildly, Masterson asked, “Which bastard might that be?”

“That no-good friend of yours. Wyatt Earp. He walked away. Just walked away.”

Masterson cleared his throat.

“What?”

“Son, you need to stop maligning your friends and start using that over-educated head of yours.”

“Wyatt’s no friend of mine.” Alan struggled to sit up.

“You’re not dead, are you?”

“What?”

“Dead Hat Joe’s not in the habit of accepting insults of any variety. He leaves a trail of dead bodies all over New Bodie. Now, you’re not dead. Why is that, do you suppose?”

Alan opened his mouth, closed it again.

“That’s right,” Masterson said, encouragingly.

“He didn’t walk away?”

“Wyatt never walked away from a fight in his life, and he certainly never left an innocent to fall to unnecessary harm. What kind of man do you think he is?”

“But…”

“He let you get hit a few times. Served you right. Did it hurt as badly as the Undertaker’s table?”

Alan winced. “No!”

“Then what are you complaining about?” He frowned and peered more closely at Alan. “You growing that beard on purpose?”

“I don’t know how to shave with that damned real razor.”

“So, learn. You sure do seem to have something mighty powerful against trying new things.”

“I might cut myself.”

Masterson laughed loudly. “Son, you got the shit beat out of you not six hours ago. Guess what? You survived. You think any little nick you give yourself is gonna compare with the pain of a beating? You seem to forget you’re in hell. This whole place is here to hurt you. The sooner you embrace that, the sooner you’ll stop pussyfooting around and start living again.”

“‘Living?’ You’re joking, right?”

Masterson seemed to hold his breath a moment, then expel it in a gust. "I just might have to beat some sense into you myself. What part of 'for all eternity' didn't you get? Wake up! Why do you think all those power struggles are going on all over New Hell? Because this is our new life, and if you don't step up to the plate and make something of it for yourself, then you truly are damned."

Alan swung his legs off the bed and sat up.

Masterson softened his tone. "What do you feel for Sally?" Alan looked up sharply and Masterson grinned at him. "Because you sure moon around like a lovesick calf whenever you get in sight of her."

He couldn't deny it.

"So, if you can still fall in love, what's that if not life? Isn't that worth fighting for? And besides," Masterson added. "you got yourself the best part of it right now. All the bloom and spring of a new, untried infatuation, where everything's still a discovery and nothing's a disappointment. Yet. It'll wear off quickly enough, and you already know consummating your affection ain't gonna give you a good goddamn; but right now, right here, for this brief moment in your eternal damnation, it's gonna be as good as anything you had back when you were alive."

It was true, though Alan was loath to admit it. His own thoughts on happiness from just that morning flitted accusingly through his memory. He probed at his jaw, fingering the extent of the bruising. He hurt. Face, stomach, ribs – but Masterson was right about that too. It wasn't anything like the pain of a visit to the Undertaker.

Masterson got to his feet. "So, come on, get up. Let's head over to Josie's for a drink and a card game."

"Why would Wyatt want to play cards with me?" He knew he still sounded resentful, but he couldn't help it.

"Son, he doesn't want you lawyering for him, but that's a whole sight different from winning your money from you."

"I don't know how to play."

Genuine anger flashed on Masterson's face. "There seems to be a damned awful lot you don't know how to do."

Alan flared. "I know how to be a lawyer, a good one."

"Which is why you need to lie in court to win?"

The anger twisted to despair, and Alan sagged back against the pillows. "It's my torment."

"You lost me."

"It doesn't matter."

"Maybe it does."

"Back … I got out of law school with a few stars in my eyes. All those big wonderful words – truth, justice, honor, honesty, integrity. I wanted to make a difference. I wanted to help people find justice through the law. The law was their ally, the law was designed to protect them … It didn't take me long to find out how wrong I was. Honesty didn't win cases. Truth didn't win cases. I'd lay the truth right out there for a judge and jury, only to be destroyed by a dishonest lawyer who used lies to weave a more convincing story, to make me and my client into fools because … Look, here comes the defendant, sworn to tell the truth on a holy bible, in tears on the stand, fabricating a fraudulent story, whole cloth, that would prevail on technicalities. Everything I believed in could be undone by clever coaching and manipulation because no one else believed that the truth belonged in the courtroom. We weren't playing by the same rules. It wasn't justice they wanted. It was winning.

"Oh, sometimes, truth still won out, but I watched and I learned, and one day, I tried lying myself. I won that case. I won it while, inside, I hated myself. I died a little that day. And each case thereafter."

Alan sighed. "Well, it carried down here. I was told upon my arrival that as long as I lied in court, never told the truth, I'd win my cases. But every time I did so, I'd lose a little bit more of my soul. One of these days there'll be nothing left, and then…" Alan pointed up at the ceiling, where above the roof the brilliance of Paradise would be shining. "That will be out of my reach forever."

Masterson kept quiet, and Alan was grateful. He didn't want sympathy or more advice. He stood and paced, fighting against the nausea caused by his movement. After a moment, he continued, "You know what happens to the attorney when you *lose* a case down here? You suffer the same punishment as your client. The sentences I've seen handed down …." Alan shuddered. "I don't want … I couldn't bear a worse fate than what I already have. So … I lie in court."

"And your soul whittles away."

Alan nodded miserably. "I figured *that,"* he pointed up again, "was so far out of my reach, I wasn't giving up much."

Masterson shook his head. "You're a bigger goddamn fool than some of those poor cowpokes outside. You're throwing away the *only* thing that's still yours. Come on, get your boots on. We're going out. I'll tell you a story about Wyatt while you get ready.

"You heard of Curley Bill Brocious? Damned dangerous man, one of the worst in those days. Caused a heap of trouble in real life, still causing trouble down here. You probably know what grief he caused Wyatt and his brothers after the whole O.K. Corral incident, from the motion pictures, right?" Masterson grinned at Alan. "Anyway, one night before any of that happened, he got rowdier than usual, and the marshal in Tombstone tried to arrest him. The marshal pulled Brocious' gun out of the holster to disarm him, it went off, and the bullet caught the marshal square. He died shortly thereafter. Wyatt was involved, saw the whole thing. He told me he believed the shooting was an accident. Wyatt got Brocious out of Tombstone and up to Tucson before he could be lynched. When it came time for the murder trial, Wyatt told the truth about what had happened, and Brocious got off. Case was ruled an accidental homicide.

"Brocious was as bad as they came, and Wyatt knew it. A lot of men, they'd have lied on the stand on general principles and gotten that bastard convicted and hung and made the territory a lot safer place for everyone. It would have been justifiable as a public service, really. Not Wyatt. He believed Curley Bill wasn't guilty of the murder charge he was on trial for, and that was what mattered. But that's Wyatt. His honesty got repaid with treachery and murder, but one time I asked him, if he'd known what was going to happen in the months to come after Brocious got off, if he'd have changed his mind about what he said in court."

"He said no," Alan murmured.

Masterson let the silence grow, then asked, "Now, you coming?"

"No," Alan said suddenly, remembering. "I can't. What time is it? The opera's got to be starting soon! I promised Sally." He reached for his boots before Masterson could roll his eyes again.

*

To his surprise, the opera house was packed. Not even standing-room-only remained. From the stories Masterson and Sally had told him, he figured most of the attendees weren't actually there for the music, but for the excitement and rowdy brawl that was sure to break out instead. He peered in over the sea of heads, then gave up and backed out of the theater, turning instead toward the stage entrance. She would be disappointed that he hadn't gotten there in time to get a place in the audience, but there would be plenty of other performances. Besides, Masterson's parting refrain still echoed through his mind: *you haven't heard her sing yet.* Maybe he could keep it that way.

He had wanted to bring her real flowers, but that idea hadn't lasted long. There weren't any, and even if there had been, he knew they'd only have poisonous thorns or smell like offal. He'd done the only thing he could think of – drawn her a bouquet of round-petaled daisies on a piece of paper supplied by the hotel front desk. The sheet was folded carefully in his pocket.

He pushed through the back door into a cramped hallway that opened into a large backstage storage area crowded with props, set pieces, and costumes. The chorus singers milled around, indistinguishable – except for their makeup – from the denizens out on New Bodie's streets. He could hear the orchestra warming up, if the nails-on-chalkboard shriek of violins qualified as tuning. Amid the cacophony of the backstage preparations, Puccini's voice rose, haranguing someone in Italian again. Alan pushed his way toward the dressing rooms lining one wall. Anticipation at seeing Sally again sent a thrill through him.

A gunshot cracked.

Alan stopped dead, frozen as much by the instant silence that descended backstage as by the report itself.

The door to Sally's dressing room banged open, and the round man Alan had seen once before on stage burst out. Eyes bugged wide and hair disheveled, he hesitated, faced with the rest of the cast. A wild sob escaped his throat, and he shoved his way through the singers, past Alan, and out the stage entrance into the street.

Alan ran to the dressing room door, beating the nearest chorus members through the doorway by inches. They shoved in behind him.

Sally knelt, lifting a pistol off the floor. Just beyond her, partially hidden beneath a rack of costumes, Puccini lay dead, shot in the chest. Even as Alan stared, the body dissolved and disappeared, returning to the Undertaker, leaving nothing but a wet stain behind on the floorboards.

Turning, Sally met Alan's gaze, her jaw slack. "He shot him!" she said. "Luigi shot him!"

*

Alan paced outside the stage entrance, waiting with the throng of onlookers. Several shotgun-toting deputies kept order, but the crowd seemed mostly curious, not riled up. Finally, the marshal escorted Sally out, long fingers clenched around her upper arm. She was still costumed as Minnie, her blonde hair mussed and falling out of its braids. She appeared lost and vulnerable in that sea of big men, and Alan would have done anything to grab her and run away to safety with her.

Behind her came two more deputies, and the man who had run earlier, whom someone in the crowd had identified to Alan as the tenor, Luigi Bonzoni. He was a short, round man, with curly black hair, a dark complexion, and a thin swooping moustache under a Roman nose. Unlike Sally, Bonzoni did not appear to be restrained. Quite the contrary. He was talking openly in broken English to the deputies, the panic he'd displayed earlier gone, replaced with a self-assured confidence. Alan took an instant dislike to him and his smug attitude.

"Alan!" Sally called.

He pressed forward until he could catch her free hand in his. She squeezed it hard.

"Please!" she said and burst into tears. "They're charging *me* with the murder. I didn't do it! Help me! Promise me you'll take my case."

"Don't worry," Alan said. "Of course, I will."

A burly deputy straight-armed him out of the way, and Alan watched Sally escorted down the street, Bonzoni, the deputies, and the onlookers following close behind.

"Said you wouldn't hurt for clients."

Alan turned to see Masterson joining him. Alan gestured after Sally and murmured, "I didn't think my first client would be somebody I cared about."

"This is hell. You think it would be somebody you didn't care about? Where's the torment in that?"

He sure couldn't argue with that statement.

"Come on," Masterson urged. "That earlier offer still stands. Come on over to Josie's and let's play some cards."

Alan nodded. "I will. But later. I need to talk with Sally first."

*

He expected to find the marshal's office a small hole-in-the-wall affair, but it was abnormally spacious inside. The potbellied wood-burning stove squatted alone and ignored in the center of the room. A padlocked gun rack hung on the wall behind the marshal's desk. Two deputies' desks stood on the other side of the room, and there were even two cots in the corner. To Alan's surprise, the marshal was the only one inside. The crowds had dispersed. Alan supposed murder was so common that unless it was something really unusual, it didn't keep the mob entertained for long.

"You the young man Missus Lockett retained as her attorney?" the marshal asked.

Alan nodded.

"I'm Marshal Lee Hall. You know that Luigi Bonzoni says she did it."

"She said *he* did it," Alan said.

"I know. And no other witnesses, unless the Undertaker sends the deceased back here fast. That would sure settle it! But somehow, I doubt it'll be that straightforward. It'll be the tenor's word against hers, and since this isn't the first time this has happened to her, her credibility's not holding up too well."

"What?" Alan felt the floor start slipping out from under his feet. "She's … she killed someone before?"

Hall shot him an incredulous look. "This is New Bodie, sir. Who hasn't killed somebody?"

"But, what happened?"

"The last time? Oh, she shot the last tenor. I forgot his name. She claimed he was upstaging her. No one was sorry to see him go. She got off. This time she won't be so lucky." The marshal shrugged. "Or Luigi Bonzoni won't."

Alan closed his eyes, a pit of despair opening in his stomach. This wasn't good. He recalled the scene in her dressing room, the way she'd been picking up the pistol. It hadn't looked like she'd shot it herself, but then he had a hard time picturing the petite woman wielding a gun. Then again, he remembered her temper and how quickly she'd tried to grab Dead Hat Joe's gun straight out of his holster. She seemed to know her way around a firearm.

"Got any weapons?" Hall asked.

He held the sides of his coat open for inspection, and the marshal waved him through a door. The hall beyond had at least ten cells, most of them with snoring occupants. Sally had been given a cell to herself, down at the end. Hall clanked the barred door shut behind Alan, and she rushed into his arms. She smelled of gunpowder and blood, but under it he detected a hint of flowers. He held onto that. Alan took her arms from around him and sat her beside him on the cot. "What happened?"

"That damned composer. I don't care what his problems are; we got our own too, you know? He just wants to put on a decent performance, break free from his torment for one night. Well, he's not going to get it, not in hell. And I don't want to sing any more. I can't! I'm done, Alan. He just pushed back one time too many."

"How did he die?"

She ignored the question and checked the others cells to make sure no one was listening. Quietly, she said, "The bartender at Josie's told me he overheard you tell Wyatt that you can't lose a case."

"What? How –"

"I like you." She blushed slightly. "I asked around to see if I could find out more about you, is all."

"Sally, you're changing the subject. This is important."

"So is this," she said. "Is it true? You can't lose a case?"

Reluctantly, he let her coax the admission out of him: "It's true. If I lie in court."

She traced the side of his bruised face with a gentle touch, then a dimpled smile spread across her face, and she leaned in and kissed him. Startled, he tried to pull back. She giggled and said, "Then it's perfect. I wanted to check with you first, but Giacomo was just yelling and demanding that I sing what he wrote for once, and I just couldn't stand it another minute. So I took a chance the bartender had heard right."

"What are you talking about? Are you saying *you* killed him?"

"Well, Luigi sure didn't have the guts, even if he was as tired of singin' that opera as I was. But that's why it's perfect! It's just his lawyer's word against my lawyer's, and your word, honey, is golden. You can lie in court and say Luigi did it, and we'll win the case, easy as pie!"

He stared at her.

"Don't look at me like that," she said. "You saw him. You saw the way he treated me. The way he yelled and screamed at all of us. That happened *every day*. That's abuse, ain't it? I got a right to defend myself according to some law or amendment somewheres, ain't I?"

He was at a loss for words.

She snuggled into his arms and rested her head against his chest. The scent of her hair tickled his nose with the fragrance of bruised roses. She was so warm, and all his. So, what was the problem? he asked himself. This was all he'd been doing for the last year. He'd lied for people he didn't even know, let bits of his soul slip away for nothing. Not like this. Sally was his girl. Now lying mattered. Now the price was worth something. Wasn't it?

"Sally," he said suddenly, "will you sing to me?"

Her gaze darted around the jail, the rise and fall of her breathing accelerated. "Right now?"

"Yes. Sing anything."

"I..." Her hand touched her throat self-consciously. The color in her cheeks darkened. She opened her mouth, then closed it, and shook her head. "Not now, Alan. Not here, in this awful place. Please don't ask me to. Please?"

He forced himself to nod, disengaged her arms from around him, got to his feet. "I need to go."

"It'll be all right, won't it?" she asked, her expression so crestfallen, he leaned down and kissed her. She was so beautiful.

"It'll be all right," he echoed.

*

Josie's interior glowed with the amber light of myriad lamps.

Smoke drifted in a gray haze along the ceiling planks, and the clink of bottles and glasses warred with the rise and fall of a dozen conversations. Every gaming table was crowded, except for the table in the far corner, where Wyatt Earp and Bat Masterson sat alone.

Bat pulled out a chair, and Alan dropped into it. He didn't see either man signal, but a barkeep plunked a whiskey glass down on the felt tabletop a moment later. He drank the shot down, coughing and gasping as the fiery, foul-tasting alcohol burned all the way down.

"She did it, didn't she," Masterson said, and it wasn't a question.

Alan looked up. "How did you know?"

"Son, Wyatt and I have been lawmen a long time. A liar is easy to spot, even when they're fetching and have tears streaming down their pretty faces."

Alan gestured to the bartender for a refill.

"Why are you so distraught? Isn't this a perfect setup for you? You can't lose," Masterson said. "You told me so yourself."

"I know. But if I do, Luigi Bonzoni will hang." He slammed the empty glass down against the table. "Why does that bother me? I don't know that guy from Adam."

"If you don't lie, Sally Lockett will hang," Earp said.

But she's guilty, Alan wanted to say. Damn it to every corner of hell, she *was* guilty. She'd murdered the composer in cold blood, for no good reason, knowing she had an ace in the hole to get her off. She was counting on his love for her.

But love had no bearing on truth. The law was supposed to be objective, and it was supposed to protect the innocent. Even in hell, he had to acknowledge there were still innocents. Luigi Bonzoni was innocent. It had been a long time since Alan had felt that passion: it was what had made him go into law in the first place. He remembered those early days of enthusiasm and even joy, when he had reveled in the cleanness of the law. He'd lost that perspective while he'd still been alive. His time in hell had driven the remainder of it right out of him.

He glanced up again, studying Wyatt as if seeing him for the first time. "How do you do it?" he whispered. "You've been down here for a lot longer than me. How does it still matter to you? Right, wrong, truth, lies … how can it matter down here in hell?"

"Not down here," Wyatt said. He tapped his chest. "In *here*. The only place that still matters, the only place that is still yours. If you didn't learn that in life, then you oughta learn it now."

"But Sally … I love her," Alan said. "Damn it all, I love her." Moodily, he reached in his pocket suddenly and pulled out the paper with the bouquet he had drawn for her. He smoothed it on the table top.

"No one said doing the right thing is easy," Wyatt Earp said softly. "If it was easy, everyone would do it."

And what choice did that leave him?

He listened to the swell of conversations and the rattle of a ball rolling around a roulette wheel, the simultaneous shouts of approval and disappointment when it pocketed. The pop of a cork tugged from a bottle at the bar. The purr of a deck of cards riffled together. And from the streets, the faint claps of gunfire.

Alan lifted the paper and tore it in half, then half again, then let the shreds fall to the floor.

Masterson, watching, murmured, *"Addio, fiorito assil."*

"What?" Alan asked.

"Nothing." Masterson shook his head. "Just something I heard in another Puccini opera, once upon a time." His voice brightened. "Did you know *The Girl of the Golden West* premiered in New York City with Enrico Caruso? Arturo Toscanni conducted. I remember the hoopla, though I didn't attend myself. Maybe when Puccini's resurrected this next time, the powers that be will let him switch operas."

"Maybe they'll reassign him somewhere else," Wyatt said. "Surely we've been tortured enough?"

Masterson rolled his eyes. "Wyatt, I don't have to remind *you* where we are, do I?"

"Just wishful thinking." Wyatt smoothly shuffled the cards. His blue-eyed glance flicked to Alan. "You in or out?"

Alan took a deep breath. "In," he said. "Teach me how to play this game."

The Adjudication of Hetty Green

By

Allan F. Gilbreath

Edward (Eddie) J. O'Hare, Esquire trudged slowly up the chipped stairs to the overly worn door at their top. The slightly crooked lettering on the age-etched glass stated that he had arrived at the Office of Adjudications, New Hell Branch. Eddie jiggled the door handle until he felt the internal workings connect so that the door would actually open. He stepped over the small pile of hand bills and envelopes slid under the door during his absence. He picked them up and crossed the yellowed, unwaxed linoleum floor to yet another aged door, hanging precariously near collapse. As this door opened, its hinges squeaked at the exact pitch that sent involuntary shivers up Eddie's spine.

Eddie sighed as he sat at a military-style all metal desk that had seen better days forty years ago. The chair creaked and groaned with every move he made. After tossing the papers to the desk, he pulled a gold colored pen from its cheap wood-grained stand and attempted his first notes of the day on a legal pad that looked like each page had been slightly moistened, then allowed to air dry. The minute bubbling effect on the paper's surface made the pen skip every so often.

No sooner had he begun than Eddie caught sight of himself in the small, dirty mirror askew on the wall over his desk. Eddie looked at the forty-six year old face. Anything that had been attractive about his forty-six year old face while alive was now twisted and drab in afterlife.

Eddie was relatively new to hell (after a lengthy stay in limbo while his final disposition was decided). Looking at the squalid office reminded him of the days after he'd first passed the bar. If this was hell's idea of hazing, Eddie didn't really mind. He'd soon figure out the best watering holes, whom to associate with, and how to rise through the ranks. Certainly, most of his old business associates were here in hell someplace. He'd run into them sooner or later. In the meantime, he would handle his cases, make contacts, and watch for opportunities. It had worked for him before, it would work again. This was hell, after all, and he'd had a lifetime of helping people enjoy their vices.

Oddly, New Hell reminded him of his last home, Chicago. Both were full of unhappy people who were always up to something. There weren't a lot of vehicles, so you paid attention whenever you saw or heard one going by. And there were certain people or hellish entities you had to avoid. Following his instincts, so far Eddie seemed to be adjusting fine.

The adjudication department had been established to help place clients whose problems were complex. Regardless of faith or beliefs, most people basically committed the same kind of sins over and over again. This made assigning their punishments fairly easy. However, a minority of sinners achieve hellish goals during their earthly lives and therefore may qualify for custom-tailored damnation. To add to the mess, each level of Purgatory has it quotas to meet and damnation departments to keep busy. A junior adjudicator such as Eddie must weigh the evidence, gather information, negotiate with claimants, and issue a summation to the Judgment Panel. Hell, if nothing else, wanted to make sure that each soul got exactly what he or she deserved.

Eddie glanced at the clock. Time to get to work. Of course, time-keeping was a bit dodgy in Hell. Time had a way of shifting back and forth that managed to keep everyone off balance. Eddie picked up a battered leather portfolio from the desk and flipped it open to reveal the latest H-pad. Its screen displayed pertinent information about his case for the day.

To his surprise, he knew this woman. While he had not met her personally, he knew her story. He touched a few icons on the screen and her profile flipped by: Hetty Green, The Witch of Wall Street, had a variety of claimants for her soul. He touched a few more icons and the list appeared. Before he began his review, he got up, walked over to the coffee pot, wiped out a white coffee mug with a dubious-looking dish rag and poured it full. A perk of the office, the pot immediately refilled itself. He took a sip: the dark liquid was tasteless. So far, all the food and drink he'd had in hell was devoid of flavor. With his routine needs met, Eddie got to work learning about his client of the day.

Several hours later, Eddie had a good grasp of Hetty's time in limbo. He leaned back in the chair and stretched a bit as the chair complained. A growl from his stomach hinted it was time to eat. Eddie closed the cover on his H-pad. He turned it over a couple of times. He still hadn't figured out how the damned thing actually worked. He assumed it got its information like a telephone, but this thing didn't have a wire. Perhaps it worked like a wireless crystal set and received signals out of the air. But it had both pictures and sound.

Eddie shrugged: what did he care? It might as well be hell's own black magic. The H-pad reminded him of a Tommy gun – all he had to know was how to work it, not how to build it. He shoved the H-pad aside and picked up the top envelope. It obviously contained more than paper. He tore open one end and dumped out the contents. It was his new Bastardcard – accepted everywhere in hell you want to be! He looked at the small plastic rectangle. There was a place on the back for his signature. Eddie sighed. He hated official signatures in Hell. He pulled the "signing" pen out of its base and stared at the razor sharp nib. No use in waiting. Eddie touched the nib to his other hand and immediately felt as if he had been stabbed with a dull ice pick. He grimaced and signed the back of the plastic card in his own blood then returned the pen to its base.

A flyer on his desk caught his eye. The ad promised a unique dining experience at the Inferni Club. Eddie smiled at the tag line – *Fais Ce Que Tu Voudras: Do What Thou Wilt*. He fondly remembered the many clubs in Chicago that felt the same way. Since he now had a way to pay for his meal without having to haggle over the current exchange rate for diablos or denominations of hellnotes, it seemed as good a time as any to check this place out. Besides, he could take the H-pad with him. If the H-pad didn't need a wire to work in the office, it shouldn't need a wire to work anywhere else. He stuffed the H-pad in his battered case and left.

Walking anywhere in hell was never boring. Again, Eddie felt oddly at home. Hell, like most places of his time, was perpetually either dilapidated, destroyed, or being rebuilt. Several men in togas moved purposefully across the street. Eddie didn't stare. You had to get used to seeing the damned in all kinds of clothing; anything from a grass skirts to capes to flayed skin if you were going to make it down here.

Eddie disturbed hell's pigeons, lizard-looking things that flew, squabbling over an amputated hand lying in the gutter. They scattered until he passed, then returned to their prize. Eddie had walked by bodies before, both in Chicago and in hell. It was just another day.

Eddie arrived at his destination without trouble. The instructions on the flyer had been amazingly correct. *Interesting looking place,* thought Eddie as the Inferni Club's massive church doors swung open easily under his hand. He looked around and it hit him: this place was *old.* Not old like his time; old like paintings he had seen in museums. A man dressed as a monk stood just inside.

"Greetings, please step this way. Party of one?"

"Um, yes. I got one of your flyers."

"Excellent. Would you prefer a table, booth, or room?"

"I think a booth would be fine."

"Wonderful choice. Please follow me." The monk picked up a menu and silverware wrap and led him back into the cavernous space. Eddie liked the retro décor. He saw the buffet table in the center with a few patrons circling it. It smelled good, if nothing else. How long had it been since anything had smelled good to him?

"Will this do, Sir?"

Eddie looked at the cozy booth, complete with fine leather seats and hardwood table. It may have been the finest furniture he had seen in hell.

"Yes, thank you. This will be just fine."

Once Eddie had settled into the booth, the monk signaled to someone in the room that Eddie couldn't see and then turned his attention back to his guest. "My name is Francis. If you need anything please let me know. Valeria Messalina will be your she-devil today."

As Francis the monk walked away, a striking woman in classic Roman attire arrived at the table with a glass of water and small basket of rolls. "Hello, I'm Valeria and I am your she-devil for today. On the back of our menu are all of our specials. Our drink menu is inside the front cover and, of course, we have the buffet.

What can I get you started with?"

Eddie liked her accent and her aristocratic attitude. Another aspect of hell that Eddie had discovered was linguistics. You might speak with an accent, but you were understood by almost anyone you talked to. "Do you serve egg creams?"

"We certainly do. I'll give you a moment with the menu."

Eddie watched her glide across the club. He flipped over the menu to see the specials. Apparently, the club offered daily themes: Holy Ghost Pie; Breast of Venus; Devil's Loin; Friar's Frivolous Fancies; Aphrodite's Appetizers; Roast Pope; and a variety of other edibles populated the page.

Valeria reappeared at his table with his drink. "Here you go, my dear. Have you decided?"

Eddie scratched his head for a moment then went for the default answer. "I think I will try the buffet, this time."

"Very good. I'll leave the menu with you for a drink later, perhaps." Valeria added a wink on the last word. "Please help yourself to the buffet."

Eddie watched her saunter off before heading over to the food. His hopes rose slightly. Perhaps it was being in the familiar surroundings of a club, but he could swear that he could make out different foods by the smells from the table. His nose and eyes told him that those trays held chicken thighs and breasts in quite titillating display. The short ribs left nothing to the imagination. Eddie couldn't help but smile. A lot of work went into making the Kama Sutra of food before him. He took pains with his selections and returned to his booth.

Eddie stared at the food on his fork for just a moment. Then he put it in his mouth. He sighed; at least it smelled and looked good. He would take what he could get.

As he finished his meal, he heard the H-pad make a pinging noise. Apparently, he was right: that H-pad worked just fine here. He had received a message. The message told him the claims on Hetty Green's soul were available for review. He pushed his plate to the side and made room for the H-pad. Eddie tapped the Environmental Services icon to return the call. The screen flickered a few times before the ES logo appeared on the screen.

The pleasant countenance of the standard hellish paralegal

appeared on the screen.

"Eddie O'Hare with Adjudications, returning your call about Hetty Green."

"We have been expecting you, Mr. O'Hare. Please give me one moment while I pull up the file."

"Please do, by all means." Eddie was from an era in which you were polite. You may murder your dinner guest before dessert but until then, you were polite.

The perky paralegal looked up. "Yes, here we go. We are filing a claim on Henrietta Green's soul for the wanton pillage of natural resources."

"I have that noted. Are there any special considerations that your department feels it is due?"

"We are claiming the rights to continued sin."

"On what grounds do you feel this applies?"

"Hetty was born into a family that owned a fleet of whaling ships. As we all know, there is no greater example of the wanton pillage of natural resources." The perky paralegal's countenance changed as she spoke. It shifted from that helpful look to the zealous look of a prohibitionist. Eddie knew that look all too well.

"Are there any other considerations to be addressed?" Eddie couldn't help himself. His career as a defense lawyer had been based on exonerating the guilty. He could already drive a truck of bathtub gin through the Environmental Services claim.

The perky paralegal rolled her eyes as if to ask, 'What more do you want?' Instead, she said, "Missus Henrietta Green did nothing to atone for the prior heinous acts committed during her lifetime. In fact, if the whaling business in the developed world had not been supplanted by other products and technologies, her fleet would still be out there committing a wide variety of odious acts. I'm sending you all the specifics, page and line, now."

Eddie carefully viewed the Environmental Services claims as they popped open on his screen. He took a moment to look everything over and see if he had any further questions.

The perky paralegal interrupted his train of thought. "When can we expect delivery of this sinner? We have a very special place all picked out for her."

Eddie pursed his lips for a movement before he spoke. Old

habits die hard, harder in hell. "I will take your claims into consideration; however, I have several other claimants for her soul."

"I understand that you wish to give the other claimants a fair hearing, but I am sure you can clearly see that she belongs with us. Her entire life is a deplorable example of profiteering from environmental exploitation and wanton destruction of any species not human."

"That may be true, but you can not apply later ethics to the era in question. She and her family were well within the rights of her society at the time to commit, without sin, all of the acts you cite as damning. As a matter of fact, her family's beliefs were in line with the standards of the time."

The paralegal no longer looked perky. If looks could kill (and they just might in hell), Eddie would be a smoldering heap under her self-righteous glare. Eddie smiled inwardly while his face remained impassive. He hadn't lost his touch; he could still get anybody off the hook.

"Thank you so very much for your time," Eddie told the ES paralegal. "The Judgment Panel will let you know the status of your claim soon." Eddie saw her hand move across the screen and the connection abruptly ended.

Eddie smiled outwardly now. As he typed the last of his notes, he saw Valeria approaching.

"Let me clear these away." Valeria offered, picking up his plate. "Would you like another soda?"

Eddie looked at his nearly empty glass. The egg cream had been just as tasteless as his coffee earlier. It just didn't matter what it was. The color may be right, the texture may be right, but nothing had any enjoyable flavor. "Yes, please; that would be nice."

"It will be just a minute. Do let me know if you see anything else you want?" Valeria added a touch of professional emphasis to her question. Eddie couldn't help himself: He took a quick glance at her backside as she walked away.

He shook his head slightly then pressed the next series of icons for the Family Avarice Department (FAD). After an annoying moment of screen flicker, the ornate logo for the FAD appeared on the screen. Eddie took a last sip of the tasteless soda. He looked in the glass and shrugged. The video chat window opened.

"Eddie O'Hare with Adjudications calling about Hetty Green."

An older man with a bow tie and disheveled hair stared quizzically at the screen for a few moments. Then his face brightened as he identified the correct icon to press on his end.

"Eddie. I believe you said your name was Eddie. Well, Eddie, my boy, we here at the FAD believe that we have numerous claims upon the soul in question," the speaker drawled slowly like a politician from below the Mason-Dixon line.

Eddie winced slightly. "I have that noted. Are there any special considerations that your department feels it is due?"

Eddie winced again as he saw the lawyer on the screen take a deep breath. This one looked like a true pontificator.

"We believe, I say, we believe that the evidence is quite overwhelmingly in our favor. After all, she wasn't knee high to a grasshopper when she was reading her daddy the financial pages from the newspaper. Our claims begin at the moment of her beloved daddy's death. Somehow, over the objections and obviously legal claims of her entire family, Hetty was the recipient of seven and a half million dollars. I don't care who you are, that's a lot of money to bequeath to a young lady. This is an obvious sign of family avarice."

"Are there any other circumstances you would like to be considered?"

"Any other considerations? Any other! Why when her dear Aunt Silvia departed the mortal world, your dear Hetty tried her hand at inheriting once again. She contested the part of her aunt's will that left two million dollars to charity. Well, I say, she contested the will by producing a will of her very own. Don't you know it, the case wound up in court and was a landmark. It was a landmark, I tell you. Those intelligent investigator boys used forensic mathematics on her version of the will and proved beyond a reasonable doubt that poor Silvia's signature was indeed a forgery, the act of a charlatan. Her own cousins tried to have her indicted for this heinous act. She tore her new husband up by the roots and forced him to flee across the Body of Water with her, so to speak. Hid from her crimes in London, she did. This woman truly belongs with the FAD, as you can plainly see."

Eddie entered his notes quickly while the bushy headed

claimant waited, an air of complete confidence on his face. He remained silent until Eddie looked up into the screen.

"I say there, Eddie, my boy, when can we expect delivery?"

"As I am sure you are aware, there are a number of requests for this soul. I am required to hear from all the claimants." Eddie waited for the rebuttal.

"And I am sure you will give them all a fair ear, a good listening to, as it were. However, I am quite sure you can see the clear facts – that she truly belongs with the FAD for final damnation."

"While I agree that there are overtones of avarice, your claims lack factual, hard evidence. Since she was obviously a favorite of her father, the favoritism was the sin of the father, not of the child. If the rest of the family had wanted to share more deeply in the father's inheritance, they should have taken a more active role. I see her first inheritance as legitimately earned. In the events surrounding the bequest of her aunt: yes, the will that Hetty Green produced was ruled to be a forgery – by new and untried and at that time unreliable techniques. It was never proven that my client, Missus Henrietta Howland Robinson Green, actually forged the signatures on the will. My client may have been as much a victim of the act as the rest of the family. It is also entirely possible that family members could have meant to entrap Hetty by providing the fake will in order to get back at Hetty for her original inheritance. And, yes, the family did object again legally, but without a conviction to support their case, there remain many unanswered questions. As for residing in London, a great number of Americans with means have resided in other countries." Eddie covered each and every point while the man from FAD stared at him in utter disbelief.

Before the Southern gentleman could take a deep breath to begin a counter attack, Eddie gave him the slight nod that had terminated many an interview: this exchange was completed for now. "Thank you so very much for your time. The Judgment Panel will let you know the status of your claim soon." Eddie saw the FAD man's hand move across the screen and the connection abruptly terminated.

Eddie settled back into the leather booth for a moment. He felt some of his old confidence returning. As if on cue, Valeria arrived with another egg cream.

"Here you go." She set the glass down and removed the empty. "Enjoy."

Eddie wasn't sure if she meant the soda or the view of her leave-taking. He leaned forward and looked at the H-pad to see who had queued up next. The screen flickered a bit then revealed the icon for Tactical Profiteering. If this was a special department of damnation, then he knew it would possess some of the greatest if most misguided minds that ever lived. He might have to pay them a visit in the near future. He pressed the icon and waited for the flickering to clear.

"Eddie O'Hare with Adjudications calling about Hetty Green."

Add twenty years to the standard hellish paralegal and that is who just appeared on screen. The hair had been pulled back in a stark fashion that gave her face a certain accountant-like appearance.

"We've been expecting your call. Mr. O'Hare. I have the file right here. It looks like this soul was tailor-made for the Tactical Profiteering Department."

"I have that noted. Are there any special considerations that your department feels it is due?"

"Her entire living career is a textbook case of tactical money making. However, there are a few outstanding cases I would like to point out."

"Please proceed." Eddie liked her approach, direct. He made a mental note to find this part of Hell and pay it a visit.

"During a difficult time for her country, she managed to earn over one and a quarter million dollars in greenback bonds in one year alone. She parlayed those profits in further exploitation of rail-bond purchases. That act alone had far-reaching effects for the country and its indigenous peoples. She even facilitated the failure of a major financial institution and had been profiteering from her own husband. In nineteen oh seven, she actually managed to hold the City of New York in her debt in the amount of over one million dollars in short term bonds."

Eddie watched the woman from Tactical Profiteering closely. She obviously had a firm grasp on financial concepts. She even moved with conservative effort, no wasted motion. Eddie made his notes quickly. “Thank you for the additional points.”

“I am sure you have already been asked this, but I would be remiss if I didn’t inquire as to an estimated delivery date for the soul.”

“As you know, the final disposition of this soul is actually up to the Judgment Panel. However, I will point out that while she certainly did profit from unfortunate circumstances, none of these circumstances were the direct result of *her* actions or machinations. As a matter of fact, most of her activities were at the invitation of those from whom she profited. Most investors at the time of the greenback bonds were reluctant to speculate on a struggling government. She had no such reservations and her investments helped to stabilize a nation. Yes, the rail-bonds had far-reaching effects. In her defense, these events in history were already in motion with or without her money. She was merely wise enough to keep her financial position positive during a turbulent time. Even the City of New York came to her. The city was fortunate that she was in the position to take them up on their offer; not once, but several times.”

The strict female on his video chat screen showed no reaction to his rebuttal. Eddie appreciated a good poker face.

“We appreciate the additional information, Mr. O’Hare. We are anticipating a favorable outcome from the Judgment Panel. Thank you for your time.”

“It was a pleasure.” Eddie meant his response. So far, looking over his collected notes, he felt that he could argue her out of all the charges. As he looked over the remaining icons for claimants, one that caught his eye – the very last one. It was labeled only ‘JPM.’ Eddie shrugged to himself, then touched the icon: “Eddie O’Hare with Adjudications calling about Hetty Green.”

The image in the video chat box wobbled, out of focus, then stabilized. A jowly male face appeared: “Sorry about that. We don’t normally get calls from Adjudications this early. Now, who did you say? Hetty Green? Oh, yes, I have her right here. We placed a claim on her soul under the premise of ‘Just Plain Mean.’”

Eddie made a quick entry about the department. Being just plain mean could be enough to land you in hell? If so, they must have a bumper crop of souls.

"I have that noted. Are there any special considerations that your department feels it is due?"

"Any special considerations? How long do I have? This was a very busy person. I could cite hundreds of examples."

"Let's try to be brief. Are there any outstanding incidents that exemplify your claim?"

"In a nutshell, we can start with the fact that she was a renowned miser. Even though she was worth millions, she dickered over the price of everything. She would beat down anyone on price. Since most people were far poorer than she, this was 'just plain mean.' She was so cheap that when her son broke his leg, she tried to take him to a charity hospital for free treatment. The poor fellow eventually lost that leg. She was so miserly, she didn't keep an office. She did all of her profiteering out of trunks and suitcases piled up at the bank she liked to use. Imagine. She wouldn't even pay to have any one of her dour black dresses washed completely; she'd pay to have only the dirty parts washed. She interfered with both her son's and daughter's love lives for years. She made her son-in-law sign a prenup. What can I tell you? That's 'just plain mean.' She wouldn't even have her own hernia operated on because it would have cost a hundred and fifty bucks. And as if that isn't mean enough, she died of apoplexy while arguing over skim milk." The jowls shook slightly at the final words. The heavy-set lawyer on the screen assumed the expression of a litigant staring down the jury to make his point. Eddie continued jotting down his notes. After a few moments, he looked up and met the eyes of his learned colleague from the JPM. This guy had done his homework.

Eddie took a breath and launched into his response, "Thank you for the information. I will agree that this soul led a unique lifestyle. However, in a male-dominated industry and society, she beat the boys at their own game. She had to use every tactic she could imagine to level the playing field. She remained true to her frugal roots and upbringing. Thank you for your time. The Judgment Panel will let you know the status of your claim soon."

Jowls pulled outward into a knowing smile. "Thank you for your time and consideration. I am sure that the Judgment Panel will reach an appropriate decision."

Eddie found himself nodding as the video screen went black. He picked up his soda and sipped. How in hell did they manage to remove the flavor from everything? Perhaps something from the dessert bar would have a semblance of taste; he doubted it, but it was worth a try. He perused the dessert table at the buffet, selected a pastry baked in a lurid shape, and took it back to his booth There he sat back down.

And froze in his seat.

The H-pad screen hadn't just gone dark; it was now a *liquid* black. Eddie stared at the unit for another minute before leaning closer. The icons, lines, and definition between screen and frame had melted completely away. Eddie debated the wisdom of touching the liquid surface. Eddie's self-preservation instinct took hold and reminded him that touching *any*thing in hell that was fluid, black, and held its shape couldn't possibly be a good idea.

"Thank you, Mr. O'Hare, for your effort and expertise in this matter." A sultry female voice emanated from the now quivering blackness.

Eddie flinched. Sliding the pastry across the table, he focused on the liquid darkness. "Um, thank you for the kind words." He watched the surface ripple as he spoke. Nothing like this had ever happened to him before.

"The disposition of this soul has been decided."

Instinctively, Eddie refrained from objecting to the statement. However, he had to know: "May I ask about the final disposition?"

"This soul has been assigned to the financial and accounting department of the main Administrative department. We feel that her level of expertise will be of great value to our ongoing efforts."

"I'm happy to have helped." Eddie really didn't know what to say. He had never been contacted like this before, but it seemed that someone serious liked his work.

"You will receive another assignment soon. However, a standard bonus will be deposited to your account. Have a hellish day."

Before he could respond, the H-pad returned to normal. Eddie looked for the next case. No icons appeared in the pending category. Had that voice actually been the voice of the Judgment Panel … or something more? This was hell, after all; he might have just spent all day arguing with other damned lawyers from other damned departments as part of his own personal damnation. On the other hand, since no new icons had appeared, he might as well take the rest of the day off. He could use a drink. Eddie picked up the menu and looked at the drink selections. He wondered what Valeria would serve him if ordered the 'slow comfortable screw up against the wall with a twist.'

Before he could order, a woman waddled over, flush-faced and unkempt, in a severe black dress with foody stains. "Edward J. O'Hare," she said, looking disapprovingly at him and the bawdy pastry he'd selected. "I'm Hetty Green from the Financial and Accounting Department of the main Administrative Department of Hell's Department of Infernal Revenue. I'm here to talk to you about your deductions for food, drink, and entertainment.... And I am obligated to tell you, as of this moment, you are being Audited."

Plains of Hell

by

Bruce Durham

The building was a ramshackle wood and brick structure with saloon doors and grime-streaked windows. Over its entrance a pitted metal sign creaked under a stiff breeze, the words on its facing faded and worn.

"Roadhouse Six-six-six," mumbled General James Wolfe. "Looks as good as any."

Nudging his hell-horse to a hitching post, Wolfe dismounted and tied off the reins, pointedly avoiding the beast's serrated teeth and over-sized mouth. The creature promptly swung on a second tethered hell-horse and launched into a ritual of dominance assertion common to the breed. The neighboring beast eagerly took up the challenge.

Wolfe ignored their hissing and spitting while slapping at his red coat and white pants. An exercise in futility. The fine sheen of ochre dust, accumulated on his trip from New Hell, merely ingrained itself deeper into the fabric and caked his hands. Grumbling, he gave up. The tavern patrons would have to accept him as he was, if they cared. Something he doubted, based on his brief time in this vile place.

Maneuvering between two dented, rusted vehicles, Wolfe mounted a series of crooked steps. On the porch he lurched to a stop. "Not now," he groaned. A sickening wave twisted his stomach, crept along his throat and filled his mouth with a sour taste of bile. Reaching into his coat, he produced a well-used, blood-stained handkerchief and coughed, a hoarse hacking that had him doubled over, one hand braced against the door frame. The fit passed. He straightened and gingerly dabbed at the corners of his mouth, ignoring the smear of bright red blood staining the silk. Pocketing the handkerchief, he briefly inspected his pants for specks of blood and, pronouncing himself presentable, entered the tavern.

The place was dimly lit and sparsely filled. To his right a bar ran the length of the paneled wall, its brass foot rail tarnished and dented; its half-dozen stools unoccupied.

Wolfe's nose twitched at the heavy smell of body odor and tobacco smoke. Most tables were vacant. Three Mongols argued incoherently in a corner by a fireplace, a jug of *kumis* between them. A second table held half a dozen Scots, their claymores resting against high-back chairs as they roared heartily at some private joke. By the far wall a man slept at an upright piano, his head resting on his arms, crossed on the keys.

Nearer the bar sat two men. Wolfe cocked an eyebrow, feeling a sudden kinship toward one: a vague sense of recognition. This man was clearly British, tall and elegant in a white blouse, white pants, and an elaborately powdered wig. An ornate blue coat lay folded over the back of his oak chair. His companion was dressed equally as well, but in shades of brown; smaller and thinner, with a long, pinched face framed by a similarly flamboyant wig.

Wolfe stepped up to the bar.

The bartender glanced his way and nodded. Short and round, he resembled a ball on legs, his hairless head contrasted by a sweeping handlebar mustache. "What's your poison?" he asked in a raspy voice, swiping at one of many stains marking the counter.

Wolfe examined the collection of bottles lining a shelf. "You have no wine, sir?"

The barkeep snorted. "You kiddin' me, bub?" He waved a meaty hand. "What you see is what we have."

Why did I bother asking? Wolfe thought. During his short time in this damnable existence he had determined everything was supposed to taste like shit. Sighing, he pointed. "I'll have one of those."

"Right. One Labratt's Blew comin' up. You startin' a tab?"

"No, sir," Wolfe mumbled. Reaching into his pocket, he produced a handful of *diablos* and tossed several on the counter.

The bartender swept them up and walked away, offering no indication of returning with change.

Shaking his head, Wolfe took the bottle and raised it to his lips, praying the vile taste wouldn't trigger his consumption. Last thing he wanted was another coughing fit. He drank; no second fit of coughing wracked him. Setting down the bottle, he stared into the counter.

Hell.

Hell wasn't what he'd expected. He remembered the battle on the plains outside Quebec. Remembered taking three bullets. One in the wrist, one in the stomach and one in the chest. A brief moment of darkness, followed by the vague memory of a leering, diseased and cackling face; followed by waves of excruciating pain, and then waking in a small room in a twisted building on some narrow street in a decayed section of a town called New Hell. A handful of strangers took the time to explain cars, hellphones, old dead, new dead, Satan, politics and what have you. And rumors of an audit from Above, whatever that was about.

It was too much, too soon, and he fled, taking this dirt road to nowhere. He needed time to think, to understand his place in this brutal nightmare. Most of all, to understand what in God's name he had done to find himself consigned here, rather than knocking on some pearly gates.

Rising from his melancholy, Wolfe focused on the two voices of the two men behind him. Their conversation was the casual banter of friends, loud enough that he could hear without being accused of eavesdropping.

"Malplaquet," said the Englishman wistfully. "Now that was one *hell* of a brawl. Sent many a soldier down here with that one."

"Don't I know it," replied his companion. "Pyrrhic victory, that. French chewed up my boys, bad. Would have been worse if it wasn't for you." There was a clinking of bottles. "I preferred Oudenarde, myself. Much cleaner. Good victory." A pause. "We made a good team, my friend. A toast to old times, eh?" Another clink. "Ah, hell, I'm dry."

Wolfe, intrigued at the mention of two famous battles, turned to face the speakers. Clearing his throat, he said, "I could not help but overhear, good sirs. May I join you? I believe we have something in common."

The seated Englishman took his measure: Wolfe was in afterlife what he had been in life – a tall, slim man with a thin face and pasty complexion. The Englishman exchanged a look with his companion, shrugged, and waved at an empty chair. "By all means.

Of course, courtesy dictates you must stand us a drink."

Wolfe nodded. It had been his intent anyway. "What will it be?"

The Englishman said, "Sludgeweiser."

His friend, in a subtle French accent, said, "Make mine a Helliken."

Minutes later, bottles in hand, Wolfe settled into the vacant seat. Setting down the beers, he extended a hand to the Englishman. "I am James Wolfe, General in his majesty King George the Second's army."

The Englishman snorted. "The second George? Hah. I knew his father, the pompous ass. I am John Churchill, the Duke of Marlborough. You may have heard of me. Or not. And this dour personage is Prince Eugene of Savoy. You may have heard of him. Or not."

Wolfe stared, his mouth hanging open. *Marlborough and Eugene? The two greatest generals of their age? Seated here, in some out-of-the-way dive drinking beer and chatting of old times?* Snapping his mouth shut, Wolfe composed himself and shook both men's extended hands. "A pleasure, truly. I have studied your battles in detail. Both of you. They were inspirations for my own career."

Churchill's eyes lit up at the compliment and leaned forward. "Really? So, what did you think of Blenheim?"

Before Wolfe could respond, Eugene raised his index finger and said, "We commanded fifty-two thousand men in that battle, you know. The French had us outnumbered, but we kicked their ass. They lost some twenty thousand, the poor sods, to our forty-five hundred. How about Ramillies, Wolfe? What do you know about Ramillies?"

Wolfe opened his mouth, but Churchill sat back, inspected a finger nail, and said, "Commanded sixty-two thousand men, Wolfe. Only lost one thousand. French lost another twenty thousand." He raised an eyebrow. "Oudenarde?"

Wolfe hesitated and looked at Eugene.

Eugene swallowed a mouthful of Helliken and burped. Wiping a sleeve across his lips, he said, "Ah, Oudenarde. What a joy. One hundred five thousand to a hundred thousand. Only lost three thousand. French lost another fifteen thousand." He chuckled. "You see a pattern here, Wolfe?"

There was a pregnant pause as Churchill and Eugene clinked bottles and drank.

Wolfe ventured, "Tell me about Malplaquet."

The generals exchanged less than pleasant looks. Churchill mumbled, "We don't talk much about Malplaquet. It was the bloodiest European battle of the eighteenth century. We won, but the butcher's bill was enormous, for both sides. Victory isn't always glorious, Wolfe."

"But –"

Churchill waved a dismissive hand. "We won it, all right? That's all that's important. Now, enough about us. What battlefield honors have you accrued, Wolfe?"

The general shrugged. "Well, there was Dettingen, sir. We beat the French in that one."

Eugene nodded enthusiastically. "Good show. One can never tire of beating the French. Was that your first command?"

"Not exactly. George the Second commanded. I was a lieutenant at the time."

Eugene steepled his fingers. "A lieutenant? How quaint. Anything else you wish to share, or was that it?"

Wolfe noticed an elaborate carving someone had at one time etched into the table. Idly he traced his finger along the outline. "There was Falkirk and Culloden, sirs. I was a major, then."

Churchill belched and rubbed his belly. "Any details with which to regale us? Oh, and don't finish tracing that. Last person who did was whisked away by something with four arms and fangs as long as my, er, pistol."

"They were short fangs," Eugene commented.

Churchill raised his middle digit. "Go to heaven."

Wolfe jerked his finger from the carving. "Details? Nothing, really. That is a time I am not particularly fond of."

Eugene drained his bottle of Helliken and slammed it on the table. Looking expectantly at Wolfe, he said, "You introduced yourself as a general, remember?" His eyes drifted to the empty bottle.

Wolfe sighed, caught the barkeep's attention and held up three fingers. Returning to Churchill and Eugene, he said, "I was promoted to major general for the invasion of New France and siege of Quebec."

Churchill pursed his lips and nodded. "The New World, is it? Did you know I was a Governor of the Hudson Bay Company?"

Eugene frowned. "Hush now, John. Bore us with that tale later. Let's hear about this siege of Quebec."

Wolfe looked away. "There is not much to say. I lured the French out of the fortress. We fought a battle. I won."

Eugene clapped his hands. "A battle? Excellent. Numbers? Details?"

Wolfe felt his face grow warm and knew he flushed. Embarrassed, he glanced about the tavern, his eyes settling on the man asleep at the piano. For the first time, he noted a chain running from one heavy wooden leg to the man's ankle. At that moment the piano player stirred, raised his head and cast a weary eye toward the bar.

An impatient throat cleared and Eugene repeated, "Numbers?"

Wolfe sighed and faced them. Churchill and Eugene had their eyebrows raised in expectation. He put a hand to his mouth and mumbled, "Five thousand to forty-five hundred."

Churchill leaned forward. "What was that? Didn't quite catch it. Did you say fifty thousand to forty-five thousand?"

Eugene snickered. "No, I think he said five thousand to forty-five hundred."

Churchill sat back and belly-laughed. "So, you commanded a skirmish, then."

Wolfe opened his mouth to protest.

Eugene reached over and clapped him on the back. "Don't be ashamed, Wolfe. We can't all lead enormous armies." His lips twitched into a smile. "So, what happened next?"

Wolfe shrugged. "I don't know. I died." In the sudden silence he waited, expecting sympathy. Instead, he received the opposite as Churchill and Eugene shrugged, before casually reaching for their beers. Wolfe's mood darkened. "You find my death irrelevant? I assure you, it was not. I was young. There was a wonderful woman back in England I was to marry. I am insulted by your indifference, sirs."

"Hold your water, Wolfe," Eugene said over the lip of his beer bottle. "We meant no disrespect, did we John? There's something you must understand. In hell, death is never death."

Wolfe knit his brows together, confused. "What do you mean by that, sir? Are you implying we are immortal?"

Churchill reached into a coat pocket and produced a pipe. "In a manner of speaking, yes. Now, don't get me wrong. You can die, all right. Eugie and I have been down that path twice already. It's just that hell has a rather twisted way of bringing you back, usually in the most undelightful manner."

"Oh," Wolfe managed to say as everyone lapsed into awkward quiet.

Moments later a series of tentative notes rose from the piano. The random notes soon trailed off. What followed then was an angry hammering on the keys, a madly chaotic cacophony of sound that gradually evolved into an inspired rendition of Johann Sebastian Bach's *Goldberg Variations*.

Wolfe, wincing at the initial blast of noise, closed his eyes as he was swept up by the music, amazed at the clarity, speed and deftness of playing. He was familiar with Bach, had enjoyed several pieces performed on harpsichord at various social gatherings during his time in England. But this … this was remarkable.

There was a tug on Wolfe's coat. Opening his eyes, mildly irritated, he saw Eugene motion at him with his finger. Leaning close, he asked, "What?"

In a raised voice Eugene replied, "Don't get yourself too involved."

"Why? What do you mean?"

As if on cue, the piano's keys began to move of their own volition, striking up a loud and lively ragtime piece that clashed with the pianist's own performance. For several moments the tunes conflicted with one another in an obscene dissonance until the pianist abruptly quit, punching the upright before shaking his fists in a fit of anger. Meanwhile, the piano continued its toe-tapping number.

Over the din, Wolfe asked, "What was that all about?"

Churchill leaned back in his chair and crossed his arms. "Glenn Gould."

Wolfe spread his hands. "Who is Glenn Gould?"

"Some prodigy born well after we died. One of the *moderns.*" Churchill shrugged. "Apparently someone at the Hall of Injustice saw this as a fitting punishment. Not sure of the reason for the punishment, and I'm not about to ask."

"Me neither," Eugene agreed. He tapped his empty bottle and looked at Wolfe. "I thought you ordered another round?"

Wolfe scowled and turned to signal the barkeep. He didn't get that far. His attention was drawn to a succubus. He'd been warned about succubi. The strangers back in New Hell had explained them: female demons who controlled men through sex. The red-skinned demon temptress stood just inside the tavern entrance, the saloon doors swinging to a slow rest behind her curvaceous body. Scanning the room, her yellow eyes locked with his. Flashing perfect teeth, she approached, her hips swaying enticingly.

Despite himself, Wolfe felt the initial stirrings of arousal. He swallowed and looked to Churchill and Eugene. Both men were busy inspecting their fingernails.

The succubus glided to a stop beside him and purred, "Are you General James Wolfe? *The* General James Wolfe?"

Wolfe swallowed again and wondered if this had anything to do with the rumored audit of hell from on high. "I am," he croaked.

The succubus nodded and produced a scroll.

Hesitantly he took it from her slender red hand, determinedly ignoring the long, sharp fingernails.

"A pleasure, Mister Wolfe. You've been served." Turning on her heel, she departed for the door, her alluring hips swinging with each seductive step.

Wolfe tore his eyes from her captivating backside to study the scroll. It appeared very official: vellum secured by a red ribbon and sealed with the stamp of the Hall of Injustice. The strangers had told him about the Hall of Injustice, too. His hands turned clammy. His stomach twisted. The uneasiness triggered an onslaught of bile and blood, rushing up his gorge. Wolfe dropped the scroll on the table and scrambled for his handkerchief. Turning his back on Churchill and Eugene, he hacked into the stained silk for several long moments.

The fit passed. "My apologies," he muttered. Turning back to the generals, his eyes widened. "I say!"

Churchill and Eugene, chairs together, had the scroll open before them, reading its contents.

Eugene glanced up, "That's a bad cough, Wolfe. You should see someone about it."

Wolfe made a grab for the scroll, but Churchill snatched it away, lips silently moving as he continued reading. Wolfe sat back and snapped, "I have consumption. I had it when I was alive. My brother died from it." He lapsed into silence as a sudden thought occurred. *I wonder if my brother is here.*

"Tee Bee," Eugene explained.

"What?"

"Its official name is 'tuberculosis.' That's what doctors call it now."

Putting thoughts of his brother from his mind, Wolfe said, "Consumption sounds simpler. Is there a cure for this … Tee Bee?"

Eugene grinned. "Is there a cure for anything in hell?" He turned serious and leaned forward. "You don't get out much, do you?"

"What do you mean, sir?"

"It's obvious. Your manner of speech, your lack of knowledge." Eugene's fist hammered the table, causing the Scots to pause and look over. "I wager you believe you don't belong here. You're in denial, aren't you, Wolfe?"

Wolfe flushed. Flustered, he said, "I am not in denial, sir. I am new here. I woke up in this world but several days past. And what if I am in denial? Do you two gentlemen believe you belong here?"

Eugene nodded enthusiastically. "Of course we believe it, don't we John? Between the two of us, we were responsible for tens of thousands of deaths. It doesn't matter if we were right or wrong, good or evil, innocent or guilty: we ordered men to die. And let's not forget the ancillary effects on the innocent lives lost to looting, starvation and disease."

Wolfe pursed his lips as he absorbed that, his fingers nervously drumming the tabletop. *An interesting perspective, though clearly misguided, since responsibility ultimately belongs to the commanders-in-chief and the governments they represent. A point of view worth pondering, however.*

Churchill asked, “Who is this Marquis de Montcalm character?”

Wolfe’s head shot up. “What?”

Churchill laid the scroll on the table. “Louis-Joseph de Montcalm. Marquis de Montcalm. It says here he’s requesting a trial.”

Wolfe took the scroll and read it. His lips moved as he struggled through the legalese. Minutes later he laid it on the table, his mind racing. He glanced at Churchill and Eugene, who watched expectantly. “This subpoena is preposterous…” he began.

Two demons, large, scaly, red and horned, burst through the saloon doors and took positions to either side of the entrance. The tavern occupants fell silent. The player piano abruptly stopped. Gould seized the moment to begin an aria, but the key cover slammed down, nearly taking Gould’s fingers off at the knuckles. His solitary curse was the only sound.

Another two demons entered, smaller cousins to the burly specimens stoically guarding the entrance. They scanned the interior.

Wolfe noted one of the small demons lacked a horn, while the other missed an ear.

One Ear pointed at an unoccupied area. The two demons rushed over and slapped a pair of tables together, placing a chair behind them. They promptly cleared out several more tables, dragging the heavy furniture across the wooden floor, creating an open space. Nodding in satisfaction, One Ear returned to the entrance and pushed through the saloon doors while the demon with the missing horn placed a second chair beside the joined tables. It sat. A moment later, a battered stenotype appeared on the table in a curling puff of smoke. The demon arranged itself before the device, cracking knuckles and flexing fingers.

One Ear returned, a man following closely on its heels. The man was old, his stooped body clad in an ill-fitting and dusty suit. A length of chain ran from a button hole on his threadbare vest and into a pocket. His drawn face sported a prodigious white beard, contrasted by several dark strands of hair peeking from under a battered straw hat. Hobbling with the infirmity of age, he moved to the table and sat heavily in the lone chair.

A series of papers appeared before him. Producing a pair of spectacles, he bent forward to read the top sheet. Muttering to himself, he set it aside and quickly leafed through the remainder. Returning the spectacles, he wagged a finger at One Ear, who leaned close. They conversed for a moment before the man nodded and the demon stepped back, taking a position slightly behind the old man's right shoulder.

In a voice like gravel on tin, One Ear announced, "This court is now in session. All rise for the honorable Judge Roy Bean."

Wolfe exchanged looks with Churchill and Eugene, then glanced over at the Mongols and Scots, who appeared equally confused.

The two burly demons snarled and took one step forward from their posts at the door. Chairs scraped as everyone stood. The big demons stepped back, regaining their positions.

Bean's demon assistant said, "Court may be seated. Except you." The demon pointed at Wolfe. "You will approach the bench."

Wolfe looked to Churchill and Eugene for guidance. Both men had found something interesting on the floor. Swallowing, Wolfe approached.

One Ear held up a clawed hand. "Close enough."

Wolfe stopped.

Judge Bean picked up a sheet of paper and cleared his throat. "You are James Wolfe, son of Edward Wolfe?"

"Yes sir."

For the first time Bean set eyes on him. "Your Honor."

"Yes, Your Honor."

"And do you understand the charge brought against you?"

Wolfe shuffled his feet. "Not exactly, Your Honor. I had little time to read the document. To be honest, sir, I do not understand what this is about."

Judge Bean grunted and looked back at his assistant. "Where is the Plaintiff?"

"*Ici, Monsieur le president.*"

Wolfe's neck hairs stood at the voice and confident tread of leather boots pounding across the wooden floor. The footfalls stopped, and he sensed a presence near by. A quick glance confirmed his suspicion. It was Montcalm. Adversaries in battle, they had spied one another from afar, but never personally met. This was the closest he had come to the French general.

Judge Bean grunted again. "Good of you to attend, Mister Montcalm."

Montcalm sketched a bow. "Apologies, Monsieur le president. I was detained by –"

Judge Bean raised a hand. "I am not the President. You will refer to me as 'Your Honor.'"

Wolfe allowed a slight smile at Montcalm's rebuke, until Bean's stern gaze shifted his way. The man may have had the look of someone old and tired, but his eyes were sharp. This judge still retained his faculties.

"Mister Wolfe," Judge Bean began. "You have been summoned before this court to answer the charge of cheating."

So the outrageous accusation on the scroll was true. "Your Honor, that is a ridiculous –"

"Silence," Bean growled. "You will not address this court until ordered." Scowling, he cast about the table top. "Where's my gavel?"

One Ear said, "Missing, Judge. I have my best imps looking for it as we speak." A sudden puff of smoke revealed a claw hammer, close beside Bean's hand. "I believe that will suffice for the time being, Judge."

Wolfe heard Bean mumble something about his gavel and not some bloody hammer. The demon assistant remained silent.

With a throat clearing harrumph, the judge continued. "The charge is cheating. To-wit, Mister Montcalm has accused you of cheating your way to victory at the, er …" a shuffling of papers, "at the battle on the Plains of Abraham. How do you plead?"

Wolfe's mouth opened and closed soundlessly, his indignation growing at such a preposterous claim. Suddenly he felt his gorge rise anew. Panicking, he fought to control it. He would show his weakness to no one. Especially now. With supreme effort he wrestled it down, a silent victory, save for the bitter taste lingering in his mouth. Drawing himself up, Wolfe said, "Not guilty, Your Honor."

Judge Bean drew his lips into a thin line. "Very well. Mister

Montcalm, present your case."

Where Wolfe was thin and sickly, the Marquis de Montcalm was fit and sturdy, possessing a round face, large nose and generous mouth. Sketching another bow, he began, "Your Honor, my case is simple. On the night before Monsieur Wolfe and his men ascended the bluffs near the said plain of Abraham, he lied to my guard standing watch on the river."

"Lied? How so?"

"It is like this, Your Honor. We had expected a flotilla of supplies that night. Sadly, there was a change of plans I was unaware of, and the flotilla delayed. My guard, not informed of the change, saw Monsieur Wolfe's boats and issued a challenge. One of Monsieur Wolfe's men was fluent *en Français* and answered the challenge. The guard, not knowing better, and having no clear view in the dark, allowed them passage. Thus, by trickery and deceit did the British gain the plains and force me to do battle." Montcalm crossed his arms and shot an accusing look at Wolfe.

Silence descended as Judge Bean's jaw worked, his smoldering eyes burning into the Frenchman. In a low voice he asked, "And?"

Montcalm spread his arms. "And what, Your Honor? Is that not sufficient?"

Judge Bean launched out of his chair and ground his knuckles on the table. His face flushed as he spit, "And *that's* your case? Some British soldier lied to your guard? Your poor little guard? Oh, the horror." He barked to One Ear. "Where's that box of Snotex? I think I'll go cry for a minute." He swung back on Montcalm. "What kind of fool do you take me for, you idiot?" Nostrils flaring, he snapped, "An assassin plunging a poison knife into your back might be cheating. Wolfe bribing your men to turn on you might be cheating. Why, if Wolfe here challenged you to a duel and had one of his snipers shoot your damned head off, then *that* would be cheating. But, lying to a guard?" Bean reached for the hammer. "I should fine you for wasting the court's time." He raised it. "This case is –"

One Ear's hellphone went off, its ringtone playing cheery notes from *The Devil Went Down to Georgia*. Bean paused, head turning to fix the demon with a withering glare. The assistant raised a finger, asking for a moment while it took the call on its remaining ear. It listened, nodding repeatedly before terminating the call and approaching Bean. It leaned over to whisper in the judge's ear. Slowly Bean lowered himself into his chair, his features passing from anger to puzzlement to reluctant acceptance. As the assistant stepped back, the judge spent several moments staring hard at the table. Looking up, he snapped, "That was the Big Guy. He wants you two to refight the battle."

Montcalm bowed. "*Bon! Tres bon*, Your Honor."

Wolfe stammered, "That is impossible, Your Honor. There are no Plains of Abraham here, and we have no men."

Bean glanced up at the assistant. One Ear whispered into his ear. Bean nodded. "I am informed there is a field located some three miles west of us. It will be altered to approximate your Plains of Abraham. You are ordered to meet there in two days time."

Wolfe swallowed. "And the men?"

"Your Honor," Judge Bean reminded him.

"And the men, *Your Honor?"*

"Yes, well, the court agrees that assembling the original combatants on such short notice is impossible. Therefore, you will have at your disposal a number of revenants equal to the numbers of men that took part in the battle."

Wolfe felt light-headed. *Revenants?* He knew about revenants from English folklore. "Revenants?" he squeaked. "Revenants are undead beings, Your Honor. Mindless, undead beings. They have no capacity to give orders. I warrant they can barely follow one. No, Your Honor, I cannot command an army of revenants. It is impossible. I would be all over the field issuing instructions."

Chairs scraped behind Wolfe and two sets of footsteps approached. A reassuring hand clapped him on one shoulder.

"Your Honor," Churchill said, "Prince Eugene and I will stand with General Wolfe and assist him in commanding his – troops."

Judge Bean contemplated the request, his gnarled hand stroking his white beard. He nodded. "Very well. Mister Montcalm?"

"*Oui*, Your Honor?"

"As Mister Wolfe has acquired assistance in the prosecution of this upcoming battle, the court will allow you the same privilege."

Montcalm bowed. "*Merci*, Your Honor." He paused, his forehead breaking into a map of wrinkles.

"Your Honor, *quel sont* revenants?"

*

"This is ridiculous," Wolfe mumbled. "This is a circus. A bloody circus."

Standing slightly apart from Churchill and Eugene, Wolfe shook his head at the vast multitude of wagons, cars, giant metal constructs known as buses and countless hell-horses streaming along the road from New Hell in a dust-stirring chaotic mess, a mess exacerbated by metal-twisting accidents and furious fistfights.

Those managing safe arrival were treated to a carnival-like atmosphere resplendent with colorful tents and countless concession stands erected by merchants, hawkers and opportunists offering all varieties of food, drink and cheap souvenirs.

Wolfe groaned at the sight of a t-shirt with his image emblazoned on the front and the words *Hour of the Wolfe* in elaborate scroll stretched across the back. A second t-shirt making the rounds had Montcalm's visage and the words *French Fried* on the reverse. Wolfe found that one mildly amusing.

But what Wolfe didn't find amusing (in fact, mildly disconcerting), was the growing influx of spectators and morbidly curious. He had no clue how word of the upcoming battle could have spread so swiftly, until Churchill calmly mentioned something called the *information age*. Whatever that was.

And, oblivious to the chaos, two motionless armies of revenants stood like terracotta warriors from the reign of Emperor Qin Shi Huang, separated from each other by a span of several hundred yards. These undead waited quietly, patiently, completely unaware of the sights and sounds of the throng gathering along the sidelines.

To Wolfe's further dismay, his revenants represented four formations of soldiers drawn from various periods of English history. Some of the uniforms and weapons he recognized, others he didn't. Fortunately, a look at Montcalm's army showed that the Frenchman had fared little better. To all appearances they were on equal footing. So, now he had to determine the best use of this hodgepodge of undead.

Putting his disgust aside, Wolfe approached Churchill and Eugene. He heard the generals share a laugh, even as they acknowledged him. "Does nothing ever intimidate you two?" Wolfe asked, a hint of irritation in his voice.

Churchill appraised Wolfe before smiling. "Relax," he said. "This is hell. Even if you die you'll come back. Eventually." He waved an arm at the gathered crowds. "Think of this as a show for the masses."

Wolfe frowned. "And what if I lose this rematch before these masses, sir? I have my pride."

Eugene chuckled. "If you worry what people shall think of you if you fail, don't. They don't care. All they want is a good show. In time this will become a distant memory. Enjoy it for what it is. Entertainment."

Wolfe snapped, "Easy enough for you, sir. It is obvious that you, men that I admire, have succumbed to this nightmare place and take what it offers in stride. I, sir, have not." He pointed at the motionless revenants. "And what, pray tell, do I do with these?"

"Use them," Eugene replied.

"Use them? I do not even know what era half of these things belong to."

Churchill shrugged. "You have little choice, Wolfe. This was the hand dealt you. Surely you know a general has to make do, however unpleasant that is. Hmm. What have we here?" Reaching into his coat, Churchill produced a pair of binoculars and trained them on Montcalm. Turning the focus ring he said, "It appears our opponent has solicited help. I see another Frenchman. From his uniform I'd say he's from the time of Napoleon. The other? Let's see. Grey greatcoat. Hat. Massive beard. A gambling man would wager he's from the Civil War."

Eugene asked, "Which one?"

"The American. Wait, there's a third. Hmm. Not sure, but I think he predates us, Eugie."

"Let me see." Eugene took the binoculars from the taller man. "That's Count Tilly. I met him back in New Hell. He fought in the Catholic-Protestant wars back in the sixteen hundreds. He's a good one."

Churchill stroked his chin. "Tilly. Magdeburg. Yeah, he's a mean bastard all right. Not sure of the credentials of the other two. Perhaps we should go say hello."

Wolfe, his attention divided between the strange-looking binoculars and the banter between Churchill and Eugene, reacted sharply. "What was that? You want to say hello? To Montcalm? Are you serious, sir?"

Eugene shrugged. "Why not? Have you ever met the man?"

"No, I have not. What purpose would it serve?"

Eugene winked. "Well, you could always gloat. But on a serious note, I think it would benefit us to learn who our opponents are."

Wolfe nodded, slowly. "Of course. You are right, sir. That makes sense."

Churchill clapped him on the back. "It's settled then. Come along."

Montcalm quickly spotted their approach and, gathering his companions, hurried to intercept them. The groups slowed to a stop, facing off several paces apart.

In the ensuing silence, as each side measured the other, Wolfe realized Churchill and Eugene, great generals both, were deferring to him as commander. A lump settled in the pit of his stomach, a nervous reaction to this sudden and overwhelming show of confidence.

Montcalm, on the other hand, was anything but nervous. The general gracefully removed his tricorne and bowed. The men behind him nodded. Replacing his hat, Montcalm said, "Bonjour, Messieurs. How may we help you?"

"Monsieur Montcalm, I believe you have us at a disadvantage. You have met the Duke of Marlborough and his esteemed companion the Prince of Savoy. However, *we* have not had the pleasure of making the acquaintance of your associates." Wolfe nodded toward Tilly. "Though I understand you to be Count Tilly."

Tilly, a bearded man of medium build and finely chiseled features, grunted.

Montcalm said, "The Count Tilly is a man of few words. Now, let me present Marshal Ney and General Longstreet."

Ney, his fiery red hair blending with the ruddy sky above, merely nodded. Longstreet, however, stepped forward. Removing a clay pipe from his mouth, he said in a soft and controlled voice, "A pleasure, gentlemen. Mister Churchill, I have read of your campaigns and battles, and I wish to express my sincerest admiration for your exploits and career – the same admiration I extend to your compatriot, Prince Eugene of Savoy. Mister Wolfe, forgive me, but I know little of your military victories, though I trust they are substantial." Stepping back, the pipe returned to his mouth and sweet smoke curled from its bowl.

An awkward pause ensued as Wolfe simmered at the subtle, if unintentional, slight. Wolfe decided he had seen enough, and turned to go.

Montcalm flashed a smile. "Be ready, Monsieur. Time grows short." He pointed toward the crowd.

Wolfe followed Montcalm's finger. A ten-foot-high hourglass rested on a pine table beside a rusted cube van. A mountain of sand formed a cone in the bottom half of the glass, the upper glass was nearly empty.

A man separated from the mass of spectators and approached. He was dressed in a British uniform not dissimilar to Wolfe's own. As he neared he smiled widely and held out a hand. "Greetings, General Wolfe. You look rather sharp today."

Wolfe shook the proffered hand. "And you are?"

"Arnott. General Benjamin Arnott. I see you require an extra body, and I come to offer my services."

"Should I know you, sir?"

Arnott stepped back. "Not likely, sir. I fought some years after your – death."

Wolfe frowned. Reminders of his death always left him chilled. Gesturing at the uniform he said, "You are British, obviously. Who were your opponents? The French? The Austrians? The Prussians?"

Arnott gave a slight, embarrassed shake of the head. "Nothing so illustrious. I fought the Americans during their war of independence. Miserable ingrates and turncoats that they were."

Wolfe chewed his lip, wishing he had some knowledge of the military personnel who had existed after his time on earth. He looked to Churchill and Eugene for advice, but they had returned to the English lines. Hesitantly, he said, "Very well. I can use you, General Arnott."

Arnott clapped his hands. "Good. What do I command?"

*

Wolfe stood with his back to the enemy, critically eyeing the revenants and contemplating their use. Eugene and Arnott stood apart, waiting patiently. Churchill studied the French through his binoculars.

Wolfe's four undead formations included British musketeers from the eighteenth century, soldiers with whom Wolfe, Churchill and Eugene were passingly familiar. Beside them stood a battalion of Colonials, drawn from an era of British expansionism that existed well after Wolfe's time. Beside the Colonials, on the far flank, stood a regiment of pike from the fourteen hundreds and, on the near flank, by Wolfe, some five hundred longbow men from the same era.

Wolfe, deciding his force would excel at defense, turned to Churchill. "Your thoughts on the enemy, sir?"

Churchill lowered the binoculars, letting them hang by a leather strap against his chest. "Near as I can tell, they have two formations of muskets, one of men-at-arms and a lot of crossbowmen."

Wolfe gestured for the binoculars. "May I look?"

Churchill raised the strap, careful not to disturb his powdered wig, and handed them over.

Wolfe, following the example of Churchill and Eugene, placed the strange instrument against his eyes. The image was blurry. "I cannot see very well, sir."

Churchill leaned over and touched the focus ring. "Use your finger or thumb to turn this."

Wolfe did so, and choked off a gasp as an image snapped into view, much sharper than any telescope from his era could produce. Idly he wondered how much more technology available in hell was beyond his experience and understanding.

A horn sounded. Wolfe lowered the binoculars and looked at the hourglass. The last sprinkling of grains had slipped through its neck.

Arnott announced, "Showtime."

Churchill looked askance at the general. "A touch eager, are we?" His heavy brow knit into a 'v' of wrinkles. "Arnott … *Arnott?* You know, I've read as much military history as I could get my hands on since arriving here, and I don't ever recall coming across a Benjamin Arnott."

Arnott shrugged. "I was no big player in the war."

Wolfe, closely following the exchange, said, "Well sir, as your capabilities are an unknown quantity, you will command the pike."

Arnott frowned briefly before nodding. "Understood, General. The pike it is. What are my orders?"

Wolfe pondered that. They would be most effective against the opposing men-at-arms. "Hold steady for now. Montcalm made the first move when we fought last time, let us see if he will do so again." Moving to Eugene he said, "Sir, I would ask you to command the muskets."

The French-born Austrian smiled grimly. "With pleasure, Wolfe." Eugene set out after Arnott, both departing for their respective positions.

Wolfe approached Churchill. Handing over the binoculars, he said, "I would have you command these Colonials."

Churchill raised an eyebrow. "And here I thought you would assign me the longbow men."

Wolfe managed a thin smile. "That would be a grave error of judgment on my part, sir. No, I am satisfied with the longbows. They will match up well against the French crossbows. You and General Eugene will duel the French with your musket formations."

Churchill grinned and jerked a thumb at his contingent. "These Colonial British have a rifle called the Lee-Metford. Unlike our muskets, they hold more than one bullet and they have superior range. Montcalm may have a surprise coming his way." He paused and straightened, scanning the French ranks with his binoculars from one end of the line to the other. "Montcalm's men are giving directions to their revenants. I see movement. They're on the march."

"We had better see to our men, then."

Churchill chuckled. "Easy, General. We have ample time."

Wolfe turned. "What do you mean?"

"Have you seen a revenant march? They are undead, remember? Their motor skills are, to put it mildly, lacking. They're coming, all right, but at this rate we could enjoy a nice cup of tea well before they reach us. Well, a cup a tea, anyway. Can't vouch for its taste."

Wolfe, however, was not convinced. "Look, General, if our side received a formation of troops like the Colonials, wouldn't it be safe to assume the French may –"

At that precise moment, a curling cloud of white smoke erupted from a French formation, followed by the staccato reports of rifle fire. Bullets whizzed past, one buzzing by Wolfe's ear like an angry hornet.

Churchill, unfazed and untouched, lowered his binoculars. "Damnation, Wolfe. You're right. Well, so much for outgunning them with the Lee-Metfords. Who are those guys?"

Wolfe, shaking his head, said to Churchill, "It would appear we are evenly matched, sir."

Churchill, eyes yet fixed on the French, said, "I would agree. Ah, I have determined our opponent: Legionnaires."

"Romans? I thought they used spears."

"Pila. The Romans used pila: six foot long javelins. But these are not Romans. They are French mercenaries. And Wolfe, there's something else. They're using multi-shot rifles, like our Colonials."

"So?"

"Well, do you find it strange they have not yet fired a second volley?"

Wolfe crossed his arms. "Yes. That *is* strange."

"It has apparently baffled the French, too. At this moment they argue furiously among themselves. However, I believe I have the answer."

"And that is?"

"It is possible these revenants can only comprehend one command at a time. They are undead, after all."

Wolfe pondered that. He knew no more of the inner workings of the undead than he did of hell, but Churchill's idea was oddly plausible. "So, by your reasoning the Legionnaires must receive repeated orders to fire. They lack the capacity to extrapolate."

"In a nutshell, yes."

"Therefore, by your reasoning, the Legionnaires must still be stationary, having been given the order to fire and not an order to advance, while the balance of the French army approaches, having been given the order to march and not to fire."

Churchill scanned the French lines. He lowered the binoculars. "You have a knack of complicating something simple, Wolfe, but the answer is yes."

Wolfe clapped his hands. "Then let us get to work before Montcalm and his crew figure that out."

*

It took three successive volleys from the Colonial revenant's rifles before Montcalm and his team caught on and raced back to their formations, arms waving and fingers pointing.

The first two Colonial volleys tore into the French Legionnaires, causing much damage but few deaths. A long look by Wolfe through the binoculars determined that the dead had sustained head wounds. Armed with this knowledge, Churchill issued a series of precise commands to the comprehension-challenged revenants, and gave the order for the third volley. This produced the desired results. Heads exploded. Bodies dropped. *Advantage, British.*

Leaving Churchill, Wolfe joined his longbows, walking in that calm, determined stride expected from powerful men, the kind of nonchalance in the face of enemy fire that resulted in so many battlefield deaths among high-ranking officers. Except, in this case, Wolfe had little to fear. This wasn't some historic conflict fought on the fields of Europe. This was a silly little rematch, a skirmish between undead soldiers who could barely grasp one-word commands.

A heavy thrum, the sound of bowstrings released under high-tension, alerted him to danger. Wolfe instinctively dropped to the ground. *So much for nonchalance.*

Twisting his neck, he watched a cloud of incoming bolts slam into his silent formation of longbowmen. Many along the front row lurched a step back, the leather fletching of deeply embedded bolts protruding from their decaying bodies. Others dropped to the ground, bolts piercing heads, mouths and eyes. Throughout all this, not a sound was uttered, not a scream or cry of pain.

Unnerved by the eerie silence, Wolfe leapt to his feet and shouted, "Nock arrow." The revenants slowly, painstakingly reached down to pluck standing arrows embedded in the ground and fit them to their bow strings.

Wolfe pointed at the enemy crossbowmen and raised his arm. "Aim."

Silently they obeyed. Even undead, the revenants remained masters of their craft, and single-mindedly understood the role expected of them: they knew no other.

Wolfe dropped his arm. "Release."

The deep drone of unleashed bow strings punched the air, its reverberating hum not unlike a swarm of angry bees.

Fascinated, Wolfe watched the mass of arrows rise high into the ruddy sky before arcing into a deadly descent.

A chorus of oohs and ahhs drifted up from the spectators.

The arrows slammed into the crossbowmen, driving many to the ground. One landed by Montcalm's feet. The French general looked up, startled, and shook his fist at Wolfe.

Wolfe held his finger and thumb an inch apart. "That close, you bastard," he mumbled. Viewing the results, he was disappointed by so few deaths. He knew his revenants would be hard-pressed to exclusively target heads until the enemy was within range for a decent horizontal shot. Still, with the maddeningly slow pace of the revenants, he knew his side could manage two or more volleys to each volley from the enemy crossbowmen. *Another advantage, British.*

Once again Wolfe commanded, "Nock arrow." Maybe this time they would strike Montcalm, whose death would put an end to this farce.

An unexpected hue and cry rose among the spectators.

Wolfe paused, looking their way. Many among the crowd were on their feet pointing, jumping and gesticulating wildly. Unsure why, Wolfe examined the French forces. Nothing appeared out of the ordinary. The French men-at-arms continued their slow advance as General Longstreet fiercely stalked the formation, unsuccessfully encouraging the undead to advance faster. The French muskets had engaged, the uneven pop of their fire drifting across the battlefield.

Moments passed while Wolfe waited. Eugene's contingent failed to return fire. Stepping several paces away from the longbow men to capture an overall view of his lines, Wolfe cursed, suddenly understanding why the crowd had reacted.

Arnott!

Wolfe was betrayed by the late-comer to his cadre.

The British pikemen under Arnott were rolling over the thin red line of Eugene's formation from behind, their steel-shod weapons tearing into undead bodies and punching through undead heads. Eugene, caught unaware, now struggled to reposition his revenants in a vain attempt to repel the assault, their slow response making the task nearly impossible.

Churchill, hearing Eugene's frantic shouting, was slowly refusing a portion of his own flank, turning his lines to face the pikemen and support his friend. However, this repositioning left the balance of his Colonials facing the enemy, with no commands to guide them, and exposed to the weapons of the Legionnaires. *Advantage, French.*

Wolfe cursed again. These revenants were just too slow. Looking to Montcalm and his crossbowmen, he noted they were still reloading. His longbows, however, were ready with arrows nocked. Issuing the necessary orders, Wolfe had them fire another volley before setting off for Churchill.

Prying a Lee-Metford from the undead hands of a fallen Colonial, Wolfe came up to the beleaguered general and said, "The only way to end this is to kill Arnott." He held up the weapon. "Do I just pull the trigger?"

Churchill, his powdered wig matted and askew on his head, furrowed his brow, puzzled. "It's a rifle. Of course you pull the trigger." Sudden understanding dawned as Churchill remembered Wolfe's unfamiliarity with 'advanced' technology. Taking the rifle, he checked its magazine before handing it back. "It's loaded. Eight rounds. Just aim and shoot. Keep shooting if you have to."

Nodding thanks, Wolfe skirted the front rank of musketeers in search of Eugene, praying the man was not a casualty of Arnott's treachery. He discovered Eugene of Savoy on the ground, barely thirty paces from the slowly advancing pikemen, clutching his side as blood spread through his brown jacket. "You hit?" he asked.

"What do you think?" Eugene snapped.

"Sorry. Where's Arnott?"

Eugene raised a shaking hand. "Somewhere over there, hiding among the pikemen. Damned if I never saw him reposition his revenants. Too much going on to expect a backstab."

Wolfe had few words of comfort, only an unspoken responsibility for involving these great men in Montcalm's mad quest for revenge. "Hold on, friend, I must find and kill Arnott, lest we all die." Patting Eugene's shoulder, Wolfe sprinted before the pikemen.

Finding Arnott nowhere in view, Wolfe placed himself before the advancing pikemen and shouted, "Halt. Halt, damn you." Slowly, in clusters of two or three, then in larger groups, the revenants lumbered to a stop. Silent and motionless, pikes facing forward, the revenants halted. Their steel blades displayed a variety of undead trophies: torn arms, meaty pieces of decayed flesh, and skewered heads.

A flash of motion and the crack of gunfire tore a yelp of surprise from Wolfe as pain lanced across his left wrist. Wolfe glanced at the bloody furrow caused by the round. A bare quarter inch lower and the wrist would have shattered. "Not again," he mumbled. This was the exact spot where his first wound occurred at the Plains of Abraham. He shivered, remembering.

A second shot rang out. Wolfe grunted as something slammed into his stomach. Eyes welling with pain, he looked down. Dark blood spread across his shirt in a growing stain. *I don't believe this*, he thought. *My second wound, just like last time*. Was this to be his punishment? That history would repeat itself? Even in hell?

"You still standing?"

Wolfe peered through pain-filled eyes as Arnott stepped around a statue-like revenant, pistol gripped firmly in one hand, approaching with the casual air of a man in control. Wolfe eyed the weapon and saw that it was no flintlock. This weapon was small and darkly metallic, something from Wolfe's future.

A wave of nausea suddenly overcame him, and his gorge reacted violently. Fighting to keep his bloody coughing spell under control, he spit out, "Why?"

Arnott smiled. "A promise of money, advancement, a key place in a growing empire." Arnott shoved a revenant by the shoulder. The undead soldier stumbled a few feet before resuming its motionless state. "I mean, think about it, Wolfe. Revenants? This whole rematch was a joke from the start. Nothing more than a money-making opportunity for the right people."

Wolfe dropped to one knee as another wave of nausea overtook him. The muzzle of his Lee-Metford touched the ground in his limp right hand. "Who are the right people?" he managed.

Arnott lowered to his haunches, maintaining eye-level with Wolfe. "Those who have a hand in just about everything legal and illegal in and around New Hell."

"Criminals, then."

Arnott shrugged. "If you must. Brilliant criminals, though. You're new to hell. Suffice it to say, they fixed this battle, and stand to make a lot of *diablos*, as do I from wagering on the outcome. Anyway, enough chat. I have a battle to win."

Wolfe felt light-headed. "Have you no – honor?"

Arnott laughed. "Honor? In hell?" Leaning forward, he touched Wolfe on the knee with a finger. "I'll let you in on a little secret, Wolfe. My name's not Benjamin Arnott. It's Benedict Arnold." He paused, smiling. "Well, I can see by your blank look that my name means nothing to you. I'm not even offended. Let's just say that betrayal is no big thing. Been there. Done that. Really good at it." Leaning back, he raised his strange weapon and aimed it at Wolfe's chest. "Sorry. Have to go."

The consumption Wolfe had fought so hard to control won out, and he coughed violently, blood and bile flying from his mouth to splatter on the ground. He coughed again and again, every breath becoming a strained wheeze between each sharp intake of air.

Arnold paused and lowered his pistol. A humorless grin played across his lips. "That's some deadly sickness you have there. Can't be the belly wound. Tuberculosis?"

Wolfe nodded. The violent wave subsided. As he wiped at his mouth with the back of his sleeve, he noticed Arnold's gun pointed off to the side. Firming his grip on the Lee-Metford, he forced himself into another coughing fit. Arnold continued to watch, taking sadistic satisfaction from Wolfe's state.

Wolfe suddenly reared back, tilted the Metford's barrel up and squeezed the trigger. The resulting blast and report wrenched the weapon from his hand. He threw himself sideways, expecting a bullet to strike his chest, thus completing the trio of wounds accrued during his final moments on the Plains of Abraham.

No shot came.

Instead, Benedict Arnold lay sprawled on his back, his head a bloody mess, the lifeless eyes fixed on the reddish sky.

Wearily, Wolfe sat up. The wound in his belly ached. Blood pooled on the ground between his crossed legs. Another bout of nausea wracked his body; roaring filled his ears. He lay on his back. Moments later he opened his mouth in wordless surprise at the sight of several figures slowly crossing overhead, high in the sky. One paused, as if watching.

Then came a deafening roar, and the ground heaved.

As Wolfe felt his body pitch through the air like some rag doll, he remembered Churchill saying that death was not final, that he would be back. However, this time he prayed it would not be in that lousy little room back in New Hell.

*

"And finally, this just in:

"Disaster struck the much-hyped Plains of Abraham rematch today when a chasm opened under the battlefield, swallowing participants and spectators alike. Among the casualties was our crew from the Perdition Broadcasting System. While the cause of this tragedy remains under investigation, a survivor claims to have witnessed at least seven apparitions appear overhead and, I quote, 'One of those bastards spread his arms and all hell broke loose.' More on this story as details follow.

"Until then, good night and good luck."

"And that's a wrap, Mister Murrow."

Edward R. Murrow merely nodded and, reaching for his pack of cigarettes, lit another.

The Register

by

Michael H. Hanson

NIH (Not In Hell) Field Assignment 662
Chrysler-Smith, Alistair
Newport News Rest Home, State of Virginia
Class 1 Topside Transit Visa

It is a proud and lonely thing to be a field agent for The Hell Register of Preeminently Damned Lawyers, thought Alistair Chrysler-Smith, a blond-haired man of medium height and build, who strode out of the Virginia nursing home with a weary smile and a wealth of new data on his bright-red electronic hellpad. Four former paralegals, two law clerks, a judge, five defense attorneys, and all of them dying from the smorgasbord of illnesses, cancers, and failing organs that define the closing act of the play known as old age. Bitter, angry, and weathering a lifetime of professional regret: a nice crop of potential recruits indeed.

Alistair hopped into his car, a black, fully restored 1957 King Midget Model III (the Register's middle management had no shortage of comic bureaucrats and smartass requisition officers). He drove his folded-steel compact with its nine horsepower motor down the driveway and out onto the I-66 highway.

Consulting his hellpad while scratching his well-groomed white beard and mustache, Alistair calculated he had less than twenty minutes to cross three state lines, park, and reach the Newark New Jersey courthouse in time to watch a sleazy lawyer get a child-killer acquitted on a technicality. Punching an aftermarket switch on the dashboard, Alistair activated an under-the-hood, supercharged amulet to create a small, shimmering portal. Driving through the portal, he crossed roughly three hundred miles in a matter of heartbeats, to emerge on the Garden State Parkway.

Part actuary, part statistician, and part psychologist, a field agent for the Register had a great deal of operational leeway and discretionary equipment at one's disposal, as long as one was discreet. His job was prestigious and important, but demanding; the accuracy of the Register's field agents was rigorously scrutinized by hell's performance monitors. Consequently, Alistair sported the latest in hand-held computers to supplement his eidetic memory and rapid-firing neo-cortex. In short, Alistair liked to cover his ass.

*

NIH Field Assignment 663
Chrysler-Smith, Alistair
State of New Jersey/Newark Courthouse/Summit Diner
Class 1 Topside Transit Visa

Leaving the courthouse hours later, Alistair smiled. True, the murderer had choked under cross-examination and it looked like a death sentence was in the making. But it was the behind-the-scenes machinations that concerned the Register.

The prosecutor, an unrepentant sinner, had secretly broken several chain-of-evidence statutes in her pursuit of a guilty plea (and concomitant political advancement). The defense attorney had come close to getting an acquittal, but considering that he was sleeping with the very attractive D.A., there wasn't much venom in his bite. Oh, and the judge had taken bribes via his clerk for three upcoming cases.

Alistair found a nearby park bench and began recording his day's observations

Half an hour later hunger pangs became a distraction and he left the park bench to hit the road for New Jersey's number-one eatery.

*

Sitting by himself in the back booth of the Summit Diner, finishing off a gravy-soaked steak with a large side of soggy fries, Alistair clicked his forked tongue (one of several physical idiosyncrasies meant to keep him from getting intimate with the natives) and ran his eyes down his daily numbers spreadsheet: potential acquisitions; countdowns to demise; breaches of standards of professional conduct and ethics; cases won; cases settled in favor of client (or self); payoffs; bribes, threats and intimidations;

destruction of evidence; subsidiary sins; taking the Lord's name in vain....

"Mind if I join you, handsome?"

Alistair's large green eyes registered mild surprise.

"Gefjon," Alistair said, "of course."

The stunning, young brunette in a tasteful Chanel suit slid onto the booth's opposite bench.

"Still wearing those atrocious off-the-rack outfits, I see," Gefjon said.

"Don't knock Valentino. He's the fashionable businessperson's best friend."

"Please. He's the Wal-Mart of the upper middle-class." Gefjon raised her hand. "Waitress!" she yelled. "Coffee. Black."

Alistair set down his electronic notepad and studied the apparently twenty-something satanic judgment counselor. He'd known her professionally for over 200 years, subjective time, which really didn't mean much, considering the amount of temporal jet-setting required by their respective jobs.

"So what brings an uptight snob like you into a delightful dump like this?" Alistair asked. "Slumming?"

"Insults are beneath you, field agent," Gefjon snapped. "Besides, this little trailer seems good enough for an employee of the Register...." Her upper lip curled as a grimy trucker left a four-dollar tip on the front counter before sauntering outside.

"I like the ambiance," Alistair said, "not to mention, I used to eat here back in my soft-body days."

Her eyes opened wide.

"A telling admission," Gefjon said, leaning forward. "Either you're finally losing your edge, or you're up to something, Alistair. Spill it."

Alistair smiled and sipped his coffee. Gefjon's day-job ensured that they crossed paths at least five times a week. Where Alistair's information-gathering activities were purely passive in nature, Gefjon used every trick in her arsenal to aggressively recruit qualified personnel for hell's burgeoning legal system. As an earthly manifestation of a hell-spawned succubus, Gefjon was legendary for leading good mortals down the brimstone path. What free time she could scrounge was spent seducing register staff in hopes of getting inside info and a jump on her competition.

A lower-order demon, Gefjon had strict limitations placed on her access to "topside" earth, including having to check in with her superiors below every six hours. Her situation was analogous to being on probation with an ankle monitor, quite different from Alistair's status as special field agent, the infernal equivalent of full ambassadorial rank.

"If I've said it once, I've said it a thousand times…" Alistair said.

"'Register staff maintain the highest security standards in the deepest pit of hell,'" Gefjon laughed. "Yeah, sure."

"I lived a good portion of my mortal life in New Jersey." Alistair sighed.

Gefjon leaned forward, intrigued. "You practiced law here?" she asked. "You passed the Jersey bar?"

"Why no, in fact, I was never a lawyer in life." The look of shock on Gefjon's face was fully worth the price of admission.

"B-b-but … but …" she stuttered, "I thought all Register staff are former lawyers! Are you saying you were never a judge or even a legal advisor?"

"Correct," Alistair said. "Nor a stenographer, nor a legal clerk or paralegal, or patent modeler, or any of a hundred other jobs in the biz."

"Then how…?"

"When I first moved to New Jersey – and no, I won't tell you from where – I got a job as a staff editor for the Martindale law directory."

"No way!"

"Way," Alistair said, "and it was definitely an overrated position. We were more data-entry clerks than real editorial staff."

"And that's why you…?"

"Not so quick," Alistair said. "After four and a half years of that mind-numbing work, I became an editor for the Services and Suppliers Catalog. That lasted three years. Then I moved on to eventually become a senior editor on the…. Are you ready?"

"I'm all horns."

"The Bar Register."

Gefjon gasped. "So *that's* why you were recruited to work on the...."

"Nope," Alistair said. "I was a loyal, conscientious, hard-working, and downright honest employee during my eight years with the Bar Register."

"Sounds like you were a prime candidate for the, uh, other side." Gefjon frowned.

"Possibly," Alistair said. "But then the big move came."

"You murdered your boss," Gefjon guessed, "chopped your wife into little parts, went on a molestation rampage across Rutgers University. No, you got caught on 'To Catch a Predator.'"

"I was given a position in the company's lawyer and law firm ratings department."

Gefjon let her breath out slowly. "The penny drops."

"From a great height."

"And I take it that – like our Register's own ratings department –"

"In a word, yes," Alistair said. "Processing peer review questionnaires was the public face of ratings, and it was definitely a more egalitarian process of information-gathering than my current paranormal barnstorming investigations."

"You said, the *'face.'*"

"Yeah. That's the rub," Alistair said, signaling for a coffee refill, "and there my downward spiral began."

"The ratings system was compromised, wasn't it?"

"Not at first," Alistair said. "But the financial demands of life, a handful of screaming kids, my spendthrift, upwardly-mobile wife, the price of cocaine.... I needed the money."

"You could have robbed a bank, Alistair," Gefjon sniffed.

"You're such a romantic, sweetheart," Alistair smiled. "I was never prone to theatrics. Within five years I'd bugged every computer on the floor. Once I had undetectable access to all the databases, it took me a year of tracking ratings applications before I found my marks. Three thousand lawyers and law firms desperate to garner a rating, and not necessarily an A, but a B! or even a C! People who wanted to join the golden crowd so very much...."

"And for the right price...."

"I offered them legitimacy," Alistair said, "and what followed was a glorious reign of twenty years where I raked in millions."

"Your bosses never found out?" Gefjon asked.

"Nope," Alistair said. "It was the IRS who finally caught on. My backstabbing second ex-wife cut a deal and ratted me out. I stuffed a shotgun in my mouth right before they raided my home."

"And so you departed ratings, leaving it to fester under some other corrupt, replacement boss."

"On the contrary," Alistair said, "I was, ironically enough, the only criminal in that department, that building, and that company." Alistair left a large tip on the table, escorting Gefjon out of the diner and into the cold night air.

*

NIH Field Assignment 664
Chrysler-Smith, Alistair
State of New Jersey/Howard Johnson, North Plainfield
Class 1 Topside Transit Visa

Alistair stuffed a warm cinnamon-raisin bagel swabbed with cream cheese into his mouth. If there was one thing he liked about Hojo's, it was the bottomless continental breakfast.

"I swear you pick these tacky establishments just to offend me," Gefjon said.

Alistair looked up to see her leafing through the New York Times. The far windows showed the sun beginning to crest the horizon.

"You were particularly frisky last night."

She smiled. "You've given me more insight into the Register in an hour than I've scraped up on my own over the last hundred years."

"Have I now," Alistair asked. "And what do you think you know?"

"Just that this world-hopping reporter routine of yours is only half of the equation," Gefjon spat.

Alistair smirked but remained silent.

"Fine," Gefjon said, "play it close to the vest, but don't think I haven't figured you out. The ratings system was corrupted right here in this lowbrow state and I'll bet you've done the same thing with the Register down in Hell."

"A nasty accusation from one so low on the totem pole," Alistair said. "You know, I could report you on a number of violations – attempting to seduce a superior officer of the court being only one of them."

"Don't be an idiot," Gefjon said, "your not-so-subtle little past-life story last night did the trick: I want in."

Alistair's face took on a ghastly smile and Gefjon swallowed nervously.

"Do you really, my dear?" Alistair asked. "Even considering the potential repercussions?"

"Are you kidding me?" Gefjon squealed, then lowered her voice to a whisper: "Status means everything to the arrogant pricks strutting around the infernal Hall of Injustice. There isn't a prosecutor, defense attorney, or judge in hell who wouldn't give their left cloven hoof for a chance to one-up their colleagues. Besides, I'm sick of being an errand girl on a tether. I want some freedom, like you have. Damn it, I've paid my dues."

"You could be right," Alistair said, sipping his orange juice.

"Please," Gefjon said, "I *get* it. You've been playing me like a trout. You wanted to see how discreet I was, while bedding me over all these decades. Well, have I passed?"

Alistair smiled. Glints of red sunrise reflected off his teeth. "You're in."

*

BIH (Back In Hell)
Field Agent Repatriation 665
Chrysler-Smith, Alistair
Priority 1 Recall
Pandemonium, In Transit

Barreling up Nile Boulevard, Alistair's demonic taxi driver, a tiger-striped, wolverine-faced monstrosity named Matali, paid scant attention to his bureaucrat passenger. Only operatives with the highest of hell's security ratings ever traveled this narrow, mostly empty road that led directly to the lower garage caves cut deep into the base of Pandemonium's grand City Courthouse. Matali knew it was best not to get chummy with these spook types. Besides, the infernal mange eating its way across his buttocks and lower back was more than enough to worry about on this pothole-covered road.

Alistair looked up from his hellpad to take in the surrounding mix of skyscrapers, warehouses, and volcanic parks. If New Hell was hell's Manhattan, then Pandemonium was its Chicago, smaller, no less corrupt, and a lot less hypocritical in its immorality and venality.

The colossal courthouse slowly came into view. There were five hundred Doric columns, fifty feet high, marking the perimeter of the imposing building. Phidias, Iktinos, and Kallikrates had used every spare soul from hell's massive population to build this monument to Tartarosian justice. Unlike the stacked-cake approach they designed for the Parthenon's columns back in mid 5th century BC, each of these towering pedestals was carved as a single piece of black-speckled, white granite, mined from the slopes of the stunted mountain that serves as the courthouse's foundation.

Alistair rubbed his temples for the fifth time this morning. He never should have had that eighth drink last night at the Death Rattle, but it couldn't be helped. The popular back-alley dive had a two-drink minimum per act, and Alistair had to sit through some atrocious performances before his favorite band, the Ungrateful Dead, started their set. It was an ear-numbing cacophony and perfect for covert conversation.

Alistair examined his hellpad intensely. Gefjon's erotic and highly experienced colleagues (Malfean, Alalahe, and Gemmeul) had done their job well. Playing the pimp was a new trick for Alistair, but then, much about him had changed since he'd first transubstantiated into existence down here. Nothing was beneath him now. He'd always been a survivor in life. Deep in the Inferno, his instincts for self-preservation had been honed sharp.

Matali stopped his taxi as two security demons gave him and his passenger the once over. Looking like tuxedoed, upright rhinoceroses suffering from *erythropoietic porphyria,* they motioned Matali onward with pus-covered claws.

*

BIH Departmental Debriefing 666
Alistair Chrysler-Smith

Priority 1 Recall
Pandemonium, City Courthouse
Hell Register/Ratings

Alistair sat before the Hell Register ratings department's review committee – six coldly beautiful female demons renowned for their successes as interrogators, debriefing specialists, and torturers.

Right now, this judgmental sextet did not look happy.

It had taken Alistair a full five minutes of elevator descent to reach this deepest of courthouse sublevels. Former Truman White House contractor John McShain and thousands of deceased employees from the Laborers' International Union of North America spent over fifty years in the secret excavation. Alistair considered it a point of pride that his division of the Hell Register of Preeminently Damned Lawyers merited the most secure of concealed office locales. The rating of incoming lawyers was a redundantly-secure activity, hidden from all surveillance equipment, eyes, soothsayers, and remote viewers.

"We've downloaded your latest statistical analyses, Alistair" Mayet, presiding demon and committee chair, possessed the body of an exotic dancer and a green haired countenance sporting a single, large yellow eye. "You've done more work topside in one year than our entire task force has processed in a decade. Recent conversations in the higher court's cafeteria paint you as a real fair-haired boy."

Alistair swallowed nervously. He sat in the interrogation chair, a monstrosity of black obsidian and ebonite. His red hellpad lay upon the wide right arm of the throne. His fingers rubbed the edge of his tablet computer every few moments.

"So, would a raise be out of the question?" Alistair asked.

Astraea, a multi-limbed demon (renowned for her erotic excesses in Pandemonium's after-hours scene), took a step forward and displayed a smile filled with dagger teeth. "The problem, handsome, is your pre-death rep. We have high standards down here. We're sure you've heard what happens to those seeking to corrupt the, ummmm, sanctity of our activities."

Alistair looked up at the far wall, where a startling eight-by-thirteen-foot oil painting was hung. It was a perfect reproduction of William-Adolphe Bouguereau's horrifying 1850 painting, 'Dante and Virgil in Hell.' The painting depicted the fifth circle of hell, where the wrathful are destined to fight eternally on the surface of the river Styx while the slothful watch from beneath. The crimson "sky" of hell glowed hot in the artwork's background. In the foreground were two naked Caucasian men in vicious combat, one biting the other's neck vampire-like. On closer examination, Alistair could see that the victim's eyes were alive and blinking. Every now and then the figures of Dante and Virgil would animate for a few seconds and lean forward to whisper in the victim's ears. Alistair fancied he heard their hushed message, "…right to remain silent. Anything you say can and will be used…"

Mayet followed his gaze. "Mister Moore is the loser in the painting, Alistair," the demon said. "Moorie thought he could sell premature ratings data for favors in the higher circles. Now he suffers his punishment under our watchful eye."

"Yes, well … point taken," Alistair said. He tapped his fingers nervously over his hellpad. "So, if there is nothing else to discuss?"

Astraea took a step forward and pointed four of her eight arms at Alistair. "We're on to you, pipsqueak. You may not have sold any information yet, and we're sure our blade servers are sacrosanct, but we got over a dozen off-the-record snitches who think you're up to something."

"And you think this will hold up in court?" Alistair asked. "I protest. Besides, I'm innocent."

Mayet stood taller. "There will be no court review, Alistair. We police this division. We're judge, jury, and … executioner. Even if you are innocent today, your true nature will eventually come out. You can't be trusted. Besides, I think Mister Moore could use a little company in my favorite painting."

Alistair's fingers rubbed the surface of his notepad. "Then I guess I have nothing to lose by saying you're a bunch of bloody hypocrites. I don't know how you get away with it, but it's been obvious to me from Day One that you're all corrupt and have been abusing your oversight of ratings for some time."

"Nice try, loser," drawled Myndie, a petite, naked demon with skin mottled like desert camouflage and a strong West Virginian accent. Her right hand pointed at Alistair like a loaded gun. "Nobody knows what we do in here."

"Then you admit your crimes," Alistair asked, "that you're all guilty of abusing your positions?"

The sextet laughed uproariously.

"So what, punk?" Mynndie spat. "We're at the top of the pyramid, and we're here to stay."

"You're a fool, Alistair," Andraea said. "You think recording us on your little toy is going to save you? *We* pull the strings from down here. We're the real power behind the throne. There isn't a lawyer in hell who doesn't owe their current position to our selective rating system ... and they repay us daily with innumerable favors."

"Andraea's right," Mayet said. "Our electronic and thaumaturgical countermeasures make this the safest of safe houses ... the ultimate panic room. There is no deeper or more secure pit in all of hell. Your silly little device can't transmit anything through these walls, and nothing you've learned will ever see the red light of day."

Alistair looked up from his hellpad, but not with an expression of defeat.

"Whoever said this was an electronic notepad, ladies?" Alistair asked.

"A talisman then," Mayet spat, "no matter. There is no captured spell or magically charged 'juju' that can pierce these barriers."

Alistair slowly and carefully picked up his device, popped off the false cover, and held up what appeared to be a rectangular slate of polished black rock.

"Oh crap," Mynndie said, "the jig is up."

"We repeat: charms and fetishes will not work here." Mayet growled.

"I... I was instructed by persons in higher ranks," Mynndie yelled. "Besides, this is hell. I've done nothing out of the ordinary!"

"This isn't a mere talisman, ladies," Alistair said. "It is one of the nine black tablets of the Apostasies, Hell's Supreme Court. Rumor has it these ebonite slates were carved from Lucifer's own tears, shed at the end of his great fall, each one crystallizing into a large black diamond upon contact with the fiery lake. Had one hell of a time convincing Justice Taney to loan it to me. Seems he always wanted a four-way with two succubi and a seraphim. And to the best of my knowledge, everything witnessed, heard, or seen by one of the black tablets is immediately known by them all. A nice function for when the justices need an emergency conference."

"Liar!" Mayet screamed.

Alistair smiled. "Your superiors are being contacted as we speak."

"Boy," Mayet snarled, "you just bluffed the wrong demon."

Mayet stepped away from her five colleagues and charged Alistair. The field agent leaped from his chair and braced for impact. A moment before reaching him, Mayet raised what appeared to be a small, wood hammer in her right hand.

"Roy Bean sends his regards," Mayet shouted.

Alistair raised the black tablet like a shield, two handed. Gavel and tablet met with a thunderous explosion and a roar.

The resulting shock wave floored the sextet.

Mynndie was tossed clear across the conference table to strike the far wall. Her neck snapped audibly. According to Alistair's research, this would make the tenth time she would wake in the hands of the Undertaker, naked, blindfolded, and facing degrading humiliations.

Andraea lay slumped in her chair. The handle of the gavel had impaled her right eye and now protruded from the back of her skull. Several spasms ran through all eight of her hands, belying her death. She too would face a horrific awakening in the Undertaker's hands.

Her sister demons, Vali, Naru-Kami, and Chantico, were struggling to stand upright, moaning about their bruised and broken limbs.

Shaken, but still standing, Alistair smiled down at Mayet.

"I wasn't bluffing, Lady Chairman," Alistair said, "and this all could have been much more civilized."

Alistair reached down and, grabbing Mayet by one wrist, dragged her toward the wall where the Dante and Virgil painting hung.

"Please," Mayet begged. "No! No … not *that.*"

"I personally prefer the Impressionists," Alistair said, "but I suppose one must make allowances when it comes to taste in art."

Alistair slammed Mayet's right hand against the painting's frame.

There was a blinding flash of white light.

Into it, Mayet disappeared. In her place crouched a slim, naked man of indeterminate age.

Wide-eyed, he screamed with joy.

"I'm free," former defense attorney and Miranda Rights trailblazer Alvin Moore yelled. Then his eyes fell on Chantico, whose head sprouted red serpents and cactus spikes. *"You,"* Moore gasped.

Moore launched himself across the room and tackled the wounded demon. "Everything you've done to me will now be done to *you.*" Before Chantico could protest, Moore's teeth fastened on her throat.

The demon couldn't even scream.

The foundation and walls of the interrogation room shook violently. The black tablet in Alistair's hand pulsed with a dull, green light.

"I wouldn't crawl too far, ladies," Alistair said to Vali and Naru-Kami. Vali's zebra-skinned hide and Naru-Kami's rainbow plumes shivered in terror. "Your own canvases are on their way."

Alistair turned away. He'd thought this victory would be sweet; instead, it tasted bitter.

The exchange of victims removed much of the painting's original homoerotic charm, but Mayet's bright green hair and huge weeping eye leant a wonderfully macabre flavor to this new rendering of a fine work of dark art.

*

BIH Staff Briefing: 001
Pandemonium Courthouse
Register Ratings Department

Alistair sat at his new desk and appraised his twelve recruits. Foremost in the group was Gefjon, among the most seductive of succubi, and yet somehow looking as natural as ever in her

Chanel outfit.

"Under direct supervision by the editor-in-chief of the Hell Register of Preeminently Damned Lawyers," Alistair said, "I have been tasked to revamp this department, rewriting standards as well as official rules and regulations. We'll be creating much of this as we go along, but rest assured I plan to make the systematic assignment of lawyer ratings far swifter and more efficient."

Alistair smiled wickedly at his new staff and waved his hand in the air. "As the recent redecorating of my office shows, corruption of any kind will not be tolerated."

Gefjon gulped as she assessed the six huge paintings strung across the surrounding walls, all depicting variants of the same scene. Each showed one of the former committee who had ruled the ratings department. In each painting, one female demon's throat was being torn out by a ferocious, naked man. The three-dimensional eyes of the two-dimensional female demons bled and blinked.

The staff listened, mesmerized, as Alistair continued.

"But before we begin our planning session," Alistair said, "I want you each to place every single electronic device in your possession on my desktop."

The recruits hurriedly obeyed.

Alistair tossed a small sledgehammer onto the pile of notepads, tablets, and personal electronic assistants.

"Now … smash those damned things to bits!"

Island Out of Time

by

Richard Groller

The Oracle at Delphi screamed a scream…

…a scream that could evoke nightmares for eternity. Nichols stood frozen by her stare, looking into the eyes of a woman who beheld infinity and found it totally mad.

When first approaching the temple of white marble overgrown with moss and ivy, Nichols had sensed no danger in its decrepit splendor. Even in hell, he put no store in sibyls. And here he was, about as deep in hell as you could get, in the old dead's mythic realms. Nichols trusted only logic and his five senses, first in life, now in afterlife.

His boss, Dick Welch, had sent him to this oracle to determine the source of the time perturbations troubling Satan: "Go to the oracle at Delphi, Nichols. She'll tell you something," Welch had ordered.

Temple steps. Brackish water in green and murky pools, barely reflecting Paradise's ruddy light. The temple caretakers must not venture out much.

A fresh-faced female acolyte, nubile in her green linen chiton, appeared from shadows and led him through an anteroom, past white marble benches, to a bronze door, ten feet tall, with bas relief scenes from Greek mythology. Vintage old-dead theatrics.

Doors opened before them, anticipating their approach like sentries, channelizing their progress until they stood in a *big* domed chamber: hundred foot ceiling; central dais of dead-black marble. Nice touches. So were the gold sconces for unlit torches every ten feet. Very Hollywood, or very Greek, or very overdone – take your pick. Light shone from behind Corinthian cornices.

On the dais sat a throne, carved from the biggest chunk of rock crystal Nichols had ever seen. And on the throne sat the oracle herself, mostly naked, too sexy and too muscular by half: golden nimbus glowing from her skin.

The oracle said in a ringing voice, "You wish to know the Nature of Time. What you ask is not without price. What does my lord offer in payment?"

Nature of Time? Shit, she knew before I asked.

Nichols replied, *"My lord,* Satan himself, requests the information."

The oracle was staring at him as if his face held the key to eternal salvation, which it sure as hell didn't. But he had to say something more, because she was waiting for it.... "Oracle, my lord will allow you a just reward – if you tell us what we want to know. Something valuable, something relevant to stabilizing time perturbations."

At this the sibyl raised both hands flat before her, and the lights went out. All that could be seen was her nimbus and the water atop the altar, bathed from below in a luminous glow.

Silently the Delphic Oracle rose and bent over the water on the altar, staring into it.

She babbled in a hushed tone: first in ancient Greek, then in a language he didn't recognize. He understood some Greek: fighting in Tartaros beside Alexander and his heroes, Nichols had learned Koine Greek, the lingua franca of the Hellenistic old dead, but he was at a loss to understand this gibberish. Too bad Welch wasn't here: his boss had had lots more linguistic training....

The oracle started calling out numbers and what sounded like equations. Nichols pulled out his hellphone and keyed the video function for later analysis by linguists because he couldn't go back to Welch saying the oracle blabbed her head off but he had no idea what she said.

Then something went very wrong. Her hushed tones turned cacophonous. She was shuddering, writhing; contorting her body, tearing at her face and eyes; screaming and shrieking.

"Kill me," she sobbed. "Kill me, emissary of Satan. Now. Please. Relieve me of these frightful visions, I beg it of you."

Sure, honey. Just hold on a sec.... But then he realized he wasn't sure if he should kill her. Welch hadn't said anything about killing this oracle.

A dull foreboding crept up his spine. Since Welch hadn't

prepared him for killing the oracle as part of this mission, then killing her *wasn't* part of his mission. Her antics turned nightmarish. She raved and screamed and shook and threw herself at his feet. She frothed at the mouth. Her head wagged, her body thrashed. The acolytes stationed around the room broke formation, put their heads together, and started toward her.

Enough was enough.

Croesus, king of Lydia, would be pissed, for sure, but Croesus damned well needed a new oracle anyway. Blood poured from the oracle's empty eye sockets. She couldn't see the acolytes converging on her. They grabbed her as she struggled.

Nichols knew exactly what to do.

While the acolytes held her head still, he fired two quick shots from his Desert Eagle, hitting her cleanly and perfectly between the eyes.

She slumped like a puppet whose strings had been cut as his gunshots reverberated throughout the suddenly silent chamber, reechoing off the dome above.

*

Back in New Hell, safe and arguably sound, Nichols reported to his boss, tucked away in the deepest recesses of Admin in an unmarked office. After seeing Nichols' hellphone video, Welch replied "None of this means shit to me – deliver that video to Zeno of Elea personally and answer any of his questions regarding this incident."

So Zeno had already been tasked to work the problem.

Nichols had Achilles pick him up in his stealth-equipped Huey Cobra to expedite the rendezvous with the old dead philosopher. Nichols could soldier on: it was what he did; but he couldn't shake the memory of the oracle's eyes.

*

Pythagoras arrived late at the Infernal Observatory on the snow-covered peak of Mount Sinai. With a hellpad under his arm, he seemed a thoroughly modern version of the ancient philosopher who had inspired so many sects of Pythagoreans, including the *Mathematici* in whose name Hippasus was drowned for documenting the irrationality of numbers. Pythagoras was paying a surprise visit to Zeno of Elea, whose *ad hominem* attacks on the technical doctrines of the Pythagorean School still infuriated him: Pythagoras believed that reality was fundamentally mathematical.

Demons standing guard outside Zeno's lab at the Department of Apparent Time, were having their obscenely explicit way with a pair of human-looking snowmen. Something was amiss here.

Zeno was in no mood for company. "Do you know what He asks of me, Pythagoras? The fabric of Infernal Time has somehow become unstable, and Satan himself has commanded *me* to fix it or face the consequences." Zeno nodded toward the hall where more demons stood guard: "I can't work under these conditions!" Out tumbled details of Satan's last visit and the effect of the temporal disturbance on Satan's pet, Michael. "Satan was toying with me – he showed up in a black robe and powdered wig and pronounced sentence upon me. There is no justice in hell, Pythagoras. None. I suffer undeserved punishment without benefit of even a trial. I didn't cause hell's temporal perturbations. How does Satan expect me to stop them?"

"Shall I ask the Legal Aid Society to petition the Mount Sinai Appellate Division?" Pythagoras proposed. "File a Writ of Mandamus against Satan for travesty of justice? With your august status, perhaps Daniel Webster will defend you."

"Go up against Satan? You fool, will you never learn?" Zeno glared at Pythagoras as if about to bodily expel him for suggesting such a thing.

Just then a man named Nichols showed up with a video for Zeno to see. This was a soldier, big and broad and muscular, and clearly discomfited by Pythagoras' presence, barely acknowledging him.

Nichols herded Zeno into a corner and spoke with him, *sotto voce,* then left hurriedly.

Once Nichols was gone, Zeno was in no mood for company. "Please take no offense, but I have no time now for the pleasure of your company, friend Pythagoras."

"Good frater, time here is eternal! What else could we possibly have more of here, than time?"

Zeno answered simply. "Almost anything. At the moment, so to speak," Zeno grimaced mirthlessly, "time itself is the problem – it appears to be undergoing increasingly less subtle perturbations. I'm at a loss trying to quantify the boundaries of the problem."

Pythagoras, bowing smartly from the waist, said, "Perhaps I can offer some assistance, then? It would be a pleasure to tackle a real challenge." With a wink, he added, "Besides, why should you have all the fun?"

"I must caution you about consequences, since you can't take a hint." Outside Zeno's window, several demons were performing unnatural acts upon a debauched snowman. "The problem is serious, its implications not well understood. Satan himself is very concerned. He is determined that efforts will be unflagging until a solution is reached. And His Satanic Majesty promises unending torment to those who fail him, so his man Nichols tells me."

Pythagoras smiled. "A joint effort to solve an impossible problem, the stabilization of Time itself? Sounds interesting. And, should we succeed, far more ennobling than most hellish pursuits. Besides what can he *really* do to us? Kill us and send us to hell?"

Zeno clapped his hands. "Then, let's be about taming time itself: a small feat, for you and me."

The two old dead turned their attention to the video left by Nichols, Satan's emissary.

*

The words of the Delphic Oracle on the recording were cryptic but not incomprehensible. Pythagoras understood her. She spoke of an island appearing, an island of myth: "Onogoroshima – a self-forming island, the handiwork of Daikok – The Great Black One." And she spoke of something else as well – an opening between worlds, a "Demon Gate."

So far, no such island or gate had been reported to Authority, or so the devil's henchman, Nichols, had assured Zeno.

Pythagoras didn't trust Nichols.

Where was this island, this gate? Another place, another space, perhaps another time? "'Why this is Hell, nor am I out of it,'" Pythagoras muttered absently, a quote from Christopher Marlowe. Could there be place, space, and time beyond hell … accessible to the damned?

The unknown beguiled Pythagoras. Thoughts of a new world, perhaps even a new dimension, filled him with hope. Whatever the risk, he needed to know the truth of it.

First, he must find this island, if it did exist on this plane. Then, having verified its existence, he must set foot there. Not so easy. If he found the island, he could volunteer to join in any ensuing investigation of such anomalous loci. If he discovered the place, Agency would surely let him go along….

Using Gurgle, Pythagoras found that some of the numbers given by the oracle included a latitude and longitude (49 degrees, 50 minutes South latitude; 128 degrees, 33 minutes West longitude); along with a height, several hundred feet below sea level. The numbers were given in polar coordinates, reversed and inverted, but this was to be expected: a good oracle is always inscrutable.

He took his data to Zeno's monastic cell in the observatory: "Zeno, consider the possibilities! An expedition! We volunteer our services. Once the existence of a site at these coordinates is verified, we're the discoverers of a whole new island, perhaps even dimension. Your friend Nichols can assure us a place on the exploration team."

The Stoic Zeno was much less adventurous. Traveling hell's ocean was perilous at best, suicidal at worst. Seaworthy vessels and crews foolish enough to undertake such voyages were few; most travelers flew or went by land across the infernal reaches of hell's multilayered continent. But even travel by land would be difficult to arrange.

Zeno looked at Pythagoras and said, "You have fun, my friend, chasing ancient gods of the netherworlds – I am chained to my desk, overseen by demonic taskmasters. And here I shall stay, by order of Satan, wrestling with the nature of space and time. Studying the paradox of reality in hell is more appealing to me than meeting forgotten gods face to face."

*

Welch's instructions to Nichols were explicit: "Pull together the assets you need, using every resource available. Determine whether or not a real threat to Satanic authority exists. Assess the situation and get out – don't be a hero."

Pythagoras' eagerness to volunteer made Nichols suspicious. But Pythagoras was willing and motivated. One thing was sure: Pythagoras' coordinates were right on the mark.

The SATSATPHORECNET (Satanic Satellite Photographic

Reconnaissance Network) confirmed the existence of an island at those coordinates, where no island existed a month ago. This island was lush and green. A scant five degrees above the tree line, this island was covered with trees – in the sub-polar region where hardy grasses and other tundra plants should be struggling to grow. None of this data made sense.

And this diabolical brain-teaser just kept getting better: the *USS (Underworld Satanical Ship) Arizona,* on a run from Satanic Samoa, had disappeared without a trace, two days past. Was there a connection? Although the course of the *Arizona* (through the "Roaring Forties" and "Furious Fifties") lay within the turbulent ocean storm track, no storms had been reported and no SOS broadcast. NUDET (Nuclear Detonation) sensors had reported no activity.

Nichols' head hurt: he hated data that made no sense.

Nichols pulled strings to berth a team on the *IJN (Infernal Japanese Navy) Yamato,* en route to investigate the disappearance of the *Arizona.* With Achilles' tricked-up Huey and a team of four specialists, he'd reconnoiter the island and get out, hopefully without involving the *Yamato's* crew.

The *Yamato* was big for a ferry but, if push came to shove, Nichols wanted plenty of firepower available.

*

Pythagoras ventured into New Hell's theatrical district, to find a friend he'd known long enough to trust. Erik Weisz was small, intense, and accustomed to accomplishing nearly impossible feats. In life, he'd been world famous as the master showman, Harry Houdini.

When Pythagoras found him in a joke shop on Forty-Second Street, Houdini was morosely slumped over his counter, staring at a well-worn photo of his beloved Beatrice, once his wife and partner in the act known as "The Houdinis."

"How are you, Harry?" Pythagoras inquired.

Houdini, looking up: "Pi! Could be worse. What's the occasion? Have you found a way to transmigrate our doomed souls out of here?"

Pythagoras just smiled. "Maybe…." Then he made Houdini the offer: "Not the chance of a lifetime, but of many lifetimes. Join me. Pull off the greatest escape in infernity's history."

Hearing Pythagoras' proposal, Houdini's eyes widened: "Pi, I'm eager. Your scheme is far preferable to selling magic tricks that won't work to the desperate damned, to pay for my sins of pride and lust for glory. The challenge is irresistible."

"And should we succeed, my friend," Pythagoras said softly, "the prize is freedom."

*

It took Nichols hours to identify candidates for his ops team. And hours weren't reliably passing at the same rate.

By the time he had his short-list winnowed to two, he was diabolically pissed off. The two candidates he adjudged most qualified were: Captain John B. Merkerson, late of the 10th Mountain Division and the 10th Special Forces Group; and Major John Wesley Powell, late of the U.S. Geologic Survey. These two men were experts in their fields, apparently fearless, and combat veterans.

Merkerson was the son of a ski instructor in the Colorado Rockies. A mountaineer with an iconoclastic bent; he sought solitude but played well with others. While assigned to a Special Forces A-team during Vietnam, Merkerson received a battlefield commission and was decorated for gallantry. After the war, he transferred first to the 10th Special Forces Group (Airborne) and then to the 10th Mountain Division at Fort Drum. He was killed in his prime during that tour by a drunken ambulance chaser. When Nichols interviewed him, Merkerson's only condition was that if they survived the mission, Nichols would help him find the ambulance chaser who'd killed him.

Next, Nichols tracked down Major John Wesley Powell, the quintessential exploration geologist. Like Merkerson, Powell had explored the Rockies widely. Fighting for the Union during the Battle of Shiloh in 1862, Powell lost his right arm. In 1869, he led the Powell Geographic Expedition through the Grand Canyon and up the Green and Colorado Rivers, then wrote the definitive book on the Colorado Rockies. Later, he became director of the U.S. Geologic Survey and founding director of the U.S. Bureau of Ethnology. If Powell had a personal stake in the outcome of this expedition, Nichols could easily enlist him. Powell's DIS file noted that since the onset of the time perturbations, the missing right arm had begun "ghosting" in and out of existence, disappearing and reappearing randomly. Powell assumed the ghost arm was part of his personal torment.

Nichols was going to convince him otherwise.

*

"You're useful," Nichols conceded to Pythagoras. "But now you want me to bring an escape artist on a caving expedition to an unexplored island? Why?" As Nichols got up, his heavy Desert Eagle snagged his ladder-back chair. "Houdini'd be excess baggage. A wild card with no training in rock climbing and spelunking. The last thing I need is a damned magician. It's too risky."

Pythagoras pouted. "Fine, just leave me behind, too." Nichols needed an expert on time perturbations and all matters temporal. Pythagoras was Nichols' first, best choice. And Pythagoras knew it.

Satan was already on Welch's back, demanding results. The window for reaching the *Yamato* via Huey on schedule was rapidly closing. Nichols wouldn't bother Welch with administrative detail. Pythagoras had Nichols over a barrel, and the stubborn little Greek with the comb-over and the long nose knew it.

"Fine, Pythagoras. You're responsible to see that this Erik Weisz Houdini guy doesn't get in the way. The magician pulls any shit, or wimps out, we leave him behind – wherever or whenever. A spectator on this mission is something I won't fucking tolerate."

*

The helicopter gunship moved stealthily on its flight path from the *IJN Yamato* to the mysterious island, giving Nichols too much time to think, and rethink, and wonder how he got into this fact-finding junket.

If his prima donnas followed orders, everything would go fine. Get in, reconnoiter, get out. That's all there was to it … but his hackles were up. Bad sign.

So far it had all gone like clockwork. Shipboard, Merkerson and Powell clicked immediately and became fast friends, a geologic mutual-admiration society. Houdini was quiet and intense: agile, and physically strong enough for the task ahead. Despite his oldish bookworm's body, Pythagoras was in reasonable shape.

So what had Nichols so torqued? Maybe it was killing the

oracle. Maybe just nerves. Pre-mission jitters. Still, he needed to shake his forebodings. His team couldn't be allowed to guess that he harbored doubts about this mission.

On initial approach, Nichols had Achilles swing wide and circle the island. It was about five miles wide by about seven miles long, with a large rock outcropping off shore on the leeward side, a small mountain rising a thousand feet at its center, and forested with deciduous trees, wrong for this latitude. A white sand beach with a scummy black border encircled it like a dirty collar.

There were structures on the beach. Or rocks that looked like structures. Nichols had Achilles put the Huey down on the beach near the offshore outcroppings, to get a better look. He ordered Houdini to stay with Achilles, and Merkerson and Powell to reconnoiter the adjoining woods.

He and Pythagoras then got out and walked toward the rocks.

Structures?

*

Merkerson, with Powell, beside him, encountered utter silence in the woods. Normally, even in hell's bleakest regions, you heard something: birds, beasts, insects.

But here nothing howled or peeped or even fluttered.

Could he and Powell be the only living things in this forest? The trees around them, trees that shouldn't have been growing here, were twisted unnaturally. The deeper they trekked, the weirder the forest became.

Time to get back to the beach. If they could find it.

*

When Nichols and Pythagoras reached the rocks, they found a series of altars or ceremonial stones there, inscribed with kanji characters, sigils, runes and grotesque figures. The large upright slabs had shackles attached. The stones were stained dark with blood.

Nichols looked up and away, his attention drawn to a spot at the center point of the horizon. A face like the face of Chaos itself arose from the ocean and filled the entire horizon before him.

That face scared the devil out of him.

The vault above darkened to an ominous crimson. A shimmer

of gold wreathed the great head rising from the sea.

Nichols trembled. Suddenly, he was cold.

Pythagoras shook him: "Are you all right, Nichols? You look like you've seen a ghost."

Nichols shook his head, as if he could shake the fear out of his brain. The apparition disappeared (if it had ever been there). The horizon was merely horizon: sea and sky, nothing more.

Nichols didn't daydream. Something had been there; now it wasn't there.

He grabbed Pythagoras by the arm, dragging him toward the helicopter: "I'm fine. Let's go – we've got work to do."

*

As the party reassembled at the helicopter on the beach, Nichols outlined his plan of action: "First, we emplace a data-link repeater on top of the mountain. This will be the only conduit that permits real-time communications with Achilles on the *Yamato*. Then we set up a VHF data transceiver and digital image transmitter outside the mouth of that cave entrance we spotted from the air. Within mutual line-of-sight of the repeater and the transceiver antennas, we can control the transceiver remotely via the comm link. Same for the multi-spectral video recorder we'll carry into the mountain with us." Everything depended on a MIL-SPEC fiber-optic cable, rugged enough to be unraveled as they moved through the cave, but light enough not to bog them down.

Nichols continued: "Second: Achilles, after the comm link is in place and we're working our way into the cave, you return to the *Yamato*. With you in reserve, at least part of the team will be safe and Welch will have his report for Satan. Stay alert. Be prepared for an emergency extraction if things get too hot."

Achilles, hero of the siege of Troy, began bitching: "Here we go again – you guys go off and have all the fun while I have to cover your rear. Why can't I –"

"At ease, cowboy," Nichols cut off Achilles in mid-sentence. "We're running a military expedition here. You know how to play the game. If you didn't want to come, you shouldn't have let Welch volunteer you."

Achilles scoffed but said nothing more.

"Third: Powell, as our geologist, you'll lead the party into the cave system and determine the most expedient course to our destination."

Nobody argued the details. Achilles and Merkerson took the helicopter up again while the rest of the party remained on the beach.

*

Nichols handed his binoculars to Pythagoras, who winced as he watched Merkerson execute a rappel out of the helicopter: quickly drop face-down from the helicopter to the top of the mountain. When the repeater and antenna were emplaced atop the mountain, Nichols angled the antenna so the main lobe would have maximal line of sight to the repeater.

With the comm check apparently successful, Merkerson grabbed the rope, put his foot in its loop, and Achilles ferried him back to the beach at the mountain's base. Pythagoras was certain that Merkerson would fall any second to a grisly death.

In a wash of stinging sand and beaten air, Achilles gently lowered the helicopter. When Merkerson was low enough to comfortably drop into the midst of the team assembled on the sand, Achilles released the line suspending him.

With the last team member safely disembarked, the helo went invisible, as if by magic: no sign of it was left save the residual sand its rotor blades kicked up.

*

Meanwhile Powell, undertook a cursory inspection of the cave mouth, pronouncing it a natural entrance based on the exposed karst resulting from limestone dissolution, and kept up a running dialogue in Nichol's earbud: the cave descended in a gentle incline for as far as he could see, and appeared totally unremarkable.

"No matter how natural it looks, stay alert, Powell," Nichols said into his wire. Now was not the time to let down their guard: he knew damn well that in hell appearances could be deceiving.

The party donned helmets with headlamps and connected a safety line among them in thirty foot intervals; Nichols took the rear: they'd be screwed if the fiber-optic cable tangled with the ropes they'd need to stake off for any upcoming vertical descents.

Several hundred meters into the subterranean void, Powell reported the first vertical chasm. Powell warned that he was lighting a flare and dropped it into the hole, revealing the chasm was several hundred meters deep, and ended in water. Saying that the cave system still sloped ahead of him, Powell asked for and received Nichol's permission to continue down the gentle slope.

At the rear, Nichols played out his comm cable, hoping that the makers of the altars outside were long gone.

Another five hundred meters in, the tunnel widened into a long horizontal gallery. Lights from their helmets illuminated stalactites and stalagmites, glorious and eerily serene. They trekked through an enchanted forest of crystalline columns, sink holes and helictites until a wall blocked their path, featureless but for a narrow squeezeway.

Traveling through the squeezeway set Nichols' teeth on edge: weapons were useless in such close confines. Persevering for thirty meters more, they then found themselves in a second gallery (lower-ceilinged and much shorter), leading to a long, tight crawlway.

From here, they must belly their way forward. After forty meters, the second gallery abruptly opened up into a downward sloping cavity, leading to a crevasse dropping fifty meters, straight down, to a solid floor leading into a tunnel.

Powell swung his rock hammer, firmly anchoring a piton into the cliff top, then undid his safety to allow Merkerson to come forward. Powell was good, but Nichols couldn't take the chance that his ghostly right arm would disappear during the abseil – not without a belay-man to prevent his fall. So Nichols had Merkerson make the initial descent and take up the belaying position.

Pythagoras and Houdini were next, with Powell talking them through the procedure, checking the safety of their sit-slings and carabiners and murmuring encouragement.

As Pythagoras expected, Harry Houdini didn't hesitate to take the initial step over the edge: Houdini was a veteran escape artist and had thrilled many an audience straight-jacketed, suspended high in the air.

As Houdini's body disappeared over the edge of the cliff, Pythagoras heard him call, "Don't worry, Pi, just lean back into it. This is the fun part. Relax and enjoy it."

If you weren't worried, you didn't understand what was happening, Pythagoras thought as his feet went vertical against the face of the precipice. He froze there, unable to move, equally unwilling to go back up or follow Houdini down.

Powell coaxed Pythagoras from above and Houdini coaxed him from below. His clumsy progress down the cliffside to the waiting team members seemed never-ending. Safe. Relatively.

From high above, Powell called, “Let me show you how it’s done,” and descended the entire distance in two bounds.

Pythagoras, still queasy, muttered “braggart” and opened his canteen to water his painfully dry mouth.

Nichols, still at the top, unreeled the fiber-optic cable and lowered the box-spool casing to Merkerson. He then mimicked Powell’s fast-bounding descent.

Leaving the ropes in place for their return, they ventured into the tunnel. The tunnel fed into a wide circle; the circle in turn opened into yet another passageway, sloping sharply downward.

While Powell staked a piton for a safety line to facilitate a hasty rappel down the sharp incline, in the light from his headlamp, Pythagoras noticed something strange.

A dead thing, so far below ground? The carcass was not fossilized, yet somehow preserved. And it was grotesque. Perhaps it was a deformed ker or harpy, or a stunted erinys, some supernatural personification of the anger of the dead. But no, it was too ugly for that. Perhaps it was a baby phorcyde, one of Phorcys and Ceto’s monstrous children. Or a member of some more ancient demon race? A pair of wings was attached to its headless round body; its belly had a gaping mouth, frozen open in death; its leathery flesh was grayish, almost invisible in the light of their headlamps.

Houdini prodded it gingerly with the tip of his survival knife and said quietly, “What in the underworld is this?” to Pythagoras.

Pythagoras shrugged, saying, “It might be some unknown species of subterranean bat. Don’t let it bother you, Harry. We have more immediate concerns. Look there.”

Ahead was a steep incline of about a hundred meters, opening into an intermittently self-illuminated cavern. Stalactites and their shadows appeared to dance in uneven rhythm, as if the light was moving randomly.

Powell, up ahead, slowed to a stop where the tunnel opened onto a ten-foot ledge.

When Pythagoras joined Powell, he discovered the source of the eerie light.

*

Below Powell was a pool about a hundred feet in diameter, with a phosphorescent glow and a thousand eyes. Beside Powell was Pythagoras, frozen in shock at what they both saw. Was this pool alive? Cognizant? The thousand eyes on its surface roved in every direction. The ground around the pool was shrouded in mist. Lights bobbed around its edges. Its surface became agitated as its eyes looked up at them.

Now the pool's surface moved constantly – creating creatures, limbs, organs at random in horrific combinations: winged eyes; clawed tendrils; fleshy feet and arms, all spewed into the air above, only to be swallowed up as the protoplasmic pool created razor-teeth to devour the grotesques as fast as it created them. Some few creatures escaped the beastly pool that mothered them.

These landed on the cavern floor, flopping helplessly. Some oozed back into the swirling protoplasm. Others, self-propelled, wandered into the several tunnels that dotted the base of the cavern surrounding the roiling lake of pandemonium.

The horror below Powell was whispering to him, crooning at him to come join the fun. In the pool, he'd never be alone again, it promised. The thing in the pool had gotten into the mind of a solitary man and was promising his heart's desire….

Powell had to get out of here. Now.

He tackled Pythagoras, dropping the philosopher to his knees on the ledge, then slammed into Merkerson's chest, hoping to escape into the tunnel.

Merkerson shook him, but Powell just shrieked, "Got to get out! Out!!" and tried to push past, more terrified than he'd ever been before. On the narrow ledge, Merkerson stepped aside to let Powell get past, then cold-cocked him.

Powell barely felt it when they dragged him into the tunnel's mouth and left him there.

*

Merkerson watched Nichols sweating the result: one man short, with Powell out of commission. Nichols wasn't happy.

Pythagoras scrambled to his feet, less interested in the

protoplasmic being below than in a circular area scintillating on the far wall of the cavern at roughly the height of their ledge. Turning to Nichols and Merkerson, Pythagoras said, “Mister Nichols, if you please, ignore the beast below us. Rather, have your Captain Merkerson fire a stake into that turbulence over there.”

“Do it,” Nichols ordered.

Merkerson was happy to oblige. As he painted that nebulous region of space on his smoothbore piton projector with its laser rangefinder, the laser registered infinity.

Merkerson fired. His “plain-vanilla” piton shot forward and out of sight as it entered the suspended circle of ever shifting space on that rock wall.

Pythagoras whooped. “Just as I thought! I believe *that* is the dimensional doorway or time portal we seek, and I’m fairly sure it is the source of the time perturbations that have Satan tied in knots – or if not the source, the *way* to the source. Come, we must be like my frater Aristotle: ‘espy, see, behold, remark and observe.’”

*

Discipline was breaking down. Nichols was now shifting to Plan B, his go-to-shit plan, as fast as he could, stuck on this six-by-ten ledge with a bunch of fools. Powell, the stolid major, had turned out to be the liability, not the batty old-dead philosopher, who was now giving orders as if this was his mission. Hell of a note.

“Friend Merkerson,” Pythagoras commanded, “use your rangefinder to give me a distance to that large stalactite there in the center. Also, to the far wall of the cavern.”

Then Pythagoras sat down cross-legged at the ledge’s edge and opened his hellpad on his lap.

Houdini in tow, Nichols edged forward to get a better look at this ‘dimensional doorway or time portal,’ as Pythagoras called the glitter on the far wall. Dimensional gateway or time portal be damned: hell was full of anomalous regions. You didn’t name them and claim them; you avoided them.

Houdini stared blankly, awestruck.

Nichols let out a strained, almost inaudible whisper: “Devil take me.”

Nichols’ concerns about team stability and Powell’s breakdown were instantly overshadowed. Satan’s demons could make a strong man void his bowels, but this…?

What in all the blazing netherworlds of creation was this? A willful incursion into hell – from the outside? Who'd want to do such a thing; more to the point, who *could?*

Nichols promised himself that the next time Welch looked at intel and told Nichols: "None of this means shit to me," Nichols was going to take sick leave, not volunteer to find out what was what. Welch was an operational master and the smartest damned soul that Nichols had ever met. But Welch had stayed home on this one, sending Nichols in his stead because Welch was busy trying to keep a lid on Satan's troubles. So, being Welch's right-hand man, Nichols got command on this operation, because he was accustomed to being sent on missions requiring field experience and Welch trusted Nichols to ride herd on whomever, whenever."

Harry Houdini knelt beside Pythagoras and asked him what the next step would be. Pythagoras said, *sotto voce,* a single word, "Freedom."

But Nichols heard it, loud and clear. Great. Mutiny. Here it was, the hidden agenda he'd been sensing: fools in hell are three-for-a-penny.

Still, mission trumps all. As the two conspirators talked, Nichols set up a multipurpose video surveillance camera to record multispectral digital images of the portal as well as the pool for analysis later. To insure that the information would survive even if they didn't, he sent the digital data back via ruggedized fiber-optic cable over the VHF line-of-sight data link to Achilles on the *Yamato.*

Have fun, Achilles. Only an ego of heroic proportions like yours could be jealous about missing this cluster. Pythagoras meanwhile, finished computing the exact length of rope needed to swing from the ledge to the twinkling point in space. Merkerson fired a depleted uranium piton, with climbing rope attached, into the base of the twinkling rock outcropping.

On impact, the rock-penetrating piton imploded at the base of the stalactite, embedding a brace that would hold if the rock was solid.

Putting his hellpad into his backpack, Pythagoras stepped forward, grabbed the rope and said, "Fraters, we extend the boundaries of knowledge from hell itself! I salute you!"

And the old dead Pythagoras stepped off the rock and swung, like a decrepit Errol Flynn, until he reached the nadir of his arc....

A large tentaclelike pseudopod shot straight up from the pulsating mass of flesh and congealed around Pythagoras, pulling the philosopher into its gelatinous mass. The climbing rope, rated for eight thousand pounds, snapped.

Pythagoras screamed.

Powell had regained consciousness. Now, seeing Pythagoras consumed, he crawled to the edge of the ledge. Before Nichols thought to intervene, Powell grabbed his entire satchel full of explosives, affixed a det cord and tossed the bag into the heart of the beast.

It 'swallowed.'

Then there was a phantasmagoric display as flesh and limbs and organs exploded into the air in a deafening mix of concussion and screeching. Writhing bits of flesh showered the pool, wriggling and pulsing as they returned to their source.

The pool devoured each and all, hungrily sprouting new razor-toothed mouths.

Everyone in the party fired at will, unloading several clips before realizing that the rounds, slamming mercilessly into the writhing protoplasm, had no effect.

Nichols watched Powell, not the pool, until Powell collapsed against the wall of the ledge, eyes glassy.

Nichols realized that the pool creature probably considered them a threat as it deliberately spewed forth a gilled and scaly humanoid, about seven feet tall, with a face like a carp, who proceeded to climb the sheer wall to their ledge.

Nichols fired his Desert Eagle into the scaly creature's crested head.

The creature fell back into the writhing pool and was lost.

Merkerson and Houdini were shouting that the only way to reach the time portal was to build a one-rope bridge and crawl across before the monster tried something else.

The protoplasm pool below spawned a man-sized lump of flesh, with arms and legs for locomotion but no other visible organs, which scrabbled across the cavern floor, away from its progenitor and down a tunnel at the cavern's base. Two more followed it.

Nichols let them go. He was conserving ammo, playing sentry while the other two readied the rope bridge. If the bridge failed, they'd all be dumped into the protoplasm pool, where they wouldn't exactly get dead. Not getting dead meant no express trip to Slab A, no way out of that pool. And Nichols had no intention of being stuck here in a pool of spare parts.

Something Nichols recognized crawled out of that pool: an ogre demon, with red skin, rippling muscles, a black spade beard, two horns on his head, fangs and claws. It too stormed out into one of the cave openings.

Nichols absently noted that each time a creature emerged from the pool, the glowing lights in the surrounding mist flickered and danced. Then he'd shoot each creature. It would fall down or fall back, more like a video game or training film than real life. After staking his line to the ledge with his piton and tying it down, Merkerson fired a depleted uranium piton at a stalactite about six meters out, and pulled himself, hand over hand, across to the stalactite.

Below, the creature spewed out two more gill-men. Nichols was grinning as he changed magazines and shot the gill-men before they could climb more than a few meters up the cliff face. He was counting rounds now. Each Desert Eagle clip had eight .44 magnum rounds, and he had only two clips left of the six he'd brought....

Merkerson took aim on the second stalactite that had been used by Pythagoras in his failed attempt across. His piton hit home, and he quickly tied off the end of the rope to a freshly-embedded spike. Re-attached, he painstakingly began the second leg of his trip.

Nichols kept one eye on Merkerson, the other on his targets and the rest of his team. Houdini had begun his commando crawl out from the ledge. When he was three-quarter of the way across to the first stalactite, trouble raised its damned head.

This menace was standard hellish issue: nine-foot, night-black, taloned, bat-winged and horned, it reminded Nichols of a Tartarosian. Its smooth skin glistened like fresh tar, and its body muscles rippled with great apparent strength.

As it rapidly climbed into the air toward Houdini, Nichols fired. Magnums fire dirty: smoke and flame belched from the

Desert Eagle's muzzle. The single magnum round ripped through the ebony demon's wing and it tumbled helplessly into the protoplasmic pool below.

Merkerson took the safety off his Ingram; the Mac-10 was now ready to rock and roll. He sank another piton into a stalactite about ten meters away.

The portal in the air shimmered like a summer's day.

Nichols saw Merkerson secure the piton just as he was targeted by a Heikegani crab with a human-faced carapace and the wings of a hummingbird. In life, Nichols had pulled duty in Japan: according to legend, each Heikegani held the soul of a samurai warrior killed in the battle of Dan-no-ura. It moved toward Merkerson. Nichols fired and missed, leaving him only six rounds.

"Merkerson, heads up!" Nichols yelled.

Merkerson grabbed his Ingram and followed the Heikegani's progress toward him through the MAC-10's scope. When the giant, winged crab was about ten feet away, Merkerson fired a continuous burst.

Nichols always loved the sound of a machine pistol burping: the creature, torn to shreds, tumbled headlong into the pool below.

As Merkerson resumed his crawl and Nichols shot four more hybrid crabs (leaving him two rounds in his clip); Houdini reached the first anchor point, and Merkerson got to the third stalactite and attached a safety line to it.

Eight feet from the opening.

Merkerson hammered a new spike and tied off the line that would complete the last leg of their journey. Houdini was at the halfway point. Merkerson had just begun his next crawl when another bat-winged demon arose from the abyss, followed by yet four more hybrid horrors.

Nichols immediately fired on the large demon, which left him one round and not much time to change clips when fractions of a second could mean an eternity as protoplasm in the pool below.

The other four hybrid horrors attacked Nichol's two suspended companions, two on one.

Houdini, anchored to the stalactite, fired his .45 at the winged crab closest to him. It shattered and fell. The second blind-sided him, slamming Houdini into the rock outcropping. He dropped his gun and his mouth opened wide as he gulped for air.

Nichols had one round left in his Desert Eagle and no time left at all. The hovering samurai crab was descending on the dazed Houdini. Nichols took careful aim and squeezed.

The crab splattered all over Houdini as it died, and Nichols had a moment to change clips.

Merkerson was flanked by two more crabs that came at him from opposite sides. He annihilated the wing of one with the Ingram.

It tumbled. By then, the second was upon him. Merkerson couldn't withstand the sudden impact. He dropped into a monkey crawl, but it couldn't save him. Merkerson lost first his balance and then the Ingram and the piton projector.

The creature lunged at his feet. Merkerson dropped his legs, hanging suspended from the line by his hands. As the creature made another spiraling pass at him, he hung by one hand and with the other, grabbed his climbing hammer.

Meanwhile, although he had eight more rounds, Nichols couldn't shoot at the crab or he'd likely hit Merkerson. Merkerson lodged his climbing hammer in the crab's carapace on the second lunge and lost that too. But crab and climber were still too close for Nichols to risk a shot.

As the crab spiraled in once more, Merkerson grabbed a survival knife from its scabbard and punched the razor-sharp knife into the creature's shell. The creature slammed into him, breaking his grip on the life line. Man and monster tumbled, each pummeling the other until they met the writhing surface of the protoplasmic pool.

The pool opened a hundred sudden mouths to consume its prey.

Nichols shouted, "Houdini! Get your ass back here. I can't protect you any better than I did Merkerson. I don't have enough ammo for every monster in hell. Out of there. Now! Move!"

Houdini called back, "No, my friend. Now is a time for daring. I shall leave this place, but not to return to hell." He then stood up and deftly tightrope-walked the entire distance to the third stalactite.

Below, the pool spewed out two more fish-faced gill-men. Nichols was staring in disbelief after the crazy escape artist, so he didn't see the first gill-man creeping up the rock face until it was almost upon him. "What? You're hungry? Want a snack? Here you go," Nichols said. He stepped back and, as the creature's head popped above the edge of the abyss, he shot it face first with the Desert Eagle.

He was getting cranky, he knew, but enough is enough. And this carnival was more than enough. Nichols shot the second creature in the top of the brainpan as it scrambled up the cliff toward him.

Fools in hell are ever at home: Houdini was now at the final stalactite. As he prepared a rope to swing the final few feet into the portal, a pair of night-black wings emerged and flew at him.

Nichols was losing count of his rounds, which he hardly ever did. He thought he had six rounds left. He fired twice at the demon's wings from the ledge but his .44 mag rounds didn't slow its ascent. And he knew he hit it. Both times. So now, maybe, he had, five, maybe four rounds in his clip and two clips on his belt before he was in deep shit here. When Nichols got home to New Hell, he was going to have a serious talk with Asmodeus, the demon king, about what demonkind was getting up to these days.

The black-winged demon arose at such an angle as to come between Houdini and the shimmering portal.

Then Nichols remembered Pythagoras recounting the Delphic Oracle's ravings about 'an opening between worlds, a Demon Gate.' *Demon Gate? For damned sure.* The portal that shimmered before him was this so-called Demon Gate.

Terrific. Now he could satisfy Welch's curiosity and Satan's need to know – if he lived long enough, or died clean and recycled to Slab A in the good old Mortuary. He'd even welcome the Undertaker's halitosis right now.

But there was still Houdini, unarmed except for a knife, who thought he could use the demon gate to escape. That figured: what's an escape artist want to do most of all in hell? Escape.

Nichols decided he'd shoot Houdini himself: it would be kinder.

Houdini was now positioning himself high on the stalactite, with his feet on the final piton driven by Merkerson.

Nichols couldn't risk wasting one of his bullets, and he didn't have a good shot at Houdini's head – yet.

Houdini was waiting for something, too. Poised. Ready for … what?

The black-winged demon flew to within five feet of him and Houdini jumped directly at it. His feet landed squarely on the demon's massive shoulders, between its wings. Pushing off from the demon's shoulder he vaulted into the portal – and was gone.

Vanished without a trace. Not even a disturbance of the portal to show he'd ever entered it.

The demon wheeled smoothly about, seeking new prey.

Four or five bullets in his gun; two eight-round clips on his belt. Big demon that seemed immune to gunshots. Nichols did the math. With great effort, he slung the catatonic Powell over his shoulder and ran for the inside of the tunnel. Somewhere back there was Powell's plasma rifle, lost in the melee. If Nichols had had that rifle, the argument with the big black demon could have gone differently.

Then the black demon was on top of him before Nichols could react.

Flailing its spiked tail, the demon impaled the unknowing Powell, disemboweling him as he ripped the unconscious man from Nichols' back. Nichols stumbled in the gore and his legs went out from under him.

He landed flat on his back. "Hey, Joe, come give me a hug."

The demon came on.

Cursing in Satan's name, lying in his companions entrails, Nichols emptied the remaining rounds in the Desert Eagle's magazine into the demon's face, shooting two-handed.

Nichols had been right: he had only had four rounds left, not five.

The demon reeled, the shock of the weapon knocking it back, and it tumbled from the cliff. The eviscerated body of Powell, still skewered on its tail, sped its descent into the proto-soup below. Nichols discarded his empty magazine and slapped a full one into the Eagle, whistling "Hey, Joe" softly between his teeth. With his hackles risen, determined not to look behind him in case looking at the protoplasm pool triggered the creation of the beasties, he grabbed the camera and scrambled up the tunnel as quickly as he could.

When the tunnel was once again nothing more than a crawlspace, nothing had flapped or slithered or bounded after him.

At a safe distance beyond the tunnel's mouth (if there was such a thing), he lobbed a frag grenade behind him. When the tunnel mouth didn't collapse, he lobbed a second, then a third, until there was enough rubble to block the opening.

Bottled up tight – at least for now.

He had one magazine in his Desert Eagle and one in his belt. The plasma rifle was long gone, left on the ledge, dropped over the edge, or grabbed by crazy Powell. He took only the memory card from the camera and ditched the rest. He still had a climbing hammer, his survival knife, plenty of line, carabiners, plain pitons, his spelunker's helmet, clips for the Uzi he no longer had, three more grenades, some det cord and the comm link. He used the fiber-optic line to send the data he'd recorded and an encoded message through the fiber-optic line to Achilles – 'Code 2:120/Code Red/Code Black.' Then he began climbing back to the beach. Though his back was wrenched and both his legs hurt like hell, he might make it out of here yet.

Or at least had a damned good chance of it.

Just then heard a noise behind, and looked back: three gill-men had broken through the rubble blocking the tunnel's mouth. And behind them rolled a Jeep-sized spherical glob.

*

Nichols' signal for emergency pickup pleased Achilles, who was tired of drinking no-proof Saki with off-duty Japanese crew members and hoping for a little action, although he was startled by Nichol's request for a Code Red/Code Black.

In the Huey, Achilles grinned as he laid the special backpack on the seat beside him … just as Nichols had requested. Then he started his safety check, preparing to return to the island.

*

Nichols was running as fast as he could, but each stride across the sand made his angry leg muscles burn more.

Somehow he must keep ahead of the gill-men chasing him, with a weird ball of amorphous flesh behind them. A well-placed round from his Desert Eagle might stop one of the gill-men, but then they'd be reabsorbed into the sphere.

The gill-men with their spherical caboose relentlessly pursued him. He was out of grenades and nearly out of adrenaline.

Nichols considered escaping into the surf. But the surf was black and oddly viscous along the beach. The waves rolling near shore resembled the protoplasm in the pool. He couldn't risk it.

He tried raising Achilles via comm link, but the line was jammed by someone or something. If Achilles hadn't received his original distress call, Nichols was fucked.

Too tired. Lungs aching. Despite his pursuers, he had to stop, catch his breath. He couldn't outrun those things forever.

So.... Nichols took off his helmet and began emptying the powder from his remaining Uzi rounds. Fingers shaking, he cobbled together a fragmentation bomb, using his helmet, the brass, the spikes and the detonation cord.

He threw it like a bowling ball. It rolled toward the gill-men and the blob, and exploded between them. Pieces of blob and gill-men showered the beach.

As Nichols was already running toward his extraction point, slowly and erratically, black shadow covered him. He looked up and saw a bat winged demon.

If it had a face, it was smiling. It swooped down, smashing into his back with its claws.

The impact knocked him to the sand. Its claws had torn his clothes. Blood ran down his back. Trying to catch his breath, he grabbed his pistol.

The demon dived at him.

His lives flashed before him. Bullets ripped the air. The Huey's thirty millimeter Gatling fire center punched the creature and pushed it backward as it tumbled to the beach. Nichols shielded his face from the Huey's sandy rotor-wash.

He could see Achilles in the cockpit. Scrambling into the chopper, trying to catch his breath, he gasped, "Did you bring it?"

Achilles replied, "As the devil is my witness." He slapped at the backpack beside him. Achilles was too savvy to ask what had happened to the rest of Nichols' team.

Nichols grabbed the backpack and cradled it, sliding into the second seat, then began to prepare its contents.

When it was prepared, he gave Achilles the coordinates and got ready to lean out the door.

*

A mushroom cloud blossomed behind the Huey.

Achilles cursed as its electromagnetic pulse took out several electronic systems, including the Huey's stealth capability. Panels sparked as backup systems tried to compensate.

The thirty-kiloton nuclear munition had done its job and they were still aloft. Almost home free.

When the *Yamato* came in sight, Nichols was counting his cuts and bruises.

As Achilles tried to raise the *Yamato* on the comm link, he heard a single scream in Japanese in his helmet's headset, *"Umibōzu!"*

As they watched, a huge tentacle wrapped itself around the great battleship and pulled it into the sea.

Achilles said flatly, "We may not have enough fuel to make it to safety. Closest landfall is the mainland. Some call it TazzMania. Or the ice floes of the south polar region. Nobody home to help us, either place."

"Try TazzMania and hope we don't have to swim part of the way." Nichols started ditching anything expendable, to lighten the Huey's load. If he drowned, he'd make it back to Slab A and the Undertaker, which was the best death he'd been offered today. Then Nichols buried his helmeted head in his hands waiting for whatever would come to pass.

*

On Halloween night, a delegation from the Society of American Magicians held its yearly ritual, encircling the grave of their past president, Harry Houdini.

Every year they kept this vigil, on the anniversary of Houdini's death, in hopes that he would send them a sign from the great beyond. A lawyer representing the Committee for the Scientific Investigation of Claims of the Paranormal (CSICOP), no friend of the Society, attended, assuring that the magicians played no tricks.

The ritual's climax was to break a wand in half. As the ranking magician stepped forward, flexing his wand dramatically, Houdini's grave was encircled with light.

The magicians reflexively covered their eyes. Within the circle of light, a figure appeared. An intense and familiar figure: Harry Houdini.

Houdini reached forward. Snatching the wand from the ranking magician, Houdini held it before his face and bowed deeply.

The crowd of magicians muttered and ramped, awaiting the inevitable speech from the triumphant Houdini or whoever had staged this grand illusion.

Before Houdini could straighten up, the night sky cracked apart in a burst of light; a hole opened; from the bright hole came two huge black talons.

The lawyer from CSICOP lunged forward and grabbed Houdini around the waist as those talons pierced Houdini's shoulders. The talons lifted Houdini up into the sky, the lawyer still clinging to his waist.

The hole was gone. The light was gone. Houdini was gone. And so was the lawyer.

The bemused magicians looked at the grave, at the sky, and then sadly at one another.

No one would ever believe them.

Appellate Angel

by

Edward McKeown

Arkiel, the angel, stood and tucked his wings behind his suit jacket, picked up his briefcase and left his quarters, headed for the Hall of Injustice. In hell, court was held every Sinday: there was literally no rest for the wicked, including, unfortunately, him. Arkiel was an angel sentenced to hell; he worked here. Being cast down was harsh punishment, he felt, for teaching humans forbidden knowledge, taking a woman to wife, begetting a nephil, and then, eons later, indulging in a few weeks' dalliance with a visiting succubus. Mating with human women and teaching forbidden knowledge weren't the worst things an angel could do. There were the minor downcast, fallen angels such as he, watchers and helpers of humanity, and then there were the great fallen angels who'd contested with the Highest…. Arkiel wasn't all-powerful. The demonic temptress had been on earth, carrying a message when he'd chanced on her in a valley he was watching. After that, well … succubi were what they were and while Arkiel had never been a human, his animus was male. At the time it had seemed worth the risk.

Now, on another dreary Sinday, their spectacular pleasures seemed fleeting compared to his continuing punishment. He opened the door of the transients' compound and stepped into hell proper. Before him lay Pandemonium, stretching out to the horizon. An enormous city, where all the taxi drivers were from NYC, all the trains were run by Slamtrack and the potholes had been known to eat vehicles and occupants alike. The street shimmered in the heat; moans and shrieks filled the air.

His chauffeured black limo waited for him at the curb.

Gravelog, his scaly-skinned demon driver, opened the door and Arkiel slid inside. As usual, the rehabilitated demon said little. He saved his voice for the relentless, and for him, joyful task of howling abuse at the other denizens of hell during the commute. With demonic driving, they made it in record time to the courthouse, a massive, columned, white-speckled granite edifice from whose upper floors unsuccessful litigants were often defenestrated.

Arkiel got out of the limo and walked up the front steps, nodding to the uniformed guards who stared vacantly at the damned souls queuing up for court. The officers passed him through.

"Have a hell of a day, counselor," said one sergeant, a ghastly soul with haunted eyes who had died only days before full retirement.

Arkiel sighed. The sergeant always said that to him. A bailiff let the angel into his assigned courtroom. He took his seat and unpacked his brief at the prosecutor's table. His paralegal was absent today, but Arkiel was well-prepared and needed no help with today's case.

The doors swung open and Arkiel's plans for an early lunch flew out the window as the androgynous demon, Yoko, one of hell's highest-ranking advocates of evil, walked in. The demon wore an impeccably tailored suit and too much jewelry. It was followed by its client, an Aztec priest in his ceremonial robe of flayed human skin – in hell, the skin was his own.

Trailing them was a succubus, and like *all* succubi, she was enough to raise the dead, in every sense. She wore a pin-striped jacket and Arkiel couldn't tell if she wore tights on her fantastic legs or merely dye. Her tail with its heart-shaped tip floated behind her; she was erotic perfection incarnate: only the best for Yoko, hell's ranking demon of lust.

Yoko gave him a jagged smile that suggested the demon knew every detail of why the angel had been assigned here. The three seated themselves on the defense side.

The doors behind the dais opened and in floated a softly glowing ball the size of a man. Its dull gray surface resembled the clouds of a summer storm.

A bailiff and a skeletal clerk followed it. "All rise," the bailiff intoned. "The Appellate Section of the Grand Court of Hell, Pandemonium Division, is now in session."

Arkiel stood, leaning forward on the table in front of him,

grateful for loose trousers. The succubus smiled and winked at him. He concentrated on thoughts of ice and snow, remembering his last case in Niffelheim.

The skeletal clerk, dressed in black, frowned. "Are counsels present and ready in the matter of Hell versus Huemac?"

"Demon for the defense is ready," Yoko said.

"The prosecution is ready," Arkiel said.

"Oral argument having been requested," a somber voice rolled from the cloudy ball atop the dais, "counsel for the defense may proceed."

"Oh, Great Demonic Being –" Yoko began in wheedling tones.

"'Judge' will do," said the ball.

"Ah, yes, Judge. We merely wanted to demonstrate our respect for this high court of hell."

Arkiel sighed – it was going to be one of *those* cases.

"We come before you, in the final act of this longest-running case on the docket," Yoko said, "to finally make an end to these persecutions of my client, Priest Huemac, wrongfully convicted –"

Arkiel shot to his feet, ignoring the stirring in his trousers, which was adding to his damnation with every thrill he felt: lust was sin for an angel, and Arkiel was living the doom.

"Objection. My learned colleague seeks to distort the record. There is no question of guilt in this matter, only severity of the sentence. It is uncontested that Huemac slaughtered four thousand, one hundred and fourteen men, women and children in ritual human sacrifice."

"Ah, but the defense," Yoko said, advancing around the table, "contends that those are merely facts and separate from the issue of guilt."

"Counselor Arkiel," the judge said, his glow brightening, "please remember this is an appellate court with no jury to sway. Displays of righteous anger only waste the court's time. I will hear this."

Wonderful, Arkiel thought, *the great glowing gasbag is in a mood today.* "Yes, Judge."

"Judge," Yoko resumed, "my client is a man of true faith. His people looked to him, with approval – with *approval*, mind you – to explain the world to them, for protection from the elements, from their enemies, from the supernatural. It is true that, as with so many earthly religions, the early practices were somewhat … sanguinary. But whose fault is that? What power is it that blocks the eyes of men to the truth and misleads them?"

"That would be demons like you and your master," Arkiel interjected.

Yoko sighed theatrically. "Judge, could you remind the learned advocate of the concept of a rhetorical question?"

"Counselor Arkiel, please restrain yourself."

"Yes, Judge."

"But to address the point raised," Yoko continued, "even my dark master is a creation of heaven and operates under the mandate of the Creator. All the Almighty need do is raise its little finger to lift the curtain hiding the truth, and we demons would be ended.

"I submit that my client," Yoko turned to the Aztec, placing one clawed hand on each of the small, dark man's shoulders, "is a good and devout man, a pillar of his community, indeed at the apex of his society. He was falsely led, by a religion he merely inherited from his parents before him. Through innocent error and the primitive state of his culture, he did not know better. The requisite evil intent for the severe punishments of hell is simply not there. We beg this court to overturn this sentence and release my client from further torment."

"Counselor Arkiel?" the judge said.

Arkiel rose, trying to hold back his anger. "'A pillar of his community?' Indeed, he took members of that community, tied them to pillars, and had their intestines pulled out. 'At the apex of his society?' Too true. He stood at the apex of their ziggurats and with a piece of sharpened rock, ripped through their living skin, cracked their ribs and dug out their internal organs before their dying eyes, for no purpose –"

"He did not know that," Yoko said, leaping up. "He thought he was warding off famines and drought –"

"Silence, Counselor Yoko. You've had your say."

"Your Honor," Arkiel said, pacing before his table, "if the universe has one immutable law, it is that to kill without need, slowly, with the intent of causing pain, as did this man –" the angel jabbed his finger at the dark-eyed priest, "– is inherently evil. The youngest children quickly learn that to hurt others is wrong and wrongs are punished. Only adults seek to find justification to excuse evil behavior.

"Counselor Yoko would have us sympathize with this butcher of humans. I ask you to take a different perspective. You are a man, a woman, or even a child, seized by men dressed in jaguar skins for no reason other than being too close to the land of this priest. Sometime later you are dragged in front of a blood-maddened mob to the top of a ziggurat. You are thrown onto a slab before a crowd hungry for blood and entertainment. Then this… this… priest, begins to vivisect you … and smiles while he does it."

"Counselor, enough theatrics, confine yourself to the case," said the glowing ball.

"But that *is* the case, Judge. Counselor Yoko seeks to excuse evil with sophistry, invoking cultural relativism, on the grounds that terror, violence and ignorance were the norm in this priest's world. How many other societies, with even less understanding of the universe, developed humane punishments, instead of rituals of institutionalized murder that required them to war with all other peoples to feed their cultural appetite for human sacrifice?

"Plainly stated, Judge, there is no new evidence to consider in this appeal. Evil has been done and is again admitted by the defense. This issue has been raised and disposed of by this august court before. This case is no different from the cases of millions of damned souls in hell who are currently being gassed, shot, starved and worked to death repeatedly, suffering the same torments they inflicted on others in life. If this court respects its own precedents, it can show no more mercy to this villain than he showed to those under his knife."

The globe pulsed with more light and less gray. *"Surrebuttal,* Counselor Yoko, to Counselor Arkiel's appeal to *stare decis?"*

"Surely, Judge," Yoko rose and said smoothly, "there can be no comparison between those new dead penitents to whom my colleague alludes – who were beneficiaries of the Enlightenment and other moral advancements – and my client's Neolithic culture. Look at him. Can you hold him to the standard of people raised in the age of Einstein, Gandhi, and so many other humanitarians?

"My client was merely a cog in a machine, following orders.

His choices were to comply with the norms of his society or end up on those very same sacrificial altars. How easy it is for us here, safe, to say how bravely we would have resisted evil.

"'We would not have wielded the knife. We would not have fired the rifle. We would not have turned on the gas.' Hypocrisy!" said the demon. "All beings are entitled to survive. There was no resistance movement for Huemac to join. Yes, it is easy for us to be brave here. Even accepting that my client had any awareness that his acts were evil, he had no choice."

"Well argued," the glowing judge said.

"If I may, Judge," Arkiel said. "Counselor Yoko has indeed argued well, saving the best arguments for last and they merit a response."

"All right, Counselor, but make it snappy," the judge allowed.

"My colleague seeks to excuse Huemac for his Neolithic culture, as if kindness and decency are inventions of later societies. The earliest hominids, who shared their food, and cared for the elderly when they were no longer useful, were more moral than the people of many technologically-advanced countries.

"Man is gifted with choices. While this fiend in human form, or Torquemada, or Jim Jones may claim the mantle of heaven to exonerate their actions, heaven denies them. Humans have free will and must lift the curtain on good and evil themselves. It is ludicrous to claim that any person can believe cutting apart another person is not evil.

"'I was just following orders.' 'I was given the choice of being victim or victimizer.' Can expediency excuse evil? Can we exonerate a man of evil-doing because that evil was done while choosing between his own life and the lives of others?

"Each day that choice of self or other is made a million times. The universe does not protect one from choices, or from consequences. You're not automatically rewarded for making the right choice.

"Anne Frank died young; the man who turned her in lived a long life, in the home he denied her. Yet who would choose to be that man?

"Huemac saved his own life at the cost of over four thousand other lives. The price was too high. His enjoyment of the sufferings of his victims, documented by those victims themselves, is too well-established to ignore.

"'I was just following orders,' excuses nothing. 'It was them or me.' Well, some sympathize with that argument. I submit that this case merits no sympathy. To each soul may come the choice to succeed in a bad cause or be destroyed in a good one.

"This case has been delayed by every conceivable legal device for too long. Let justice be done now."

Yoko rose, black eyes gleaming. "To paraphrase Melville:

> 'Is it I, God, or who that lifts this arm? But if the great sun move not of himself; but is as an errand-boy in heaven; nor one single star can revolve, but by some invisible power; how then can this one small heart beat; this one small brain think thoughts; unless God does that beating, does that thinking, does that living, and not I. By heaven, man, we are turned round and round in this world, like yonder windlass, and Fate is the handspike. And all the time, lo! that smiling sky, and this unsounded sea! Look! see yon Albicore! who put it into him to chase and fang that flying-fish? Where do murderers go, man! Who's to doom, when the judge himself is dragged to the bar?'

"Counselor Arkiel hands out mighty burdens to humanity. Let him who is without sin cast the first stone. Yet even the appellate angel falls short of these marks, or he would not be cast down among us damned souls. He wants humans to be angels while he himself, giving in to temptation, is a fallen angel."

A rumble rolled from the judge. "No *ad hominem* attacks, Counselor Yoko, or I will hold you in contempt. Arkiel is cast down for lust; he is no fallen angel who contested with God."

"I thank Your Honor," Arkiel said. "I am glad the court knows the difference between a fallen angel and one who has merely been cast down for a time to pay penance. Indeed, I am grateful to my learned adversary for bringing a 'succubus slash paralegal' to court today. Perhaps my own transgressions seem more … understandable with her standing there and, after all, I harmed no one else –"

"And that will be quite enough digression, counselor," the judge said, a prim note creeping into the voice of the glowing ball.

"Ahem. Yes, sir."

"The court has heard sufficient for its purposes. This appeal is denied. The defendant is to be taken immediately to continue serving his sentence. He will be sacrificed as he sacrificed others … four thousand, one hundred and fourteen times."

Huemac gave an anguished scream and sank to the polished marble floor.

"Let me lodge but one more plea before this learned court," Yoko said. "Fifty-seven of his sacrifices died of natural causes while being dragged … er … accompanied to the temple. Another thirty-two suffered mental collapse and never knew what disemboweled them."

"Counselor Arkiel?"

"The prosecution does not see how scaring a person to death is a mitigating factor: no reduction of sentence is appropriate. As regards mental collapse, so long as he absorbs the suffering of the families, we raise no objection."

Yoko grimaced. "So stipulated."

Huemac's mouth opened but no sound came out.

Arkiel looked down at Huemac. "I'd save those mental collapses for the end. Give yourself something to look forward to."

The brazen doors at the far end of the courtroom were flung open. Five demons, caricatures of the priest with flayed skin robes and large obsidian daggers, seized Huemac and dragged him out. The doors led not to Pandemonium but to a verdant jungle under a harsh red sky. Stone buildings lined a road leading to a ziggurat. People thronging the streets stared silently: Huemac's victims and their loved ones, waiting for their revenge. The doors clanged shut on Huemac amid the throng and the Neolithic vista.

"Court adjourned," said the globe, drifting toward its chambers.

"All rise," demanded the bailiff.

Arkiel leaned against the table as Yoko and the succubus rose.

Yoko looked at the paralegal, saying, "Would you mind waiting outside, honey? I have to congratulate opposing counsel and you might prove to be too much distraction for Arkiel."

She laughed, a tinkling sound like crystal near a waterfall.

Arkiel watched appreciatively as she swayed out of the courtroom.

Yoko walked over, extending a red-clawed hand. "Well done, Arkiel, though you did start with the upper hand."

"You argued well too. I was worried by the victim/victimizer speech."

"Nah, the guy was too much of a prick. He deserved the obsidian enema he has coming."

"What, no sympathy for your client?"

"That little shit? No, really not much for any of 'em. I mean, I've got a job to do."

An odd thought struck Arkiel. "I know how I got here. How did you?"

The demon looked embarrassed. "Truth is, kind of the same thing, opposite side. I mean the cut on me is I'm too … sexy for a demon. So I drew this job, defending these no-account little weasels. Screw them, I say."

"Looks like we have more in common than I suspected."

"Maybe even more than you think, Angel. You know, a body could get used to Hell. There are some pretty decent parts. Yeah, admittedly they're in the 'burbs and the commute is … well, hell."

"What are you saying?" Arkiel asked.

"Just that there's two sides to the bar and maybe less difference than you expect. I could use an advocate with your passion and intelligence. I can't trust anybody at my firm. They're all evil, of course. After all, hell is other people, just like Sartre said. It would be nice to have a straight guy on the team."

Arkiel laughed. "Oh, please, Yoko. Me? Work for a law firm run by the demon of lust? Not even a downcast angel would stoop that low, especially one with a clemency review coming up."

"Come on," Yoko said. "Tell me you won't miss the old place, the variety, the action."

"I'm in hell," Arkiel shouted. "Hell, hell, hell!"

"Relax, Arkiel. I'm just saying that after hell, heaven would bore you silly – if you ever got there. Anyway, good case, and I'll see you around the circuit."

"Sure, Counselor."

Yoko left and Arkiel gathered up his things, bemused by his

conversation with the demonic advocate. Buoyed by his win, he only barely winced when the guard sergeant said, "Have a hell of a night, Counselor."

Gravelog was out front with the limo but he wasn't alone. Yoko's succubus was there, leaning against the fender, studying Arkiel with ruby eyes.

He walked up, holding his briefcase in front of him, thinking icy cold thoughts, baseball scores and anything else that could distract him. Every time his body betrayed him, his sentence in hell got longer.

"Hello," she said in a voice that thrummed on his nerves.

"Can I help you?"

"I do hope so. I'm Malfean, and I'm bored, lonely and new in Pandemonium with a Sinday night to kill and no one to help me." She reached forward and slipped a card into his lapel pocket. "That's my number. Call me. I might bc waiting." She strutted off, her heart-shaped tail tip swaying from side-to-side while three cars piled into each other on the other side of the street.

Arkiel recovered the power of speech and looked at Gravelog. "I'm never getting out of here. Am I?"

The homely demon looked back at him. "They tell me there's always hope, sir."

With Enemies Like These

by

David L. Burkhead

Wendell waited in the bushes and rubbed at his sore back. A long night's work had paid off. The hastily dammed stream (not the clear stream of a mountain brook as he'd known in life, but one of the fetid streams common in hell) had overflowed its banks and flooded the road. After flowing across the road the stream tumbled over a low bluff into a ravine. The heavy rains of the day before, now faded to a light sprinkle, made the flooding seem plausible.

The target would be coming soon and Wendell could then spring the second part of the trap.

How had he gotten involved in this plot? Wendell wondered. First the long years working in research at the Hall of Injustice, then finally being assigned to try cases … but scarcely had he begun litigating when he was fired. Each step after that had led inexorably to this point but Wendell still could not see just where he had taken the wrong turn. The plot, whatever it was, would fail – they always did – and where would that leave Wendell?

The light rain, threatening to turn into sleet, had no answer.

Wendell assumed he was a sacrificial goat – working alone, on a minor mission, without adequate equipment or support. Nothing ever went right in hell, at least not completely. Someone must have thought that setting up Wendell to fail might allow some more critical part of the overall plot, whatever it was, to work.

Or maybe the plot was just run by idiots.

Wendell ceased massaging his back at the drone of an approaching car. The time was right. This could be the target.

A dingy yellow car, exactly matching the description Wendell had been given, rounded a bend in the road and came into view, blue smoke pouring from its exhaust. As it neared the flooded section of road, it slowed to a stop.

As the car started to reverse, Wendell pulled the trip cord that activated the second part of the trap. Spiked boards shot out from concealment on the roadside just in time for the car to back over them, puncturing three of the car's four tires before the driver could stop. From his own concealment, Wendell dashed for the car as it spun once before coming to rest against a large rock.

The driver's door was already opening as Wendell reached the car. He grabbed the driver's arm and pulled. The driver of the car managed to stay on his feet as Wendell pulled him from the car.

"Unhand me, sir." Then, impossibly, the driver jerked free of Wendell's grip before Wendell could twist him to the ground.

Wendell reached for a new grip with his left hand while his right sought the large knife suspended from his belt. The driver, in turn, grabbed for Wendell's arms catching both. Wendell, trying to jerk his own arms free, was surprised at just how strong the other was.

They grappled for some time before Wendell stepped backward to find empty air under his foot. He fell, clutching the other and taking him with him.

The fall took an awfully long time.

*

Wendell woke flat on his back on stony ground. His chest felt as if somebody had lit a fire in it; his right arm burned as if it had been used for kindling. At least he wasn't on the Undertaker's table. So he had survived the fall.

It was cold here, wherever "here" was – not freezing, but decidedly uncomfortable.

Wendell opened his eyes. The first impression was one of gray: fog and mist in a dim twilight. Occasionally, shadows moved in the mist. He looked himself over. No fire, just a remarkable burning pain with every breath and every movement. *Oh. Broken ribs.* Then the burning in his arm would be.... He tried to move it. *Yes. Broken arm.*

"Awake at last?" The voice came from behind him.

Trying not to move his body and arm, Wendell twisted his head to see who had spoken. It was his target, the person he had been assigned to capture. The target, who had Wendell's knife and sidearm, was wearing his greatcoat and sitting cross-legged, watching him.

"I know you," the target said, "the author of that book everyone was having vapors over. 'The Common Law' wasn't it?"

"That was a long time ago," Wendell said.

"Oliver Wendell Holmes, Jr.," the target said. "Upstart young justice on the Massachusetts Supreme Court."

"You're out of date." Suppressing a groan, Wendell used his good arm to push his torso upright. Now he was panting in pain, sitting on the rocky ground. "I was an Associate Justice on the U.S. Supreme Court before I died."

"Supreme Court Justice? That quick? Or, no, not so quick. Time does run funny here."

"Oh?"

"I've only been here maybe … a year or so, I think. You?"

"Longer than that. A lot longer."

The target waved a hand. "Doesn't matter. So they made you a Supreme Court Justice? Then the country really was going to hell. Appointing someone who thought that the whim of the moment superseded the written law of the land – including the Constitution – to the highest court in the land? Disaster waiting to happen."

"That's *not* what I wrote," Wendell said.

"No, but it's where what you wrote leads, inevitably. And now the high and mighty Yankee Supreme Court Justice is reduced to kidnapping – or worse." The target, drew Wendell's sidearm, a revolver, similar to the ones Wendell had used during the war, and sighted along the barrel. "Was it kidnapping? Or murder?"

"Some people wanted to know what you know about current operations in the Hall of Injustice. Nothing personal. And you have the advantage of me, sir. You know me but I am afraid I do *not* know you. Who were you? Who are you?"

"Nobody important. Not then, not now. William Simpson, William Dunlap Simpson. Lieutenant Colonel William Dunlap Simpson, Fourteenth South Carolina Volunteers."

"Um."

"Do you want to know why I haven't sent you to the Undertaker, Holmes?" Simpson rose to his feet. "Do you really want to know?"

"Whether I do or not, it's quite clear you want to tell me." Holmes clenched his teeth to prevent their chattering. The cold was starting to get to him.

"You're right I do." Simpson waved an arm expansively. "Look around you, Holmes. Take a good look."

They were on a small hillock; the mists blocked vision more than fifty yards or so in any direction. One shadow was becoming larger and more distinct, approaching them.

"You're not going very far with that arm and those ribs," Simpson said before Wendell could mention the approaching shadow. "It's cold enough for exposure to kill you, but not cold enough for it to do so quickly. You are going to spend a long time dying, Justice Holmes, and I want you to think about me the entire time."

The shadow resolved into an emaciated man dressed in heavy furs. "Give me food," the man said. "Please. I beg of you."

Simpson started and turned to face the man. "Get away, you." He shoved the man away.

The man stumbled and fell, rolling down the hill. Out of sight in the mists they heard the sound of thrashing and screams, then silence.

"What did you do that for?" Holmes said. "All he wanted was food."

"Well, we don't have any," Simpson said, then stopped. "Wait a minute. You understood him?"

"Of course. Didn't you?"

"Pure gibberish. Sounded vaguely … German maybe?"

"I heard English," Holmes said, "the English of the Boston of my youth."

Simpson shook his head and sat back down. "Somebody's playing games with us. Looks like I need to keep you alive for a while."

*

Wendell had his greatcoat back. Although he still felt the cold, his teeth had stopped chattering.

"We haven't got anything to splint that arm," Simpson said. "You'll just have to tuck your hand in the belt and try to keep it still."

"I'll manage," Wendell said.

"You'd better. Having someone who understands the local

gibberish while I try to find my way out of here is a convenience, not a necessity. Don't become 'inconvenient.'"

Wendell nodded and did as Simpson had suggested. With his arm thrust as far as he could through the waistband and the belt cinched tight around it, his arm stayed fairly still. The pain was a railroad spike driven through his arm with each step. "Which way do we go, Simpson?"

"Down the way that fellow fell," Simpson said. "Now that I know you can talk to him, he may have some answers for us – if he's still alive."

Wendell did not say that being able to understand the people here did not mean he could talk to them. Better not to say anything that might make Simpson decide he was "inconvenient."

A few yards down the hill, Wendell froze. A large snake lay curled on the ground a few more yards further along, barely visible in the fog. "Careful," he said.

"I see it," Simpson said. "This way." Simpson veered to the left, but they proceeded scarcely five more yards before another snake came into view. Simpson veered again but this time two snakes lay in their path.

Simpson stopped. "Where did all these snakes come from?"

"We're in one of the lower hells," Wendell said, "one that features a lot of snakes, I would say." He looked around, then back up the hill. "They seem to avoid the hilltops."

"It's a bit warmer down here," Simpson said. "Snakes don't like the cold. I expect we'll find more as we go down the hill."

"Then how are we going to get anywhere?"

Simpson cast Wendell a look of mixed pity and disgust. "City boy, aren't you? Snakes are cold blooded. When it gets cold they go torpid." Simpson knelt to examine one of the snakes in front of him. "As long as you watch where you put your feet and don't step on them, they won't bother you." He stood up. "Let's go."

Wendell hesitated.

Simpson looked back. "Or not. It's up to you."

Despite the chill, Wendell licked sweat from his upper lip and followed Simpson down the hill.

*

"We're going in circles," Wendell said. The snakes had

become a virtual carpet over the muddy ground as they got to the lower reaches of the valley, requiring care to avoid stepping on any. True to Simpson's word, however, the snakes had remained still.

"Nonsense. We may be wandering around a bit but...."

"That's the third time we've passed that hill."

Simpson sighed. "I didn't want to admit it, but I think you're right. It's this fog. It's hard to keep a straight line if you can't see where you've been or where you're going." He stooped to look more closely at one of the snakes. "Now that's something. Come take a look."

"I'd rather not," Wendell said.

Simpson looked back over his shoulder. "Developing a case of Yankee Chills on me? Come take a look. I promise you won't get bit."

Wendell crept forward and knelt next to Simpson.

"Look at that," Simpson said, pointing at one of the snakes.

Wendell did not recognize the species of snake. It lay with its head tilted to one side, its mouth open, its fangs extended. As Wendell watched, a teardrop slowly grew at the end of one of the fangs, then fell to the muddy ground.

"Do you think this mud is all from...?" Simpson reached down and touched the mud with one finger.

"Jehoshaphat!" he shouted, springing to his feet, shaking his hand. He caught himself before taking a step back.

Wendell stood and watched warily as, with teeth clenched, Simpson swore while continuing to shake his hand. Eventually Simpson stopped and raised his hand to examine the finger. From where he stood, Wendell could see an angry red blister growing at its tip.

"Snake venom," Simpson said. "All this mud is from snake venom, and worse than any I've ever heard tell of." He raised the finger toward his mouth, then apparently thought better of it.

"Hadn't you better, I don't know, suck out the poison or something?"

"I wasn't bit, Holmes. This –" he held out the blistered finger, "– was simply the venom in the mud. Imagine what it would do to the inside of your mouth. Still, I suppose I should do something." Simpson drew Holmes' knife and, with a quick stroke, sliced open the tip of his finger. He let the finger drop to his side, where it dripped blood in a steady stream to the mud at their feet. "We have to get out of here." He shook his head. "But finding our way...."

Wendell grinned. "You may know snakes, Colonel, but do you know your Euclid?"

*

"This had better work, Holmes," Simpson said.

"No reason why it shouldn't," Wendell said. "It should at least keep us going in a straight line. Whether that straight line leads anywhere or not is another matter."

They had climbed to a nearby hilltop and gathered as many rocks as they could carry. At Wendell's direction, Simpson had built a small pile of rocks. They had then proceeded down the hill about half the distance. There, where the pile was still visible, they built a second pile of rocks. From that point they continued downhill, glancing back frequently to ensure that they stayed in line with the two rock piles. When the first pile was just barely visible, they made a new rock pile, in line with the first two. Whenever they ran out of rocks, they'd make the long, weary trudge back to the last hillock they had passed to gather more.

The stream caught them by surprise: a small, fast-flowing stream, clear and inviting.

"I can't remember the last time I was so thirsty," Simpson said, "but somehow I'm not inclined to take a drink."

Wendell looked around at the snakes, dozens in view. They had passed thousands in their trek, all dripping venom onto the ground. "Can't say as I am, either."

"Back in the army, the sergeants always said to dig the latrines downstream of the camp."

Wendell nodded. "It made the coffee taste better."

Simpson laughed, "Yours too, eh?"

"What did you expect?" Wendell sighed. "It was the same army before ... well, before things went terribly wrong."

"'Before things went terribly wrong,' indeed." Simpson shook his head sadly. "That's one way to put it. A country torn apart by war and more than half a million dead."

"Follow the stream?" Wendell waved in the direction of the stream's flow.

Simpson nodded. "Follow the stream."

After several minutes of walking along the stream, Simpson said, "I suppose there's the quick way out of here."

Wendell stopped. "Quick way?"

Simpson turned to face him. "The Undertaker."

"Have you actually *been* to the Undertaker?"

"Well, no, but…."

Wendell shook his head. "I have. Several times. It's not pleasant."

"Worse than this?" Simpson's gesture took in their surroundings, the snakes, and the probably poisonous stream.

Wendell nodded. "Worse than this. Besides…." He stopped.

"Besides?"

"Every time I'm restored, I end up waist deep in that same damn lake of boiling blood. Every time."

"Good Lord!"

"I guess it's some kind of personal punishment," Wendell said. "I have no idea what I did to deserve it, though."

"What do you do when you end up there?"

Wendell sighed and shook his head. "Mostly I scream a lot. Eventually, I'm able to drag myself out and make my way back to New Hell. Last time, though, well, looks like I was taken in by the wrong crowd." And the plot he had been pulled into had put him here, where one incautious step could send him right back to the Undertaker and the lake of boiling blood. Yet. again.

The dim, unchanging light made time hard to judge, but Wendell guessed another hour had passed before Simpson hauled up short. "What's our supply of rocks like?"

"My pockets are full," Wendell said. "Why?"

"I think I see some color over there." Simpson pointed in the direction of a looming shadow in the distance, a shadow that seemed to go up forever.

Wendell squinted but all he could see was gray, darker where the shadow was, and lighter elsewhere. "Your eyes must be better than mine."

Some time later, Wendell carefully stepped over yet another snake. "Are the snakes getting thicker here?"

Simpson didn't answer.

"Colonel?" Wendell looked up and froze.

While Wendell had been watching the ground for the increasingly numerous snakes, the shadow ahead of them had resolved into the largest tree Wendell had ever seen, its trunk so wide that its expanse was lost in the fog. Its height? Well, there was no imagining where the tree's canopy might end, somewhere above them.

It was not, however, only the tree that drew Wendell's attention. There was a snake gnawing on the tree's root. And what a snake. The head alone was the size of a two-story house. The body? The body of the snake was lost in the distance. How far it extended Wendell did not know. The snake was the source of the color that Simpson had said he saw. Its head was black with a bright yellow band around the neck. The body alternated in bands of black, then yellow, then red with irregular black spots, then yellow, then black once more.

Simpson stood frozen, staring at the snake. "Red touches black, he's a friend of Jack." Simpson whispered, "Red touches yellow, he's a deadly fellow."

"Colonel?" Wendell said again, touching Simpson's arm.

"We need to go back to the stream now," Simpson said, "very, very slowly."

That would do you no good, Midgarders, the voice sounded in Wendell's head. "Midgarder," Wendell vaguely remembered the term "Midgarder" from Norse myth. He did not know much about Norse myth having studied Classical in college. The snake released its hold on the tree's root and turned toward them. *I could snatch you before you could take a single step.*

"He's talking in my head!" Simpson said.

Yes, Midgarder, the snake said. *I am talking in your head. And you are talking with your mouth, a rather crude and noisy way of talking but all you Midgarders are capable of.* The snake reared up until its head was almost lost to sight in the fog then lunged toward them, stopping with its mouth a few feet above their heads. Its fangs, though small for the size of that head, were nevertheless longer than one of Wendell's arms. At least these fangs did not drip venom.

And now, Midgarder, is there any telling you can tell for why I should not swallow you, small though you are?

"Who are you?" Wendell said.

I? I am Nidhogg, the World Serpent. Nidhogg withdrew slightly. *I am the one who crawls at the base of the World Ash Yggdrassil and gnaws of its root, filling it with venom that will sicken the tree and bring about Fimbulwinter in the End Times. I am the death of the nine worlds. Although Surtr, the fire giant, is fated to bring about the final burning, he could not, save for my work here.* The snake pulled back still farther. *So it is to be the game of questions? Very well. If I win, I shall devour you. If you win, what shall be my forfeit?*

Simpson broke in, "We just want to get out of here."

Then so be it, Nidhogg said. *If you win the game of questions, I shall provide you with a guide who will show you the paths out of Niffelheim and to the worlds above.*

Since you have asked first, I shall ask now. Who are you?

Wendell looked at Simpson, who shrugged and motioned to Wendell to answer. Wendell thought for a moment. Nidhogg's answer had had a poetic tone to it. Very well, poetry and allegory it would be. He would do his father proud. "Wendell is my name. I am the reader of law and the lawgiver. I came from the preserver of life and became a giver of death. I spoke with few and spoke for many. I fought to preserve the law and fought to change the law. I slew men with balls and three times the ball passed through me. I went into death and came out alive."

Well answered Midgarder, Nidhogg said. *And now, your question.*

Wendell rubbed at his mustache as he thought.

Come, come, Midgarder. Your question, please.

"Very well, serpent," Wendell said. "Long ago a sailor sailed to the west, seeking the East but found instead a new West. Name him."

Ah, you think to trick me, Midgarder. Nidhogg swayed above them. *You are not the first New Dead to come before me and, like Wotan gained wisdom from Mirmir's Well, so too do I gain the wisdom of those I devour. His name was Bearer of the Slain God. And Dove was his name.*

Wendell had to think about the answer for a bit. The Slain God would be Christ. Bearer of Christ. And Dove, in Latin, was *Colombanus.* Nidhogg had simply translated the name. "That is correct, Serpent. Your turn."

Very well, answer me well, if your wisdom avails, who is it that rules over the nine worlds, from his throne on high?

Simpson spoke before Wendell could form his reply, "The Almighty God."

Such a simple answer?

"The Almighty God," Wendell said. "The father of men. The bearer of burdens. The most wise. The Lord of all the Earth. The Lord, protector of the faithful. The Most High. The One and the Three. The answerer of prayers. The mover of the stars. The ruler of heaven. The Slain God."

Oh, Wonderful, Midgarder! Nidhogg pulled back farther and laid his head down on the ground next to them. This did not reassure Wendell, as it merely emphasized how truly enormous Nidhogg was. *All kennings of Wotan and yet also names for the God of so many of the New Dead. Very clever.*

Wendell caught his breath. That had not been his intention. He did not know what "kennings" were, let alone how they might apply to Wotan. He had simply been using terms for God in ways that seemed to fit what he was coming to understand were the rules of this contest. He supposed most beliefs of a supreme deity would be described in similar terms but he had been lucky. He must be more careful in the future. Luck was something on which he could not rely, not here, not in hell.

"Tell me, Serpent, if you know the answer, who brings despair to the damned in hell."

A tricky question, Nidhogg said. *Some believe this and some believe that. But all their beliefs fall short of the truth. One of plagues shall come down. Seven weapons shall he wield. Lightning death will he deal and bright blue will his lightning burn.*

Wendell hesitated. That did not sound good at all. He had heard of nothing like that, yet he suspected that to question it and yet have it prove true would be to lose the contest. "Very well, snake. Your question."

Wendell lost track of how long the contest continued. With

each question Nidhogg asked, Wendell found it more difficult to form a meaningful answer. From the expression on Simpson's face he could see that Wendell was beginning to panic.

Well, enough, Midgarder, Nidhogg said at last. *Although I fear our contest shall soon draw to a close. Ask your next question.*

Simpson spoke up, "What have I got in my pockets?"

Nidhogg reared up. *What question is this?*

Simpson placed his hands on his hips and looked up at Nidhogg. "You heard me. What have I got in my pockets?"

Three guesses, Nidhogg said. *You must permit three guesses.*

"So you accept the question," Simpson said. "So be it. Three guesses it is."

"What are you doing?" Wendell whispered in an aside.

"I met a writer shortly after I got here," Simpson whispered back. "He had a similar game in one of his books. I remembered how it was won."

"But…."

"We were losing, Holmes," Simpson said. "Don't deny it. I figured it was worth a shot."

What do you have in your pockets? Nidhogg said. *Hands.*

"Nope," Simpson said holding his hands out to the side.

I know the track you have been laying so I will say 'rocks.'

"Wrong again. I used the last of those back that way."

Perhaps you thought to be tricky, Nidhogg stretched forward, his tongue flicking out and the barest tip touching Simpson on the head. *Very well, I say you have nothing in your pockets.*

"And, wrong, a third time," Simpson said. Slowly, he reached into his pocket and pulled out a single Diablo coin. "I believe that means we win."

Nidhogg pulled back yet more and settled his head to the ground once more. *So it does, Midgarder. So it does. Very well, you shall have your guide, a guide to show you the ways out of Niffelhel and further out of Niffelheim. Remain here.* Nidhogg turned and disappeared into the mist.

"Should we leave now, before he gets back?" Simpson said.

"I don't think so," Wendell said. "If he wanted to kill us, he could have done so easily enough. A lot of these old religions hold things like this contest as sacred. He may try to twist the meaning, hold to the letter while twisting the spirit, but I don't think he'll out-and-out cheat."

*

Their guide was almost as disturbing as Nidhogg himself. Of roughly human appearance the guide stood twelve feet high at the shoulder. The shoulder was the highest point on him because his neck had been severed, and the giant carried his head in his arms.

This is Vafthruthnir, Nidhogg said. *He will show you the path out of Niffelhel and further to the bridge across the Gjöll, the river which borders Niffelheim, beyond which are the caverns that lead to the upper world.*

"These are Midgarders," said the head in the giant's arms. "I am to help such as these?"

You are to show them the paths, Nidhogg said. *See that they reach the bridge safely. Your duty ends there.*

"But...."

Challenge me not on this, Nidhogg said. *There are far worse fates one can face than having to carry one's head until the coming of Ragnarok.*

Vafthruthnir seemed to sag. "As you wish, Noble Serpent, the Death of the World. As you wish."

"What did he say?" Simpson asked Wendell. "You understand them, right?"

Wendell nodded. "The giant – his name's Vafth– vafthtroo–"

Vafthruthnir, Nidhogg said.

Wendell looked up at the snake then back to Simpson. "The giant doesn't want to help us. The snake insisted."

"A concise enough summary," Vafthruthnir said. He turned to face Wendell and Simpson. "Come, Midgarders. We have far to go."

Wendell started to nod then stopped. The giant wavered in front of him. A moment later, he found himself sitting on the ground, his arm and ribs throbbing in time with his pulse.

"Holmes?" Simpson's voice seemed to come from far away. "Holmes? Oliver! Look at me!"

Wendell looked up. There were two of Simpson. He giggled.

Simpson was beside himself. One Simpson. And another Simpson next to it. Beside himself. Wendell giggled again.

"Snake!" Simpson shouted. "Is there anything…?"

This is your problem, Midgarder, Nidhogg said. *I have my own task to attend to.*

"Useless serpent," Simpson said. "How about you, giant? Can you help my companion…?"

Vafthruthnir did not respond.

"Of course. He doesn't speak English." Simpson turned back to Wendell. "Focus, Oliver. Stay with me."

"Wendell," he said.

"What?"

"I go by Wendell. Oliver's my father."

"Okay, *Wendell*," Simpson said with a slight smile. "Stay with me. Focus."

Wendell nodded. The two Simpsons slowly merged into one.

"I should have expected this," Simpson said. "A forced march on top of your injuries. You must be one tough bastard to have lasted this long." He slid around until he was on Wendell's uninjured side. "If I help you, do you think you can stand up?"

"I'll try."

Simpson nodded and pulled Wendell's arm across his shoulder, holding it at the wrist with one hand while reaching across Wendell's back with the other to grasp his belt. Wendell grunted as the movement jostled his broken arm.

"Sorry about that," Simpson said, "but this is going to hurt."

"I'll … manage."

"Forget what I said about Yankee Chills. On three?"

Wendell nodded.

*

The travelers took a break at the top of a small hill. A cluster of men, dressed in shaggy furs, retreated before them at their approach and huddled at the far end of the hilltop, staring fearfully at the giant. They had picked up large stones and held them in their hands, prepared to throw, pitiful weapons indeed against a giant of Vafthruthir's size.

Wendell sat shivering on the ground, drawing breath in ragged gasps while his arm throbbed in time with his pulse.

"Your companion should kill you and move on," Vafthruthir said. "You will not live to reach the ice fields, let alone cross them. And neither of you will cross them alive dressed as you are."

"What did he say?" Simpson crouched next to him.

"Kill me. Won't live long anyway."

"Much as I'd like to, how will I understand the giant without you, or him me?"

Wendell snorted. "Not sure if you're joking."

"When you figure it out," Simpson said, "you tell me."

"There's more. Ice fields. Said we won't survive them dressed as we are."

Simpson looked across to where the other occupants of this hilltop were huddled. "Not dressed as we are, huh?"

"What are you thinking?"

"We need warmer clothes. They have warmer clothes."

"You can't. For one thing, they outnumber us and…."

"Relax, Holmes." Simpson stood up. "I'm not like your General Sherman. I plan to trade for some of their furs. But first we've got to get you strengthened up and that means getting you fed."

Wendell suppressed a laugh. "Have you seen anything to eat around here?"

Simpson laughed. "Not only a Yankee, but a city boy. You just wait right here." He stopped to gather up some rocks then walked down the hill, disappearing in the mist.

"Where does your friend go?" Vafthruthnir asked.

"He said he's going to get food," Wendell said.

The group at the other end of the hilltop started whispering together. One of them took a few steps in their direction. "You have food? Please, can you give us some?"

"Go away, Midgarder," Vafthruthnir said. "We have nothing for you."

Wendell faded in and out of consciousness several times before Simpson returned and squatted next to him. "Can you sit up, Holmes?"

Wendell struggled upright.

"There's no fire, so you'll have to eat it raw, but here." Simpson held out several cuts of meat roughly cylindrical in shape, about an inch to an inch and a half across and about six inches long.

"What's that?"

Simpson said nothing, simply held out the meat.

"Snake!" Wendell said after a moment. "You can't eat that. Those things are poisonous!"

Simpson sighed. "City boy. The snakes make their poison in the head. As long as you don't eat that they're fine. You Yankees had better supplies than we did in the war. A lot of my boys would catch snakes and eat 'em, because that's all they had. Now we need to get your strength back up. So eat."

Wendell took a piece in his good arm and tentatively bit into it. The meat was stringy and had a somewhat fishy taste. Before he'd half realized it, he had gobbled the meat from the bones and was reaching for another piece.

After Wendell finished the second piece, Simpson held up a hand. "That's enough for now. Feeling better?"

"A bit," Wendell said.

Simpson nodded. "As I remember, you said that first fellow wanted food? Well, these look just as hungry." Simpson stood and held down a hand to Wendell. Wendell took it and, with Simpson's help, rose to his feet. "It's time to do some bartering, I think."

*

Wendell knew that eventually he would regret the food he'd eaten. In the meantime, the meat, along with the furs for which Simpson had traded more pieces of snake, renewed his strength. His ribs and arm still ached but his vision no longer had the disturbing tendency to go double.

Simpson had traded snake meat not only for furs, but also for a pair of woolen breaches that he had converted into a crude backpack, the legs serving as straps. He had stuffed additional snake meat into the pack.

"Time to take a break," Simpson said when at last the three travelers returned to the stream. He shrugged out of the pack and set it on the ground, then pointed at Wendell. "You, sit. Rest."

"Yes, sir, Colonel," Wendell saluted.

"I'll be back shortly," Simpson said.

"Shouldn't you rest too?"

"I'm not injured. I'll rest a bit when I get back." With that, Simpson walked upstream until he vanished into the mist.

"Your friend is a strange one, Midgarder." Vafthruthnir said.

"Strange? Maybe." Wendell squirmed where he sat, trying to find a comfortable position. "And he's not exactly a friend. We're more like old enemies."

"Old enemies, you say?"

"Different sides of a war. His side lost."

"So both of you were warriors?"

"Soldiers," Wendell said. "Lawyers. Judges. Different sorts of politicians." He shook his head. "'The player on the other side....'"

The giant sat next to Wendell. With his head in his lap he was almost at a comfortably conversational distance. "What do you mean, 'player on the other side'?"

"It's from an essay by an old professor, Thomas Huxley. 'The player on the other side is hidden from us. We know that his play is always fair, just and patient. But also we know, to our cost, that he never overlooks a mistake, or makes the smallest allowance for ignorance. To the man who plays well, the highest stakes are paid, with that sort of overflowing generosity with which the strong shows delight in strength. And one who plays ill is checkmated – without haste, but without remorse.' We made our share of mistakes in that war, but in the end, it was Simpson's side who lost. In the end, they didn't have the industry, or the manpower to win."

"But they had valor?"

"Oh, yes," Wendell said. "Valor they had, in plenty."

"Then he should remain here, as should you," Vafthruthnir said.

"What? Why?"

"Ragnarok, the Fate of the Gods, is coming, Midgarder. Whether soon or late, no one knows, but its coming is certain. The hosts will set sail from Niffelheim on Naglfar, the Ship of the Dead, and join with the sons of Surtr and with my giant kin, the Jötuns, and we shall march on the abode of the Gods, Asgard, and Asgard will fall. And a new day shall dawn for all that is goodly and beautiful in the gold-thatched hall of Gimle." Vafthruthnir sighed. "And yet for many years few have come to swell our ranks. Two doughty warriors would be a welcome addition." He raised his hands and spread them out. "This place of mists and darkness, Niffelhel, is not the whole of Niffelheim. While we do not have the pleasures of Valhöl, one can wait in peace for the coming of Ragnarok."

Wendell thought better of saying what he thought, that he had no intention of staying in this place. "You have given me much to think about."

*

Simpson returned with an armload of dead snakes, which he immediately set about skinning, gutting, and cutting into pieces about six inches long. Once done, he packed the snake pieces into his makeshift backpack and shouldered it. "Trade goods," he said in response to Wendell's questioning look. "We may need them. Ready to proceed?"

Wendell nodded and got to his feet.

"This way," Vafthruthnir said, and proceeded downstream along the bank.

After three more breaks, at each of which Simpson killed more snakes to add to their store of meat, the stream they had been following joined a large river.

"Touch not the water," Vafthruthnir said. "You will not die, but the agonies will make you long for the mercy of death. We continue this way." He pointed downstream once more.

"Is it just me or is it getting colder?" Wendell asked.

"Not so many snakes anymore," Simpson said.

"Aye, it is becoming colder," Vafthruthnir said, "and much colder yet will it be, before we are through. The ice fields lie ahead, and beyond them what remains of Ginungagap, the yawning void from before the world was. Only there can we find our way free of Niffelhel."

Soon they encountered the first frost in hollows along the riverbank. When asked, Vafthruthnir admitted that the frost was free of venom and safe to swallow. Wendell and Simpson scraped loose handfuls to suck on. The frost relieved the thirst that had been building in the sight of so much water that they dared not drink.

As they continued, the edges of the river became rimmed in ice. The ice extended up the banks and before long they were walking on a sheet of ice broken only by the dark trace of the river, curls of mist rising from its surface.

When Simpson called another halt, the river had finally frozen completely. The river ice had a yellow-green cast, in contrast to the blue-white of the ice elsewhere. Although the sky remained a murky gray, the mists had cleared in the cold.

Frost rimed the furs around their heads and the cold burned in their noses as they breathed. Vafthruthnir, despite his light clothing, did not seem to experience any discomfort from the cold.

"Does it get much colder than this?" Simpson asked.

Wendell repeated the question for Vafthruthnir who answered, "Not much colder, Midgarder. We have only a few more leagues for this leg of our journey, and then you shall see a wonder such as few Midgarder eyes have witnessed."

"Press on, then," Simpson said when Wendell translated.

True to the giant's word, as they crested a small rise, the ice dropped away before them in a jagged cliff. Here the river broke free of the ice and fell for miles before disappearing in the depths below.

To his right more than a dozen miles away, Wendell saw an irregular wall of gray-brown. The wall extended both down into the gap and up into the sky above them for as far as the eye could see. Ahead, more than twice as far loomed a second wall of dark red. Wendell could not see where bottom of the … canyon seemed such an inadequate word … might be in the miles below them.

"Ginungagap," Vafthruthnir shouted over the roar of the waterfall, "or what remains of it since the creation of the World Ash." Vafthruthnir pointed at the gray-brown wall in the distance to their right. Wendell sucked frigid air over his teeth as he realized that Vafthruthnir meant that wall, extending beyond sight in all directions, was the World Ash, or part of it, and that would make it the same tree on which Nidhogg had been gnawing.

The river that the three had been following was not the only cascade breaking from the near wall. To their right, stretching out into the distance were four others; to their left, six more. Vafthruthnir pointed to the farthest one on the left. "There. That is where we must go, the Gjöll, the river resounding."

*

The crossing to the Gjöll was harrowing, across the treacherous ice, close enough to see the precipice, but no closer. The Gjöll, when they reached it, was not completely frozen over like the other rivers, but filled with ice floes that howled as they ground against each other before tumbling over the falls and into the depths. The noise of the ice, and the river running beneath it beat at their ears. They turned to follow the Gjöll upstream.

The unchanging light provided no clue to how long they marched. Wendell thought it was days. The pain in his arm and in his side had receded to a dull ache by the time the ice had finally receded and they gained the rocky shore of the river. On this side of the ice there were no snakes. Instead, small stands of scrub provided wood for fire to warm them and cook the snake meat that Simpson insisted Wendell eat.

The Gjöll broke over rapids frequently. The roar of one set of rapids did not completely fade behind them before the roar of the next began. They walked in the constant bellow of water crashing over rocks.

When they left the riverside, they left the ice behind, so the thirst they'd avoided while crossing the ice returned to dog them.

"Isn't this water safe?" Simpson asked at one of their rest stops. "Look at all those fish in it." He waved toward the slender silver shapes that flitted through the water.

"Those are not fish, Midgarder," Vafthruthnir said when Wendell had repeated the question.

Wendell looked at the slender, silver forms running down the river. "Not fish? Then what are they?"

"They are knives, Midgarder. The Gjöll is the river that flows with knives. The water here is poisonous. You cannot drink this water, nor can you swim in it, nor wade. The only place to cross is at the bridge, the Gjällerbru."

On their march, they came upon a black wall of dressed stone to their left. It ran until it vanished into the distance. Ahead, it curved and followed roughly parallel to the river. The wall was unbroken by window or door and Wendell guessed the height to be about fifty feet.

"That wall marks the border of Helheim, the abode of Hel and the dead who did not die in combat," Vafthruthnir said. "There the dead await the coming of Ragnarok. We shall soon be at the Gjällerbru, where I shall be quit of you."

They had made four rest stops and were close to making a fifth when they rounded a bend in the river and a bridge came into view. At this point the river was, Wendell judged, a little over a quarter mile across. A covered bridge of post and beam construction spanned its width. The sides of the bridge were covered in wood planks and the roof was a thatch of glittering yellow that caused Wendell to catch his breath.

"Yes, Midgarder," Vafthruthnir said on noticing Wendell's stare. "The Gjällerbru is thatched with gold." The giant sighed. "Once Helheim was a place of rest and contemplation for those who did not die in combat. It was a place of beauty. Then, some say, your Christian beliefs started infecting the Norsemen. Over time, Helheim became a place of darkness and of cold. Then the souls stopped coming."

Vafthruthnir stopped. "There is your way out, if you can manage it. Cross the bridge and there is a cave angled upward which leads to the upper realms." He smiled, a grim smile, made all the more ghastly being on a severed head. "The giant Modgud guards the bridge, and will allow none to leave. And should you somehow pass her, Garmr waits at the top of the cave and will allow none dead to pass out and none living to pass within."

"Wait a minute!" Simpson said when Wendell had repeated Vafthruthnir's words. "The snake said to show us the way out."

"And to see you safely to the exit," Vafthruthnir said. "I have done so. He said nothing of seeing that you pass through that exit. That is your affair and none of mine."

Simpson drew Wendell's revolver and pointed it at the giant. "How about we make a new deal right here."

"Put that away," Wendell said. "He's walking around with his head in his arms. Do you think a forty-five Long Colt is going to bother him much?"

"No more will it discommode Modgud." Vafthruthnir said with a shrug.

"I've got an idea," Wendell said. "Giant, you say that no souls have come here?"

"Not for many years."

"Then I have a proposition. It is likely that no souls have come because no one venerates the old gods any more. If you will help us to get past the bridge, then I will swear by whatever oaths you agree are binding to tell others of these old gods, to tell them that Helheim has been a place of rest among the hells rather than torment and that they can share it if they but believe. When they are killed in hell, as many are, it may be that they come here. And your ranks will swell, bringing closer the day of Ragnarok and the final death of Odin, the one who took your head."

"Are you out of your mind?" Simpson said. "You can't...."

"It's the only way," Wendell said. "We'll never get out of here without help and if this is the price of help, what else can we do?"

"Very well, Midgarder," Vafthruthnir said. "Swear your oath and place your hand in the Gjöll. If you speak true, it will not harm you."

Wendell swore and, holding his breath placed his left hand in the river. True to the giant's word, the venom in the water did not burn him.

"As you say, one named Wendell. I will draw Modgud to me. With no fresh dead brought to us, her vigil is a lonely one and to speak to one of her own kind will be a relief. When she comes to me, cross the bridge swiftly. Be warned: the floor of the bridge is made of knives, edge up. If you cross with boldness, then you will take no hurt, but if you hesitate they will cut deep, leaving wounds that do not heal."

"Boldness," Wendell said. "Can't be any worse than the battle of Ball's Bluff," (where he had been hit by three musket balls, one passing completely through his chest). "And Garmr?"

"That I cannot help you with," Vafthruthnir said. "I am bound to this place and may not cross the bridge."

"Garmr is a giant dog, is it not?" Simpson said when Wendell had relayed Vafthruthnir's words.

"A very great dog indeed," Vafthruthnir said, "and the most terrible of all the beasts in the nine worlds."

"I think I know how we can deal with him then," Simpson said.

"Then wait here," Vafthruthnir said, "and do not be seen."

*

Wendell crouched just behind the summit of a small rise. Simpson crouched next to him. Below, Vafthruthnir approached the bridge. They heard the giant shout but could not make out his words. A few minutes later another giant arrived, this one even larger than Vafthruthnir. Vafthruthnir's shoulder came only to her mid-chest. This must be Modgud, Wendell thought.

Vafthruthnir gestured as he and Modgud walked slowly upstream, apparently absorbed in conversation.

"Now!" Wendell said and, steeling himself for the pain from his broken bones, began to run for the bridge, Simpson sprinting at his side.

Simpson was slightly in the lead when they reached the bridge. As Simpson's foot touched it, the bridge began to shout: "Help! Intruders!"

"Trickery!" Wendell heard the voice boom behind them followed by the resounding thud of running footsteps.

"Run!" he shouted and set action to his words, drawing upon what reserves of strength they had left.

They were halfway across the bridge when the sound of the footsteps behind them changed, from the dull thud of feet on rocky ground to the sharper sound of boots on the deck of the bridge. Almost blind with pain, Wendell continued to run, expecting a giant hand to close on him at any moment.

But the hand never came. He reached the rocky shore at the other end of the bridge and dashed another hundred yards before slipping and falling, barely managing to twist to his left to land on his good side. Wendell nearly passed out from the pain.

When Wendell sat up he saw the giant Modgud, who had halted at the near end of the bridge. "You may have escaped me, Midgarders, but Garmr will not be so easily bested."

"Holmes?" Simpson said. "We'd better get moving before she comes after us."

"I don't think she will," Wendell said. "My guess is that bridge is as far as she goes."

Simpson nodded. "Still, I think we should get moving. There's that dog to pass yet."

"You said you had an idea?"

Simpson nodded again.

"All right, let's go." Wincing at the renewed pain, Wendell slowly forced himself to his feet.

A few hundred yards from the riverbank, the shore rose in a sheer cliff to invisible heights above them. As Vafthruthnir had promised, a cave pierced the cliff, angling upward. Stalactites and stalagmites rimmed its mouth like giant teeth.

Inside the cave, the dim light of Helheim soon faded, replaced by even dimmer light from luminous fungi. Even when their eyes adjusted to the murk, they could barely make out their path.

Eventually they could see a ruddy light ahead, growing brighter and forming a lopsided oval as they approached the upper end of the cave.

"Come ahead, Midgarders," a voice said from ahead of them.

Wendell froze and glanced sideways at Simpson. A shadow detached itself from the wall at the exit and stood silhouetted, nearly filling the oval before them.

"Come ahead. I am hungry."

"Now's the time for that idea of yours," Wendell whispered.

"What idea would that be, Midgarder?" the voice said, and then chuckled. "Did you think to keep secrets from me? Only Gold Teeth has ears better than mine."

"I understood that!" Simpson said quietly.

"Of course you can understand me, Midgarder," the voice said. "Men and women of all tongues have passed my way since the dawn of time. I am Garmr, the Hel Hound. It is my duty, given by the Norns, who create the destinies of men and gods, to challenge all who seek to pass into and out of Hel, to see if their business is meet. And it is my duty to devour those whose business is not. So come forward. If your business is acceptable you have nothing to fear. If it is not, you may then choose between me and the Jötun below. There is nowhere else to go."

Wendell looked again at Simpson, who nodded. Together they walked slowly forward. As they neared the exit of the cave they could see that the shadow was the shaggy head of a great dog. The dog's muzzle glistened with gore. When it stood at their approach, this dog was twenty feet tall at the shoulder. Its chest and forequarters were agleam with blood.

Simpson cast a quick glance behind them, into the cave, then looked back up at Garmr. "The most terrible of all beasts?"

"Ah," Garmr said, "you think that because Nidhogg is larger, that Fenris the wolf and Jörmungand the world serpent are vaster than I … that they are more terrible? Know this, Midgarder: they may be greater in size than I am, but all men and all Gods face me in the end. Fenris and Jörmungand are fated to die in Ragnarok, but I shall abide. My first howl shall herald the coming of Fimbulwinter, the three year freeze that shall destroy the world of men, my second, the assault on Asgard, and my third, the renewal of the world. I am the ending of all things and their rebirth."

"Very great and terrible indeed," Simpson said, "and yet you hunger."

Garmr lowered his massive head. "I hunger. Few have come this way in an age. And those few I try to devour vanish from my very jaws."

"How fortunate for you, then," Simpson said, "that I have meat that will not vanish away when you eat it. We have come to give it to you. Is that not a meet business for us?"

Garmr laughed softly, his doggy breath stirring around them like a foul wind. "Oh a meet business indeed. And when I have devoured this meat, I shall then devour you – and see if you will vanish from my jaws as well."

"Oh, I am so sorry, great one," Simpson said. "Our task is to give this meat only to one who swears to allow us to pass. If you will not swear, then we cannot give you this meat."

"What need have I of oaths?" Garmr said. "I can simply slay you and have the meat you carry whether you will give it or no."

Seeing Simpson at a loss, Wendell spoke up. "That is terribly unfortunate. We stand here within a cave, which your majestic size will not allow you to enter. You may keep us here if you choose … but that will not win you the meat."

Garmr stood looking at them for several seconds. "Very well. I swear by Yggdrassil, the World Ash, to allow you to pass this once, if you give me meat that does not vanish from my jaws."

"Both of us," Wendell said.

"Both of you," Garmr agreed.

Wendell looked at Simpson, who nodded.

"Very well." Simpson removed his makeshift pack, opened it, and removed one of the pieces of snake. He tossed it to Garmr who caught it in the air and swallowed.

"More!"

Piece by piece, Simpson threw the snake pieces to Garmr. Eventually, all the snake meat was gone.

"Ah, it has been so long since I have had meat in my belly. While it has not the taste of hero or thief, it is better than the nothing I have had for so long. Very well, you may pass." Garmr stepped back and to the side, clearing the way out of the cave.

"At the end, so easy," Wendell mused as they left the cave. "What do you plan to…?" Pain exploded against the back of his head and Wendell was falling. He hit the ground and rolled onto his back. Simpson stood above him, holding Wendell's revolver. Smoke curled from the muzzle and cylinder as Simpson took aim again.

"You've sworn to convince people to believe in the Norse Gods so they'll go down there when they die. I can't let you do that," Simpson said. "I just can't."

The revolver thundered once more.

*

Wendell woke on a stone slab that felt all too familiar. He had been on such a slab several times before, in such a place … in this place. He knew where he was, beyond a shadow of a doubt: the Undertaker's table. As before, he couldn't see, move, or feel, but he could hear raspy breathing … and he could smell. The fetid breath of the Undertaker burned in his nostrils.

"What have you done to yourself this time? The wound in back's not bad – just a scrape really – but this one? I'll be forever putting these little pieces of bone back together. Do you know how hard it is to reconnect all the neurons in a brain? I always seem to lose something. Should I leave you the piece of lead as a souvenir when they reassign you? Shall I? Or perhaps not."

The Undertaker did something. The sound and smell of the raspy breath started to fade. "Now this won't hurt a bit."

Always does, Wendell thought, just before losing consciousness again.

He woke once more on chilly ground. Without thinking, he

reached up and probed at his head with both hands. No sign of bullet holes. His broken arm worked perfectly. His ribs no longer grated against one another.

He looked around. Instead of a lake of boiling blood, he was surrounded by cold and mist – a definite improvement. That Norse hell, he was back in that Norse hell.

He tilted back his head and laughed. Then a light caught his eye, and another: light, like flashes of blue lightning far away in the sky. A sense of foreboding clutched at his heart, seeing those blue lights against the dim, gray sky. Nidhogg's words came back to him:

One of plagues shall come down. Seven weapons shall he wield. Lightning death will he deal and bright blue will his lightning burn.

Wendell was certain something very bad was about to happen.

The Dark Arts

By

Kimberly Richardson

"Ah, my dear Clarence," said a voice from behind him. Clarence Darrow, fierce litigator and civil libertarian, turned to face his client, a fallen angel named Penemue. The fallen angel was long-limbed and exquisite, lounging amid the luxurious library of his Lost Angeles mansion, into which Darrow had been spirited without warning. "I called you here for a most serious matter." Penemue leaned back into his chair and closed his cats' eyes. "I need your professional services. It would appear that I am being sued for plagiarism." The fallen angel opened his beautiful eyes and focused them on Darrow's grizzled face. "Another author charges that I have taken his work and claimed it for my own." He cracked his fingers then laid them in his lap. "As you know, my own work is just that: mine. I have no reason to steal from another."

"Who made such a claim?" asked Darrow, trying to get to the heart of the matter.

"Some lesser being of no particular repute, who claims that *I* stole from *him*. Can you imagine that, Clarence? The nerve!" Penemue got up from his chair and paced through the room, which looked a bit unnerving due to his height and facial expression of beautiful disgust.

"So, how did you find out about this charge?" asked Darrow. The fallen angel stopped pacing, and blinked his red eyes at his lawyer.

"That damned fiddler, Paganini, told me last night," he hissed. "I am the fallen angel who gave man the use of ink and paper. It is absurd to think I would then steal the work of a mere human. Will you aid me in this matter? You have been quite a capable representative before and I see no reason to call upon anyone else for this."

Darrow closed his eyes and ran a hand across his jaw, rubbing the stubble. This might be the most interesting case he'd encountered since he defended the right to teach Darwin's Theory of Evolution in public school in the famous *scopes* trial. Someone dumb or crazy enough to accuse a fallen angel of plagiarism had to be taken seriously; the game was most assuredly afoot. He opened his eyes, pushed his hair to the side of his face and said, "I'll take the case."

*

Penemue refused to have the case heard at the Hall of Injustice like a common criminal. Changing Penemue's mind was like asking a demon to smile, so Darrow met with the plaintiff's attorney at Thanatos Library to agree on a venue to discuss the case. When Darrow walked into the hallowed halls of the library, he was immediately greeted by opposing counsel, another damned soul, wearing a wrinkled suit with several grease spots.

The other lawyer saw Clarence and rushed up to him, grasping his hand with a vice-like grip. "I'm Boulder! This is a real honor, Counselor Darrow!" he gushed.

When Boulder released his grip, Darrow's hand was covered in a thin and slimy goo. Darrow peered into the shadowed face of the lawyer with his piercing eyes then said in a low voice, "Well, shall we get to it, then?"

Boulder led him amid rows and rows of books with various forms of flesh used for the covers. Some books on library tables had faces eternally locked in torments their own minds had devised: faces with sunglasses grafted upon them; faces slack-jawed from drink and vacant from drugs. Punishment suited to crimes against literature. Darrow shuddered. The scourges of literati were not his problem. At least, not today. Today he had a plagiarism defense to prepare and a case to win.

He sat down across from the greasy opposing counsel and now noticed that the slime on Boulder came from boils and sores on his face and neck and possibly the rest of his body. Darrow looked down at his own slimy hand, wiped it on the chair and said gruffly, "So. What's this about your client claiming my client committed plagiarism?"

Boulder reached into his battered briefcase and pulled out several yellowed documents. He glanced at them for a moment, then handed them to Darrow without a word. As Darrow collected the documents, he noticed an unpleasant odor emanating from them. The first document was a hand-written statement from one Mr. John Ginger, a damned soul and struggling writer in Lost Angeles, who claimed he could not afford a computer and thus wrote all his manuscripts in his own blood with a quill pen. He lived alone, had yet to secure a book deal, yet asserted he had written brilliant novels. His testimony further claimed that Ginger's works all suddenly disappeared, thanks to a certain fallen angel named Penemue who lived on Rue de la Mort in Lost Angeles. Darrow glanced up.

The opposing counsel was staring right back at him: at some time, for some crime, Boulder's eyelids had been cut away.

Darrow glanced through the testament one more time, then handed it back to Boulder, who returned the document to his briefcase, which clicked closed.

"My client was told by Nicolo Paganini, the composer and violinist, of accusations that Penemue had stolen works from someone else. Is your client the one spreading these rumors?" Darrow asked.

Boulder shrugged innocently. "My client figured that, since Paganini and your client were enemies in the arts world, the mad violinist would prove to be quite an ally during this matter."

"I see."

The lawyer leaned forward in anticipation. "Do you, Mister Darrow?" Darrow peered into the lidless eyes of the lawyer. Boulder, misreading Darrow's silence for puzzlement, folded his arms on top of the table, leaned forward and said in a hushed tone, "We're ready to settle for appropriate compensation."

"Settle? Are you mad?" exclaimed Darrow, and received several orders to *"Hush"* from the faces in the books strewn about. He leaned closer to the greasy lawyer and said in a lowered voice, "Settle? Your client *does* know who my client is, correct?"

"But of course, which is why my client expects a very large award."

Darrow leaned back in his chair and ran a hand through his hair. *He really thinks he has a chance*, Darrow thought to himself. "Look, Mister –"

"Boulder," said the attorney who reached out his greasy stained hand again for Darrow to shake. Darrow refrained. "Just call me Boulder, if you don't mind."

"I don't mind at all, but you must know that your client does not have a chance in –"

"Ah, ah, ah," interrupted Boulder, wagging his finger at Darrow.

"All right, fine, but still, your client's accusations are preposterous. My client would never steal work from anyone, let alone a being he deemed inconsequential." Darrow allowed himself a smug smile as he said that; sometimes, it felt good to have certain clients – the kind who possessed a goodly share of the powers of hell.

"What if I told you, Darrow, that my client not only knows your client stole from him but right under his nose? Called my client a lowlife form of algae whose only purpose was to be stepped on and then later scraped off while walking at a jaunty pace.

"Mister Ginger also claims that he saw Penemue holding Ginger's latest work and that, when he approached Penemue, the fallen angel only laughed in his face while cursing him out in some archaic language."

Darrow's smug smile faltered a bit; that *did* sound like something Penemue would say. He rubbed his grizzled jaw again, trying to think of an appropriate response, then said, "My client would like the proceedings to take place at his home. He refuses to have them heard at the Hall of Injustice." Boulder held up a hand and this time, it looked to be even dirtier than before.

"My client knew that a fallen angel would feel that way and refuses the location. He wishes the hearing to be held at the Hall of Injustice, where his case can be heard in a public forum." Now the greasy lawyer looked every inch a hard-ass as his eyelid-less eyes focused on Darrow with an eerie sense of calm. "We will not accept anything less than that. Tell your client either he agrees to the conditions or he can admit his guilt and we can settle out of court. Your client has made quite a nice living writing books and we want half of his wealth. Nothing less than that. Good day." Boulder picked up his beaten-up briefcase and walked out without a backward glance at the disconcerted Darrow.

Darrow cursed inwardly then grabbed his client's business card out of his pocket. One touch to the card sent Darrow immediately to his client's home just as Penemue walked into his library with a grin on his face and blood splattered on his crisp white shirt.

"Ah, Clarence," Penemue purred, "so amazing is the female body. How supple under certain stress." He looked at his bloody hands, then carefully licked them clean. "So, Clarence, how did the meeting go?"

"It did not go well at all!" he said in a disgusted voice, not caring if Penemue took offense. Darrow walked over to the liquor counter, made a glass of what looked to be whiskey, and drank it all down in one gulp.

"That's a special blend created by *you know who*," Penemue said carefully just as Darrow realized his mistake and began to gag and cough. He glanced at his glass and watched the remains of the liquid slide up and down the glass as if it were alive. He lowered his head, trying desperately to breathe, but the liquid clogged his throat. He coughed, holding his glass over his mouth, and spat out the angry liquid that now attacked the glass with great and rare abandon. Darrow placed the glass on the table with shaky fingers and vowed never to do something so foolish again. He smoothed his hair to the side and fixed his gaze on his client.

"Penemue, our terms on the matter were rejected," said Darrow in a softer voice; his throat felt as though it were on fire. He rubbed it tenderly then continued, "Mister John Ginger makes a claim that he saw you carrying pieces of one of his documents around and confronted you. According to his attorney, a Mister Boulder, you ridiculed Ginger, then cursed at him in an unknown language." He found a chair and sat down, "And, he refuses to meet you here. He wants to meet at the Hall of Injustice."

"What?!" cried Penemue as he began to pace back and forth. "This is ridiculous, Clarence. What should I do? I never made any such remarks to him or about him to others. I'd never even heard of him 'til that damned fool Paganini told me of the matter. I have no intention of lending his client credibility by having the case argued in public."

"He said that he knew you would want to meet at your home rather than the Hall of Injustice, so if you refused his venue, you could admit your guilt and they would meet you here to settle. He's after half of your wealth." Penemue stopped pacing and his cat-like eyes bored into Darrow's soul. Darrow felt his mind wanting to snap into pieces as his bowels turned to jelly; mortals were never meant to bear up under a fallen angel's full attention. This day was no exception.

"So, what should we do?" asked Penemue in a soft but still deadly tone.

"You'll have to meet him at the Hall of Injustice, unless you want to admit your guilt and have him meet you here." Penemue blinked a couple of times then his face erupted into a wide grin. He clasped his hands with glee.

"Marvelous! Tell him that is exactly what we'll do!" Now Darrow was stunned.

"What? So you actually *did* commit plagiarism?"

"No, no, but I shall admit my 'guilt' and once he and his damned lawyer arrive here, I will show them just how wrong this claim is." Darrow looked at him questioningly then actually grinned when Penemue revealed why he was so confident.

*

Darrow contacted Boulder and informed him of Penemue's decision. He could actually hear those eyes rolling around in their sockets as Boulder expressed his gratitude for bringing swift justice to this devastating matter. Mr. Ginger would be pleased as blood-punch when informed.

"Yes, that's right," said Darrow with a lazy tone to his voice, "my client wants to make his admission of guilt formally, but out of court. He asks that you and your client arrive later today, if possible."

"What of the funds?"

"We'll handle that, don't worry."

Boulder paused for a moment. "So, Darrow, your client actually admitted to it, huh? How does it feel to represent a liar?" Darrow was glad Boulder could not see his shit-eating grin.

*

Penemue had just finished "playing" with one of his slaves, a young woman with dark brown skin that rippled in a certain way when he toyed with her like a cat with a mouse. Darrow could still hear her screams as Penemue closed the door to his bedroom and walked into the living room to join Darrow sitting nervously on the couch.

"My dear Clarence," he said as he entered and made himself a glass of his 'special blend,' "do calm yourself. I have shown you all you need to know about this trifling matter."

"Yes, I know, but are you sure *he* doesn't know?"

"If he did, this case would not be in existence now," Penemue took a sip of his harsh liquid then sighed as he swallowed the liquid. Darrow could actually see a small bulge sliding down the angel's throat. He looked away just as a servant arrived, accompanying two damned souls.

The servant bowed low and said in a muted tone, "Master, Mister Boulder and Mister Ginger to see you." Penemue waved his hand at the servant, who then disappeared in a flash with an anguished cry, leaving behind a puddle of reddish gore on the floor. All eyes locked onto Penemue, who merely smiled and said, "What I do with my own servants is no business of yours."

First Boulder, then his client, Mr. Ginger, stepped over the puddle and entered the room. Darrow got a good look at the young man who had made the plagiarism claim. Ginger was an emaciated soul with sunken cheeks and an odd clump of hair attached to his head, while his eyes appeared to roll loosely around in their sockets.

Boulder looked at his client. Since Penemue had agreed to confess his guilt, Boulder still assumed he had a case … as long as he could keep his client under control. Darrow blinked once then set his piercing gaze upon the man who dared to threaten a fallen angel.

Ginger focused on Penemue's unnaturally beautiful face, grinned like a madman and said, "You! All those manuscripts! You took them from me and now I want them back!" His voice rose into a screech. Darrow held his hands over his ears while Boulder and Penemue merely glanced at Ginger as though at a rabid dog.

Even his own attorney believes his client is a fool, thought Darrow.

Clarence pulled out two chairs for Boulder and his client then sat back down on the couch while Penemue stood, nursing his drink. For too long, no one spoke.

Finally, Penemue finished off his drink and said in a low voice, "So. You are here to accept my plea of guilty, correct?"

Before Boulder could respond, Ginger jumped up, shaking his finger at Penemue and cried out, "You stole my work and I want money! *Money!"* He screamed the word over and over again until Boulder placed a hand on Ginger's shoulder to calm him.

"Yes," said Boulder, "money. In cash, please. Now."

Darrow glanced at Penemue, knowing what was about to happen. Dread, anticipation and revulsion swept through him. Penemue smiled at his lawyer then walked casually over to Boulder and Ginger and began to remove his shirt in front of them.

Boulder glanced at Ginger, realized that the poor fool was frothing at the mouth, then back at Penemue. Darrow watched from behind, knowing what was about to happen only because Penemue had warned him earlier.

As Penemue unbuttoned each button, Boulder and Ginger got a look at his chalk-white skin … and something black swirling around on it. Then, they noticed that the swirls were words moving of their own accord. Finally, Penemue threw aside his white shirt and raised his arms.

Then Boulder knew he had been assigned a fool for a client, but it was too late.

Words scrambled all over Penemue's too-perfect chest while gaping red holes appeared here and there all over his body. Darrow noticed two long reddish gashes down his back that seemed to be fresh and oozed something darkly purple in color.

To fall so hard for so long, Darrow thought.

"Do you see now?" said Penemue in a harsh whisper. He then jerked his head at Darrow behind him; this was Darrow's cue. Clarence arose, walked to a small table and picked up a manuscript. He handed it to Boulder so he and his client could look at it. Before Ginger could respond with more unsubstantiated accusations, Boulder said, "Yes, and…?"

Darrow then calmly walked over to Penemue with the manuscript and touched it to Penemue's torso; as the paper made contact with Penemue's skin, a large hole the size of the manuscript appeared in the middle of the fallen angel's chest.

Darrow, as previously instructed, placed the document against the gaping red hole and it was sucked in loudly, then the hole closed. Suddenly, the words from the manuscript appeared alongside the rest of the words that were showing all over Penemue's body. Penemue sighed as the manuscript returned to its master. For the manuscript had literally come from the fallen angel's mind and body.

The fool named Ginger sat up straight in his chair, watching with wide eyes as his case fell apart like a wet deck of cards. Boulder stared. Then, knowing the case was lost, he wordlessly dragged Ginger from the room and the house.

Penemue shouted, "Run! Run away!" He was convulsed with laughter and roared, "this is *hell*. There's no place to hide!" Darrow watched them leave and turned back to his client's swirling body. Still smiling, Penemue turned to Darrow, saying "Am I not still the fallen angel of ink and paper? Surely, you never doubted me, Clarence?"

Penemue squeezed shut his eyes, satisfied to his very essence. Perhaps he moaned softly. Perhaps not. Darrow stared at Penemue's skin. Words faded and appeared repeatedly all over Penemue's body while more red, puckering holes of all sizes opened here and there, transiently revealing other documents of various sizes and content.

No, Clarence Darrow thought, *there is no doubt.* His client was truly a master of the dark arts.

Heads You Lose

by

Michael Z. Williamson

Captain Joseph McCarthy shouted, "Ready men, this is a combat drop. Hostile territory." Over the angry buzz of engines in the C130, McCarthy was hard to hear.

Lieutenant Roger Upton Howard, III, Esq. rolled his eyes at that. *He says that every damned time. We know it's hostile. It's hell. We're lawyers.*

In life, Roger had never imagined he'd wind up like this. It was a joke, then: Sell the devil your soul. The lawyer asks, "What's the catch?"

The catch was, hell was real, and he hadn't even signed a contract. Those vague maunderings about ethics were all it took. Was it right to defend drunk drivers and petty crooks he knew were guilty? Apparently not, since the universe had seen fit to have a drunk driver crush him. Death had been close to instantaneous. He recalled a moment of pain, and then waking here. Here, pain was part of the scenery, and it seemed eternal. He couldn't say how long he'd been here, just 'a lot of days.'

Then Roger stopped reminiscing, because it was time to jump. The light blinked, and McCarthy shouted, "Hook up!"

This was hell: he couldn't die permanently, and every drop was terrifying because there were endless new ways to suffer.

The Coordinating Legal Airborne Platoon (CLAP) shuffled forward toward the paratroop doors, and Roger's guts and sphincter clenched. He joined the shuffle, hit the door, and jumped out over the choking clouds of hell – or, more accurately, Ashcanistan.

The ripcord tugged his canopy open. He didn't realize his leg straps were loose until they suddenly drew up and yanked his groin. He gasped, flinched, and tried to separate them. By then he was directly over Henry J. Summers, II. He dropped, scrambling through Summers' canopy as it blocked the air. They didn't quite tangle, and Roger made it into the open.

That was worse.

Now he could see that the denizens of nearby Kabum were expecting them. They didn't like lawyers in death any more than they had in life: What price repercussions to the already damned?

A rocket ripped past him with a roar of white noise, and ripped HJS, II's canopy into flaming shreds. The elderly poet and civil servant plummeted faster and faster as the rushing wind fanned his chute to flames, then embers. Roger tugged a riser to slip away from those glowing sparks. He didn't want to catch on fire.

In moments, flak started bursting around them, spit from crude but functional anti-aircraft guns. All Roger could do was shudder as they dropped. Then they got in range of rifle fire, catapults, javelins and arrows. He pulled the release on his ruck and prayed to no one in particular. He'd never known how. At least he'd known how to parachute; he'd been in the 82ndAirborne. Most of these poor bastards jump-qualified the painful way.

The earth below was a cratered landscape: hell's Ashcanistan had been a battleground for eternity. The sky above twisted in nauseating lavender and green moirés.

Then they were landing in heaps on the rocks. Some caught on promontories. Others bashed into cliffs and tumbled into sharp valleys. Roger was lucky. He descended smoothly into the bottom of a shallow gully.

Two monkeys hopped to the gulley's edge and threw.... He grimaced as feces splashed across his chest and spattered his chin.

He overheard one of the primates say, "Not like that, Phil, you clumsy monkey...." Then Roger hit the ground, landing on a sharp rock, and his knee ...

Electric jolts shot through his leg. He heard and felt his knee pop. He collapsed to the ground, whimpering.

General S.V. Benet (not the poet, but his grandfather), hopped over to shout at him, and a poor trooper nearby, whose leg was blown off.

"Pick up your leg and get moving, Horace!" Benet shouted. "And you, Howard, on your feet and –"

A bullet grazed Benet's throat, then two ripped his uniform, scoring his torso, and tumbled by. "Bloody repeaters!" he gargled in a spray of blood as he bounced away on his pogo stick.

Roger drew the metal frame from his ruck and assembled his own pogo stick, ducking as bullets whacked past. Then he crawled over to help Horace with his. The poor man was on his first jump and in excruciating pain.

"Hold your leg in place," he said. "It'll heal, re-attach. And hurt. Lots." He made sure the kid held the leg in place, while he assembled Horace's stick.

"Now, up," he said.

How they managed, he didn't know. He never knew. In short order, though, they were astride their metal steeds and bouncing ignominiously across the rockscape, joining up with others and forming a loose column. Satan had decreed that CLAP's ground transport would be pogo sticks only. It was undignified, inefficient, liable to make one puke, and excruciating on injuries. Every bounce sent spikes of agony through his balls and up his spine. The only positive aspect was that the pogo stick's bounding, irregular motion made the rider harder to hit.

He caught sight of Henry, barely recognizable, a mashed sack. He cringed in fear and revulsion. Cringing hurt, too.

Just behind him, Horace said, "Sir, my leg is healing already, like you said, but it's healing crooked."

Roger nodded, looked over his shoulder and said, "Yeah, sooner or later it'll get shot off again and maybe it'll heal straight next time." It would heal. After all, pain would be less effective if one got used to it.

He felt sorry for Horace. The poor guy had it worse than the rest. He wasn't even a lawyer. He was an accountant.

*

The transit to the site was worse. Whenever you felt at your lowest in hell, the minions of hell found a way to make it lower. Your only option was to do nothing, sit still, and ferment. Except that didn't work well, either. Something would come along to displace you or crush you or otherwise deepen your suffering.

CLAP's deployment here would make things worse, not better. Hell wasn't supposed to be fair, or even unfair. There was some kind of algorithm at the head office as to how fair or unfair hell was supposed to be, when. Said algorithm probably changed regularly.

Everything else did.

So CLAP rode pogo sticks in Ashcanistan, because the sticks caused the troopers more pain. They'd had camels once, in Sinberia. In Hellaska they'd had fast dirt bikes, but no Arctic clothing. CLAP's missions were recorded in the scars on his body: some healed crooked; some wouldn't heal, and just oozed.

That fucking Benet: He was as atrocious in afterlife as he'd been in life. While alive, Roger had never heard of Benet. Apparently, it was his brilliant idea to issue single-shot rifles at the Little Big Horn and at several other battles during the Indian Wars, insisting (despite evidence and pleading troops) that "aimed single shots" were better than repeating weapons. The locals here had hellish copies of AK-47s, RPGs, that Russian .50 caliber machine gun whose designation Roger could never remember. 'That Fucking Benet,' as everyone referred to him, insisted they use .45-70 Springfield rifles, single shot. The rifles were accurate enough, except when gravity or the laws of explosives suddenly changed, but the CLAP were routinely slaughtered by peasants with better weapons. And That Fucking Benet would never learn. "Aim better!" was his only advice.

All Benet did was tell you to aim better. McCarthy ran everything else, constantly ranting about Communists. He was doing so now, voice shifting and syncopating as he bounced along. They could hear McCarthy through the speakers in their helmets. CLAP had the highest tech gear imaginable, sometimes….

"Remember … that the Commies … had a huge … operation in ... Afghanistan …. Probably did … here, too … Be on the lookout…. We'll need to ask … that question of anyone … we meet."

Seemingly, the local damned would never run out of ammo. However, while progress was infuriatingly slow, pogo sticks did make the CLAP harder targets.

Certain ways to approach indigs don't seem like invasions. Of course, in the best traditions of armies in hell, they didn't use those. Who could one complain to in hell? In fact, their task here was to "ensure that unfairness escalated."

Given the idiots in charge, unfairness would certainly escalate. Roger pounded across the landscape, the pain in his knee like a red-hot rod, jabbing through the side of the knee joint. He kept Horace slightly ahead of him, watching the poor kid grimace rhythmically in agony. It always sucked to be the new guy. Although Roger wasn't that seasoned, himself.

He had no idea how long he'd been here. Why think about eternity? He hadn't been here long enough to get philosophical about the stabbing pain or the stupidity. Though he wasn't sure one ever did. The discomfort changed regularly, so you never got used to it.

Roger dove for cover: a trained reflex. He was in the air before his mind told him there was incoming fire. But his body knew ... as it knew he was about to smash into hard desert and sharp rocks.

He shouted and groaned, "Contact, right!" Others yelled the same warning simultaneously.

Roger found his cover, rolling behind a slight hummock. He skinned a shoulder: the new pain counterpointed the pain in his knee; every movement felt like fire.

His military training came to the fore. The designer of the ALICE pack he wore should be somewhere here in hell, wearing one for all eternity; and that dumbass Springfield rifle he carried was a bitch when you had to roll on it.

He pulled its sling from around his shoulder and opened the breech, then fumbled for ammo. He had twenty cartridges, which That Fucking Benet had determined were all one needed, if every shot counted. The man predated suppressing fire.

Unfortunately, the enemy didn't. The locals were pouring out fire from a hell-made Russian-style Dushka, and he thought he recognized AK fire.

Between bursts, Roger heard Benet shout, "... precise, aimed shots ..." and gritted his teeth. In his opinion, they needed a machine gun to lay down fire, then maneuver, suppress, and riddle every enemy in sight. This 'aimed shots' crap was not going to work – again.

He wriggled out of his ALICE pack, with the frame gouging him as he did. They had no body armor, of course. Most couldn't die permanently; obliteration was a mythical fate, or at least very rare. If you did die, you were recycled through the Mortuary and usually sent right back to your unit. So CLAP wasn't issued body-armor. Why carry the extra weight? Why bother?

Why bother with anything?

Then someone started screaming as he was hit.

That's why.

He slid his pack up near the ridge of his little hummock, raised his rifle carefully, and tried not to flinch as he shot. He didn't shoot at anything in particular. He just felt better doing something, instead of nothing.

Benet whacked him stingingly with a swagger stick and shouted, "What are you shooting at, trooper?"

"A general," he snapped.

Poor Benet was condemned to try to lead lawyers, accountants and philosophers into battle for all eternity. A more prestigious post in the regular military always eluded him. That didn't make the jackass pleasant.

Ba-boom!

The explosion blew a huge ball of dust into a rising cloud, followed immediately by a concussive slam that shook the ground and punched his ears. Overpressure slapped him with hot gas and ammonia. The *ba-boom* would be the calling card of the Supervising Legal Airborne Group ("SLAG"), dropping aerial judgment on the opposition.

Then it got quiet, very quiet – and not only because he was partly deaf: there was no opposition left alive anymore.

The deafness was always temporary. Hell liked its residents to experience every sensation to the fullest, like that Britney Spears song playing incessantly at full volume for a week. He'd never get that insipid tune out of his mind.

Benet had been blown flat and no one was disposed to help him get up.

Helmet off, Captain McCarthy took over, slicking his hair self-consciously: "We are here to provide the damned with the benefits of modern legal judgment and, I hope, to promote the American way of life. I –"

"Shut it, Tail-dragger Joe, America ain't no part of perdition," someone shouted.

McCarthy spun, then must have decided to ignore the heckler.

With a muscle ticking in his jaw, he shifted his speech to practical matters: "Before we start, let's find a building and organize our files. Thurmond, go ahead, please."

Catcalls went up throughout, though they'd all known this was coming.

Crusty sergeant Thurmond bounded away, two flankers at his heels. It was hard not to respect Strom Thurmond, even if he was a stubborn old womanizer. The man had volunteered for the Airborne in WWII while in his 40s; then served in the U.S. Senate until he was over a hundred.

Roger grabbed his ruck, gingerly easing it on his blistered and battered shoulders. He found his pogo stick (sadly, still functional), and joined the rest of CLAP, bouncing into town. His slung rifle banged his shoulder and head with every leap, until he was in a murderous rage.

Up ahead, Sergeant Thurmond picked a convenient building from several still standing, made of low, thick brick, on the near edge of this once-sprawling hive of scum and villainy. Within a hundred yards, Roger gave up bouncing. Holding the stick over his shoulder like a ladder, he sprinted for the designated headquarters through jolts of pain and tumbled through its doorway in a tangle with Horace – and McCarthy, who never waited to be last.

Benet, the jackass, was at least man enough to wait outside until everyone entered. Counting them, his bushy beard fluffed with every word.

A hiatus between bombardment and confusion. They seemed safe, for now. Troopers stood watch at the high windows. Medics treated casualties.

Roger waved one nurse away: he didn't need a clumsy lawyer-medic probing his knee. The knee was intact; little would improve it; and, with no anesthetic, treatment would be agonizing.

Speaking of which, Henry Summers looked pretty bad. Half his face had been shot off. Now the remaining face was healing, crushed and twisted, with a drooling smile that exposed broken rear molars on the right side. Missing teeth and crushed bone made his jaw asymmetrical. Added to the wrinkled ruins of his leg and torso, Henry's situation was nightmarish.

Henry would adapt to living with his disfigurements. Roger

would get used to looking at him Eventually. But not quite yet. Guiltily, Roger dropped his eyes and busied himself with his gear.

Everyone was preparing for the next phase of their mission. They carried the necessary legal codes with them, in those brutal ALICE packs. Roger reached for his, safe in a lockbox with sharp corners, then bound in an accordion file, sealed with a Perdition Seal that burst into flames when he released it so he could access the several binders within.

Each of them carried two hundred pounds of documentation. All documents must be accounted for, because those were their only references: the infernalnet was, of course, unreliable, even if they could get signal out here.

Pages were always out of order. Any file might contain any page, and the pages were differently printed and spaced, so it was hard to tell which followed which. It was an administrative nightmare.

Suddenly, McCarthy screamed like a girl and kept screaming: "Nooooo! Eeeaaaaeeiii!"

They all stared at Tail-dragger Joe. Had McCarthy melted down again? On McCarthy's pants were telltale stains of wetness at the crotch. Wonderful.

"Sir?" someone asked. "Captain?"

McCarthy hummed or cursed to himself and nobody else spoke or moved for far too long.

Finally, Benet stepped over and lifted the cover letter from the dirt floor of the makeshift headquarters. Smoothing out the wrinkles caused by McCarthy clutching it like a doll, Benet read aloud: "'The operative legal code of the day is that of the USSR, nineteen sixty-five.'"

McCarthy was curled on the ground, whimpering, "Commies … commies … commies …."

While Benet alternated between cajoling and kicking the worthless old radical, Roger sorted his papers, leaving appropriate gaps where pages were missing.

Crooked-legged Horace and Rehnquist, CLAP's paralegal, came around to sort, stack and box. Boxing was necessary to keep the papers in order, but the boxes were held together with duct tape that had degraded in this dusty, gritty hell of hells. Horace and

Rehnquist did the best they could.

Roger snuck his phone behind his raised knees. Perhaps there might be some brief infernalnet connectivity. Worth a shot. He slid out the keyboard and pulled up DisgraceBook, on the off-chance of connecting. He recognized no names. He had fifty invites for dates with succubi, Insecurity Service surveys, and suggestions of souls to bedevil. He clicked on the first one of those.

The page came up on his screen, where a grizzled old man leapt naked out of a bathtub. Hurling enough invective to merit notice even in hell, the nude senior snagged an old Garand rifle from the corner and rasped, "Get off my page!"

Roger shut off the phone.

Quiet persisted until a relief platoon of infantry arrived to assist with insecurity. They remained outside for the most part. He avoided meeting them, but caught a glimpse of them when their lieutenant came in to talk to Benet.

Among the New Dead, infantrymen spent the afterlife getting shot up. One – with dark, curly hair and a Greek accent – was horrifically scarred. Appalling injuries were part of this hell. Roger wondered if he'd eventually end up looking like the Greek. He tried not to be disgusted by the poor guy and waited for lunch.

As always this year, lunch was a stiff stick of jerky and a piece of dry bread. So was breakfast and dinner. He sighed as he chewed slowly, wondering when the menu would change, and to what. Last year they'd had only raw tuna, past its peak. One ate because nerves and habits compelled it – *if* you could: Some guys in hell had no stomachs; some had no anuses. Some starved to death, becoming more and more helpless and easy prey in the process....

"Howard, wake up," someone snapped, too loud.

Roger jerked upright. He'd been napping against the wall, and now had a crick in his neck.

McCarthy glowered at him and moved on.

"Yes, sir," Roger said to his back.

Next to him, mashed-up Henry said, "Get ready."

Roger knew what Henry meant. He turned away, trying not to look at Henry's twisted face. Poor bastard.

Get ready – to work. Hell might have too many lawyers, but none were in residence here. The locals wanted their grievances heard. And CLAP would hear every one, rendering injustice as best they could.

Crooked-legged Horace started a roster, so the locals could lodge their complaints and seek resolution.

The good part was that the shooting had stopped. The bad part was the cases ranged from sad to bizarre to disquieting.

McCarthy grabbed the first dozen and read them off. Then…

"Next we have a classless action lawsuit by the remaining eight lives of a hell-kitten for attempted genocide of mice; suit brought by said tabby hell-kitten (striped-winged variety) called Lucky, who wanted to grow up. Countersuit by one 'Sneaky,' the desert hell-fox, who determined that Lucky's life number three will be the tastiest and he, Sneaky, has been unfairly deprived of it. Howard, can you handle this?"

"Yes, sir. I can." You knew you were in hell when you were a lawyer defending litigious animals badmouthing one another.

McCarthy read on: "A Mohammed (… why is every third male in hell named Mohammed? …) alleges that a prostitute did *not* give him, and I quote, 'a poetically succulent release,' and *did* give him several nasty diseases. She says because, in hell, orgasm …" McCarthy hesitated over the word, "… is commonly unattainable, and the diseases were the weekly special, she's innocent: she only provides a service. Summers?"

"I can do that, sir," Summers mumbled through smashed lips.

"A certain ... former … presidential candidate, Democratic (presumably a Communist), insists an election wasn't run fairly. Regulatory Statutes of Unfairness say that elections in hell are supposed to be rigged. I'll take that one."

Roger felt sorry for everyone in that case. McCarthy would rant.

Benet said, "In here are our primary mission orders."

You could hear a feather drop as he ripped open the package. These were never good. A flash and a nauseating whiff of sulfur attested to its authenticity.

Benet scanned them, sighed in relief and read aloud: "We are to bring back the head of the most honest man in hell for deposition."

"It's a trap!" McCarthy scoffed. "An honest man in hell?"

Roger muttered, "Certainly neither of you." Nor himself, but he was honest enough to admit it.

Horace said, "Evil and dishonesty don't have to go together. The only hurt I caused was some fractional percentage of shortage to the IRS. It benefited my clients. Not evil, but dishonest."

"Who are we going to find here who's evil but honest? Peter the Great? Julius Caesar? Those Greeks from that famous battle?"

Horace said, "I can get on the infernalnet and see who's around here."

"Do that. You young kids know how that stuff works."

"Yes, sir; we do," Horace agreed, though he'd been fifty at the time of his death. "Young" in this case meant "more current."

*

The next morning, in a red-painted mud-brick hall, domed and spired, Roger conducted his trial as barrister for the tabby hell-kitten named Lucky, using the legal code of the UK, 1923, complete to powdered wig. Standard procedure, most days but, today, the minor demon serving as judge was glorying in his role.

"Your Dishonor, we –" *Zap!* Lightning singed Roger's butt. "Your Dishonor, we object –" *Zap! Zap!* "My Lord Judge, we propose –"

Zap! Zap! Zap!

At noon, the code switched to that of King Kamehameha of Hawaii. Roger steeled himself for horrors to come. The Hawaiian death penalty was even more terrifying when you knew you *couldn't* die from it.

Mercifully, he was able to argue the stripe-winged hell-kitten's case well enough for the case to be dismissed before the Kamehameha rules kicked in. He doubted that poor little Lucky would really enjoy his victory, since after his eight more legally-mandated lives came and went, the hell-kitten would face innumerable lives with no legal protections: the restraining order against the fox would lapse.

And the smiling desert hell-fox would be waiting.

*

That evening, back in CLAP's compound, now wired and sandbagged, they chewed their jerky and discussed their mission.

Benet said, “Satan wants the head of the most honest man in hell. By specifying head, should I assume he wants this head *sans* body?”

“I believe we must, son,” Sergeant Thurmond drawled in his scratchy voice; ancient skin wrinkled around his beady eyes. “I always take His Satanic Majesty at His word.”

“The next question is: who’s the most honest man in hell? Accepting that ‘good,’ ‘honest’ and even ‘kind’ don’t necessarily overlap, who would meet the criterion of ‘honest’?”

Roger thought about that. Nearly every damned soul in hell thought he was doomed unjustly to eternal torment; they sinned and died and sinned more and died again; the damned dead never learned; new sinners arrived constantly. Everybody in hell lied constantly, if only to himself. So could there even be a soul in this backwater of New Hell who was honest?

Crooked-legged Horace said, “I have it: Gandhi.”

Roger tried to smile but smirked instead. “Gandhi. Of course.”

McCarthy muttered, “That skinny little Communist bastard.”

Roger didn’t think Gandhi qualified as a communist. The father of *ahimsa* (nonviolence) as a political strategy, yes. Liberal, certainly. Pacifist, mostly. Of course, McCarthy accused everyone of being a communist.

Benet said, “I have only once heard that name. Who was he; what’s he about now?”

Roger said, “In India, Gandhi pioneered *satyagraha*, which means resisting tyranny with passive disobedience. He led his people to civil independence from the British. Nonviolent. Persuasive. Unassailably consistent in his beliefs.”

Benet snorted, but said, “He certainly sounds promising. Where do we find him?”

Horace answered: “I believe he’s right downtown, protesting something.”

Hardly surprising.

The day turned cold; its chill bit Roger’s lungs. They met no resistance on their way ‘downtown.’ Factions abounded in Kabum; after their landing the day before, they were just one more clutch of damned souls among the doomed from everywhere. Distant battles raged, as residents of hell fought over metaphors or territory or eye-color or infernal affiliation: men made hell familiar, and war was familiar to every soul from every era.

They walked downtown. Roger preferred the blisters from his boots to yesterday's parachuting and pogo-sticking. Streets here were convoluted and narrow and, as usual, their maps were wrong. So they walked in the general direction of downtown, among mud-brick facades and teetering high rises with blown-out glass, guided by eye and ear and instinct to where the damned were congregating.

They found an open plaza surrounding a parliament building: in it was a flagpole; on the pole flapped a tattered flag showing a black devil dancing on a red mountaintop: the symbol of Ashcanistan.

Only the flag was familiar. Roger had never before served in Kabum. They'd not been briefed for this foray. On the whole, the town felt ancient, but then there were the gutted high-rises ... stupidity from every age, chockablock on the streets.

A protest was ongoing, involving thousands upon thousands, old and new, in the costumes of human history. CLAP went unremarked and unchallenged, despite weapons, as they patrolled the perimeter looking for their witness: nonviolent demonstration or not, sarrisophori and demons and bedawi and ifrits and kaffirs and modern soldiers prowled among the throng: helmets with horsehair crests and metal wings and slitted visors and horns and feathers and spikes and chinstraps and faceshields and MOP re-breathers turned to them and away again. Kindred souls.

"I see him," McCarthy said. "At the base of the steps. A scrawny little weasel, sanctimonious in his cowardice."

Gandhi was wearing homespun, despite the day's chill. From old photographs, Roger recognized some of Gandhi's dedicated disciples. Ahead, people squeezed toward demon guards. Closer to Gandhi, his followers were organized in ranks, climbing low stairs in formation.

"Very much like communists," McCarthy commented.

"Or soldiers," Roger threw out. McCarthy's paranoia and obsession was really irritating to him.

As marchers reached the top, demons on risers flanking the podium held up pokers that flashed orange-hot and stabbed the leading wave of demonstrators. Screaming, the damned protesters thrashed and rolled down the steps. Some got to their feet and stumbled toward the rear of the line, to repeat the process. Others crawled away.

"What the hell is this?" Benet asked.

"It's called 'passive resistance.' They seek to overwhelm the demons without fighting."

"Does that work?"

"Only against a civilized enemy worried about public opinion."

"Isn't it rather ridiculous? You'd think he'd learn."

So are single-shot rifles against repeaters, you jackass. "It did work against the British in India. His proposal to use *satyagraha* against the Nazis in World War Two was never tested."

Benet said, "So I'd suspect. Well, let's see if he's our man."

Sobs from the non-violent seared by pokers sounded, strangely disturbing.

McCarthy said, "Roger, you seem to know something about this man. Introduce us, on the double."

"Yes, sir." Probably a good idea. Benet knew virtually nothing about Gandhi or his time. McCarthy had the manners of a pig. Even a simple, reasonable request came out of McCarthy's mouth sounding pompous.

Surprised by his own calm, Roger led the way. He hadn't yet died in hell, though he'd suffered numerous indignities. He sighed. There was going to be a first time. Maybe today.

Roger stolidly led the party from CLAP forward, edging through the throng.

Gandhi noted them approaching, faced them, and inclined his bald head.

"Mister Gandhi," Roger said, "or do you prefer *Bapu*?" 'Bapu' was Indian for 'father,' and the whole nation had once called Gandhi that. But Gandhi was complex, and also demonstrably racist. Nor was Gandhi a pussy. 'I do believe,' he once wrote, 'that where there is only a choice between cowardice and violence, I would advise violence.' So Roger figured that between the racism and the exhortation to violence, canny old Bapu had earned his way here, just like everybody else.

Little Gandhi was all beatific smiles. His cohorts stood nearby but made no move to interfere. "I answer to either. How may I help you?"

In the midst of this mayhem, Gandhi tried to be reassuring: Roger could smell roasted flesh, hear the wails, and yet the leader seemed undisturbed.

Benet asked, "Mister Gandhi, sir, is the mob going to be a problem?" CLAP moved in, creating a wall between their target and the *danse noir* on the steps.

"The 'mob'?" Gandhi asked, still beaming. "Right must battle might, or lose all legitimacy. They are but supplicants for decency, presenting a rational request to the demons. This 'mob' is not a problem, though certainly the demons may decide to make them such, for their own purposes."

"Well then, sir, we were sent to bring you."

"'Sent'? Ordered? You do not yourselves choose to come for me?" He tsk'd knowingly, and Roger understood it was an attempt at debate. Among doomed screams and demonic violence, this tableau was bizarre, even for the netherworlds.

Benet looked confused and annoyed. McCarthy looked apoplectic.

Roger stifled a grin. That sight was worth enjoying. Pleasure in hell was hard to find.

Benet faced the little Indian and said, "Come with us, or face unimaginable pain and suffering. I personally try to avoid pain and suffering." Benet must think Gandhi didn't understand.

Gandhi said, "You could choose to endure it, however. You could choose not to participate in hell's charade. New Hell, they call this place, but nothing is new here. If people refuse to take part in Satan's games – that would be new. If all souls do that, the devil, by any name, becomes powerless."

Incorrect, but inspiring. Torment didn't require assent on the part of the tormented: you like it, you don't; you run, or you fight. Didn't matter: this wasn't a world to win by intimidation and press manipulation, by inspiration or steadfastness. Right and wrong didn't matter here: Erra and the terrifying Seven were ripping their way through all the hells, sent from Above, meting out injustice to innocent and guilty alike.

So Gandhi *didn't* get it. He was doing in afterlife what had worked for him in life, like so many others. Kabum was a part of the greater underworld, in all its manifest complexity. No debater's trick or fillip of law could change that. Roger admired Gandhi, the way you'd admire a diorama. It took exceptional strength of character to behave this way in hell. Or sheer insanity. Impressive, either way.

McCarthy muttered, "Damn commie."

Gandhi heard McCarthy and responded: "Indeed not. I am no communist, nor a capitalist, a monarchist, nor any other type of statist. I am myself, and only myself. You serve another, by choice. I serve myself, by choice."

Realizing that Benet was confused and McCarthy about to burst a blood vessel, which in hell meant literally and messily, Roger stepped in: "Bapu Gandhi, we have been asked to find the most honest man in hell. Your name was mentioned, and I took the liberty of presuming you might be he."

Gandhi laughed in delight, in a low resonant tenor.

"Oh, young man, I can make no such claim."

Modesty, but perhaps false. All men lie. "No?"

The wizened elf sighed and smiled and said, "I was once a lawyer. I lusted and lied to protect my sordid dalliance." Ghandi shrugged. "I manipulated truth for effect, for my nation. I made statements deemed racist. I do not regret any of it, even now, but I am here because I was not as honest as I was effective. And I am in New Hell, subject to Satan's will, when Naraka is the place of torment, or proper hell, for Islamists and Hindus and Sikhs and Jaines and Buddhists – Yama should be my judge, not this Father of Lies who rules in New Hell. The underworld's mistake, or my own? No matter. Here I am, among the other New Dead, liar that I am, opportunist that I am, with the flock that died believing my lies all around me."

McCarthy asked, "Who, then?"

Little Gandhi shrugged his skinny shoulders. "Only the press thinks it knows who is honest. Walter Cronkite is somewhere in New Hell. He is a most trusted judge of honesty and keeper of opinion. He haunts the battlefields, beyond the minefields. He would be a good bet. If one wanted to bet in New Hell. What is there to lose, in afterlife?"

"Very well. However, we must bring you along as well, just in case."

"With respect, I refuse to comply."

McCarthy motioned to Benet. Benet drew his saber and swung smoothly; he'd had much time to practice his technique here.

The anti-communist crusader looked down at the head of Gandhi, rolling on the ground, and said, "I should think it was obvious, and now demonstrated, what one could lose." He wore a shit-eating grin. "Yama, Kali, Satan – whoever you wanted to invoke – What an asshole."

Gandhi's head came to rest, face up. Gandhi's face smiled wanly at them as his body, vomiting blood, collapsed next to his head. His eyes tracked his corpse, calm and resigned, as his head was stuffed into the sack Thurmond had in his hand.

Roger felt nauseous. McCarthy had enjoyed the beheading.

Then they looked around them. They stared hard at Gandhi's followers, who stared back, silent and ominously unmoving. CLAP wasn't supposed to use violence, except in self-defense. Self-defense might be needed any second. Roger had only his slung, single-shot rifle, no long bayonet at his side like That Fucking Benet.

Another Indian moved through the crowd as if he were parting the waters of the Red Sea: Gandhi's assistant or his successor: Roger couldn't tell which.

This Indian guy took a deep breath and said in a booming voice, "Bapu will come back to us in time. Meanwhile, we shall continue our sagratyha." He turned and walked up the steps, heedless of the writhing wounded around him or even the final twitches of Gandhi's body in its pool of gore. The devotees followed.

So they weren't even going to bury their beloved leader, just leave his body on the steps. Roger was shocked; he didn't understand it.

Benet said, "So we proceed to the battlefield beyond the minefields."

Roger understood that.

*

The minefields were easy to find. South of town was a large, vacant area, pocked with craters.

They dismounted, stacked arms – well, sticks – and approached carefully, stepping from existing crater to existing crater. They stepped over a Bactrian's corpse, newly dead; the corpse squished and slid, its skin loose from the meat beneath. Roger nearly retched.

Behind and to the right, a muffled blast threw a shifting shadow. Roger wheeled in time to see somebody flail in midair, then fall, and explode as the damned soul landed on a live mine. Pieces blew skyward and fell to the minefield again, and some hit more live mines and were cast heavenward again, only to crash back to earth....

Seeing someone fall from the sky and smash on the minefield brought Roger a moment of clarity. The human body was intelligently designed, if the purpose of the design all along had been to easily inflict maximum pain and damage. So maybe life was just hell's kindergarten.

Benet interrupted Roger's epiphany: "Howard, get on that gadget of yours and find where this Bronchitis fellow is."

"Walter Cronkite. Famous reporter, and actually very well respected. I do think he's a good bet, sir."

"Well, get on with it."

This being New Hell, at the critical moment Roger had trouble manipulating his phone, with its intermittent connection, the shifting sunlight and a sack with a wiggling head in it nearby, as well as a staring, belligerent McCarthy and a confused, frustrated Benet cleaning his saber.

After a few minutes of swiping, typing and cursing, he had video. Cronkite looked good, as he had at his prime, which was about when Roger had been born.

"He's reporting live from the eastern front, where a battle is."

"Which battle?" McCarthy wanted to know. "Battle against Commies?"

"Who knows? There are so many battles."

"Well, let's proceed. Back out the way we came, then a blister break."

Roger tried not to think about blisters. Blisters in hell were worse than blisters in life. They infected, oozed, scarred over abscessing pockets. He could feel them blossoming inside his stiff leather wingtips, and along the edge of the upper. They'd pop and peel. You could ignore the burn, and the layers of skin coming off. The necrotic-tissue damage was something else.

You wanted to be first for treatment. Treatment hurt a lot, but was over quickly. The later patients got to anticipate the pain. Shrieks from each victim primed the next to expect agony. Benet always went last and, to his credit, never uttered a sound. That Fucking Benet had never commanded in battle, but he did have courage.

He was also stubborn, after a century and more, about those stupid single-shot rifles.

Roger wondered about Gandhi and his obsession with passive resistance and Benet with his single-shot rifles. Neither could help you in hell. So was hell meant to break the damned of their sinners' habits? Satan never offered explanations. The CLAP handled petty cases to no useful end, for eternity; and, with the endlessly shifting legal codes, botched most of them. Like that hell-kitten named Lucky.

When they stopped to lunch and to treat their feet, their shrieks and screams seemed to please the locals. Hawk-nosed men and gray-eyed women in indigo watched in delight as lawyers suffered.

When Roger's turn came, their company's combat medic punctured Roger's festering sores and poured alcohol over them. Roger tried not to howl when the alcohol hit his liquefied flesh. He flushed and sweated; his brain spun; nausea washed over him like surf. Then he spun down a deep dark tunnel into unconsciousness.

In his nice black comfy place, a shoe prodded him. "Howard, wake up."

He groaned, tried to rise and failed with the pack holding him back, rolled on sharp rocks and stood. His feet were numbed now, so he felt the pokes in knees and elbows all the more.

There were no showers or clean suits in hell, either, and his tie was too tight.

They bounced endlessly across the craterscape. The water in his canteen tasted like a combination of mud and urine. In coldest weather, they got moldy iced tea. In extreme heat, it was sometimes boiling Drownin' Numbnuts coffee with curdled cream no sugar, and a dead mouse. He'd like water. Clean, safe water. Just once.

Without warning, sniper fire ripped from cover across the wasteland.

Henry fell over, making whistling noises, his shoulder blown apart. Thurmond grabbed his shoulder and held it so it might heal reasonably straight. Three CLAPpers returned fire and, despite the single shot nature of their rifles, the massive .45-70 rounds succeeded in scaring away the enemy.

They bivouacked under a shivery chill vault, red like clotted blood with heaving violet and pink swirls. Not pretty like an aurora. Just disorienting and vomitous. He shivered miserably for hours on end, trying to recall black starry nights and crescent moons smiling at him.

The next morning they munched their rations and moved out. His feet were lumps of rancid meat in his shoes at this point, and his knee had stopped hurting, and stopped bending.

Far ahead, though, was a defensive line of rocks, sandbags, mortars and other weapons, and thousands of Ashcan troops trying to protect their little piece of hell from an onslaught of Chinese and Zulu and punk kids.

"Damned commies!" McCarthy muttered deliberately loudly. "If we can find something to charge them with, I'll haul them in for hearings."

Roger really wished McCarthy would forget communism. Even communists were victims in hell. The past of a sinner paled before his netherworldly sins. The damned butchered hapless victims because they could. Because they always had. Because they always would.

Roger had never been a hero. He'd been too clever by half for that. But in hell, if he could find some heroic path, he'd take it. If it could get him out of hell. But then, heroism isn't about premeditation. Holding "hearings" of alleged communists was about premeditation.

Ahead, though, was a small civilian truck bristling with gear. It didn't look like a 'technicals' truck; he saw no machine gun rising from its bed. As they got closer, Roger identified its fancy satellite dish and antennae. Not irregulars, then: too much expensive gear. They dismounted and proceed on foot, pogo sticks under their arms. It felt strange to walk, to see a stationary horizon. What twist of physics let them pogo so well, without falling and exacerbating their injuries more? Or was it just personalized torture for men who'd enjoyed limousines and first-class travel?

A short distance away, someone stood in front of a camera, a pop-filtered microphone trained on him, pointing to the outgoing fire. It was definitely Cronkite: handsome and dignified. He seemed in fine shape.

Then when he turned, Roger realized that Cronkite was shot to hell. His camera-loving face was perfect, unmarred, yet battlefield butchery covered his body. Par for the course in Ashcanistan, but anywhere else in hell he'd be dead and recycled by now.

Cronkite's voice was deep, resonant, familiar: "Greetings, Soldiers. Are you here with the Forced Unified Central Kabum Emergency Resistance…?"

Cronkite's next words were drowned out by mortar fire and the basso whoosh of a round incoming.

The round landed far behind them. Roger flinched but didn't duck.

After he stood, Benet nudged him. He said, "No, sir, we're lawyers."

"Ah, yes. The lawyers. CLAP. I've heard of you. You are almost as popular as I, myself." Cronkite's voice sounded avuncular.

McCarthy stared at Cronkite wordlessly.

Roger spoke up: "You are *the* Walter Cronkite?"

"If you mean the reporter, I was; yes. What I am now, I'm not sure. But as you can see, I'm still reporting. It's what I do, wherever I am."

"I'm Roger Howard, sir. I remember watching you while I was growing up."

"You're making me feel old."

"Sorry, sir."

"No apologies necessary. I assume, though, that this is a professional visit? Am I being sued again? That happens more here than it ever did in life."

"No, that's not why we're here. We're here to –"

McCarthy finally said, "Cronkite … weren't you the understudy of Murrow?"

"I was," Cronkite nodded. "I recognize you, sir."

Roger noticed Cronkite hadn't greeted McCarthy.

McCarthy did too: "Polls proclaimed you the most trusted man on television, Cronkite."

"I was called that. I certainly tried to be."

"So tell me the truth, Mister Cronkite, now that it doesn't matter. Was Murrow a communist? A sympathizer?"

Cronkite rolled his eyes and feigned surprise: he must have heard the slurs in life.

"Murrow? Not to my knowledge, no."

McCarthy shifted uncomfortably. "You're certain?"

"Quite certain. But what does any of this matter now, in hell?" Cronkite waved his hand, indicating the area around them; he didn't even wince in pain until after he lowered his injured hand.

Roger could see McCarthy considering Cronkite's question. If Cronkite was honest, then his expressed certainty was genuine. If not, then Cronkite wasn't the soul they wanted. But McCarthy obviously hoped to harm Cronkite in either case.

What struggle must be ongoing inside McCarthy's twisted mind, between duty and vendetta? *McCarthy, you're a moron*, Roger thought.

"Are you the most trusted man in hell, Cronkite? Yes or no?" McCarthy pressed.

"I would hope not," said the famous newsie. "Not now."

"Then you admit your were, in life, on television. But not in hell, on hellevision?

Cronkite smiled sadly. "What had life to do with television? Precious little. Television in life was a lie; hellevision in afterlife is the same. I condensed the world's events each day into a small nugget of predigested facts, presented for the layman. Usually the subjects I explained were beyond my own knowledge, yet I was expected to report and comment on them, to help greater fools than I rest easy in the night. I tried to be fair, but I did have opinions."

"You sound like you might be our man," McCarthy said slyly.

"You are seeking the most trusted man in hell?" Cronkite surmised, now analytical and not avuncular at all.

Mind like a steel trap, that Cronkite. "The most honest," Roger clarified. "To depose for a trial at the Pentagram."

"I see…. Well, I'm afraid I must decline the honor. First amendment habits die hard. And I certainly can't claim to be the most honest man in all the hells." Cronkite said dismissively and turned toward his camera crew, as if the discussion were now closed.

That Fucking Benet asked, "Do you know who would be, Mister Cronkite?"

"Would be?" Cronkite rounded on them. "The most honest? No. However, in my own limited experience of the afterlife, I'd recommend Mathew Brady." The power of the word had once resided with this man; Walter Cronkite had not forgotten.

Roger had no idea who Mathew Brady was.

Benet looked as if he'd been shot: "The Civil War photographer? Abe Lincoln's guy?"

Cronkite said, "Yes, that is he. Was."

"Do you know where this Brady is?" Roger asked.

"When last I spoke to him, he was just over that rise, capturing images of the aftermath of the battle between the Taliban and the Taliwhackers."

Benet nodded. "Thank you. Unfortunately, we'll still have to take you with us."

"Oh? Very well," Cronkite said, seeming rather relaxed as he motioned his crew to take a break.

Roger looked at Benet and at McCarthy, and back at Thurmond and smash-faced Summers and crooked-legged Horace and the rest of CLAP. With the camera crew right there, there was no way to cut off Cronkite's head clandestinely.

Roger realized no one else was going to come out and say it. Sighing, he told the famous news anchor the truth: "Mister Cronkite, sir – we are supposed to bring Satan your head."

"Well," Cronkite said gravely, motioning his camera crew to start rolling: "That's the way it is, this day in hell."

Cronkite stood motionless, eyes locked on Roger, as Benet's saber sliced through his neck.

McCarthy stepped back as blood spurted and the head of Cronkite bounced and rolled at their feet: "I *still* think Murrow was a Commie. Cronkite may have been smart. That doesn't mean he was informed."

McCarthy had no decency in life or afterlife, in Roger's opinion.

Thurmond put Cronkite's head in a leak-proof bag designed for the purpose. "In better days, I always found Cronkite to be a true gentleman," he said in his scratchy Southern drawl. "He was fair, respectful. He talked to the person, not just to the politician. I had good friends on both sides of the aisle, and we all respected him."

McCarthy shrugged. "So long as we have him. I'll find Murrow sometime, too. I know you never believed me, Strom, but you were a Dem yourself at the time, hugging those union cretins. You never saw the bureaucratic communistic Frankenstein that was there." McCarthy's voice trembled: he was excited.

Tiredly, Thurmond said, "You convinced people at first, Joseph. But in the end, no one saw what you saw. Either you were alone in your genius, or mistaken." Thurmond headed back to his stick.

Roger said, "Sirs, we need to move on," ducking his head and turning his back on McCarthy while, inside, he seethed.

Amid sporadic outgoing and incoming fire, they made their way across a rocky hillside. No bullets came their way. To the north, Taliban were shooting into the town. To the south, the Taliwhackers, as Cronkite had called them, were returning fire but aiming poorly while rebel groups fought the Chinese, the Mughals, and Satan only knew who else. Apart from the racket, travel was reasonably safe.

They made it over the next ridge on foot (for once). Some distance down-slope, there was an American tent, Civil War vintage; nearby were encampments of other civil warriors: English, Irish, Russian, and Mexican.

They spotted Brady, all alone outside the American tent.

Benet said, "That's odd. During the Civil War, Brady sent teams of photographers out, while he stayed in New York. Each team was three to five. Yet Brady seems to be by himself."

Brady was handsome. His bushy hair and Van Dyke framed an aristocratic face. He didn't look wounded or disfigured.

Roger thought the large-bellows-camera mounted on a sturdy wooden tripod delightful.

Here and there in the camp were other tripods and cameras, a tent with folding wooden doors that was probably a darkroom, a supply-wagon overflowing with boxes.

Benet stalked over to the photographer: "Mister Mathew Brady?"

Brady squinted through his spectacles, then over them.

"General Benet, isn't it?"

"Indeed I am, sir."

Brady said, "You seem a bit older than I recall. I'm glad you had a long life."

"I was sorry to hear of your passing, even though it came after my own," replied That Fucking Benet.

Brady's face drooped slightly. "I'd hoped afterlife would be better than life. Instead, it seems perpetually to show me the worst of existence. I suppose that is punishment for my photographs."

"It may be. Though you always showed things honestly."

Brady's Van Dyke trembled. "That I did, or tried to. War needs no exaggeration. Nor, I found, does everyday torment."

Benet said, "So it seems. For your candor, sir, we must take you to Satan himself to be deposed."

"Deposed?"

"This is the Coordinating Legal Airborne Platoon, Mister Brady," McCarthy interrupted, puffing himself up.

"Ah," Brady said. "Yes, there are jokes one could make, but it's hardly worth doing so, is it?"

Benet nodded, without rancor or humor. "You *do* speak the truth, Mister Brady."

"Why do you need me to accompany you?"

"Actually, sir, I will be forthright with you, as a peer. We need only your head," Benet told him. "More, we are required to bring and authorized to take *only* your head with us."

"Not all of me..." Brady slumped and sighed. "I see." He looked from That Fucking Benet to Roger to Thurmond, to the rest of CLAP, behind them. "May I make a final request, then? Final for now, I suppose."

"What is that?" Benet asked.

"Would someone capture a photograph of this event? Before I go? The photo can be delivered with the others." He indicated a leather box with a large label gummed to it.

Benet said, "I can work the camera. I am familiar with the type. Mister Howard, will you take my sword?"

Roger wanted nothing less than to take Benet's sword in hand. Death might not be permanent, but suffering was always remembered. Brady's head would be turned over to higher headquarters, perhaps eventually to Satan himself. Roger looked around, hoping one of his colleagues would volunteer to do the deed. All CLAP knew what Roger wanted. Everyone looked at their feet.

"I regret this already," Roger said. "But I will do it."

The inevitable cannot be successfully forestalled. Brady led Benet to the tent. Roger followed.

"Let me prepare the plate and set the equipment," Brady said wistfully. The two disappeared into the tent, leaving Roger alone outside.

In tight quarters, the two bumped canvas now and again.

Behind Roger, McCarthy came up. "Are we ready, then?"

"Yes, sir," Roger agreed. "General Benet will take a photo of the scene as Brady's last request."

"What the devil's the point of that? Really. This is hell, if no one has noticed. Such a photo won't go anywhere, accomplish anything…."

"I suppose a paper somewhere might print it, sir," Roger said.

"If anyone remembers who this man is. And he'll be back, soon enough. I live for the day when I get to meet Karl Marx face to face."

"I'm sure you do, sir."

"What is that supposed to mean? I've been watching you for some time, Howard. Didn't you go to some fruity liberal school back east?"

"Harvard, sir."

"Harvard. Bastion of northern intellectual liberal elitists – my enemies. A stronghold of communist ideology in the decades following my death, I understand."

"Certain professors; yes, sir." *McCarthy, you understand nothing.*

"I never did trust that type. Nor artists. This fellow," he

nodded his head toward Mathew Brady, "is one like that. Always wants to show the pathos, the tragedy, the art of misery. Next thing you know, people think the aggressor is some kind of tragic hero. Who was that little bearded commie after I died? Made into some kind of tee-shirt icon for hippies and dope fiends?"

"Che Guevara?" Roger guessed.

"That's him."

McCarthy finally shut up as Benet and Brady brushed the canvas aside and came out of the tent. Brady took a deep breath and shivered slightly. Benet placed a comforting hand on Brady's shoulder. With the other, he drew his long, curved saber.

Roger awkwardly accepted the heavy blade from Benet; he had little experience handling real swords. Inexperience, today, was a problem for Roger; it mustn't become a problem for Brady. A botched execution would be too much to bear – for them both.

"Mister Brady, I am deeply ashamed," he said, and hesitated. "I must ask you to kneel."

Brady lowered himself to his knees with dignity and bent forward.

Benet was at the camera, under the hood, fiddling.

Roger asked, "General Benet, are you ready?"

"Almost," replied That Fucking Benet. "This is not the same model of camera I trained on. However, I have focus, I think. And flash powder."

Benet fumbled with the plate, reached back under the hood, and slid stuff around. He poured a measure of powder over what looked like a long match, and held it aloft.

"You may proceed, Howard," Benet told Roger.

Mathew Brady shut his eyes and started praying: "Our Father, who art in heaven..."

Prayer to heaven: both touching and ridiculous. Praying to those Above could do no good here, under the rufous vault of hell.

Tears filled Roger's eyes.

Brady stopped praying only when McCarthy made dismissive noises: "Great act."

Roger raised the sword. Its keen edge glittered in the baleful light of Paradise.

He must ensure his swing was true: drop his arm; snapped his wrist; and the blade should cut cleanly through Brady's neck.

Benet pulled the lens cap and tugged the string that ignited the powder. The flash lit the landscape and stinking sulphur filled the air.

Roger dropped his arm convulsively, making sure to keep his eyes open, and snapped his wrist.

The saber cut between Brady's skull and two protruding vertebrae at his shoulders, shearing through cleanly, and struck the rock underneath.

McCarthy snapped, "Damn you, Howard, don't nick that sword."

Staring at the crimson fountain splashing out of Brady's neck, Roger decided he'd had enough.

He'd accept a court-martial. First, he had to earn one.

Roger turned and thrust, as he'd learned in fencing class at Harvard, long ago. The saber didn't respond like a foil but, with no opposing blade, it worked well enough.

The way the smug little McCarthy grunted and convulsed as the saber pierced his guts was most satisfying. A half turn to the right caused McCarthy's eyes to bug out and dropped the little commie-hunter to his knees.

Seeing McCarthy kneeling there made any pending punishment worth the price.

Roger withdrew his blade, raised the saber again, and swung a second time.

McCarthy's head tumbled onto the rocks.

Roger stepped back to await further hellish torment. Instead, That Fucking Benet said, "Brilliant, Mister Howard. What could be more honest than monomaniacal purpose? But please do me one favor."

Roger's brain spun as he tried to parse the unexpected praise. "Yes, sir?"

"Please clean my sword. Thoroughly."

Check and Mate

by

Bradley H. Sinor

"For *God's sake,* John, please stop and sit down!" said Lieserl Einstein to John Adams. Wearing a bright red and yellow Hawaiian shirt, the former American president paced back and forth before his secretary like a cartoon lion in a cage.

Before John Adams could say or do anything in response, thunder rumbled throughout his small office on the Acme Building's twelfth floor in one of New Hell's low-rent neighborhoods.

For a few seconds *everything* shook, knocking half the contents of Adam's desk onto the floor. He had to grab the corner of his high-backed chair to keep from falling.

A few seconds later, the rumbling and tremors stopped, leaving the mess surrounding Adams as the only indication that the event had not been illusory.

"Madam, please don't use the 'G' word. I can do without the thunder and the shaking building. Haven't you learned by now there are some words that you really shouldn't say? After all, we are in hell."

"Sorry, but sometimes, Mister Adams, your infernal pacing drives me crazy," Lieserl replied.

Adams scoffed. Pacing was the way he organized his thoughts; it had been his habit since he was a young boy. Sitting quietly was no part of his nature; a fact he had long since accepted.

A tall woman, thin and dark-haired, Lieserl hadn't grabbed anything to keep her balance. When the walls and floor stopped shaking, she swept a bit of plaster from her tweed skirt, brushed a few loose hairs back into place, looked around the room and shook her head. "I hope you're not expecting me to straighten up," she said. "Even if I do, you'll have it trashed again within a fortnight."

According to Lieserl, most lawyers' offices were disorderly at the best of times. Adams had to admit, looking around at the tumbled piles of law books, papers and empty fast-food containers, that Lieserl was probably right.

If his long-suffering wife, Abigail, saw this office, Adams was certain that she'd give him a thorough tongue-lashing. But she couldn't: Abigail wasn't among hell's residents. That fact gave him some solace, although he missed her terribly.

"Are you sure, Madam Lieserl, that you were not sitting in Congress in the summer of 'Seventy-six? With your attitude you would have been right at home," Adams told his secretary.

He went to the sideboard where the coffee pot remained untouched, picked up an insulated mug and filled it with three fingers of tasteless brown liquid.

"Ja, ja … I'm sure your beloved Declaration of Independence would have had an entirely different tone had you allowed women to participate," she said.

"I'm sure it would have," he said, stone still, stifling his inclination to march back and forth before his desk. "So what did you come in here for?"

"To go over your schedule with you." Lieserl set down her steno book and pulled out her small hellpad, rapidly riffling through several screens.

"Very well." Adams nodded and finished his coffee in a two quick swallows. Thankfully, it had not hardened to a solid in his cup: on some days, his coffee set like mortar, but not on others; the problem was, you didn't know until the cup was in your hand.

One lesson he'd learned since awakening on the Undertaker's table was not to be daunted by small torments. Unpredictable food and drink were minor annoyances in New Hell's array of punishments befitting the sinners. Another lesson was that keeping to a schedule was part of making a living as a lawyer, whether the lawyer was a soul damned in hell or in the land of the living. Since completing his obligatory internship at the Hall of Injustice and opening his own office, Adams had developed a solo practice substantial enough that several of the bigger firms in New Hell had offered him partner status. He had declined each in turn.

Lieserl began his morning update: "We received word that your meeting with Mister James regarding the train robbery charges has been postponed. You still need to prepare a brief on the suit between Fine and Howard. And also you had a call from Mister Marx wanting to know if you would visit him and his brothers next Moansday."

Adams reached down and pawed through the litter on the floor until he found his long-stemmed pipe, apparently undamaged. He cleaned the bowl, refilled it from a tobacco pouch pulled from his desk drawer, and then struck a match across the bottom of his shoe.

"All right," said Adams, once the tobacco was burning. "Set up an appointment with Jesse for the first of the week. Let Harpo know that I will be happy to visit with him and his brothers: they always have the best contraband. As for the Howard versus Fine matter, that can wait. I do need you to double check when Cardozo is lecturing at the Hall of Injustice. I need to attend."

Lieserl rolled her eyes. "Given that you've cleared your day's schedule, as usual, will you have time to talk to a potential client?"

Adams looked down at his red and yellow Hawaiian shirt. It was relatively unwrinkled, though stained just below the pocket. Definitely not the garb in which to meet a new client.

"Please tell me that this isn't another pro-bono case that those pencil pushers over at the Hall of Injustice parcel out with no rhyme or reason."

"Nein," Lieserl said. "This gentleman carried a letter of introduction from a Captain Thomas Preston."

Thomas Preston: a name that Adams had not heard in a very long time. Adams had defended Preston and his men in the matter that history and the propagandists of the Colonies called "the Boston Massacre." Winning the soldiers' acquittal on charges of murder had been one of Adam's proudest moments, not just personally, but for the legal system of the emerging nation.

Lieserl passed an envelope to Adams. Inside was a single sheet of letter paper on which were a half-dozen lines written in a formal and accomplished hand:

My Dear Mr. Adams:

I hope this finds you doing well. I would like to

present my friend Aleister Crowley, and beg the favor of your consideration of taking on his case. While Aleister and I have disagreed on many things during the several years I have known him, he has become a trusted friend, although I will warn you to be wary should you face him across a chess board.

I remain, sir,

Thomas Preston, Captain, the army of King George III (ret.)

"So, what do you know of this Crowley fellow, Lieserl? The name is vaguely familiar, but I cannot place it." Still holding Preston's letter, Adams walked over to his office window with its view of the roof and buildings nearby, staring out at New Hell's urban dinginess and wishing for the green cleanliness of life in Braintree. "Tell me about him."

"Aleister Crowley? An infamous charlatan, an occultist – self-proclaimed as the 'wickedest man in the world' and the 'Beast Six Six Six.' He formed the Thelemite church and founded the Abbey of Thelema. He was a man of immoral desire, a racist and a spy for the British government. A writer of demoniacal pretensions, a self-proclaimed master of the black arts. Even in Switzerland, he was one not talked about in polite company. Notorious, not quite in the same way you were, Mister Adams. He claimed to be the devil made human or something like that. Friends of my adopted mother talked about him also being a well-known mountain climber. More than that, I don't recall," she said.

"Thank you, Lieserl. You are a font of knowledge. Please bring the gentleman in."

Adams tried to imagine why Preston would have recommended this client to him and how such a person as Lieserl described might look. Dissolute? Greasy? Sadistic? Mad? No use in theorizing without evidence.

The man who walked in his office door fit none of his expectations. Crowley appeared young, like a man in his mid-twenties. He wore a neatly-tailored Edwardian-style suit and nervously twisted a heavy signet ring, covered in what appeared to be Egyptian hieroglyphics.

Clean. Elegant. Aristocratic. Even were he none of these, John Adams could condemn no damned soul for their sartorial choices: when he was not due to appear in court or had no social obligations, he wore his Hawaiian print shirts. "Please be seated, Mister Crowley," said Adams."

"Thank you, no sir," said Crowley. "Let us ask no trivial favors from the lords of hell."

"Very well," nodded Adams as Lieserl slipped quietly from the office. "Tell me what brings you here. I'm hoping this has nothing to do with your 'church.' I prefer to stick to legal issues rather than spiritual ones."

"Of course, sir, and you are known as a man who gets directly to the point. I've always approved of that attitude," said Crowley. "Are you familiar with the Demon's Gambit chess club?"

While Adams had always enjoyed a good game of chess, he had never pursued it competitively. Most of the chess clubs he had been familiar with during his life had been nothing more than fronts for political debating societies.

"I may have heard mention of such a club. May I make the assumption that you are a member?"

"Indeed. The Demon's Gambit is hell's premier chess club; it boasts one of underworld's the largest libraries on the subject," said Crowley. "I come to you today concerning events following a recent tournament that the club hosted. I won that tournament without a terrific amount of difficulty, as I have won a number of Demon's Gambit tournaments. A few days ago I received a private, and anonymous, message via DisgraceBook accusing me of cheating during the tournament and suggesting I resign from the club or face disgrace."

Adams arched an eyebrow at his potential client. In his long life he had heard of card cheats, billiards cheats, business cheats and spousal cheats, but never chess cheats

"How does one cheat at chess, Mister Crowley?"

"It is a question that I have been racking my brain to answer, as well," Crowley said. "I have no idea, and I'm the one who is being accused of cheating. I thought perhaps it was some sort of joke and tried to track down the person who had sent the message. But I could not identify the sender of the message, even after enlisting the services of the two best computer specialists I could find. I even consulted Awaiss."

"And this 'Awaiss' is?" asked Adams.

Crowley let out a sigh. "A … demon. I once thought he was an angelic collaborator on my book *Liber AL vel Legis*, 'The Book of the Law,' but since my arrival in hell I have learned otherwise. Awaiss refused to help, saying it is up to me," chuckled Crowley. "Since this whole matter began I have ranged between moments of utter rage and extreme frustration. The *only* way I can imagine one cheating at chess would be through the use of magic. However, if I were to use magic to influence the games and were caught, I would be expelled as per the club bylaws, which I helped to draft."

If there was one thing that Adams had learned in politics both before and after the American Revolution, it was how to read people. Understand their feelings on something and you are that much closer to understanding their motivations. Here was the man who had called himself the wickedest man in the world and the Beast 666, and he was afraid of being expelled from his chess club.

"I must ask the obvious question," said Adams.

"Let me anticipate you, Mister Adams, and tell you, on my honor, that I did not cheat. Although it took all my strength to keep from it," said Crowley.

"You first said that you have no idea how to cheat at chess except through the use of magic. Now you say it took all your strength to keep you from it. So you do know how to cheat at chess using magical or occult means, is that it?"

"Three times during the tournament I felt a compulsion to cast a spell that would cause my opponent to be confused. It would have been a minor compulsion, an easy spell, but I fought off the urge and do not know its origin," said Crowley. "But, one would deem such a spell cast on one's opponent to be cheating at chess."

"Have there been additional incidents … incidents of the compulsion to cheat?" Adams asked. "Are you now saying that you may be guilty in theory and practice of cheating at chess through magic at various times and someone else knows it?"

"Incidents? Not of my being subject to a compulsion to cheat, no; nor have I used magic to gain an advantage over an opponent.

But I have found broken chess pieces, a knight and a pawn, in places in my home where they could not have been and where no one but me enters. Each chess piece was jaggedly broken in two. Then, this morning, I found *this* when I went for a walk." Crowley produced a chess piece, a black king, wrapped in his handkerchief, broken in two pieces with a note saying, 'Cheat again and this is what will happen to you.'

"I'd say someone was trying to frighten you," said Adams. "But why seek out a lawyer? I can deal with matters legal, but not investigative. Investigation is an activity which I do not undertake. I can refer you to an excellent agency down the street, run by my friend, Dashiell Hammett."

Crowley shook his head. He had a determined look, the sort that Adams remembered seeing on Ben Franklin's face from time to time. This Crowley had a plan and was determined to follow it through.

"I was once told that the best way to deal with a blackmailer is to go public. My club is sponsoring a major chess tournament in a few days. Many dignitaries will be present, not just my fellow members. I would like you present as my attorney and as a witness to the fact that I will not cheat. If anyone should accuse me of cheating, I want you ready to file suit against them at once," said Crowley.

Adams began to laugh. Crowley's request was just so bizarre that it intrigued him. He had always savored a challenge, whether in court or politics.

"Very well, Mister Crowley, I cannot promise you that I will be successful, but I can promise you will have my best efforts," he told the magician.

*

The huge cast-iron clock above the bar struck nine as Adams stood in the doorway and surveyed the current crop of customers.

For a watering hole merely three blocks from the Hall of Injustice and frequented by lawyers, the Hellegality Bar was small and intimate.

Operated by a man known in life as Big Bill Jansen, the place made Adams nostalgic for several taverns he'd frequented in Philadelphia and Boston. Real work got done in places like this.

He and Jefferson had engaged in spirited debates in such taverns.

A dozen acquaintances sat at tables and at the bar, nursing undrinkable concoctions, nostalgic for pretzels and beer, hell's unobtanium. The Hellegality offered poor substitutes for either.

"Well, if it isn't the world renowned Mister A," said Jansen from behind the bar. "Started any riots lately?"

"William, William, how often must I remind you, it was my cousin Samuel who was the rabble-rouser? I just used his bravado to the advantage of my country." Adams smiled.

He had this same conversation with Jansen every time he visited here. "I'll have a stout, William. Would Walter Gibson, the pulp writer, be here this evening?" The stout was sour, the beer was stale, and the food here could crack your teeth with one bite.

Jansen drew Adams his drink, stale when it hit the air. "You'll find him over in the corner, giving a couple of new arrivals lessons in the finer points of cards."

Adams sighted the table that Jansen had indicated. Two men in military fatigues, probably from one of Caesar's legions, sat opposite a third man, his back to the wall.

This third man, Walter Gibson, was the dealer: curly-haired, with a forever babyish face. He wore wire-rimmed glasses. On the table between the dealer and the two soldiers were three cards, face down, that he moved around and around after having held up the Queen of Hearts for their perusal. When he was finished, the three cards were in the center of the table.

"Now keep an eye on the queen. You know royalty; they like to keep moving and make sure they are never where you think they'll be."

One of the two men dropped a handful of gold diablos on the table. Adams could see the soldier's finger linger in the air for several seconds before punching down on the leftmost card.

The dealer nodded. With a flourish, he turned over the chosen card: the deuce of spades.

"I was sure I had it!" the soldier laughed.

"Private Santee, you and Corporal Gideon have been good sports," said the dealer, pushing several coins back across the table.

"Thank you, sir." The soldiers grabbed up the offered money and walked away.

Walter Gibson chuckled and an unfiltered cigarette appeared in his hand, between two fingers covered with band-aids. "You'd think that after all this time anyone in the army would know about Three Card Monty."

John Adams pulled out a chair and sat down opposite the pulp writer, surveying the man's fingers. "When are you going to switch over to a word processor? That manual typewriter is so outdated, and you certainly no longer have to turn out novels so fast it damages your fingers, do you?"

Holding up his hands, fingers splayed to show the band-aids, Gibson said, "You know that this is a little gift from His Infernal Majesty. Who knew he didn't like my pulp writing? And, anyway, aren't you the man who has been seen making notes with a quill pen in court?"

"That's what people expect me to use, but even I am learning to adapt." Adams reached into the breast pocket of his Hawaiian shirt and pulled out a fountain pen that he displayed for Gibson. "I'm starting to like the feel of it in my hand, but I wish it would stop leaking on my shirts."

"Nice," said Gibson. "I'd love to use a word processor but my new contract with Hellizdat Publishing specifies that I have to use a manual typewriter to write for them." Gibson continued, "I'm not thrilled I had to join their Union but it was the only way I could get them to accept my proposal."

"So you got a go-ahead on your proposals for that new pulp super-villain? That's excellent," said Adams. "But it's not your literary skill I need right now," said Adams. "I require your knowledge of stage magic."

Gibson smiled. As successful as he had been in his life as a writer, stage magic had always been his true love. From his sleeve he pulled a red scarf, wrapped it around the top of his empty beer bottle, and passed his hand over it twice. The scarf on the bottle was now blue.

"That's exactly what I'm talking about," said Adams. "Stage magic: no spells; no incantations – just illusions. That *was* an illusion … wasn't it?"

"Now, now, John. That would be telling. So what's going on?" Gibson leaned forward, elbowing aside his scarf-covered bottle of beer.

"I have a client who has been accused of cheating at chess. He says he's innocent and that there may be real magic involved. But, it's occurred to me that there may *not* be," said Adams.

Gibson sat quietly for several moments, gnawing the edge of his lower lip with his teeth. "Cheating at chess, now that isn't something you can easily do. I'll make a few inquiries, if you would like, to see if any of the usual crowd has come up with any new illusions that could be applied to chess, although I rather doubt it."

"The tournament is in two days," said Adams.

"Two days. Not much time. I can give you a few telltales to watch for," said Gibson. "Have you considered the possibility that it may actually be a combination of real magic and sleight of hand?"

*

A cold wind blew down the street as Adams emerged from the tavern. Gibson had given him something to think about.

A few people were drifting along the sparsely-trafficked streets around him. Most had the glazed look of clerical workers who knew that in hell there was no end to their labors. Adams doubted that most of them even noticed him.

Harmless, to the last damned soul, were these. Yet as he walked, Adams couldn't shake the feeling that someone was following him who was not so harmless. Long ago, his friend Hammett had taught him several ways to determine whether you were being followed without giving any sign that you were suspicious. Adams wished he'd paid closer attention to Hammett's tutelage. Try as he might, he could not detect who following him.

Pausing just before an intersection with a rutted main road, his shoe bumped something. Adams looked down and saw a broken chess piece lying directly in front of his left foot.

It was a rook, raggedly split in twain. Picking it up, he was certain that the chess piece was made from the same stone as the one that Crowley had brought to his office.

The distinctive snick of a switchblade sounded. Adams turned and saw a small curly-haired man in a frilly shirt and dark jacket, cleaning his fingernails with the point of his knife.

"Check," the man said, his accent betraying a South London origin. "Bad time to be out and about, mate."

Before Adams could say anything, a red sports car came screaming down the street, its spoilers scraping potholes as the car weaved its way around slower vehicles. Tires screeched on asphalt. Though the car wasn't close to him, Adams took a step back as the vehicle vanished quickly around the corner.

When Adams turned back toward the stranger, the man was gone. On the ground where the stranger had been standing was another chess piece, this one unbroken.

"Curiouser and curiouser," said Adams.

*

"I was wondering if you were going to make it," said Aleister Crowley when he saw Adams enter the anteroom of the Demon's Gambit chess club.

Adams looked up with a smile; he passed his traveling cape and tricorne hat to a wraithlike sycophant who materialized for the purpose. The creature attempted to take Adams' walking stick, but the former president retained a solid grip on it.

Adams approached Crowley. "Not to worry, Mister Crowley. I was delayed at the Hall of Injustice, with this heavenly audit going on. The bureaucracy is frenzied; mistakes are multiplying. Now, with Erra and the Seven involved, I don't want to deal with the courts unless I absolutely must," said Adams.

The high priest of Thelema seemed calm enough. He held a book in his left hand and Adams noted a slight tremor in his fingers. Nerves? Palsy? Or something else?

There was a small hand-held magnetic chess board on the side table near Crowley. The pieces were arranged in a variation of a classic chess problem.

"So, have you felt an urge to cast any spells in relation to the tournament?" Adams asked his client.

"No, I have not. I even considered the possibility of having one of my associates put a dampening spell on me that would prevent it," Crowley said. "However, I thought that might tip our hand to my enemy."

"Yes, far better to be discreet," said Adams.

The tournament would begin in one hour. The Club was filling with members and visitors. Static exhibits dominated the smaller rooms. One featured a chess-playing computer. Rumor had it that anyone who beat the machine would be entered into a drawing for a one-way ticket out of hell. So far, no one had beaten the computer. The few who tried to beat the computer and failed were reduced to Hiroshima-type shadows on the wall of the club.

A good way to earn you a ticket into the hands of the Undertaker, not to heaven, Adams thought. Since he had awoken to find himself in hell, Adams had not once returned to the clutches of the Undertaker; his single memory of the Mortuary was one he'd rather forget. He had gone to great lengths to avoid a return visit.

Adams watched Crowley work his away across the room, chatting with guests as he went. Adams spotted several Dutch and Spaniards, heads together, probably up to no good, and Walter Gibson, stage magician and pulp writer, unobtrusively following in Crowley's wake.

At the tolling of a huge clock on the wall, people took seats before the platform where three tables and boards were arranged. On the far wall huge chessboards would reflect each move made by the players so that the audience could follow the games. Several video broadcasts had utilized micro cameras at board level, but such programming had proved too boring even for hell.

To his surprise, Adams found himself interested in the progress of the tournament. When Crowley's round started, he defeated his first opponent, a captain in the personal guard of Czar Nicholas of Russia, in a dozen moves. His next two were tougher, their games lasting nearly a half-hour each.

Crowley showed no sign, during his play, of being under any kind of external, or infernal, influence. If there was a plot against Crowley, it was not evident … yet.

Two hours into the competition, Adams picked up his glass of wine and noticed the words *'I have him'* scrawled on his coaster.

Reaching into his vest, Adams got his hellphone and punched three numbers. He hoped he remembered how to work the silly thing … and hoped it *would* work. He longed for the simplicity of his quill and parchment.

Having placed the call, Adams knew it would just be a matter of time until the whole matter came to a head. So he turned his attention back to his client who now sat at the center chess table.

Crowley's opponent was a soul whom Adams had known in life: Captain Meriwether Lewis, the American explorer. Adams had approved Jefferson's appointment of Lewis as co-commander of the expedition sent to map the Louisiana Purchase.

"I call foul, sir! You are cheating!" said Lewis to Crowley.

The explorer pushed back from the chess table and glared at Crowley. A tall gangly redhead in a black suit and string tie, Lewis loomed over the board like a scarecrow.

"Cheating? Just how does one cheat at chess, sir?" said Crowley, remaining calm, per Adams' instructions. "I suspect you are far gone in your cups!"

Adams pushed through the crowd and climbed onto the platform, taking a position to the right of Crowley.

"You claim dishonor, sir? Then I would suggest," said Adams, "you explain yourself forthwith, proving your claim – or else you owe Mister Crowley and the other members of this club an apology!"

"I know you, Mister Adams. You'll not twist things to serve your own ends as you did in life," warned Lewis, his voice steady. Lewis brought out a palm-sized mirror, its surface fogged as if someone had breathed hard on the reflective surface. "I was given this by François Duvalier. It clouds up when someone within five feet tries to put a spell on me. Aleister Crowley is the only one close enough to be doing so!"

The crowd's murmurs grew louder, but Adams paid no attention.

"I think not, Captain Lewis," said the former president. "In this particular case, perhaps unlike other circumstances, my client is totally innocent."

"I doubt that. Mister Crowley is a dishonorable cheat," said Lewis. "Nothing you can do will change that fact, Mister Adams, no matter how you may twist the truth."

"I don't need to twist anything," Adams said, pacing slowly back and forth along the edge of the platform. "I fully admit that magic was involved in this incident. Mister Crowley, kindly empty the contents of your coat pockets onto the chess table."

Crowley stared at his lawyer for a moment, then complied. He had a kerchief, a notebook, a snuff box and a small yellow stone incised with a complicated sigil. "I've never seen that stone before in my life," Crowley said. "But I recognize the sign on it: it's a compulsion stone. Put there by my opponent, Lewis, no doubt, in order to ensure his victory."

"A likely story," muttered Lewis. "Besides, why would I need to use magic against Crowley to win? I'm twice the player he is, if not more so."

"I will leave assessment of the relative chess skills of Mister Crowley and Captain Lewis to those who know the game better than I," said Adams. "I will conjecture, Mister Crowley, that this isn't the first time such a stone has been among your effects, even if you haven't known about it. Think for a moment, Mister Crowley: was Captain Lewis present at your last chess tournament?"

Crowley's eyes turned up in his head as he searched his memory. "Yes, I do believe he was. We chatted before the tournament and he came up to congratulate me afterward."

"At that time, I suggest Captain Lewis was testing the compulsion stone, putting it in your pocket and then retrieving it later," Adams postulated.

"Conjecture. You have no proof," said Lewis.

"Not of your actions during the earlier tournament, but I do have a witness who saw you put the stone in Mister Crowley's pocket today," said Adams. With that, Walter Gibson pushed his way through the crowd to stand on Crowley's side of the table.

"You put it in his pocket, sir; you are good with your hands, but not good enough that I didn't see you do it. Should I be called upon as an expert witness, I will definitely testify to what you did," Gibson said.

"Yet Crowley, not I, was the one using magic. Club rules clearly state that anyone influencing games unfairly will be expelled, and your client is in possession of a magical instrument of influence," said Lewis. The smug look on Lewis' face irritated Adams no end.

"Actually, no – Mister Crowley wasn't using magic. You just claimed he was, Captain Lewis. Do you have it, Walter?"

Gibson held up a folded piece of paper.

"This is a copy of a writ, signed by Judge Roy Bean, canceling out the power of anything of a magical nature that you, Captain

Lewis, have touched in the last few hours," said Adams. "Once Mister Gibson spotted what you had done, he let me know and I texted my secretary, who was waiting at Judge Bean's court. As soon as he signed the writ, it went into effect," said Adams.

Lewis folded his lips inward and then smiled. "I know a bit about the law myself. That kind of writ is nothing more than a piece of paper; unless I am given it and am informed that I am being served, which I was not. You're bluffing, John Adams. And I'm calling your bluff."

"I don't bluff," said Adams. "If you check your inside coat pocket you will find a copy of this writ, properly signed. You *were* served with it. My associate, Mister Gibson, placed it on your person himself. He even *told* you that you had been served, as he is compelled to do by law."

Lewis stared at Adams and Gibson. "Remember?" said Gibson. "When you were crossing the room earlier, I bumped against you. We even exchanged a few words. I said, 'You have been served.' Is it my fault if you thought I was asking you a question about the waiters, rather than making a statement? Or that you weren't aware the writ was in your pocket?"

Lewis's face flushed red with anger. Without answering Gibson, he pushed away from the table and stalked toward the front of the club. Several sycophants hurried after him with his coat and top hat.

"Check and mate. Nicely done, Mister Adams. Nicely done." said Crowley.

Disclaimer

By

John Manning

The last thing he remembers is the chatter of an automatic weapon. Glass explodes from the French doors. Drywall erupts from the office walls. Paneling cracks and splinters from the opposite side of the room. Knick-knacks, pen holders, picture frames rain down on him from his ruined desk. Warm, sticky, wetness oozes from the soggy carpet beneath him. Cold numbness spreads inward from his limbs. Darkness grows, closes him in.

Closes him down.

*

Aaron "Monty" Montgomery awoke face down on a hard laminate surface. A deep rumbling vibration thrummed throughout his body. He heard a metallic rattling from somewhere above and behind him. Slowly, he pushed himself to a sitting position and looked around. He frowned. He was sitting in what looked like an elevator car. From his right he heard a discordant humming sound rather like Muzak played over an old, cracked speaker. The rhythm seemed familiar. He turned his head. Centered in the wall to his left was a pair of closed steel doors. A rectangular panel was mounted half way up the wall between the doors and the wall opposite him. Instead of buttons for different floors there was only one. It made no sense. Instead of a number, he saw just a single word:

THERE.

In front of the panel was a tall, four-legged wooden stool. His eyes followed the blond wood until he reached a pair of stone-colored taloned feet. His eyes moved further upward. On the stool sat…

"Hi."

Monty crabbed backwards to the opposite wall and tried to keep going. The *thing* sitting atop the stool could not possibly exist, let alone talk to him. It sat with its knees folded in front of it. Monty guessed it was between three and three and a half feet tall. Gray, stone-like skin covered its naked body. From between its legs rose a penis that would have made any male porn star hang his head in shame and envy. Monty guessed that made it a *he*, not an *it*. Leathery wings the color of dried blood sprouted from between its – his – shoulders and draped his back. He had arms and legs like a man. Instead of hands and feet, however, he sported claws and talons. His face was canine, although the ears were wide, pointed, and hairless. A tuft of thick, black fur ran up and over the center of its head and down its back like a Mohawk.

"Name's Rudolfo." The creature extended his right claw as if to shake hands. When Monty just stared at him, he shrugged and returned his attention to the panel before him.

"Wha-what *are* you?" Monty whispered.

"I guess you'd call me an imp." The operator looked at Monty and smiled. His teeth accented his canine appearance. "Or, a lesser demon, if you prefer. Just one of hell's many little annoyances."

Monty shuddered. He should probably play nice until he figured out what was going on. Still, he had to know. "No offense, but you look more like a gargoyle."

"None taken. I been called worse."

Monty looked around, but the car offered no clues. He could have been in any number of cheap hotels or early office buildings. Sweat trickled from his hairline and ran down his cheek. Whoever owned the building really needed to do something about the air conditioning. He sniffed. He wrinkled his nose. Rudolfo needed a deodorant. Badly.

"Where am I?"

Rudolfo's face split into a mischievous grin. "On an elevator."

"I had that much figured out," Monty grumbled. "Where is this elevator?"

"It's between destinations." Rudolfo was enjoying Monty's rising frustration.

"Okay. That means it's going somewhere. So, where is it going?"

"To hell."

Monty blinked. "But, it feels like it's going up."

"What it feels like and what it is ain't necessarily the same thing." Rudolfo twitched with repressed glee. He loved baiting the 'new dead.' It made the long elevator ride so much more enjoyable – for him.

"Shouldn't it be going down?" Monty persisted.

The imp laughed. "You new dead always get it wrong. Up, down – it don't mean nothin' here. Einstein had it figured out. It's all relative and dimensional." Rudolfo leaned toward Monty, winked, and gave him a conspiratorial poke in the ribs. "He's down here, by the way."

Monty looked around. The car was austere. The walls were bare. Dark splotches dotted the surfaces. He sniffed again and immediately regretted it. It wasn't coming from the demon.

"What's that smell?"

The imp sniffed. "Oh, that. It's brimstone. Sulfur. Goes with the territory. You'll get used to it. No, wait. You're dead." The creature chortled and snickered. "You'll never get used to it. So, get used to it."

"Dead?"

"Right. Dead. Expired. Recently departed. Deceased." Rudolfo leaned forward and breathed an acrid sulfurous cloud into Monty's face. "Dead."

The demon returned his attention to his control panel and its single lighted button. He began humming the same, discordant, familiar tune.

"What *is* that?"

Rudolfo stopped. "What's what?"

"That tune. What is it?"

"This?" He hummed a few more bars.

"Yes, that. I've heard it before."

"Oh, it's just somethin' I picked up in a bar in Sydney when I was up there doin' some harvestin' for one of th' big boys. See if this helps any." The demon cleared his throat and started singing. "*Don't mind you playin' demon – as long as it's with me – if this is hell – then you could say – it's heavenly – hell ain't a bad place to be.*" He grinned. "How'd you like that?"

"It was definitely … interesting." Monty smiled. "That was an AC/DC song, wasn't it?"

In truth, it sounded like feeding time at a large zoo.

"It's called *Hell Ain't a Bad Place to Be.* I'm thinkin' about singing it for *Demonic Idol* when the auditions come to Sinsunatti next month. What do you think? Have I got a chance?"

Monty shifted expressions, using the smile he reserved for when he told his clients everything was fine, no worries, when truthfully all had gone to shit and there was nothing he could do to save the situation. "I guess it depends on the competition, doesn't it?"

The ascent was bad and got worse. Monty had been on high-speed elevators in the past, but nothing like this. The laws of physics said this kind of speed was impossible, yet he was certain that the car had exceeded terminal velocity some time ago. Just when he thought the car must burn up from friction, it stopped.

It did not slow down.

It did not ease gracefully to a halt.

It stopped.

While he tried to come to terms with the realization that he was not a puddle of protein jelly on the car's ceiling, the doors slid open with the sound of fighting – or mating – cats.

Marty looked through the door at the empty vista beyond. The terrain that stretched before him was totally flat and featureless, devoid of vegetation or creatures. Black, billowing clouds raced overhead across the garish, red-orange sky. A bright glow shone through the clouds straight above, but he could not tell if it was the sun, the moon, a star, or a really big spotlight. The wind howled as it raced across the plain with nothing to retard its progress. The rotten egg smell filled his nose and throat. He gagged. Tears filled his eyes and ran down his cheeks. The gas mixed with the tears and turned them to acid that burned runnels in his skin.

"Here you go, Mac."

"But… but…" Monty choked, unable to speak with the burning in his nose, mouth and throat. He doubled over.

"Hey, a smart lawyer like you oughta come up with somethin' better than motor boat sounds. Step on out there."

Monty turned to Rudolfo. "You said … this … is hell. There's … nothing … here." He choked the words from his raw throat.

"You been listenin' to too many religious stories. Some people say that everyone builds their own hell when they're livin' back on Earth. If so, this is the one you made." Rudolfo sighed. "Look, Mac. I don't make the rules and you ain't the only soul I gotta pick up. This one is all yours. You own this bit of real estate. Now, get out there and claim it."

Rudolfo gave him a firm shove and propelled him, unresisting, through the doorway and spinning him around as he did so.

Monty caught his balance and looked up. An elderly woman stood before him. No, not elderly-geriatric – *ancient*. For the first time in his life he fully understood the meaning of the word 'crone.'

Her liver-spotted scalp shone beneath the thin, lank silver threads that cascaded down either side of her head in limp curls. Her seamed and leathery face bore more cracks than a dried riverbed. Pale, bleary blue eyes sparkled from below a thick, snowy unibrow. Her nose was a hooked wedge of flesh stabbing knife-like from between her eyes. Cracked, flaking lips opened in a leering grin as spittle dribbled from the corner of her mouth.

"Well, well," she cackled, exposing cracked and yellowed teeth. She leaned toward him for a better look. "Ain't you the pretty one?"

Unable to stop his natural, ingrained male inclination, his eyes continued downward over her naked flesh. The skin hung in sagging, wrinkled folds. Her breasts – dugs, really – lay flat against her chest. On the right breast the word WELCOME was branded in angry, brownish-red letters. On the left, the word was WOMAN.

Monty's glanced continued downward to her crotch. Her right hand partially covered her pubic hair in an obscene parody of modesty. Her fingers rapidly worked the protruding and sagging lips of her ancient slit. He saw more movement within the thicket of gray hair nestled between her legs – motion other than that of her fingers. He shuddered. A scream grew within his mind. Something was twisting and writhing down and out and reaching toward him.

This can't be happening, his brain screamed even as his legs tried to push him away from the squirming flesh. He first thought they were tentacles, but he soon realized his error. They were worse. They were tongues – two twitching, reaching, grasping, bifurcated, blue-black appendages.

And, they were reaching for *him.*

"Welcome to hell, Darlin'." She raised her arms and stepped toward him. "I have so many wonderful things to show you."

The old woman pressed herself against him, her sagging breasts surprisingly firm against his chest. Her left hand slid up and behind his head as she tilted her face up to him and his down to her. Her lips parted. Her pustule-covered tongue darted over their flaky surface. Despite his struggles, he felt his head pulled inexorably closer. His nostrils filled with the stench of shit and rotting flesh. Her lips pressed against his; her tongue stabbed into his mouth.

Monty screamed around the invading flesh and tried to push himself backwards into the car. The doors were already closed. He pushed helplessly against the steel panels as he felt his zipper pulled slowly down. His erection grew to a tumescence he had never experienced in life. The slippery tongues reached into his boxers. As the black muscular flesh enveloped his engorged member, darkness claimed him.

*

Monty awoke face down on a hard laminate surface. He frowned. The last thing he remembered was being raped by an ancient hag on a flat plain under a red-orange sky. The pain of his chafed, abraded organ told him it wasn't a dream. He also had the worst case of "blue balls" he had ever experienced. His scrotum felt swollen to ten times its normal size and it ached like it had been used for field goal practice by an NFL place kicker. His body screamed for release, but he was afraid to touch himself.

A deep rumbling vibration thrummed throughout his body. He heard a metallic rattling from somewhere above and behind him. Slowly, he pushed himself to a sitting position and looked around. He frowned. He was sitting in the elevator car again. A feeling of déjà vu washed over him.

Not again, he thought. *If this thing takes me to that old woman I'll kill myself.*

"Goin' down."

Monty shuddered. "Rudolfo, right?"

"Afraid not," the creature on the stool growled. "What, we all look alike to you? You racist or somethin'?"

"Um, no. N-nothing like that."

" Oh. So you think we only got one elevator, then. You think this is sticksville or somethin', don'tcha? Listen, Bud. This was a heavy duty, high class operation long before you came along. Modern guys like you an' Howard Hughes an' all th' rest think just cuz youse is th' newest deads that nothin' else before you was any good. You don't know it, but we hadda huge marble staircase that worked just fine. Yeah, it was slow. Yeah, all you newly-deads kept bleedin' an' pukin' an' pissin' an' shittin' all over it, but, hey! That only gave it character, y'unnerstand?" The demon poked a blackened claw into the middle of Monty's chest. "There's so many of you dyin' up there and comin' down here we'd never handle it with just one car."

A cold dread filled Monty. "You're not taking me to that old hag again, are you?"

"Dubbayah, Dubbayah? Nah. Fun time's over. Time t'get t'work. Th' Undertaker's released ya back t'full duty status." The creature extended a green, scaly, black-tipped claw toward the panel and pressed a button. The car halted. "You're overdue for orientation. You musta had a real good time with the Welcome Woman. I unnerstand she gives some great tongue action."

Monty felt the acid burning in his throat as his gorge rose.

The doors rumbled open revealing a massive foyer.

"Hall of Injustice, hell's Law Library. All out!" The demon kicked Monty forward. As he pin-wheeled to keep his balance, the doors closed behind him.

He managed to keep from falling on his butt – barely. As he smoothed his coat and shirt and brushed the ever present sprinkling of yellow dust from the lapels, he saw a little Greek-looking man wearing a gold-trimmed white robe hurrying toward him. He was followed closely by an Egyptian-looking kid dressed in a crimson smock, gray slacks and gray sandals. The boy wore heavy black eye makeup and there was no mistaking the adoration on his face when he looked at the older man.

What the hell, he thought. *The old guy looks Greek. Don't ask, don't tell. Unless I'm supposed to defend one of them, it's not my problem.*

"My name is Demetrius. I'm the Chief Librarian of hell's Law Library. And, you are late," the figure scolded. "Foreman and Belli are about to introduce the guest speaker. For you to come in afterwards would be a horrible insult. I ought to make you wait for the next group."

Monty blinked and looked around.

"Over there." Demetrius pointed to where a number of men and women sat watching two others standing before them. One looked to be the embodiment of every successful litigant who ever lived. The other, not quite as impressive. "Get moving or I *will* hold you back."

*

This was *not* what Monty expected. This was *not* how a lawyer of his stature and standing was supposed to be treated. He listened to the speech and the pep talk from Justice Cardozo. Yes, he, too, was a big deal in his day. He handed down many important decisions in landmark cases; wrote dozens of scholarly reviews; yadda, yadda, yadda. So, what? He died in 1938. That was almost a century before Monty had … died. The world – and the law – had moved on. In the modern world, Cardozo's only value was as a precedent and resource material.

Afterwards he had to go with Belli to receive his assignment. What was with that? Monty had been a very successful (and, well-paid) defense attorney. What was with this tort crap? That was for schmucks with no balls. Yeah, insurance lawyers and corporate geeks made decent bread, but criminal law was where the stars came out to shine. And, Monty was one of the brightest.

Then Belli gave him that slip of paper with his assignment on it and, before you could say "Goodbye, Porsche!" he was standing in a linoleum-tiled foyer. In the center of the room, four couches had been arranged in a square. A low table stood in the middle. A wide vase rose from the table's center, its glass throat filled with fake flowers on plastic stems. Dusty, tattered leaves adorned the stems and flowers in lackluster and uncaring disarray. Faded framed watercolors and bleached photographs hung crookedly on the walls.

He glanced at the slip of paper.

Golgotha Gardens Retirement Home
And Assisted Living Center

What the ... a goddamn nursing home?

Monty looked up. Men and women shuffled toward him like a scene from Romero's *Night of the Living Dead.* Some had canes; others, crutches. Walkers squeak-thumped along the floor as the dead advanced. Wheelchairs screeched their worn rubber tires as decrepit hands propelled them forward. Uniformed demons moved here and there among the creeping tide, intent on their errands and oblivious to the human detritus around them despite the crisp nurse's hats and starched uniforms each one wore.

The omnipresent rotten egg odor of sulfur was gone, replaced by the stomach-turning stench of old urine, feces, vomit, sweat, and decay.

Monty backed up until his butt hit a hard, unyielding surface. He reached behind him; his hand brushed a metallic lever shape – a door handle. Frantically he worked it until the door opened. A clawed hand gripped his right shoulder and pulled him through the doorway and into a lighted office and then slammed the door.

"Aaron Montgomery?"

The voice was feminine, sultry, and so seductive that Monty felt himself rising in response despite the intense pain of his previous encounter. With the pain and erection came the memory. He spun and placed his back against the closed door.

"Ooo. Are we jumpy?"

The source of the voice was the most beautiful woman Monty had ever seen this close. The top of her upturned head came to just below his nose. Her shimmering blue-black hair was parted in the middle and cascaded down each side of her round face. The tips of her pointed ears only added to her sex kitten charms. Dainty, pointed little white teeth peeked from behind full, scarlet lips. Her tiny bifurcated tongue darted ever so coyly – now peeking, now hiding. He decided that her delicate green scales only heightened her beauty. Her big, round, yellow eyes with their catlike, vertical slits captured his heart completely.

She took a deep breath revealing a cleavage that mortal women vainly paid thousands and tens of thousands of dollars to acquire, only to fall short of this creature's magnificence. Pain filled his brain from his already tortured penis. Even as he clutched himself in agony he knew he had to have her at any cost.

"Cool it, Mac," the succubus said, pitching her voice into a less seductive register. "You don't want this. You ain't getting this. That ain't my assignment."

After several very long moments (for Monty), the room's pheromone saturation dropped enough for him to think clearly and for his painful erection to subside. He looked around the office. Dark wood panels glistened below the wainscoting. Pale green patterned paper – possibly flowers but most likely leering demon faces – covered the walls above. A dark brown leather chair stood behind the mahogany desk. It took Monty a moment to realize that there was no computer – no office equipment of any kind – on top of the desk. All that was there were a leather-cornered blotter, 'in' and 'out' trays (the 'in' stuffed to overflowing, the 'out' bare and dusty), a pen holder, and a black, rotary dial telephone.

"Whose desk is this," he asked.

"Yours, of course. I hope you didn't think *I* was going to sit here for hours on end listening to them whine and bitch and moan, did you?"

Outside the office the lesser demons and imps gathered the residents. The line started at Monty's office door and extended down an infinite (literally) corridor as people shuffled papers, looked through valises and briefcases, and otherwise prepared for their meeting with the home's new administrator.

Monty lifted one of the slats from the mini-blind that covered his office window and looked out at the waiting people.

"Who are those people?" he asked. "And, why is there a rest home in hell?"

The succubus smiled. "These people weren't patients when they were alive. Oh, no. Far from it. These were the other ones – the nurses, the orderlies, the administrators, the inspectors, and the families of those unfortunates left to finish out their existence in squalor, indifference, and neglect."

Monty shuddered as he dropped the slat and turned around. "So, what is my role?"

"Your role is to sit here and listen to each and every one of them. You are to help them with their estate planning, trusts, and wills."

"You're kidding me, right?"

"Not at all. You will find that almost every one of them is absolutely certain that they brought it with them." She paused and licked her lips. "And, you have one other duty."

Monty groaned inwardly. "And, that is?"

"You are their intermediary, their ombudsman. It is your job to listen to their complaints, fill out the proper forms, and present those complaints to HSM for proper resolution."

"HSM?"

"His Satanic Majesty, of course."

"Of course. So, when does this farce begin?"

"It's not a farce, and it begins now. Take your seat. I'm about to open the door and let you meet your first client."

*

"This is all a mistake," the middle-aged woman in the nurse's uniform whined. Her fat rolls wiggled like Jell-O as she daubed at her eyes with a mascara streaked tissue. "I took great care of my patients. I treated them like family. I washed them and dressed them. I made sure they had clean sheets."

Monty looked at the file on his desk.

Johanssen, Maureen. Age at death: forty-three. There followed all of the expected data about school, training, experience, family, et cetera. What caught his eye was the notation regarding her reason for assignment to the home. Whenever her patients developed life-threatening conditions, she waited until the last possible moment to call the ambulance so that the institution where she worked would collect every possible penny from Medicare and Medicaid.

Glad I didn't have to depend on her for my care, he thought as he scribbled a note on the Infernal Action Request Form.

"Exactly what sort of remedial action are you requesting, Mrs. Johanssen?"

Before she could reply, Monty felt suddenly dizzy. A sensation of vertigo washed over him. The office shimmered before his eyes and then vanished.

The dizziness vanished along with his office.

Monty rubbed his eyes and looked around. He stood in a massive room. Red, polished sandstone formed graceful Moorish arches creating walls open on all four sides. Muslin sheets – bleached white and gauzy – billowed on the dry desert wind blowing in from one side. Persian rugs decorated the smooth stone floor. A low, square table covered in marble and supported by curved, intricately-carved leg stood in the center of the room. A silver coffee pitcher and two dainty demitasse cups in wrought silver holders sat on top. Thick, tasseled cushions lay on the floor on all sides of the table. A hookah-bottle of green glass trimmed in brass and sporting two tubes tipped with ivory mouthpieces stood near one corner of the table. Small silver cream and sugar pitchers rested on an ornate oval service platter. A silver ewer with droplets of condensation on its sides was positioned close. Elegant gold-rimmed crystal goblets decorated with gold filigree surrounded the vessel.

Through the arches came the distant sounds of voices, of vendors calling out their wares, the bleating of sheep and the braying camels and donkeys. He heard the clatter of hooves as horses walked on stone streets. Bells tinkled and music drifted on the wind. Although he spoke none of the Arabic tongues, the picture was clear enough to Monty. Somewhere beyond the arches was a market. It was exactly as he imagined Marrakesh or Tunis or even Cairo might sound.

"Please be seated, noble sir."

He turned. A beautiful black-haired woman (odalisque?) had slipped silently into the room. Standing less than five feet tall, she was quite a bit shorter than he. Her figure was petite, yet deliciously rounded. She wore a loose-fitting harem outfit. The diaphanous fabric revealed as much as it showed. The lavender blouse and aqua trousers were so pale they were more hints of color than actual hues. She pointed a graceful arm at the table and cushions.

"My master will join you shortly," she smiled, her cheeks dimpling and her dark eyes downcast. A kind of circlet of brass wire with tiny brass bells hanging from it circled her head just at the top of her forehead. "I am instructed to see to your comfort until then. If you wish, I will serve you coffee at the table. Or, if coffee is not to your liking, I can bring you juice or water or tea."

"T-thank you," Monty stammered as he turned and walked toward the table. Before he had taken two steps she had somehow slipped his suit jacket from his shoulders in a deft and mostly invisible motion. One moment he was wearing it; the next she had it draped over one arm.

"I will have one of the household slaves take care of your garment while you and my master converse. It shall be as new when you are ready to depart."

So, Hell has a one-hour dry cleaning service, he thought. He sat down, cross-legged, on a cushion and looked around again. He felt like a backwoods bumpkin visiting a well-to-do city cousin for the first time. He thought for a moment and then shook his head. No, that wasn't quite right. There was none of the rub-your-face-in-it garishness of the nouveau riche. This was the simple elegance of a palace – the more impressive because of its understated presence. He felt it more than he saw it.

"Coffee?"

He looked to his left. She knelt on the cushion beside him holding the silver vessel in both hands. The position pulled the fabric taut across her right breast revealing a slightly oval silver dollar-sized aureole. His breath caught in anticipation of a painful response, yet the stirring in his groin was surprisingly pleasant. He slowly, carefully relaxed.

"Please," he smiled as he reached for one of the dainty cups and held it toward the curved spout. The aroma from the thick dark liquid filled his nostrils and he suddenly realized that it was the first pleasant, appetizing thing he'd smelled since his passing over. He took a deeper breath. The girl's perfume – heady and intoxicating – washed over his senses like a tsunami. Riding the aromatic wave were notes of coffee, of course, but also notes of fruity essences and a dry spiciness he couldn't quite identify. Saffron? Sesame oil? Clove? Frankincense? All of them and more besides. He swayed, nearly reeled from the olfactory onslaught.

One thing was missing: the noxious stench of brimstone.

"So, how do you like the torture, damnation, and deprivation over there in New Hell?" A tall, dark-complexioned man asked. The newcomer walked toward the table. Monty started to rise but the man gestured for him to remain seated.

"Please forgive the disconcerting method I had to employ to bring you to me. I imagine you are – or were in life, anyway – more accustomed to having someone send a car and driver." The man spread his arms in a "what can we do" expression as he folded his long legs and sat opposite. His white linen suit was impeccably pressed. The white silk shirt fairly glowed against his dark skin showing above the open collar. His smile and open demeanor put Monty in mind of Omar Sharif, a former movie star. "The Goetic faction likes to control the comings and goings within their realm. Of course, we do, too."

"This isn't New Hell?"

"Take a deep breath, my friend." His host closed his eyes and inhaled expanding his chest fully, then slowly breathed out. "Does every breath you take here smell like flatulence?"

"No," Monty conceded. "It doesn't. In fact, it smells fantastic after breathing the daily sewer for – for however long I've been breathing it. I've wondered about that. I'm supposed to be dead. Why am I breathing?"

"For amusement."

"Amusement?"

"Of course. Anyone – excuse me, any being that runs an operation built around punishment and torture and pain and suffering must be some kind of sadist, don't you think?" Monty's host gently clapped his hands together. As the female slave filled his cup with coffee he asked Monty, "I trust that Mari has seen to your comfort."

"Yes, indeed, sir." Monty held up his cup and took a sip. The thick, dark liquid was strong and bitter. After the food and drink offered in New Hell, however, he found it ambrosial. He set the cup on the table and stared at it for a moment. He shook his head, a wan smile on his lips.

"Is the coffee not to your liking?"

"It's fine. Strong, but fine."

"Then I fail to understand your facial expression."

"Who are you?" Monty looked up. "What's *really* going on here?"

"I doubt that my name would mean anything to you."

Monty leaned back and crossed his arms. "You're probably right," he replied. "Religion was never the strongest part of my life, which probably explains why I'm in this mess. Since I've been here

I've been raped by an old woman whose pussy sprouted tongues covered in sores that felt like sandpaper. Since then, every time I get hard, the pain is harsh. Imps insulted me and took me places on elevators that only had one destination, yet delivered me to different places. I found myself assigned to work as an ombudsman and legal advisor in a nursing home filled with former nursing home owners and caretakers. My secretary is a succubus so provocative that I find myself with a perpetual erection and constant agony. I've breathed air and fumes and gasses that would gag a maggot. I've had drink that – on its best day – was flat and tasteless, although most times it had the flavor and consistency of industrial waste. I eat the food because for some reason dead people need to eat down here. Alive, I would have been afraid to dump it into the garbage for fear the EPA would hunt me down and throw me in jail.

"Suddenly, I find myself yanked out of my dreary office to a desert palace. The air smells like perfume. The hard-on I get from looking at this beautiful woman doesn't cause me excruciating pain. The coffee tastes like strong, bitter, wonderful coffee. The fruits look fresh and smell enticing.

"So, I find myself waiting for the sound." Monty took a deep breath and let it out in a long, drawn-out sigh. "I'm waiting for the thump of the missing shoe. I'm tired of being someone else's play-toy. Who or what are you? Why have you brought me here? Is it to remind me of what I no longer have? Just *how* much shit do I have to shovel for you and *where* do you want it dumped?"

His host's black eyes glittered as he looked at Monty. Despite the hand rubbing across his beardless chin and hiding his mouth, Monty could tell he was smiling.

"I realize this is hell," Monty continued. "It's all part of the grand, celestial game to make me and other sinful mortals suffer. I get it. Can we dispense with all of this and let me get back to the hell I was already in?"

"In spite of all that was done to you, you still have the courage to demand respect." The man stood. "You have the intestinal fortitude to look me in the eye and demand that I treat you as a man."

Monty shrugged. "What are you going to do to me? Kill me? Send me to hell? Sorry. Already dead. Already there. I'm not courageous. I'm just tired."

"I believe I have chosen well." The tall man spread his arms. His body shifted and changed as Monty watched. "You asked for the truth and you shall have it. Behold!"

Marty swallowed, but the hard lump in his throat refused to budge. The being in front of him could only exist in a nightmare. The head rising above the silk shirt collar and smooth lapel was a lion's – long, sharp teeth, rounded furry ears trimmed in black, tawny mane streaked with sable strands, and long, twitching whiskers. Its thin black lips curled upward in a snarl. Its nostrils flared and its gold-colored eyes with their vertical pupils sparked as it spoke. Two pairs of wings sprouted from its back and twitched menacingly. A scorpion-like tail curved back and up over the being's head. After his experience with the Welcome Woman upon his arrival, Monty really did not want to know what was squirming inside of the football-sized bulge at the being's crotch. He shuddered at the memory.

"I am called Pazuzu," the being's voice rumbled across the marble floor. "In Babylon of old, I was worshipped and feared. Believers filled my temple with gold and myrrh and silk and precious gems."

Monty scrambled backward, his eyes never leaving the horror towering above him. When the creature failed to pursue, he stopped. The more he looked at the demon, the more familiar he seemed.

"I-I've seen you somewhere," he stammered. With the light behind its wings, it formed a haloed silhouette that was mildly frightening, but more and more something of memory rather than nightmare. Suddenly, he had it. "A movie! *The Exorcist*! You were the demon that possessed that girl."

Pazuzu seemed to shrink a little. "Is that what I've come to? A motion-picture monster? Is that how I'm remembered up there?"

"Don't knock it. It was a pretty scary movie when it came out back in the seventies."

"Yes, well, that is the problem, I'm afraid. Image and following. Nothing's been the same since Jehovah sent his rejects down to the fiery pits." Pazuzu began to pace as he spoke. "First we had all of that sulfur smell drifting into our little paradise. Then,

Jehovah sends his followers all over the deserts, pillaging Palestine, eliminating the Pharaoh's troops."

Pazuzu turned with a chuckle. "I have to admit, though, that his trick with the Red Sea when he had it drown all those soldiers was classic. How stupid were those officers? Come on, even a Philistine could have seen it was a trap. I mean, could it have been more obvious?"

Monty shook his head. This was not how he expected the conversation to go after the creature changed form.

"When they came out of the desert, though, that's when it all started going to hell – literally. Sodom. Gomorrah. Jericho. I don't know what was going on in the desert all those years, but when they came out they started kicking some major ass. Yeah, they had their setbacks, but for the most part they were unstoppable. When they took on Babylon and Damascus, well…" The demon stopped and shook his head. He sighed. "I guess we've got no one to blame but ourselves. We just didn't take them seriously. And, we didn't think Jehovah would intervene as often as he did. The gods all thought there was some sort of unwritten code or something. You know, I fight you, you try to kill me, but we leave the mortals out of it.

"Things kind of quieted down for a while. Yahweh had Jerusalem and Canaan and all those countries down by the Jordan River. Ra and his bunch had Egypt. We had Persia. There was a balance of power and everyone was happy. Not Yahweh, though. It should have been enough that he had hell and the area around the Sinai and the Eastern Mediterranean. No, *he* had to have more. He wasn't going to be happy until he had it all.

"So along comes this carpenter." Pazuzu paused and looked directly at Monty. "I ask you. Who would take a carpenter and his band of hippies seriously? Would you? We certainly didn't."

"Is there a point to this story?" Monty started to refill his coffee cup but Mari was quicker. She materialized by the table and filled his cup. She held a silver tray piled with fruits toward him. He took a huge strawberry from the stack and leaned back.

"What? Do you have somewhere to go? Are you in a hurry to listen to Madame Greylocks's whining? If so, I'll send you back."

"No, no," Monty responded quickly as smells and sights and

sounds from the rest home flooded his memory. "I'm not in any hurry. I was just wondering where this history lesson was leading, that's all."

Pazuzu looked closely at him, eyes narrowed. Finally, mollified, the demon continued his discourse.

"We did not take the carpenter seriously and that was our undoing. How were we to know that his bloody death would create a sub sect of Yahweh worship that would grow until it swept around the world like a wildfire fanned by a Santa Ana wind?

"That was bad enough. We felt it had somehow missed us. None of our followers seemed interested, until another upstart god entered the contest. His name was Allah and his champion was Mohammed. Those who avoided the Christ banner leaped for the Prophet's call to arms."

Pazuzu sighed. "And, here we sit, like a bunch of Kathy Griffins on a polytheistic D-list."

"So, who is this *we* you say are on the D-list?"

Pazuzu waved dismissively. "I doubt that you've heard of them. No one cares about the old ones anymore."

"Humor me, please."

"Do the names Apsu, Marduk, Mummu, or Ba'al mean anything to you?"

"I've heard the names Marduk and Ba'al before. Not the others. As I recall, they weren't all that nice. Didn't that last one require his followers to throw babies into his statue's burning belly?"

"Propaganda. Lies spread to demonize a culture being conquered. So, you actually know nothing about them."

"I guess I don't."

Pazuzu sighed. "That's exactly what I mean. There was a time when the mere whisper of our names caused fear and anguish. Nations trembled before us."

"So, what does this all have to do with me?" Monty sipped his coffee. Despite Pazuzu's protest, he was pretty sure about the baby issue. When he set the cup back on the table Mari quickly refilled the cup. She handed him another fist-sized strawberry. "And, where do you get these magnificent strawberries?"

Monty bit into the berry and allowed the sweet yet slightly tart juice to trickle down his throat.

"Well, to put it succinctly, we want to regain our position in the celestial hierarchy, and we want you to help us."

Monty choked. Once his coughing subsided and he wiped the tears from his eyes, he laughed. "You've got to be kidding me. How on earth – I mean, how in hell am I supposed to do what you, a demon, cannot? Or will not. I'm sorry but taking on His Satanic Majesty and his legions of demons is just a bit out of my league."

Pazuzu tilted his head back and laughed, a sound not too dissimilar to a volcanic eruption.

"Take on Satan and his demons," he said, still chuckling. "What a concept. What an ego. Did you really think we would even consider such foolishness?"

"That's what it was starting to sound like to me."

"No, no, no, no, no, my friend." Pazuzu changed back to human form. "I – we have nothing so dramatic in mind.

"We know that we have neither the power nor the numbers to take on Satan and his gang in a stand-up fight. Even if we should try such a thing and find ourselves winning, Yahweh would step in and throw his angelic host into the fray. No, my friend, a head-to-head conflict is a losing proposition." Pazuzu took a sip from his cup.

"We plan to take a page from Yahweh's own book. It will take a long time, but we have eternity in which to work. We shall work from within. An insurgency, if you will. We will encourage some events already taking place, such as Che Guevara's intermittent revolution. And, we shall add to that some minor irritants – political itching powder, if you will – designed to weaken the belief that the status quo is invincible. Stir the pot a little and add a dash of promise and voila! Suddenly, the powers that be no longer exert the same control and New Hell becomes New Babylon. No muss, no fuss, no god wars."

Monty stared at Pazuzu for a long time. "Do you really think that will work?" he finally asked.

Pazuzu shrugged. "Why not? And, even if it doesn't, so what? If nothing else, it will relieve the tedium of eternity. Think about it. Do you want to spend forever listening to the same bitching and griping, day in and day out? Eating the same tasteless food?

Drinking the same rancid water? Wouldn't it be nice to have the zing and zest of a secret mission to add a tang to your existence?"

Monty paced while he considered Pazuzu's words, unmindful of the breach of protocol. Finally, he turned to the being. "So, what do I have to do?"

"Right now, nothing. Watch and wait. There will soon come a time when they pull you out of your current torment to have some fun with you. They will probably put you into some kind of no-win scenario. I don't know what it will be, but I have faith that you will recognize it.

"When they do, go along with it. Make them believe that you are trying your best, giving it your all. In the meantime, look for your opportunity to turn it in a way that they didn't expect. They are bored bullies and they are not nearly as smart as they think they are." Pazuzu chuckled to himself. "No, my friend, not nearly. When the time comes, pull your switch."

Monty shook his head, his doubts plain on his face. "How could that possibly help you?"

"By itself, it won't. But, if you do it here, and someone else does it over there, and something happens in this alley, then the actions accrue and the image that the demons might not be all-powerful begins to spread. As it spreads, their control weakens. The more they try to fight it, the worse it gets."

"So, what's in it for me?"

"In the short run, probably nothing. In the long run, maybe nothing still." Pazuzu winked. "Then, again, maybe you'll get another good cup of coffee."

Suddenly, Monty was sitting behind his desk. In his hand was an Infernal Action Request form. Opposite him Mrs. Johanssen was staring at him, her expression uncertain.

"Well, I was hoping that you would take it up with whoever's in charge of these things," she finally said. "You look like such a nice man. They're bound to listen to you."

Monty took a deep breath and instantly regretted it. The mixture of smells – rest home neglect coupled with the rotten egg stench of sulfur – was too much. He barely turned over the trash can in time as his stomach violently ejected everything he'd eaten and drunk. After several minutes of spasmodic upheaval, he was finally able to sit upright and wipe his lips with a coarse, brown tissue.

Well, he thought, *at least I have the memory.*

*

The room was huge – enormous – far larger than any office he'd ever seen. The panels of the drop ceiling were at least fifteen feet above his head. The dark paneled walls formed a cube forty feet square. Looking around, Monty noticed that the only furniture was the receptionist's desk, a massive highly-polished redwood structure. A computer monitor faced away from him at an angle. The keyboard, mouse, and mouse pad sat neatly in the center of the far side of the desk. A slender but well-endowed platinum-haired woman sat in a thickly-padded, oxblood leather chair while she typed, hunt and peck fashion, on an old IBM Selectric typewriter. The woman looked familiar, but Monty could not figure out why.

Set inside recesses in the wall behind her desk on either side stood two massive oak doors. Between them, in thick gold letters, were the words:

Asmoday, Amdusias, Amon, Marchosias,
Marbas & Zepar
Attorneys At Law

Monty relaxed. A law office! At last he was on familiar ground. A long, narrow carpet runner stretched from the elevator doors to the front of the desk. It was a garish, imitation Persian design. Twisted shapes in gold and crimson and black and orange turned and writhed like snakes or worms. He walked gingerly toward the desk expecting to feel the reptiles wriggling beneath his shoes. All he felt was solid floor.

"Do you have an appointment?" The voice was sultry, Midwestern sexy, and full of feminine allure. The receptionist had turned from her typing and now faced him. Only now did he realize how petite she was. He didn't need a hairdresser to know that her hair came from a peroxide bottle. Although she was very pretty – starlet beautiful, in fact – the retro thirties look with the too red lipstick and the rouge did nothing for him. Still, there was something familiar, something about those wide green eyes…

"Jean, is my two o'clock appointment here, yet?" the intercom on her desk buzzed.

"I think he just arrived, Mister M." The woman replied, leaning forward to speak into the machine and giving Monty a generous view of her ample cleavage. She looked up at Monty questioningly.

He shrugged. "I don't know. I guess I am. A moment ago I was sitting at my desk giving estate planning advice, and the next; I'm standing here talking to you."

"It's him, Mister M."

"Very good, Jean. Would you bring him to Conference Room B, please? And, see what he would like to drink and get it for him."

Monty glanced at a black nameplate framed in brass. The engraved white read: *J. Harlow*. Of course! The original blonde bombshell of the 1930's.

"Right away, Mister M." The woman stood and turned toward the door on the left. "Would you follow me, please, Mister…"

"Montgomery," he replied as he tried to race her to the door. "Aaron Montgomery. You can call me Monty."

She beat him and held it open with her left hand as she slipped through the portal ahead of him. He trailed behind while his eyes followed the figure eight movement of her almost perfect ass even though he knew it was pointless. After two twists, they reached a conference room. The room was large – forty feet long and twenty-five wide. In the center stood a massive conference table. The highly polished and oiled mahogany surface reflected the overhead fluorescent lights like a mirror. The top was three feet wide at either end but widened at the middle to four feet. A luxurious leather captain's chair sat at either end. Five leather armchairs graced each side. One end of the room sported a huge whiteboard with markers in the metal tray along the bottom edge. The wall opposite was plain with a low mahogany credenza between it and the end of the table. Both long walls were wood framed glass panels looking out over rows of cubicles.

The receptionist indicated the nearest chair. "Please have a seat. Mister M will be with you shortly. Would you like something to drink?"

What the hell, he thought.

"Would it be possible to get a small Scotch?"

"Certainly," she smiled. "Would you like that with cola, on the rocks, or neat?"

"On the rocks, please," he replied barely concealing his surprise.

"I'll just be a moment."

He watched as she turned and gyrated through the door.

Five minutes later she returned, placed a napkin on the smooth surface, and set a heavy glass tumbler in front of him. Ice cubes tinkled against the sides as Monty picked it up and took a sip.

He almost spit it out, but managed to gag it down. It tasted like industrial sludge. He wiped his mouth with the napkin and sat back.

He waited.

And, waited.

Thirty minutes passed. Suddenly, he looked up as the conference room door slammed open. The being striding toward him put him in mind of horror stories. It stood a little over six feet tall and had a man's torso, but that was where any species kinship ended. Rising from the neck of the tailored suit was the head of a wolf. A serpent's tail exited the seat of the trousers and writhed behind the creature. Griffin's wings rose from between its shoulders. It pulled a chair away from the table and sat next to Monty.

"I am the Marquis Marchosias," said the demon as he extended his hand. "I am one of the senior partners in this firm."

Reflexively he reached for the creature's paw. As they made contact he felt its flesh squirm and shift. Before he could pull back, however, the paw had changed to a hand and the winged werewolf to a well-dressed older – and *human* – male with silver hair and glowing, red-flecked gray eyes. The man was fit, too, judging from his grip. His olive complexion spoke to a Mediterranean or even Middle Eastern heritage.

Although disconcerted by the shape change, Monty started to rise.

Marchosias shook his head as he released Monty's hand and made an off-hand gesture for him to stay seated.

"My *legal team* – of which you are now the most junior – has been given an interesting case. Since you were a defense attorney when you were alive, this should be right up your alley."

Monty tried not to fidget. This was a demon, after all, and according to all he'd ever read or seen in movies or experienced here, their acquaintance with the truth was distant at best.

"It's a simple case. A defamation of character suit." Marchosias smiled, showing a full set of lupine teeth bristling within his human mouth. "The defendant, our client, is a writer named Bram Stoker."

Monty groaned. He could see where this was going and he did not like it.

"You've heard of him, then. Good. That makes it so much better."

"Who filed the suit?" Monty croaked through his constricted throat.

Marchosias glanced at a document lying on the far end of the table. "Let me get this right. It says here Prince Vlad III Drakulya aka Vlad Tepes aka Drakulja, Prince of Wallachia and Transylvania. I believe that is part of Rumania."

Of course. Who else could it be? Monty slumped in his seat. "Not that I think it will matter, but who is the opposing counsel?"

The demon sat on the end of the table. "It's a team. Two men – Aaron Burr and Alexander Hamilton. From what I understand they are quite good, despite their differences."

Monty looked up. "Differences?"

"They've hated each other for over two centuries."

"Maybe I can use that," Monty mused. He didn't really believe it, but the thinnest of slivers looked like a raft to a drowning man.

"I doubt it. They usually put aside their differences inside the courtroom."

"This could be difficult," Monty said, shaking his head. "The historical – the *real* – Vlad Tepes was many things. He was never a vampire. There's no such thing except in horror stories."

Marchosias leaned down until he was nose-to-nose with Monty. "You're a lawyer. What does reality have to do with anything? Besides, you misunderstand me. I don't want you to win this case. I want you to lose it."

Monty's head snapped up from looking at the papers. "Lose it?"

"Exactly."

"But, he's our client."

"Yes."

"We're supposed to defend him."

"And, we will."

"But, you just said…"

"I told you that you must lose the case." Marchosias smiled. "I fail to see your dilemma. Defend him. Just don't win."

"But, he's our client."

"So is the prince."

Monty looked down at the paper. This made no sense. It was a clear conflict of interest.

Marchosias leaned close to Monty's downturned face. "Do not even consider recusing yourself or this firm. That is not an option."

Monty didn't trust his voice so he nodded instead. His nose wrinkled in disgust. Didn't anyone use breath mints in hell?

"I will leave you to your thoughts," the demon said as he left the room. "Just remember. You must not win."

Monty remained in the leather chair. He stared at the white board while he collected his thoughts and tried to map a strategy. Obviously, he could not prove the prince was a real vampire. They did not exist.

He shook his head. He couldn't use that, anyway. It would be a win.

How common was the name Dracula in Rumania? Were the names spelled the same?

Stop it, his mind screamed. *That's a winning strategy.*

In the book, Stoker referred to him as Count Dracula. The man suing Stoker was Prince Drakulya. Obviously a count was lower on the food chain than a prince, so that was another difference. How many more discrepancies could he find? Monty glanced at the end of the conference table. The legal paper was still there. He leaned forward and pulled it toward him. He scanned until he found the name. Drakulya. Prince Drakulya, not Count Dracula. He felt his hopes lifting. Was it enough?

Quit thinking like that!

He needed to do more research. Perhaps the library was open.

Although he'd seen tens of thousands of shelves filled with books and scrolls, and clay tablets and stone, he'd also seen computers. If the database was up to date – a big if in this place – then it might not be such a daunting task. He picked up the legal documents and quickly scanned the first page.

Monty sat in the chair for a long time, afraid to move, terrified to breathe. He had time to understand one thing.

It was possible to be frightened enough to wet your pants, even in hell.

*

Monty sat at the defendant's table with his elbows on the hard, wooden surface and his hands over his eyes. So far this "cakewalk" case had been anything but. With flowery, eighteenth century oratory, Aaron Burr had stipulated all of the damning history of Prince Vlad with indifferent aplomb.

Did he kill tens of thousands of Turks? So stipulated.

Did he nail the turbans onto the heads of three of Sultan Mehmed II's emissaries for refusing to remove them in his court? So stipulated.

Was that really him depicted in the woodcutting eating his dinner while Turkish soldiers hung around him in a forest of poles, impaled and dying? Again, so stipulated.

And, in the end, irrelevant. Yes, he was a monster. Yes, a tyrant. And, yes, sadistic, even for his times.

But, was he a vampire as depicted by Bram Stoker's infamous novel, the same book as the one lying on the evidence table and marked as Plaintiff's Exhibit C?

Defense had yet to make its case. Monty shied away from the discrepancies, although it went against every part of his nature. His fiery, competitive nature screamed at him to go for the jugular. The knockout punch was easily within his reach, but he dared not swing. It looked like Marchosias was going to get his loss.

Monty glanced at his client. Stoker was a well-dressed heavy set man in his mid-sixties. He had a full head of dark hair along with a reddish brown beard and moustache. He also stank. His face bore swellings and nodules characteristic of tertiary syphilis, the disease that had claimed his life – or at least had contributed to his demise. In life, these would have been unremarkable bumps and swellings. In Hell, however, nothing was ever that simple or easy. The bumps turned into pustules that burst and ruptured, oozing a noxious thick shiny liquid that made Monty wish he could smell the brimstone once more.

He stood and walked slowly toward the evidence table, more to clear his nasal passages of the stench of his client's disease than because he had any clear strategy. Without thinking, he picked up the book.

"This book," he intoned as he absently opened the cover and slowly turned the first two pages. "This novel is the crux of this case."

He paused. A paragraph caught his eye. He read it twice, keeping his emotions in check. Was the solution really this simple?

He looked to the rear of the courtroom, to the back row of seats in the gallery. Marchosias sat in the far left corner. How much loyalty did he owe to the demon's cause?

Suddenly, Pazuzu's words echoed in his mind: *There will soon come a time when they pull you out of your current torment to have some fun with you. They will probably put you into some kind of no-win scenario. I don't know what it will be, but I have faith that you will recognize it.*

Marchosias stood for everything he'd endured since his arrival. The Welcome Woman, the belittling, the lowly posting in the rest home – all of it. What had Pazuzu done to him? Besides yank him from that demeaning task, treat him like a human being, and give him a chance to at least feel like he had value?

A snatch of song – *Won't Get Fooled Again*, by a group called the Who – ran through his mind:

Meet the new boss
Same as the old boss

Both regimes might be the same in the end but he knew one thing for sure. The current regime was full of crap.

"Your Dishonor," he began. "Plaintiff has stated – and read into evidence – this book as proof that my client defamed and impugned the character of his client, Prince Vlad III Drakulya, is that not correct?"

"It is."

"I beg the court's indulgence while I read a passage printed in the front of this book, and I quote:

This is a work of fiction. All the characters and events portrayed in this book are fictional, and any resemblance to real people or incidents is purely coincidental.

"If it pleases the court, I move that this case be dismissed."

*

Aaron "Monty" Montgomery awoke face down on a hard laminate surface. A deep rumbling vibration thrummed throughout his body. He heard a metallic rattling from somewhere above and behind him. He smiled. It would be interesting to see how long before the insurrection would take hold. He certainly had time to find out. And, maybe, just maybe, he'd get a decent cup of coffee.

Orientation Day

by

Sarah Hulcy

The Chief Librarian of Hell's Law Library was spending a tremendous amount of time and energy trying to track down every tiny crack in the Library's rock walls. Ever since Erra and the Seven sent a massive flood down the road that ran straight into New Hell, Demetrius of Phalerum had been chasing trickles of nasty, muddy, foul-smelling water (and who knew *what* else) to find the leaks and plug them until repairs could be made. The moisture threatened the most delicate contents of the Library – the ancient scrolls, parchment and papyrus recording laws from antiquity. Stone and clay tablets weren't as difficult to protect as papyri, but the modern books were almost as sensitive to dampness as the oldest materials.

Demetrius was having trouble staying ahead of the water because the Library encompassed fourteen entire floors – the *lowest* fourteen of the Hall of Injustice, where the Administration and its myriad bureaucratic departments were located. These particular floors had been chipped out of the solid rock by prisoners held in His Satanic Majesty's dungeon, over a period of aeons.

"There," he said with satisfaction. "Stopped another one." Demetrius turned to thank his newest assistant, Makalani, a lovely youth whose name – by predestination or fate? – meant "clerk" in ancient Egyptian. "Oh, no! This horrid seepage has ruined your smock," Demetrius exclaimed. "Come to my office, Sesh, and we'll find you a fresh uniform."

Makalani hurried alongside the Chief Librarian with his heart beating a little faster than normal. Demetrius had called him "Sesh," which was not only an honorific meaning "respected scribe," but was also a rather intimate use of the word. Dared he hope…?

When they reached his office, Demetrius searched through

chests until he found just what he was looking for. "Here you are; see if it fits," he said, handing an almost new, crimson smock to the excited young man.

"Oh, but sir, this is crimson.... I'm only a fourth-level scribe."

"Not any more," Demetrius smiled. "I recently lost my personal assistant when his taxi was swept away in the flood, so I'm promoting you to his position, young Sesh."

Makalani tried to control his breathing as he removed his ruined smock and slid the new one over his long, ebony curls. He adjusted the collar and sleeves, noticing how nicely his gray linen pants set off the expensively-dyed smock and smiled shyly. Then, bowing slightly, he looked up at the Chief Librarian with kohl-lengthened eyes. "Sir, I hardly know what to say. I am honored and I will do everything possible to be worthy of this opportunity."

"I'm sure you will, First Assistant, I'm sure you will," Demetrius said, well-pleased with his choice. "But now we must return to our duties," he added briskly, straightening the folds of his own robe and brushing off some dust acquired in their latest exploration. He might be working in New Hell with all these new dead, but he still preferred the dignified scholar's robes and sandals he had worn in Athens and Alexandria (even if these robes *were* made of wrinkle-resistant modern fabric).

The two descended the stairs to the third level balcony above the meeting floor of Hell's Law Library, and looked down at the newest class of damned lawyers filing in to be seated below, through a thickening haze of smoke and sulphurous vapor.

"You see them, Makalani?" Demetrius asked with scorn. "All these new dead – entirely lost without the small engines they keep in their pockets or clip to their ears, or the larger ones with push-buttons they must use to find cases, laws and loopholes in the more modern books here in the Library. They're just like my new-dead assistants, who spend all their time in the research rooms trying to get information from the Library's computer system (such as it is), instead of looking for the actual printed documents.

"At one time, I knew the location of every scroll and parchment in the entire Library of Alexandria. I didn't need *gadgets* to remind me where to find a scroll. After all, I organized that place," he sniffed, glancing smugly at his assistant. "And let me tell you, it was an enormous endeavor." Makalani looked at Demetrius with something approaching awe.

Turning back to the balcony railing, Demetrius directed the clerk's attention to the lawyers assembling on the ground floor. "First, they'll complain about the poor ventilation, the dust, the temperature, the lights and the odor down there, especially with all this disgusting liquid seeping in through the walls. Then listen for all the shocked whispers and exclamations of rage when the new class learns the rules under which they must now labor." He chuckled hoarsely, the mildew from the seepage catching in his throat. "There are *always* a few in each new group who believe that due to their prior 'lofty' status, *they* should be exempt from the probationary period required of every lawyer."

"Why is there a probationary period, Chief Librarian?" asked Makalani. "Did not these men and women learn their trade in life?"

"Oh, of course, they learned to read the law on earth – for their own ends.... Most of these people were wealthy, powerful and respected in their communities during their lives (if *not* necessarily esteemed by their peers and spouses). They foolishly assume they will continue to enjoy their previous lifestyle here in the afterlife." He scoffed. "With all the unrest caused by this audit from on high, these newly-damned lawyers should be grateful their orientation seminar is going forward on schedule. They *could* still be languishing in the morgue with the Undertaker, awaiting release. I find their shock rather entertaining – especially when they discover what their duties will be while they serve their probation," Demetrius confided.

Makalani was flattered that the Chief Librarian was taking time to share these insights with him. After realizing that his heart would never be weighed by Maat against a feather, Makalani had been ecstatic when assigned to the Law Library: here he could work under the legendary Demetrius, Makalani's personal hero, whose organization of the Royal Library of Alexandria was legend. To be named First Assistant was an honor beyond the young sesh's wildest dreams.

"Most of these newly-damned candidates are attending our 'Legal Orientation Seminar' for the first time, although a few are repeating the course – some who have died here, and revisited the

Undertaker, or have been judged inadequate and returned for 'additional' orientation," Demetrius explained as he and Makalani looked down at the enormous plaza on the lowest level.

"The ones new to hell are the most fun to watch as they learn their fate. As they straggle into the room, the saying above the door – derived, of course, from the one at the Alexandria Library – just confuses them, highlighting their woeful ignorance."

Inscribed above the entryway to Hell's Law Library was the statement: *The place of the curse of the soul.* The epithet was a source of never-ending amusement to Demetrius, a play on the words above the original library's door, which had said 'The place of the *cure* of the soul.'

"But sir, do not all men know the original words of the famous inscription in Alexandria?" asked Makalani.

Demetrius sniffed, "If these people didn't need to know something for their daily work, most couldn't be bothered to find out. All they needed to know, in their opinion, they could find using their benighted 'equipment.' It's a miracle – *sorry*," he cringed slightly while glancing up, then continued: "It's amazing if more than a few of them have been in an actual library since they studied for the bar," said Demetrius with scorn.

Makalani was still dizzy with the honor of having the famous Demetrius confide in him. In life Demetrius had revamped the legal system of Athens, where he was in charge of the city (even though a change in government forced him to leave expeditiously for Thebes, with his wife and *eromenoi).* After a decade in Thebes, Demetrius was welcomed in Alexandria, where he was appointed Chief Librarian and organized the famous Library there for Ptolemy I – until the king's heir callously fired him, an act which Makalani considered mean and spiteful of Ptolemy II.

Demetrius explained to Makalani, "When I arrived in Hades' realm, His Satanic Majesty, the Prince of Darkness, personally selected me – because of my experience in Athens with the law, and as bibliophylax of Alexandria – to be the Chief Librarian for Hell's Law Library." Demetrius made a sweeping gesture to call attention to the hundreds of thousands of shelves stretching into the distance around them. Turning to his assistant, he lowered his voice: "While not as beautiful as wonderful Alexandria," then continued at normal volume, "it does contain every law ever written on earth or in hell, whether handwritten on papyrus; incised in tablets of stone, clay or wax; drawn on sheepskin; rendered by calligraphy in ink and illuminated by hand on parchment or vellum; or printed on modern paper bound in books. So, to keep track of it all, Satan arranged for me to be assigned here. Of course, this library contains far more material than simply laws; it has reference material from all the ages.

"I do *not* want to have to explain to HSM how I allowed mold and mildew to take hold on some of the rare leather-covered books, not to mention the parchments and vellum." Demetrius shuddered. "Do you know we have the original of Danté Alighieri's 'Divine Comedy' here? All three sections: *Inferno, Purgatorio* and *Paradiso* from the fourteenth century.... *And* some of the original writings of the infamous Marquis de Sade.

"This library was in a horrendous state when I arrived, and needed my organizational skills desperately," Demetrius said flatly. "But I now know where every single scroll, parchment fragment, palimpsest, or tablet in my domain is stored. My more modern clerks are much like these newly-damned lawyers – entirely lost without their devices to find laws and cases in the printed books. I happily leave that material to their auspices. Here in hell, their fancy equipment is usually only good for *losing* the most vital piece of information they need. But they'll find out soon enough," Demetrius said as the lights in the entire library flickered, and howls of dismay were heard from the research rooms.

"It's lucky you arrived here when you did, my boy. The Legal Orientation Seminar is going to be somewhat different today; there will be a guest speaker, from 'Above,' a rarity," said Demetrius, raising his gray eyebrows meaningfully. "We'll come back later, in time to hear the lecture. The Boss has been very ill-tempered since the auditors arrived and we don't want to draw any unwanted attention, so we need to familiarize you with your duties as my new First Assistant and the steps we're taking to preserve the collections from the flood damage, as soon as we can."

Having no interest in hearing once again the same seminar given by Melvin Belli and Percy Foreman on many occasions, Demetrius was content to take his new scribe on a tour of the shelves of scrolls and other writings from antiquity – his favorites –

until the guest speaker arrived.

"I'd like to show you the new water-tight and 'crush-proof' chests I'm trying out to protect our most delicate materials," Demetrius told Makalani as they walked away from the balcony. "The containers are made of some odd substance called titanium alloy." Once again lowering his voice and leaning his head closer to Makalani, Demetrius murmured, "Since those auditors caused the flood and all these blasted leaks started… um, hmmm… what *is* that delightful spice scent…?"

*

"All right, folks, let's settle down." Percy Foreman looked out at the sea of faces representing the newest group of damned lawyers to enter Hell.

"My name is Percy Foreman and my colleague here is Melvin Belli. We were two of the best lawyers on earth, in our respective fields during our lifetimes, and we're here to acquaint you with the rules and requirements of hell's Administration for all newly-damned lawyers." Murmurs followed his statement. "I see some of you recognize one or both of our names," he said, nodding at Belli. "Nice to know they still remember us back in the real world – or does that buzzing out there mean that some of you are confused to find yourselves here? After visiting with the Undertaker, you should be under no illusions about why you're here....

"For those of you who haven't been through the official seminar before, it really will go much faster if you just let us get on with it, instead of asking the same pointless questions we've heard from all your predecessors…. But I don't suppose that's gonna stop any of 'em," he stage-whispered to his colleague, Belli.

"Before we get started, did everyone pick up a copy of the Orientation Manual for Newly-Damned Lawyers when you came in? You really want to hang on to those manuals. They're the newest edition and can sync with your hellpads. They also have a new section that can automatically display the latest rulings.

"The answers to your questions may be found in the manual, but in hell there is a certain fluidity affecting every aspect of existence, including the law. You'll just have to learn as you go. Our job is to give out assignments, *not* read through every rule and regulation in the manual. It's up to you to study the nit-picky details … in your 'spare' time," he chuckled.

As the first arms began waving enthusiastically in the audience, Foreman sighed, rubbing his hand over his large, mostly bald, head. He turned to Belli, saying quietly, "It never fails." Raising his voice he turned back to his audience, "Gentlemen and ladies, please; give us a chance to explain a few things before you start demanding answers to individual questions…. Thank you."

"Now, because I practiced criminal defense law – rather successfully, I might add – I will handle assignments for all the civil, estate, merger and acquisition, intellectual property, entertainment, corporate and any other non-criminal specialists."

At this announcement, confused looks appeared on faces in the crowd and several people looked around to see if they had heard correctly.

Foreman, the big Texan, grinned maliciously. "That's right, and if you practiced criminal law, whether in defense or prosecution, our Mr. Belli here, who was known as the 'King of Torts,' will handle *your* assignments.

"This is how it works down here: every newly-damned lawyer has to serve a probationary period working for the Administration, in whatever field of law he or she knew the *least* about on earth. How well you learn the material, find convenient loopholes for the Administration *and* how quickly you pick up on the way things function in hell, will determine how long it is before you can go into private practice for yourself or join an existing firm… That is, if you don't get killed and have to start over at the bottom, so to speak." Foreman and Belli guffawed loudly, giving each other high-fives, while their audience members looked either appalled or outraged.

Melvin Belli took the podium, an imposing figure in his custom-tailored suit, Italian shoes, silk tie and polished cotton shirt when compared to Foreman in his ill-fitting, off-the-rack outfit.

The newly-damned lawyers were already beginning to fawn, hoping to influence their placement: they greeted Belli with a smattering of polite applause.

Belli began, "A rare treat is in store for today's class. We have a visiting lecturer from on high: Mister Justice Benjamin Cardozo, who replaced Oliver Wendell Holmes on the U.S. Supreme Court, where he served thereafter until nineteen thirty-eight. Some of his decisions and opinions regarding corporate responsibility and negligence created the tort laws that made *me* so famous… and rich!

"He will attempt to enlighten you on things you might have done to avoid this place. Who knows? Maybe if you pay attention, you might someday – *way* down the line – become eligible for manumission by Altos, Hell's own volunteer angel (his friends call him Just Al), who is escorting Justice Cardozo today. But don't count on it.

"Justice Cardozo was renowned for his emphasis on the purpose of law, his insightful descriptions of the relationship between the policy and the practice of law, and especially noted for his concern for fairness in justice – something we don't have to worry about down here. Benjamin Cardozo was considered a 'lawyer's lawyer' and later a 'judge's judge,' with good reason, so you might want to pay attention."

As befitting the occasion, Belli composed his face into its most humble expression (one with which he was not particularly familiar) and raised his voice: "All rise for the Honorable Justice Benjamin Cardozo."

His audience rose simultaneously, each having learned on earth to spring to his or her feet like a jack-in-the-box at the words 'all rise.' They stood quietly while the distinguished, white-haired Cardozo was escorted into the room by an ethereal being in a glowing white robe, with the most beautiful face any of them had ever seen. The scent of a soft summer day wafted into the room as the two newcomers entered.

"Thank you, Altos," said Cardozo as he stepped to the lectern, "I'll keep this brief so the elevator doesn't have to wait too long."

"Not at all, sir. Take your time – we have a lot of it," said Altos, smiling.

*

"Please be seated, ladies and gentlemen," began Justice Cardozo. His piercing gaze swept across the room and into each soul among the convened newly-damned lawyers.

"In nineteen twenty-one, I wrote: 'The law has outgrown its primitive stage of formalism when the precise word was the sovereign talisman, and every slip was fatal. It takes a broader view today.' I see no reason to change my opinion, even after all these years.

"From reading the Register listings for some of today's attendees, it appears many of you never were exposed to my lecture series from Yale University. You believed the purpose of practicing law was to make sure *your* client would be able to get the upper hand in any dispute, by manipulating language to ensure a 'win' – whether your client actually deserved to win or not – and, not incidentally, make sure your client could afford your enormous fees."

Shaking his dignified head he continued, "I believed that, whenever possible, courts should attempt to instill fairness in an unclear dispute by analyzing and interpreting it to cover situations the parties may not have provided for specifically, in order to ensure a *fair* result. What seems to have happened, since my time, unfortunately, is that particular legal philosophy has become unimportant to some jurists and generally denigrated by the legal profession."

There commenced a shuffling of feet, ducking of heads, crossing of legs, shifting of chairs, whispers and other indications of unease in the audience.

Justice Cardozo raised his voice slightly, "But *you* people – you each made it your life's work to revise wording in contracts, laws, legislation and court documents; you made use of every loophole you could find or create and took advantage of, for instance, every *'may'* that should have been a *'shall'* or other ambiguous wording, to ensure triumph for whoever paid you, without regard for the inherent 'right' or 'wrong' of the situation. Well, *that is why you're here* – that and your consistent disavowal of the principles of fairness. You will now learn humility by seeing how it feels to lose, again and again – especially if you continue your previous behavior in *this* realm. While it may have benefited you financially and materially in your time on earth, things just don't work the same way in hell.

"In fact, it is my understanding that *nothing* works very well down here, so those gizmos you rely on – your hellphones, hellpads, and portable computers – may work sometimes; they may not work at others or, even worse, may *appear* to work, but give you erroneous results. You will be better served by doing due-diligence research yourself, in the actual books of the law, which will, I sincerely hope, instill in you some respect for how the law came into being." This time when he paused, there was total silence from the audience.

"As an agnostic in life, I wasn't convinced of the reality of 'heaven' or 'hell,' or of the precepts of Judaism – even though I was born a Sephardic Jew – or Christianity or any of the other world religions. I simply believed I should be as honest and fair as I possibly could in rendering my judgments, and live my life by the same principles, while treating my fellow man with dignity. Apparently, I succeeded well enough to be granted an afterlife in a more comfortable realm than this one.

"My message to you today is this: learn from your mistakes. You should be able to determine why you were sent here, if you think back on your life. The probation you must serve – aside from supporting His Infernal Majesty..." Cardozo looked up at the ceiling fifteen stories above their heads and shuddered, "...may expose you to the practice of law at all levels, introducing you to the dregs of hell's society. It may cause you to focus exclusively on the minutest differences of wording of laws and regulations. You will have to learn new laws and figure out how to deal with different loopholes than those with which you are acquainted.

"And my advice to you is: during and after your probationary period (however long that may last) try to atone for your behavior in life. Do something good for someone else's benefit, just because it's the right thing to do. I understand that good behavior is frowned upon down here, but it will give you the best chance of earning a somewhat less agonizing afterlife one day – *if* you gain an understanding of why you are here, sincerely regret your unworthy behavior while on earth, and try to recover the goodness and innocence you lost somewhere along the way. I thank you for your time and attention."

Not a single head rose from contemplation of a single lap as he finished. After a moment, Justice Cardozo turned to Altos, sighed and said, "Well, I hope it did someone some good...." Altos patted Justice Cardozo's arm and drew him out of the Library toward the elevator.

*

"That was quite a speech," Demetrius breathed to Makalani. "For one of the new dead, that one has the mind and understanding of a great philosopher like Aristotle, my old teacher," he said, as he dabbed at his eye with the sleeve of his robe. "But it was probably wasted on that rabble down on the floor.

"Oh, but let me show you the most wonderful scroll of the Hammurabi era, which I found behind a broken wall panel while I was sealing another leak yesterday!" And Demetrius led his assistant firmly into another part of the Library.

*

"Well, people, I'd call that an inspiring address by Justice Cardozo. It's up to you whether you take it to heart or not," said Melvin Belli as he stepped up to the rostrum.

"Now I want all the criminal defense lawyers and former prosecutors to follow me to the other end of the room so we can get started. I'll leave the rest of you civil practitioners to Percy, here." With a malevolent smile, Belli strode to the lectern at the far end of the room and turned to wait for his victims who were just making their halting way to the empty chairs facing him.

At each end of the room, a babble of questions and offended oratory rose in volume. After a moment, Percy Foreman picked up a stone tablet and slammed it on the desk next to where he stood. He shouted: "All right, y'all settle down. *Now!*"

Many in the audience gasped in shocked indignation. No one dared yell at them – ever. They were the cream of the crop, the best of the best, the wealthiest, most influential lawyers ever to have practiced civil law. And no hick Texas Criminal shyster (regardless of his incredible record of fifteen hundred acquittals to sixty-four convictions, one execution) was going to tell *them* anything!

A similar confrontation was taking place with the group gathered in front of Mr. Belli. Why should they listen to some slick, polished civil lawyer, even if he *had* single-handedly created Class Action Lawsuits and won six-hundred million U.S. dollars in awards in some of the biggest trials ever? They had collected fees in the millions of dollars themselves, representing the richest scumbags ever arrested. The former prosecutors hadn't been as wealthy a group, unless their jurisdiction afforded them regular access to bribes and perks, but they had wielded a tremendous amount of power they were loath to give up.

Each group believed it preposterous to require them to practice a type of law they'd avoided like a plague when alive. Who did Foreman and Belli think they were?

A better question would have been, *who did Foreman and Belli work for?*

When it looked like total insurrection was going to break out, and the noise level rose toward its peak, with men and women standing, red-faced and shouting at the Seminar Chairmen and each other, a bolt of lightning crackled from the highest floor of the Hall of Injustice, spearing the center of the meeting room floor, with a resounding crash.

Once again, all the lights in the Library flickered and popped, as the lightning played havoc with the electricity.

The loudest voice they had ever heard boomed: *"This is hell, you idiots! This is not Burger King. You don't get it your way – you do what you're told! The Undertaker must be slipping if none of you understands this yet. Now shut up, pay attention and take notes. Then get to work before I have to make a personal appearance...."*

As the smoke cleared from the room, silence reigned. The seminar chairmen shook their heads.

"If I may proceed now," Foreman drawled, "I will begin handing out assignments." A pen fell to the floor from someone's lap, and the woman sitting next to the miscreant let out a small yelp.

"Well, I guess we can start with you, sir," said Foreman as he pointed to the blond, too-perfectly tanned gentleman with most unnaturally white teeth, dressed in ultra-expensive 'business casual,' who was just picking up his pen. Consulting the Register of Preeminently Damned Lawyers on his hellpad, Foreman continued, "So, you practiced entertainment law in Hollywood, is that right?" Tall, Blond and Tan stood up and said with a supercilious smile, "Why, yes, as a matter of fact, I was the highest paid..."

"Yeah, yeah, that's who I thought you were," interrupted Foreman. "We have a great opening in night Demon's Court for a Public Defender. I think you'll fit right in.... It's a real pest-hole, in the worst area of Pandemonium City."

The room was treated to a clearer view of those extra-white

teeth as the first appointee's mouth dropped open in horror.

Foreman chuckled: "Of course, not *all* of your indigent clients will be demons. Some will be succubi or incubi, or your garden-variety thieves or hookers. I'm *sure* it will be a refreshing change from your previous clientele." He smiled broadly. "And just so we're clear: either get really good at your job, really fast, or you *will* stay there until someone more deserving comes along … or until one of your clients doesn't like the terms of a plea-bargain you arranged. Some of those folks in the lower echelons of Pandemonium society are quick to take offense if they feel slighted – real *personal* offense, if y'know what I mean. But don't worry. If that happens you won't be in the Undertaker's hands more than another few weeks. Then you'll be right back here, so you'd better learn fast. You have a good time, now, y'hear?"

That gorgeous tan was a sickly gray by the time the gentlemen in question disappeared with a small "pop" of displaced air. Percy Foreman, grinning, looked back at his list, ignoring the whimpers from his audience.

At the far end of the room, Melvin Belli was going through his own hellpad Register entries. "You," he said, pointing to a rather nondescript man in a cheap suit and run-down shoes who was attempting to make himself very small and unnoticeable by slouching behind a broad-shouldered, heavily-built mob lawyer.

"M-m-me, sir?" quavered a voice from behind the silver-haired heavyweight.

"Yes, you. You were a public defender in Brooklyn, specializing in doing the least amount of work for your court-appointed clients, and talking them into plea deals that weren't in their best interest, just to clear your docket, weren't you?" Melvin Belli said, as he glowered over the top of the list.

"Well, I, uh, wouldn't say, uh…."

"Of course you wouldn't," Belli snorted. "None of you ever do," he said, shaking his leonine head. "I believe I have the perfect assignment here, just for you. The Infernal Revenue Service needs some junior attorneys to go through all the older tax laws and identify any that are too favorable to taxpayers. If I understand correctly, they've asked for five new hires. It seems they have around sixty thousand volumes of tax laws that need to be updated."

"But, but, I barely passed contract law in night school. And I've never been detail-oriented enough to handle big issues like complicated taxes, and things like that…." wailed the profusely sweating thin man in the rumpled suit.

"Then I suggest you learn quickly. But don't worry, you won't be alone. There will be four more joining you to toil in the depths of the IRS archives, so you won't get lonely. Oh, and do try to stay out of the way of the Director. She can be a real bitch if she's not happy with your work…" chortled Belli, "…and you'll be reporting to her immediately." As the appalled former public defender disappeared with the newly-familiar "pop," Belli muttered, *sotto voce,* "you poor slob."

*

Demetrius snickered as he watched the assignment process continue. Sometimes this was the most fun he had all week – well, except for dallying with his new protégé. IIc wondered how many in the blur of faces, three floors below, would pass through his fiefdom again, as any more than visitors. A certain number of the fools always had to go through the process several times before they finally learned they had to play by the rules of hell to get anywhere.

When Demetrius turned to continue his discussion with Makalani, a tall, attractive man in casual black slacks, a black shirt and well-combed hair approached from one of the entrances. "How may I or my scribe assist you?" asked Demetrius.

"Well, I'm Doctor Miguel Bartsch and someone told me this was the library. Could you show me where the medical section is?" The visitor looked perplexed as Demetrius and Makalani giggled at each other.

Demetrius recovered his decorum first and said "I'm afraid you are *really* in the wrong place, sir. Most doctors of medicine end up on one of the Greek planes, ministering to the inhabitants there. I'm afraid Reassignments has made another mistake. You see, practicing medicine around here – if you actually help someone or cure them – is considered malpractice and punished immediately. So, unless you were responsible for someone's death by practicing quackery or were a money-grubbing pill pusher, you need to be sent back to Reassignments. And judging by your expression, I'll need to show you to the elevator."

As the Chief Librarian and his assistant Makalani turned to escort the doctor through the stacks and to the exit, the floor shuddered, accompanied by a rumbling sound that rapidly grew louder. Makalani quickly took Demetrius' arm, staring around in trepidation.

Dust began falling from the ceiling eleven floors above, and librarians on every floor began shouting in fear as shelves teetered and began toppling onto them. Computer screens blew out with a cascade of sparks and the lights began flickering, and failing entirely in some areas, as everyone tried to run for safety.

With a tremendous roar, the ceiling gave way under the weight of the entire Hall of Injustice above, which crashed down through the atrium, as the fourteen floors of shelves, walkways, and research and study rooms slid toward the open space in the center of the building, spilling law books onto the meeting-room occupants at the bottom, crushing them, as the Hall of Injustice collapsed into its own basement.

Demetrius barely had time to scream, "My scrolls!"

*

Absolute darkness … suffocating heat … pressure … *pain* ... groaning … remembering – falling, tumbling, flailing – Makalani tried to take a deep breath, but couldn't. As his senses gradually came back, *more pain*.... He felt something wet – was lying in something wet, felt something a little softer under his hand… more memory.

"Oh no," he gasped. The Library, Demetrius! But he *was* breathing … dust and pumice… but breathing all the same – not clean air, to be sure, but not the odor of rotten teeth and decomposition he would smell if he had died and been resurrected on the Undertaker's slab. Makalani might be buried under a rockfall of unknowable proportions facing unbelievable difficulties, but at least there was a chance to get out without waking in the morgue to the unspeakable pain of being reassembled. He sighed in some relief.

"Help… *help!*... anybody…?" Makalani doubted anyone could hear his faint call, but just then he felt a weak tug on his pants leg … heard a muffled voice:

"Sesh…? Is that you…?" Demetrius wheezed.

"Oh, sir, thank the fates!" Makalani breathed.

Remember, Remember, Hell in November

by

Larry Atchley, Jr

Guy Fawkes will always remember the day he died and went to hell. First he and his co-conspirators in the Gunpowder Plot were sentenced to be "put to death halfway between heaven and earth as unworthy of both" by the royal executioner.

He'd died on a purpose-built scaffold in the Old Palace Yard at Westminster, England, last of the four condemned plotters to meet his end there, in front of king and countrymen and church officials. Fawkes had watched from the wicker litter to which he was strapped as his cohorts' genitals were cut off and burnt before their eyes. Their bowels and hearts were removed before they were decapitated, and the dismembered parts of their bodies displayed so that they might become "prey for the fowls of the air."

Then it was his turn. Before jeering crowds, the guards cut him loose from the wickerwork frame to which Fawkes was strapped at the base of the gallows. The executioners had to hold him upright, so badly broken and battered was his body. Before being tortured, he had been tall and strong. His coarse reddish-brown hair and beard with long, drooping moustache were matted with grime.

King James I looked down at the execution yard from his balcony in Westminster Abbey and shouted: "Fawkes, how could you conspire so hideous a treason against my children, and so many innocent souls who have never offended you?"

By then, the world around him was growing dim, yet Fawkes somehow managed to reply: "A dangerous disease required a desperate remedy."

The king declared, "You have plotted to blow up The Palace of Westminster, Westminster Hall, and Westminster Abbey, myself, my family, and all the members of the House of Lords and the House of Commons. Yet you portray yourself as an instrument of God's Will? God has seen through your treasonous gunpowder plot, Guy Fawkes."

Death would be welcome, a refuge from the consuming pain of his torture. Fawkes looked up at the monarch and said, "The Devil, not God was the discoverer of our plot. I repent of and regret only that I did not succeed in blowing you all back to Scotland or to hell!"

Somehow they got him up the gallows ladder. King James I, purple with rage, decreed: "Let this traitor be hanged by the neck from the gallows, suspended between heaven and earth, for he is unworthy of both. Then, he shall be taken down alive, and his private parts cut off and burned before his eyes as he is unworthy of begetting any generation after him. His belly shall be sliced open, and his bowels and all inner parts removed and burned. He shall be quartered and beheaded, and all the pieces are to be displayed as a testament to the fate of treasonous fools. Let his remains be food for the carrion birds."

The hangman looped the noose around Guy Fawkes's head as he ascended the gallows ladder. His legs wobbled and his shoulders throbbed with aching pain from the torture of the rack two months earlier by the Royal Interrogators, and from his being dragged through the streets. Before the executioner could pull the rope taut, Fawkes found one more shard of rebellious strength: he leaped from the gallows scaffold. The rope went taut.

A sharp pain lanced through him. His neck snapped but he didn't hear it.

Fawkes was falling. Forever. Plummeting through space. Neither rope nor earth existed.

"Aaaaaiiiiiiiiiaaaaaahhhhhh!" Fawkes thought he screamed as he hurtled even faster downward, endlessly falling through nothingness and darkness for what seemed an eternity.

Then he landed with a loud 'thump' on a hard stone floor in a dark chamber, lit only by fiery torches flickering from wall sconces. A sulfurous stench rode air as hot and dry as central Spain in summertime. Before him sat a huge stone dais and, behind it, a torchlit figure gleamed, bat-like wings spread wide and black from the middle of his back. He was both beautiful and terrible to behold: proud face, massive form, manlike but distorted. A creature like a large house cat with bat-wings that mimicked his own and a bat's head perched upon his shoulder, gnawing absent-mindedly on his collarbone.

"Welcome to hell, Guy Fawkes," the winged being said with a voice like the thunder of stones in a landslide. "I am Satan. You may have heard of me: Prince of Darkness, as your countrymen say. Enjoy your stay in my domain. You've earned it."

"Hell? *Satan?* Mary Mother of Jesus!" exclaimed Fawkes as his bowels let loose in terror.

The Devil frowned. The bat-winged thing on his shoulder hissed and its spittle steamed when it hit the ground. "Too late to call upon those Above. Choose your words carefully, Fawkes."

"Why am I in hell? I'm a martyr. I should be in heaven for serving the Holy Catholic Church and the Jesuit order. Did we not help bring down the false Church of England and its evil Protestantism?"

Satan shook his head. "'Why?' For attempted murder, for the Gunpowder Plot. For choosing one group as good and another as evil and trying to kill those who disagreed with your religion. Religion brings me many damned souls who sinned in one of its manifold names. Protestantism, Catholicism: all *'isms'* are meaningless in hell. Here are only the damned. And you, Guy, are surely damned."

"But is there no appeal? No hope of reversing this damnation?" Fawkes demanded, only then realizing that his body was no longer broken, that his neck turned on his shoulders, that no wound afflicted his flesh.

"None. Or not yet. You may someday appeal your case, but first you'll pay for your sins in life. Thou art damned, Guy Fawkes, to hell!"

*

Anton Szandor LaVey awoke, lying on a black tile floor in an elevator rapidly descending. He sat up, running his hands over his body, across his shaven head, and down his Mephistophelean goatee, not quite believing he was feeling anything at all. His last memory was being in a hospital bed while a nurse told him he would pass very soon.

"But pass to where?" he had wondered.

LaVey was the founder of the Church of Satan. He'd died, he

was sure, to awake in an … elevator? He held no belief in heaven, or any afterlife, really – heaven or hell – especially not in any Christian or biblical or Dantean or Miltonesque sense. Why should human animals be punished for behaving as nature dictated? LaVey found man to be nature's most imperfect, incomplete creation. Sin, like god, was just another invention of man, designed to keep the teeming hordes compliant and guilt-ridden.

The elevator came to a sudden lurching stop; its doors opened. LaVey looked out into some kind of basement dimly lit by flickering fluorescents. The air in his nostrils was hot and dry. He stepped out of the elevator; its door sighed shut behind him and it disappeared. Where it had been, only basement remained.

"Well, hello there, tall, bald, and handsome," said a sultry woman's voice from behind him.

He jumped, startled.

A pair of arms in black full-length formal gloves wrapped themselves about his chest and locked tightly around him. Long silky hair brushed his neck. Moist lips kissed the edge of his mouth. Sweet game of seduction.

He knew this game well. Hell, he'd even written a book about it. Who was this mystery woman? He shifted to get a better look at this wanton minx.

Arms still wrapped around him, she wriggled around to face him. She was about his height. Buxom, full-figured curves filled out a slinky black evening gown, slit up both sides. Black nylons and a garter belt were visible on her thighs; six-inch stiletto-heeled boots sheathed her legs to just above her knees. Flame-red hair flowed in waves down past her shoulders. She had a beautiful, pale face, with high cheekbones and a strong chin. Bright blue eyes stared at him.

When LaVey opened his mouth to ask who she was, she planted her lips on his and kissed him ravenously. He reciprocated. Their tongues intertwined.

Her tongue flicked the roof of his mouth and probed deeper, to the back of his tonsils, and then kept going, down his throat. He gagged and fought to disengage, pushing against her arms to free himself. The long wet tongue worked its way further and further down his esophagus, choking him. Desperately, arching his head back, he broke from her deadly embrace.

He heard a slurping sound. As the woman stumbled back, she was retracting her black tongue, forked like a snake's and two feet long.

"What the fuck was that?" LaVey demanded.

She replied in soft demurring tones, "'Fuck.' To you it's profanity, but to me it's exercise." She giggled lasciviously, grabbing her ample breasts and, pushing them up toward him, offered herself once more.

"I'm all for that kind of exercise my dear, but your tongue damn near killed me. Where did you get that tongue? Surgery? Some serpentine fetish? Who are you, and *where* are we?"

The woman slid the gown off her body and onto the floor, revealing a red patch of kinky hair covering her mound, wherein something sinuous was writhing.

"I'm the Welcome Woman, Harlot Supreme, and this is hell!" she proclaimed with a haughty cackle. Her features began to shimmer and alter, warping into those of an old hag with rows of needle sharp teeth and black eyes. Long pointed horns erupted from the top of her skull. Her body swelled and bulged, gross with fat. The black nylons and garters stretched over her legs and the knee-high boots split, falling to the floor. Her breasts became flaccid; her wizened nipples split open and blood spewed from them; her feet curled into cloven hooves, and coarse black hair sprouted from her skin to cover her legs and buttocks.

"Welcome to hell, Anton!" the grotesque creature screamed.

LaVey uttered a strangled cry as a long black tongue shot from her vagina and pulled his face into the cleft of flesh between her hairy thighs. The stench of sulfur and brine was stifling.

"Kiss me, my darling," she moaned.

Anton LaVey had no choice. No woman in life had ever been able to dominate him. But this was the Harlot of Hell, infernal dominatrix. She was physically repulsive and her stench made him gag and cough, but he reveled in his subjugation. If this was hell, it suited him just fine.

"His Satanic Majesty has told me so many sinister things about you, Anton," she whispered, gyrating her pelvis against his face. "Now, Anton, you will bestow upon me the Devil's Kiss to prove your eternal loyalty to me and to His Satanic Majesty, the devil."

The harlot let him go and lay back on the floor, then turned over and thrust her corpulent buttocks up to him. She farted noxious fumes into his face. Despite his nausea from the reek, LaVey put his lips to her anus and quite literally kissed her ass.

"The Devil's Kiss is a binding pact in hell. Anton Szandor LaVey, you are truly one of the privileged damned, now and forever. Perhaps someday soon you will be numbered among the Devil's Children, Satan's own intelligence officers," she told him, her teasing smile revealing deadly teeth.

A diabolical grin spread across LaVey's face as he imagined what he could achieve in hell as a true servant of the devil.

"Hail Satan!" he proclaimed.

*

"All rise!" the bailiff announced. "The First Appellate Court of Hell is now in session, the Dishonorable Judge Roy Bean presiding in the case of Guy Fawkes versus Hell."

Everyone in the courtroom in the Hall of Injustice stood up as the judge entered. Tall, thick-middled, with a haggard, white-bearded face, he was a man once handsome but not aging well.

"Where in hell is my gavel? Bailiff! Get me another one, pronto!" Bean ordered in a voice that had swallowed too much tobacco smoke and whiskey in life and afterlife.

"Yes, Your Dishonor, right away!" The bailiff scurried to replace the judge's small wooden gavel. Bean eyed the replacement judiciously. "Hrumph! It'll not give me as much bang for my buck as my old one, but it'll have to do, I reckon." Judge Bean banged it on the wooden sounding block of the bench. "You insufferable bastards may be seated!" he declared.

"Counsel for the Appellant may approach the bench."

Icelandic lawspeaker Eyjolf Bolverksson, wearing a fine linen tunic and a rich scarlet cloak upon his shoulders, strode to the bench, case notes in hand.

"State your case before the court," Judge Roy Bean told Bolverksson.

"Your Dishonor, my client, Guy Fawkes, brings forth an appeal of his sentence of damnation in hell."

The Judge responded, "Why does Mister Fawkes think he doesn't belong in hell? What evidence substantiates this claim?"

"Your Dishonor, my client maintains that the actions resulting in his untimely death by hanging were undertaken by him in the interest of the Holy Catholic Church against an unjust and false Protestant Anglican Church of England. He believes he should have been martyred and granted sainthood by the Catholic Church, and thus should have been sent directly to heaven."

"Did the Catholic Church exonerate this man and grant him such martyrdom after his death?"

"No, Your Dishonor, it did not. However, we shall prove his lack of canonization to be an oversight on the part of the Catholic Church. We maintain that my client's martyrdom is irrefutable."

"Do you have any witnesses to support your client's claim to innocence and martyrdom?" Judge Bean asked.

"Yes, Your Dishonor. Appellant would call Robert Catesby, a peer of Mister Fawkes, to the witness stand."

"Approach the stand, Mister Catesby – and be quick about it. I ain't got all day," said Judge Roy Bean.

A middle-aged man, six feet tall with the refined features of a nobleman, approached the stand.

"Mister Robert Catesby, be warned: perjury in this court will not be tolerated. If I suspect you of lying, we will obtain the truth from you through torture. Is that clear, Mister Catesby?" asked the judge.

"Yes, Your Dishonor."

"And that goes for the rest of you damned souls!" Judge Bean added.

"Mister Catesby, sit down, damn you."

Catesby took his seat in the witness box.

"Council for the Appellant, you may examine the witness."

Eyjolf Bolverksson approached the seated witness. "Mister Catesby, I believe you know Mister Guy Fawkes, is that correct?"

"Yes sir, he was an associate of mine in life. A good friend," replied Catesby.

The lawspeaker continued, "And you were both devout

Catholics in life, were you not?"

"Yes, we were. I still am, even though I'm damned," Catesby added defiantly.

"So the Gunpowder Plot of November, Sixteen Hundred and Five, was a response by you and other angry and frustrated Catholics who were mistreated by the Protestant Church of England, which by then held powers and allegiances previously enjoyed by the Roman Catholic Church and the Pope?"

"Yes. Something had to be done about King James and the House of Commons' mistreatment of Catholics."

"What was your solution to the problem?" Bolverksson asked.

"Myself and twelve other faithful Catholics committed to destroying the Palace of Westminster, Westminster Hall, Westminster Abbey, the House of Commons and House of Lords, along with King James the First and all of the British parliament members. If successful, we would have rid England of an unjust king and wiped Protestantism from the country. It would have been a complete coup. Catholics once more would have controlled the throne and the parliament, as God intended."

"And was Guy Fawkes one of these faithful Catholics?" Bolverksson asked.

"Yes. Mister Fawkes was a co-conspirator in what became known as the 'Gunpowder Plot,'" admitted Catesby.

"What would you say was his involvement in the plot?" inquired Bolverksson.

"Fawkes was to ensure the gunpowder was properly mixed and emplaced undetected in the cellar under the House of Lords," said Catesby.

"And Mister Fawkes performed these tasks successfully?"

"Yes, he did, but unfortunately our plot was uncovered. One night, on the fifth of November, as Guy Fawkes was checking the powder, the authorities discovered him leaving the cellar. Finding thirty-six barrels of gunpowder, the guards arrested Mister Fawkes. Fawkes was questioned and tortured. When the police tried to arrest me and my fellow conspirators, I and some of my cohorts were shot and killed, the rest captured and put to death by order of the king. Had we succeeded, the Catholic Church would have lauded us as heroes.

But we failed, and history is written by the victors," stated Catesby.

"So your failed plan to overthrow the King and the Anglican Church resulted in Guy Fawkes' trial and execution by an unjust government?

"Counsel will refrain from prejudicial statements," Judge Bean instructed. "The just or unjust nature of the British government in this era is immaterial. Witness, answer the question."

"That is correct," replied Catesby.

Bolverksson took a step toward the judge. "Should failure be considered just cause for damnation? We maintain that it should not. Thank you Mister Catesby. You may step down."

Judge Roy Bean asked, "Does Appellant have any other witnesses?"

The lawspeaker called Eyjolf Bolverksson answered, "No, Your Dishonor we do not."

"Then sit down, damn it. Will counsel representing hell come forward? And don't dawdle! I've got a full docket."

William Jennings Bryan, wearing tan slacks and an open-collared white shirt, ambled toward the Judge's bench. Perspiration stained his shirt's armpits and shone on his face. He held a small electric fan, which worked fitfully, and then only when he shook it violently.

"Your Dishonor, I will show this court why Mister Guy Fawkes has been damned to hell, and why he should remain here for all eternity."

"Get on with it Mister Bryan. Who is your first witness?" demanded Judge Bean.

"Your Dishonor, I call James the First, former King of England," Bryan declared.

Fawkes gasped as James I, an august figure, tall and resplendent in regal robes, and finely woven silken clothes, proceeded to the witness box.

"James the First, former king of England, tell the court the charges of which Mister Guy Fawkes was found guilty by due process of the day, resulting in his execution by hanging," said William Jennings Bryan.

"Guy Fawkes and his co-conspirators amassed some thirty-six

barrels of gunpowder in the basements beneath the House of Lords; enough explosives to blow up the Palace of Westminster, Westminster Hall, Westminster Abbey, myself, my family, and all the members of the House of Lords and the House of Commons! His act was treasonous. His intent was to murder every high official in England so his Jesuit Catholics could take over the country," replied James I, formerly James VI of Scotland, in a resounding voice. "Fawkes shall always be remembered as a traitor and a terrorist. Mister Fawkes also took his own life, leaping from the gallows scaffold rather than face the torturous execution that was his due."

Fawkes rose and, before Bolverksson could stop him, proclaimed, "That's a Protestant lie, Your Dishonor! James the First is the traitor to the people of England who believe in the sanctity of the Holy Catholic Church and the laws of God and the Pope. It was James the First who took my life that day. My neck was broken by the providence and mercy of the Lord God almighty, and his son Jesus, may they both be praised, Amen!"

Judge Roy Bean leapt to his feet, banging the makeshift gavel on the block so hard that the handle broke. The gavel's head flew up into the air and landed on the floor with a thud. "Order in this Courtroom *now!* Guy Fawkes, you stand in contempt of court! I'll not allow you to obscenely praise Satan's opponents in this Hall of Injustice. Furthermore, based on this witness's testimony and because of your outburst, I hereby deny your appeal. You are damned and you will remain eternally damned, without possibility of redemption! This court is now adjourned! Now, you damned bastards get out of my sight before I have you all flogged!"

*

"Mother Mary, Jesus, and God Above! That didn't go very well at all," sighed Guy Fawkes, putting on his tall, wide-brimmed hat as they were leaving the courtroom.

Eyjolf Bolverksson winced and said, *"Please* watch your language here. So much for finding a judge sympathetic to your politics or to the Catholic Church."

"Hrumpf! In hell? This godforsaken place is full of Protestants and pagans. Four hundred years I've been here suffering, waiting for Jesus to set me free; hoping that one of the popes would declare me a martyr for what I tried to do for the Catholic Church in England!" Fawkes said, exasperated.

"Don't get snippy with me, Guy. I've been here a thousand years myself. Because of the things I did in life, I hold no hope for personal salvation. So I try to help others gain redemption through the Injustice System."

"For you help, I'm grateful, Eyjolf. I let my anger and frustration get the best of me. This whole ordeal has me mightily vexed."

"I understand," Bolverksson replied. "Hey, New Hell's not so bad, really. Hell isn't all like the Irish Monks described it: lakes of fire, pits of vipers, eternal suffering and torture. Okay, so it is pretty hot here, but after a lifetime in Iceland I welcome the warmth to defrost these cold old bones."

"It reminds me of summers in Spain, fighting Dutch Protestant reformists and trying to start a rebellion in England," said Guy Fawkes. "I was young and idealistic. We Catholics thought we could save the world from the evils of Protestantism – or at least save England."

Bolverksson nodded. "England always needed a good kick in the ass! My ancestors once did a fair job, though more for riches, land and slaves than for religion. But in the year of Our Lord One Thousand, my people took Christ into our hearts and became peaceful, God-fearing folk. Catholicism was good to my country, though we never truly abandoned the old ways and our beloved ancestral gods. We just added the 'Father, Son and the Holy Spirit' to our pantheon. It worked well enough."

They reached the elevators in the Hall of Injustice, New Hell's tallest skyscraper. Bolverksson paused and looked at the shiny steel doors with trepidation. "Uh … maybe we should take the stairs. My office is only a few floors up."

Guy Fawkes agreed, and they climbed the adjacent stairwell to the sixth floor. When they reached the door to Bolverksson's office, Fawkes saw the gold numbers on its door: 666.

"Surely you jest?" Fawkes breathed.

"Great isn't it?" countered Eyjolf the lawspeaker. "I worked hard to get this suite. It's in very high demand." Bolverksson opened the door and led Fawkes into a sparsely decorated but neat office, nodding to his secretary as they went through to Eyjolf's inner office.

"Let me just check the hex machine for any incoming documents." Bolverksson walked to the machine and pulled a piece of paper from the printer tray. Fawkes followed.

"Hmmm. Seems I have another potential client. I'll just send this back to him with a meeting time and date confirmed." Putting the paper in the feed tray, Bolverksson hit a red button on the machine. "Ouch! Damned hex machines, I hate these infernal things!" he complained as the button pricked his index finger and transferred a signature writ in his own blood to the bottom of the document. "Guy, I've work to do now, but perhaps you'd come by tomorrow. We can begin drafting your next appeal."

Fawkes grimaced and shrugged. "Another appeal? Judge Bean just damned me to hell for all eternity, with no reprieve, no clemency – how can I appeal? And to whom? The only 'justice' in hell is the kind Erra and the Seven have been dispensing, and I want no part of those auditors from Above, I assure you."

Eyjolf Bolverksson frowned. "They say Erra and the Seven have committed countless atrocities. Hundreds of demons slain, pestilence and mayhem spread throughout the hells, and thousands of damned sent to the Undertaker's slab – so many that there's a huge backlog in Reassignments. Some damned fool even approached me about bringing a case against Erra for wrongful death and suffering. Ha! I told him I wouldn't take on the Akkadian plague god and his seven personified weapons for all the diablos in hell!"

The lawspeaker sighed and put his hand on Fawkes' shoulder. "Let me draft another appeal. Maybe your luck will change. A different judge in a higher court could overturn Bean's verdict."

"We'll see." Guy Fawkes walked out of the lawspeaker's office.

*

Anton LaVey opened his shop, 'Hellish Curiosities & Clothiers,' in the basement of an apartment building in New Hell that was dusty and damp. The lighting flickered incessantly. The air conditioner worked intermittently. The shop was always too hot.

LaVey didn't mind the shop's heat or its malfunctioning equipment. Hell would be hell. He put a few newly-acquired items in a cabinet behind a bookshelf in the back room where he kept special objects never displayed or sold over the counter – rarities, in high demand.

Buyers for such treasures would come along. One remained cautious, dealing in illicit items: LaVey must avoid repercussions from the Administration and other dealers eager to muscle in on his *objets d'art noir* business. Old dead and demons were his main competition in hell's black market. So be it. LaVey would thrive and prosper: he'd stay on His Satanic Majesty's good side, service the Welcome Woman on demand, and make what allies he could.

The Welcome Woman had titillated him about the infernal joys of his future in hell. She'd promised him a position someday with The Devil's Children, His Satanic Majesty's own secret service, but the first task she assigned him was paltry, bereft of cloak or dagger: run this shop, selling eccentric objects and clothes to the wretched damned of New Hell. The Welcome Woman deemed him destined for greatness; he awaited a chance to prove himself worthy.

And that Harlot of Hell could screw for an eternity. He thought she might yet suck him to his second death. If the tales about the Undertaker were true, he hoped to avoid the Mortuary.

If only he could reach sexual climax.... *That* was a little detail WW had not mentioned, and which became apparent only after hours of agonizingly unfulfilled sex. Inability to ejaculate was the worst part of hell for LaVey. The Welcome Woman couldn't climax either, despite his best efforts. Never before had LaVey failed to satisfy a woman; *he* wasn't the problem, he'd thought, until he realized *he* couldn't reach orgasm with her. It was embarrassing. Still he was sure the problem stemmed from the Welcome Woman, not his own failings. Her lot in hell was to be forever frustrated sexually. He'd heard that other demons of hell could climax. He wondered what she'd done to deserve such punishment from His Satanic Majesty.

LaVey's assistant shuffled into the shop, a short dumpy woman with a broad Slavic nose, and a piercing gaze that seemed to look right through him to somewhere beyond.

"Hello, Helena. I trust you are having a hell of a day," LaVey said as she clomped around behind one of two long glass display cases at the back of the shop.

"That's 'Madame Blavatsky' to you, Anton," she said dryly. "I founded the entire Theosophist movement – you can show me a modicum of respect, you young Satanist."

"But of course, *Madame,"* he replied.

Suddenly Madame Blavatsky stood straighter, her eyes went blank, and her left hand went to her temple. *"Privyet!"* she exclaimed in Russian. "A vision!" she cried theatrically, her voice dropping an octave. "I'm seeing … a man," she chanted, "a man looking for something … something he needs, desires. He'll pay handsomely for it. Well shall you profit, but there shall be a price greater than diablos to be paid, by both of you."

LaVey shook his head and chuckled. "You old bat, it's probably just another fool trying to buy a 'Get Out of Hell Free Card.' They come in here all the time."

The front door opened with a ring of the latch bell and in waddled LaVey's first customer of the day, a middle-aged soul, dressed like one of the new dead. Madame Blavatsky snapped out of her trance and got busy sorting and hanging various outfits on racks spaced throughout the store, ignoring the newly-arrived patron.

"Greetings, my good fellow!" LaVey said to the man. "Welcome to my shop of wondrous eccentricities. What may I help you find this fine day in hell?"

"Well, I'm looking for clothes, something unusual and unique," the man replied meekly.

"Something to set you apart from the other denizens of hell, eh? I think I have something that will work for you in the ready-to-wear…."

"I am looking for something with, um, certain *redemptive* qualities. I've heard rumors that you sell such garments?" the man asked nervously, looking around to make sure no one overheard.

"Of course, I know just what you need, sir. Just one moment, while I fetch them from the back!" LaVey ducked into the back room and returned with a pair of creamy linen pants, neatly pressed and hung on a wooden hanger. On the seat of the trousers there was a light sepia-colored stain resembling a face.

"These look like they should fit you – with a few alterations, of course. Why don't you try them on in the fitting room?" LaVey motioned to an open door at the back of the shop.

The man walked in with the trousers, pulled the curtain, tried on the pants and emerged to inspect himself in the shop's single full-length mirror. "The pants … is it true what they say about them?" the patron asked wistfully.

"Some say the rumors are true," LaVey replied. "Some say a man worthy of redemption may walk out of hell if wearing the Trousers of Turin."

"I'll take them," the man whispered. "How much?"

"For you, good sir, a mere five hundred diablos, a bargain for such a rare garment and a chance at salvation –"

"I *said* I'll take them," said the customer. "I just need to get more diablos from home. If you'll hold them for me, I'll return shortly with the full amount."

"Very well, just let me measure your inseam and I'll have them ready when you return," LaVey said, pulling out a yellow dressmaker's tape.

LaVey took the customer's measurements and the man left the shop in his ordinary pants, returning promptly with a leather sack of gold diablo coins in hand. As LaVey counted the coins on the countertop, the customer changed into his new trousers in the fitting room.

"Ah, Mister LaVey, one trouser leg is longer than the other," the patron objected.

LaVey leveled a steely glance at him. "Of course it is. This is hell, you'll recall. You don't actually *expect* them to be perfect, do you?"

"I … guess not," replied his customer.

"May I interest you in something else, as well? Holy water from Saint Olaf's well, perhaps? Great for removing stains from garments…. Well, except *that* stain of course," LaVey said mirthfully. "Some matching accessories, cut from the same cloth as your pants? We have the socks of Turin, 'redemption with every step,' or the fashionable ascot of Turin? Or perhaps you would like the beret of Turin to 'cover your head in the warmth of salvation,' eh?"

"No, no I'm fine with just the pants, thank you," replied the customer. He left the shop smiling, a hopeful gleam in his eyes.

"Have a hellish day!" LaVey called to him as he went out the door.

"Another satisfied customer, eh Madame?" LaVey said.

"Ha! Another of hell's fools!" Madame Blavatsky said it like a curse.

"'A fool and his money are soon parted,' Helena. Who am I to deny them the hope of redemption?" LaVey chuckled, rubbing gold coins between his fingers. He thought about all those wretched irredeemable souls, seeking salvation and a way out of hell. They didn't know how good they had it here: an eternity of wickedness and all of hell as a playground!

*

Guy Fawkes wandered the stinking streets of New Hell's waterfront district, muddy and yet strewn with detritus from the flood, looking for a bar. He wasn't hoping to get drunk. Fawkes couldn't actually *get* drunk in hell: he shared that punishment with a majority of the damned. He was on his way to meet someone who, he'd heard, could help him achieve his own justice in hell – justice unavailable in court.

Streets teemed with hell's wretched souls. New dead with their gadgets and old dead from antiquity. Demons roamed the avenues and alleyways, tormenting hapless damned at random with branding irons, flaming pitchforks, and razor-wire whips. Fawkes was an accustomed skulker. Skillfully avoiding the demons, he gained the entrance to the Oasis Bar, guarded by a squad of Marines.

"Okay, buddy, you're allowed one gun and one magazine. Turn over everything else to us," a muscular, bald-headed Marine instructed him.

"I'm not carrying any weapons," replied Fawkes.

"We'll search you just to make sure," said another Marine, this one a crew-cut blond, as tall and ripped as his mate. "Maybe you'll like it."

The blond deftly patted him down but found no hidden weapons on Fawkes' person.

"You look familiar," commented the bald Marine. "You ever serve in Beirut?"

"Sorry, I don't know the place. I fought in Spain once, a long time ago. Well before your day," replied Fawkes.

"Spain, huh? Go on in, just don't start anything you can't finish, Spaniard!"

Fawkes walked into the chaos of the Oasis Bar. Several fist-fights were ongoing, and the place stank. Stale beer and sweat. Dim light flickered from incandescent bulbs. The air tasted dangerous.

Threading his way toward a small table in back, he was jostled and bumped by patrons. His hard-soled leather boots crunched on broken glass covering the filthy floor as he stepped around falling bodies and pools of vomit. The man sitting at the table was nondescript, the sort who could blend into a crowd unnoticed and leave unremembered. He was gangly, bony-faced and dark-haired; a thin moustache traced his upper lip as described by phone; and he was sitting at the specified table, quaffing a pint of brown hell ale.

"Guy Fawkes. Thanks for meeting me," the man said, words barely audible above the din.

"Please, call me 'Guido,'" Fawkes said.

"Very well then, Guido, I am Eric Blair, at your service. So nice to meet a fellow Englishman, no matter what political or religious differences we'd have had in life. Let's get down to business. The Committee understands you're dissatisfied with the current Administration and your appeal process at the Hall of Injustice. Certain members of the Committee think it in our mutual interest to treat those in power to our kind of injustice. It is fortuitous that you contacted us just now. There's a new revolution rising in hell. Not the romantic idealism of men like Guevera, but a genuine movement to supplant the current Administration. Perhaps you'll help us achieve that goal."

A waitress, struggling through the crowd with a tray of ales, set a pint glass down in front of Fawkes, sloshing some on the table. It didn't even froth. Fawkes took a drink and grimaced. "Aaaaggg!" he sputtered. "Flat and tasteless, like all food and drink in hell. I don't think I'll ever get used to it. I long for the taste of good ale, wine, meat and cheese."

"What I wouldn't give for a proper cup of British tea, strong and piping hot," said Eric Blair, who'd written under the pen name of George Orwell.

Fawkes stared intently at the man. "I know something of fomenting revolution to depose unjust rulers. I worked my whole life to free England from the tyranny of a foreign king who cared nothing for his subjects. If we hadn't been stopped before our labors came to fruition, our country's history – world history – would have been very different. I only hope I can succeed in hell where I failed in life. If you want revolution, what I need from your 'committee' is the means to bring down the symbol of power in hell: the tower of the Hall of Injustice. I'll require a bloody lot of barrels of gunpowder."

"Gunpowder? Guido, we can do better. The Committee has at our disposal the technology of all ages here. We know the whereabouts of a man who holds in his hands, literally, the key to our first true attack on the Administration – a personal nuclear bomb, not much bigger than a hat box. We need only to kidnap him so you can get him inside the Hall of Injustice. Then you can detonate the nuclear explosive from a remote location. We understand that you, fortuitously, know someone with an office inside the tower," Eric Blair said flatly.

"Yes," said Fawkes, just as flatly. "My lawyer has an office on the sixth floor. He'll want no part of this though. He prizes his good standing with the Administration. But I may be able to hide this man there for a short time, without my lawyer's knowledge, until the bomb can be detonated. When do we acquire this man and his bomb?"

"Soon, very soon. Take this hellphone, Guido. I shall contact you when we're ready to move. Do you know how to use that?"

Fawkes looked askance at the hellphone.

"I've had enough experience with these hellphones to operate one, yes." *These bloody infernal devices.* "I'll be waiting for your call. And I'll be ready."

"Then farewell for now, Guido Fawkes. I shall be in touch. Be very cautious. Trust no one. If our plot is discovered, there'll be hell to pay."

Guy Fawkes left the Oasis Bar, his way weaving through the

brawlers as the Marine bouncers, having finally had enough, started breaking up the skirmishes.

*

Anton LaVey was minding the store: Hellish Curiosities & Clothiers bustled with customers; Helena was grouchy, proclaiming *visions*, annoying customers. Yet sales were so brisk that not even Madame Blavatsky's delusional prophecies dampened his spirits.

Then into the busy store clanked some damned soul in full medieval chainmail and plate armor, with a long straight sword sheathed at his belt. Customers came in here dressed in fashions from all ages. Still, LaVey thought all that armor an odd choice for the hot streets of New Hell.

"And what may I help you find, Sir Knight?" LaVey asked with a salesman's smile.

"I am just browsing, thank you, good sir," said the armored man. "I'll know what I'm looking for when I see it." His accent was antiquated British.

"Perhaps you'd be interested in some of our antique swords? Or some hand-woven tapestries to decorate your house or castle, eh?" LaVey offered.

"No, I'm well supplied at present, thank you, sir," the knight replied, looking over LaVey's wares. His hard-soled boots echoed on the worn floor; the joints of his armor creaked as he walked.

"Come see these wonderful chalices, then. No self-respecting knight should be without a silver, jewel-encrusted chalice or goblet. And on sale for thirty percent off – today only, mind you – the Holy Grail!"

"No, thank you. I've already got one," the knight remarked with a smile. In the cabinet beside the chalices was something that caught the armored fellow's attention. "May I see that spearhead, the one with the nail inset near the tip and gold leaf wrapping the middle?"

"An excellent choice, sir. Some say it's the Spear of Longinus, the very lance that pierced the side of that idealist from Nazareth, whose name shall not be uttered here." Trying not to smirk, LaVey unlocked the cabinet and held out the spear. "Some maintain its provenance proves it to be the Spear of Destiny, named *Gungnir,* weapon of the Norse god Odin, and that the church disguised its true identity, attributing it to their own messianic mythology. It's said that he who holds the Spear of Destiny is invincible. Want to hold it?"

The knight took off his gauntlets, snatched the spear from LaVey, and cradled it to his chest as if clasping his newborn son.

"I will most certainly buy this, sir." the knight said in a whisper, staring in awe at the spear he held.

"Very well!" said LaVey. "This is a very special limited-edition item. I won't take less than ten thousand diablos."

"Do you take Hellcard?" asked the knight as he pulled out a plastic credit card decorated with holographic flames and handed it to LaVey.

"Of course, sir." Behind his counter, LaVey first swiped the card, then had the knight thumb a touch-pad that pricked the thumb and checked the drawn blood to verify the cardholder's identity. The transaction approved, LaVey printed a receipt and handed it and the card back to his customer.

"Here you are Mister ... Parsival. It's a pleasure doing business with you."

"Thank you. I shall tell my companions of the wondrous items your shop purveys," said Parsival as he clanked out of the store.

LaVey walked over to Madame Blavatsky and asked, "Helena, anything about that last customer seem odd to you?"

"Besides wearing a full suit of armor and paying a ridiculous amount for that rusty old paperweight?" said Madame Blavatsky.

"No. *Other* than being an armor-plated sucker," replied LaVey.

"I couldn't really read him; it was strange, like he was shielded somehow," said the Madame.

"Oh well, it's probably nothing," said LaVey. "At any rate, it's been quite a profitable day my dear."

It was getting quite late and LaVey and Helena began preparing to close up.

"Hellish Curiosities and Clothiers will be closing in ten minutes!" LaVey announced to his remaining customers, who quickly made final selections and left. As LaVey was about to lock the door, a demon, red-skinned and horned, with a long barbed tail, waltzed in and handed LaVey an envelope.

"Anton LaVey, you are herewith served by the Hall of Injustice. Have a hell of a day."

"What the devil is *this?* A court summons?" LaVey read aloud: "'The client of Meletus, attorney at law, hereby summons Anton Szander LaVey to appear at the Hall of Injustice for trial regarding the sale of goods under false pretenses, hereinafter designated as the "Trousers of Turin".' Some damned bastard is suing me because I sold him a pair of pants that didn't save his soul? Outrageous!"

The summons burst into flames in his hand, and LaVey dropped it, sucking his scorched fingers.

"I did warn you about this, but you never listen to me, you charlatan," scolded Madame Blavatsky.

"Oh, hush up, Helena, you porcine-faced hag! I have to go to the Hall and hire myself a lawyer. Finish closing up for me."

*

Guy Fawkes was pacing back and forth across the expensive Persian rug in Bolverksson's office.

"I don't see what good will come from a second appeal. Why is it going to be any different than the last one?" asked Fawkes. "And now there's a new conviction to reverse."

"Guy, I told you before that the right judge can make all the difference in a case. I think I can leverage my connections with the Administration to get a judge predisposed to our cause. We'll take this matter to the highest court in hell, if need be."

The lawspeaker's phone buzzed and his secretary announced: "Mister Bolverksson, a Mister LaVey to see you sir. He doesn't have an appointment but he *insists* on seeing you immediately."

"Yes, okay. Send him in. Sorry about this, Guy, but someone seems to be in dire need," said Bolverksson.

"No, no, it's fine," replied Fawkes.

The door opened and in walked Anton LaVey in a black suit, black shirt and black tie.

"Thank you for seeing me on such short notice, Lawspeaker. I am Anton Szandor LaVey, and I need legal representation immediately."

"Bolverksson. Pleasure to meet you, Mister LaVey. This is

Guy Fawkes, one of my clients."

"Ah, the famous Guy Fawkes, how interesting. I've read about your gunpowder plot. Too bad it didn't succeed," said LaVey. "I like seeing the socio-political order shaken up and overthrown once in a while. Keeps everyone more honest and accountable don't you think?"

"Of course I think so. Sometimes justice must be served by direct means to effect change for the betterment of the people," replied Fawkes.

"Mister Fawkes, in my experience, 'the people' don't know a good thing when it bites them on the ass," said Anton LaVey.

"That's the truth," chuckled Bolverksson. "Guy, I need to work with Mister LaVey here on my own particular brand of justice, so let's talk tomorrow."

"Yes, of course, excuse me gentlemen. I'll call on you tomorrow morning, Eyjolf. It was a pleasure to meet you Mister LaVey," said Fawkes.

"Likewise, Mister Fawkes. I hope we can meet again and continue our discussion."

Fawkes left Bolverksson's office and headed for his house in New Hell. He'd only walked a few blocks when the InfernalPhone that Eric Blair had given him vibrated on his belt. As soon as he grasped the phone, it sent a jolt of one million volts of electricity through him.

His body went rigid from the shock and he fell soundlessly to the ground. After seconds that felt like eternities, the current stopped flowing and his body relaxed.

Several people stepped obliviously over or around him before he could struggle to his feet.

"Damned Hext Message!" Fawkes said, breath ragged and shallow. "Cursed InfernalPhone!" He touched the screen to read the message: *'We have the package. Meet me in one hour, same place. Make sure you're not followed. – G.O.'*

'G.O.' stood for Eric Blair, a/k/a George Orwell.

This is it! Time to take matters into my own hands: Hall of Injustice, all its judges, and Satan be damned! Fawkes sent a confirmation to G.O., then replaced the InfernalPhone in its pouch. Turning, he retraced his steps at a brisk pace, and then kept going, toward the bar designated as his rendezvous with fate.

Fawkes walked into the Oasis Bar after the usual security pat-down by the Marines guarding the door. He sat where he and Eric had sat before, and ordered a beer. He was early. As he waited, he picked up a newspaper from the table. The date on the header read: 5th of November. The 5th of November was forever after called 'Guy Fawkes Day' in Britain, in memory of the events of November 5th, 1605. *How fitting.*

Blair walked over to their table. "Guido, our operatives are waiting for us with the package."

"Yes, let's go do this." Fawkes gulped the last of his beer.

They walked out of the Oasis and through the alleys of New Hell toward the waterfront.

An old warehouse several blocks from the bar had a service entrance in back. Eric "G.O." Blair tapped a rhythm on a rusty steel door.

A man with a jowly face and limpid eyes in black, white and gray combat fatigues ushered them inside.

"Eric, we have the package in the back office." Feminine lips twisted with his British accent. He pulled on his long nose, appraising Fawkes frankly. "You must be Guido. Welcome to the revolution, Guv'ner. I'm Jonathan Swift, once known in England as a satirist."

"This revolution has been too long coming. Now we overthrow a corrupt regime and establish a new order in hell," Fawkes said.

Swift nodded his head and grinned until his jowls quivered, then led them to a corner of the warehouse and through a door leading to a small office containing a desk and two chairs.

Sitting in one metal chair was a portly graying man with gold-rimmed glasses. His hands were bound. A rag gag was strapped around his head. In his lap he held a stainless steel box, two feet long. Cyrillic letters were stenciled on it, along with the international warning sign for radiation: a black trefoil in a yellow square background.

"Oh, m-m-my," stammered Fawkes. "Who is this?"

"Yuri Andropov," replied Blair. "He was first the intelligence czar, then leader of Russia's Union of Soviet Socialist Republics in the late twentieth century. The personal nuclear bomb he is damned to carry for all eternity is his punishment for using nuclear weapons to hold the world hostage through fear and intimidation. In his day, they called such a bomb a 'nuke.'"

"Stand up, fat man," ordered Swift, grabbing an AK-47 assault rifle from the table and waving it in Andropov's direction.

When the big Russian stood, Fawkes saw that the box was connected to his navel by a cord threaded between the buttons of his sweat-stained white shirt.

"We're going for a little ride, Yuri," Blair said to the trembling, gagged Andropov.

Swift prodded Andropov in the back with the rifle and they led the Russian outside, into an alley where a black van waited.

They pushed Andropov into the back of the van; he stumbled, almost dropping the box containing the 'nuke,' as Blair had called the bomb-in-a-box. Fawkes wondered how a box so small could contain a weapon that had held the world 'hostage.'

"Be careful with that box old man, or you'll blow us all to ... never mind," said Blair. "Just watch what you're doing, Yuri."

All climbed into the van, with Blair in the driver's seat and Fawkes beside him in front, Andropov and Swift in back. Blair turned the key and the starter stuttered, then caught.

They drove down the narrow streets of New Hell, gears grinding and suspension creaking as the van struggled along. Finally, the engine died and the van rolled to a stop in an alley a few blocks from the looming Hall of Injustice, towering one hundred and fifty stories high.

Blair tried to re-start the vehicle, to no avail.

"Shit, G.O.!" Swift exclaimed. "Time to take it on foot."

Blair got out and opened the rear doors of the van. Swift pushed Yuri Andropov from the van, while the old Russian struggled to hold on to the nuke connected to his belly with its eerie umbilical.

Fawkes searched the dim streets for witnesses as they all walked briskly down the shadowy alleys toward the tower. Swift, who had left the conspicuous AK in the van, prodded Andropov along with a semi-automatic pistol. As they neared the steps of the Hall of Injustice, they saw Anton LaVey round the corner.

The conspirators and their prisoner froze in place. Swift aimed his pistol toward LaVey just as Fawkes called out, "Fear not. He's a friend!"

"Guy, what the devil is going on here?" asked LaVey, seeing the restrained and gagged Andropov, holding the box bearing the nuclear radiation symbol.

"LaVey, remember when we talked about shaking up the socio-political order of things back in Bolverksson's office? We're about to do just that!"

Never taking his gaze from LaVey, Blair growled at Fawkes, "Guido, I *told* you we couldn't trust anyone. What part of that did you not understand?"

"LaVey's all right, G.O.," said Fawkes. "Sympathetic to the cause. Right, Anton?"

"Indeed. The occasional revolution is necessary to upset the status quo and bring welcome chaos and anarchy into play," said LaVey.

"This may be a necessary revolution, but you're no necessary part of it," said Blair. "Fawkes vouches for you. Fine. Before I change my mind, get out of here."

"Okay by me," said LaVey. "You gentleman carry on with the good work."

"LaVey, stay far, far away from the Hall of Injustice for awhile," warned Fawkes.

"Prudent advice, clearly. Thank you, Guy." LaVey wheeled and ran back the way he'd come.

Fawkes, Blair, Swift, and Andropov proceeded into the Hall of Injustice through a side door. They took the elevator to the sixth floor and walked down the long hallway to the door of the law office of Eyjolf Bolverksson, suite #666.

Swift inserted a metal shim near the door's latch and fiddled with it. The door opened. They all filed into the lawspeaker's inner office and Blair locked it once more from within. Swift shoved Andropov before him and into an upholstered client chair and stood over him, pistol in hand.

Fawkes closed the inner door while Blair rummaged in a backpack from the van, pulled out a length of black rope, and tied Andropov to the chair. From the backpack, Blair then pulled out a digital timer wired to a piece of C4 plastic explosive.

Just then a musical tone came from Blair's pocket. He fumbled for his InfernalPhone and answered it. "Yeah. Okay, we'll get back there. May take a while. The van died but we're on our way," Eric said into the phone.

"We've got a situation back at headquarters, Guido. We need to leave. You finish up here. Give us ten minutes before you set the timer. Press these two buttons simultaneously and you then have twenty minutes before the nuke blows. Good luck!"

Blair and Swift hurried away, leaving Fawkes with Yuri Andropov, eyes wide above his gag, and the nuke. He checked the time. *This wasn't how we planned it.*

After ten minutes, Fawkes nervously mashed the buttons on the timer attached to the C4. Its glowing numbers started counting down from 20:00. The descending numbers seemed to blur before Fawkes' eyes.

Just as he set the timer and C4 down on Andropov's personal nuke, the door to the office opened and in walked Eyjolf Bolverksson.

"Guy, what are you doing here? And who in damnation is that?" the lawspeaker demanded, pointing at Andropov, bound and gagged in one of his chairs, now struggling to get free. "And what's that box?"

"Eyjolf, we have to get out of here! That box is a bomb set to explode in less than twenty minutes!" Fawkes whispered in the lawspeaker's ear, looking back at the timer. Instead of reading nineteen minutes and a few seconds, the numbers indicated they had less than twenty seconds to get out of the building.

"Oh, hell," said Fawkes, turning to run out of the office and bowling over a stunned Bolverksson as he went.

As Bolverksson was gaining his feet and Fawkes was sprinting down the hall, the timer reached zero and set off the C4 charge, detonating the nuke.

Yuri Andropov was vaporized, along with the office of the Icelandic lawspeaker, Eyjolf Bolverksson, and the lawyer himself. A millisecond later, a blast wave ripped into Fawkes. The fireball followed, incinerating the entire sixth floor and expanding, disintegrating floors directly above and below in a rapidly-expanding pressure bubble.

In his penthouse on the one hundred and fiftieth floor, His Satanic Majesty, with his bat/cat/familiar Michael on his shoulder, felt the explosion rock his world. The pressure wave thrust them through the roof as the entire tower of the Hall of Injustice was reduced to flying debris.

Satan screamed with rage, "Daaaammmmmnnnnit!"

In his most classic form, all wings and fangs and fury, Satan, clutching his flailing demon familiar under one arm, rode the shock waves thirty thousand feet into the sky over New Hell, tumbling aloft, enveloped in a roiling fireball of incandescent gases. When they finally stopped rising through a sky filled with ash and dust, Satan let go of his familiar. Together, devil and pet spread their wings and glided in ever-widening circles, surveying the damage.

Where the once-mighty tower of the Hall of Injustice had stood, there now rose a black mushroom cloud of smoke, ash, and dust. The rest of New Hell looked as if it had not sustained much damage. Andropov's had been a tactical nuke with a carefully calculated yield. Even so, the entire tower had been vaporized from the massive explosion.

His Satanic Majesty and his demonic familiar descended until they reached New Hell's military headquarters, the Pentagram. Michael settled onto Satan's right shoulder, digging needle sharp claws into his master's flesh.

Satan winced with pain, but hardly cared. He stormed through the Pentagram's front doors as its armed guards fell back: No one doubted that this was their Commander in Chief. His Satanic Majesty's eyes smoldered and the temperature in the lobby rose unbearably.

Satan strode up to the front desk where a young receptionist in uniform stood frozen in horror.

"You. Soul. Call the chief of the Devil's Children. I want whoever blew up my tower!" bellowed the devil.

The receptionist fainted dead away.

"Figures," Satan said under his breath, and reached over the desk to pluck the secure phone from its cradle. Before he could dial, a voice called out from behind him.

"Your Satanic Majesty, *I know* who blew up the Hall of Injustice," said Anton LaVey.

The devil's eyes saw the soul and saw into the soul, shallow and vain. "Yes, Anton, do tell," replied Satan, without turning to face the cozening fool behind him.

"Guy Fawkes did, Your Satanic Majesty, along with two others I didn't recognize. They had Yuri Andropov, the Soviet security chief, and a nuclear device with them," said LaVey.

"Where are Guy Fawkes and his playmates now?" demanded Satan of the damned soul, although he could see the answer in LaVey's small mind.

"You should find Guy at the Undertaker's, Your Satanic Majesty, Sir. As for the others, I do not know," responded LaVey.

"Sire."

"Sir?"

"Not 'Sir.' 'Sire.'"

"Forgive me, Sire."

"Perhaps if you ask on bended knee." All around, guards stood at attention, and suited officials behind them, row after row in complete silence.

Down went Anton LaVey, on the Pentagram lobby's black marble floor. "Excellent, Anton. You'll make a fine member of the Devil's Children one day," said Satan as he quickly dialed the Undertaker.

A grating monotone came from the phone: "Slab A. Undertaker speaking."

"It's Me. Have you a recyclable down there named Guy Fawkes?"

"Yes, Sire. What's left of him. A piece or two. Odds and sods of thousands of casualties are scattered all over the damn morgue. All the little bits, glowing.... Was this a scheduled event no one bothered to tell me about, Sire? If I'd known, I'd have brought in more staff," said the Undertaker. "It'll take me some time to sort the pieces...."

"Never mind sorting pieces. Fawkes is your first priority. Put him back together and reassign him to the crater where the Hall of Injustice stood, so I can take him apart again myself – slowly and painfully, this time," said Satan.

After much effort by the Undertaker, Guy Fawkes was materialized on charred ground next to a colossal crater filled with smoking debris. Satan was waiting for him, arms crossed, wings half unfurled.

"Hello, Guy," said Satan. "Have a pleasant trip back from the Undertaker's?"

Fawkes trembled and threw himself to the ground at His Satanic Majesty's feet. "You're a-a-alive," Fawkes stammered.

"But we blew you up along with the Hall of Injustice."

"Did you? Confession, fools think, is good for the soul. As you see, I yet rule New Hell. Surely you didn't think that you and your gang of unrepentant ideologues could bring down the Prince of Darkness by destroying my Hall of Injustice," said Satan. "And don't bother trying to protect your cohorts: your mind has shown them to me, each and every one. You avoided your decreed punishment in life, but in hell, every punishment fits the sin."

Satan reached down, grasped Fawkes by the throat and, lifting him high above his head with one clawed hand, choked him until he kicked and gasped, his face turning purple. The devil then thrust a long, sharp claw into Fawkes' groin and, making a circular motion, emasculated him. His Infernal Majesty dropped the tissue into a steaming pile of debris from the Hall of Injustice.

Fawkes screamed, feeling his testicles and member burn as if they were still attached to his body.

Next Satan drew a razor-sharp claw across Fawkes' belly. Entrails spilled out upon the ground. Satan pulled out loop after loop of Fawkes' slippery intestines and dropped them into the fire.

Fawkes felt them sizzle and melt from the heat, his mind reeling. He prayed for unconsciousness, but it would not come. Prayer brought no relief in hell.

As the Devil then reached into his body cavity and threw the rest of the organs into the fire, saving his still-beating heart for last, Fawkes felt with perfect clarity every agony, every pop and rupture as his guts roasted in the flames. The sickly sweet smell of burning offal filled the air.

Satan, the devil, the Prince of Darkness, then slashed a scythe-like claw across Fawkes' shoulders and upper thighs and dismembered him completely. Another slash across his neck and his head flew from his shoulders, a fountain of bright red blood spewing from his jugular veins and carotid arteries. Fawkes felt the jarring thump as his head hit the ground, and yet could still feel his lifeblood flowing from his dismembered torso on the hot ash-covered ground.

Still, Fawkes did not lose consciousness. Death eluded him.

Satan collected six pieces of steel rebar from the rubble of the Hall of Injustice and planted their ends in the smoldering ground. He picked up pieces of Fawkes' body, each yet writhing in agony, and impaled them one by one on the steel spikes.

Satan saved the head of Guy Fawkes for last and, as it moaned and screamed in pain, the devil smiled. "Fawkes, you shall suffer for your insolence here, until my Hall of Injustice has been rebuilt. Think upon what you have done, Guy Fawkes, and remember, remember."

Satan spread his wings and took to the air then. Far below, the body parts that were Guy Fawkes still wriggled; his mouth still screamed from his severed head atop one steel pole.

*

Around the smoking pit where the Hall of Injustice once stood, mourners held a candlelight vigil for the victims of the explosion that destroyed the tallest tower in New Hell. They pined for the missing, the dying, and the dead now resting in bags and pieces in the Undertaker's Mortuary.

The Undertaker was busier than ever, sorting morsels of the newly dead. Even busier than the time Erra and the Seven wreaked havoc on the Downward Road, wantonly slaying the damned before they could reach the gates of hell.

Through it all, Guy Fawkes remained: wailing, moaning, suffering his fate.

Some souls, come to gawk, spit upon him; some threw rocks; some cursed his name. He wept on his stake, seeing what torment he had wrought upon so many helpless damned.

Every now and again, a lawyer, librarian, scribe or secretary would dig his or her way out of the rubble. Then there would be much rejoicing among those who waited, and hoped, and who found their loved ones again.

Joy is short-lived in hell, however. Six days, six hours, and six minutes after its destruction, a new Hall of Injustice materialized atop the ruins. Red polished stone rose proud again and windows gleamed bright, even in His Satanic Majesty's penthouse, where no windows had ever remained intact before.

Satan looked upon his tower with pride, and saw that it was beautiful, standing precisely where the old tower had stood, crushing under its majestic weight the dismembered remains of Guy Fawkes and all the mourners holding vigil for the dead and missing damned, promptly sending them all to the Undertaker.

Then the rubble beneath the tower gave way, and the tower settled with a tremor and a bump and a thump. At this, all the penthouse windows shattered in a cacophony of breaking glass.

"Oh, hell," lamented Satan.

Theo Khthonios

by

Scott Oden

The spear bites low and deep, slipping between bronze and leather to skewer his hip. He stumbles. The enemy surges forward. A wicker shield catches him off balance; a second spear shatters on the brow of his Corinthian helmet. "Zeus Savior and Ares!" he bellows; faces loom over him – cruel Asiatics with curled and blood-blasted beards, lips peeled back in snarls of hate. They had paid dearly for this. Oh, yes. They had paid the butcher's bill, a hecatomb of blood and flesh for every man among them. He falls to his knees, hears his own men cry out his name: "Leonidas!"

Time slows. A tracery of clouds veil the face of the sun, creating bands of light and shadow across the stony face of Mount Kallidromos. Colors flare and sharpen: the purple of Persian tunics, the gleam of scale and bronze, the warm chestnut of leather ... all nearly hidden by a pall of blood. Time's flow resumes with a scream of rage.

Leonidas struggles. He can't raise his shield. The twenty-pound aspis *hangs like a dead weight on the end of his arm. Instead, he lashes out with the broken haft of his spear. A Mede in a fish-scale corselet crashes into the mud before him. Blood gouts as Leonidas plunges the butt-spike into the fallen man's throat. He glimpses a hennaed beard, the gleam of gold. An Immortal no more. The Spartan's gaze holds a moment longer, then he glances up ... in time to see the weapon that will write his doom: a Persian* akinakes, *its blade notched and slick with blood. Greek blood. The blood of his allies, of his kinsmen, of his precious Three Hundred. A gory hand snatches at the neck of his breastplate; iron rasps on bronze as the* akinakes *pierces the hollow of Leonidas' throat.*

There is one cold moment of searing pain. Leonidas tries to speak, but his voice is silenced by a foaming tide of blood; he tries to spit in the Persian's eye, but he cannot draw breath. And as he hangs there, his life's blood pumping from severed arteries, King

Leonidas of Sparta recalls words spoken over a meager breakfast, words to bolster Spartan resolve: "Eat hearty," he told his grim-faced Spartiates, his valiant Three Hundred. "Eat hearty, for tonight we dine in Hades!"

And so they did. That night, the night of their deaths at the hands of the Mede – the night they died defending the narrow pass of Thermopylae – Leonidas and his Spartans met on the banks of the River Styx. Beneath a storm-wracked sky they dined on black broth and loaves of ashen bread. With a smile, Leonidas recalled the broth's tastelessness; in that moment, he apprehended the nature of this place called Tartaros, with its endless wars and opportunities for glory: it was a Spartan paradise.

The dead king of Sparta stood now at a table topped with sand and rock, gazing over the landscape it represented. His companion, Dienekes, had spent many long hours scouting the surrounding countryside himself and directing the efforts of the Skiritai – the cadre of scouts who were the eyes of the Spartan army. This map was the culmination of Dienekes' efforts, its creation aided by one of the new helots, a young foreigner clad in gray wool who died at a place called Verdun.

Leonidas studied the lay of the land with a critical eye. He had no frame of reference, no sun or stars to tell him which direction was north; instead, he let the nomenclature of the phalanx guide him: the Stygian Mere guarded their backs, its stinking fens nourished by the hateful waters of the Styx; on his shield side, a few leagues off sprouted a tangled and mist-girt forest, where the savage Blue Men held sway. On his spear side, Leonidas' spies had discovered a fortified citadel rising at the head of a long valley, held by men who called themselves Turks. And straight ahead, through country gashed by chasms and haunted by all manner of brigands and masterless shades, the dead of Argos made their camp.

A slow smile twisted Leonidas' thin lips. He stroked his spade-like beard and nodded. As they were in life, so too would they be in death … sparring partners for his restless Spartiates, spear fodder for their newfound helots and *perioikoi*, the infernal dwellers round about. Perhaps not a glorious campaign, but a necessary one. Even here – especially here – his Spartans needed practice in the art of the spear; they needed the Argives–

The harsh and dissonant blare of a *salpinx* scattered Leonidas' thoughts. He stirred from the table, turned to the flap of his tent as Dienekes appeared. Twenty years his junior, Dienekes had been his *eromenos* as a youth; they were companions, now. Shield-brothers standing shoulder to shoulder in the phalanx.

"What goes?" Leonidas said.

The younger man, stripped to the waist and sweating in the unrelenting heat, indicated the gates of the Spartan camp with a jerk of his head. "A herald has come."

"Who from?"

Dienekes shrugged. "He calls for you."

With a deepening frown, Leonidas followed his young companion out into the Stygian afternoon. The sky overhead was the color of bronze left too long at the mercy of the elements, and the air around them stank of ash and gall. Sulfuric clouds and the smoke of a thousand fires scudded low over the horizon. The Spartan king heard a distant rumble, like the iron wheels of Hades' own chariot thundering down the flinty banks of the Acheron.

The Spartan camp stood atop the crest of a low hill. The battle squires who were with them at Thermopylae directed the efforts of a new crop of helots, men from wildly different lands who had wept at the sight of the *lambda* scrawled on Spartan shields – the inverted 'V' of Lakedaemon. "I have searched for you, good king!" one had said, clutching Leonidas' knees in shameful ecstasy. "For three hundred years I've scoured Tartaros for some sign of you!"

Strange, Leonidas thought. By his reckoning they had been under the earth for a little more than a fortnight….

He and Dienekes passed these same helots struggling to erect defensive walls under the tutelage of a cadre of *perioikoi* from Greater Greece, engineers who hailed from a place called Genoa. They worked with stone grubbed from the hard ground and timbers cut under the watchful eyes of the Blue Men. The wall would follow the natural slope of the hill, the engineers said, to create a *glacis* that would stymie potential attackers. Not that Leonidas planned to afford his enemies time to mount such an assault – once enough arms were scavenged from nearby battlefields, the omens taken and libations made, he would lead his Spartans out against the Argives, slaughter them, then move on to the Turks.

The salpinx bleated once more, and as Leonidas neared the

gates of the encampment – little more than a barricaded ox cart – he heard a man calling his name: "Leonidas, son of Anaxandridas, come forth!"

Nimbly, the king of Sparta leapt atop the gate, Dienekes in his wake. Two men waited outside the encampment, a herald and his salpinx-bearing slave.

"I am here," Leonidas said without preamble. "Who are you, and what do you want?"

The herald was clad in the manner of an Athenian aristocrat; he was a spindly-legged fellow, small and goatish with a dark face and a bristly-black beard. He stared at Leonidas as though taken aback. "Y-you – You are King Leonidas?"

"Did I not just say as much?"

The herald cleared his throat. "I am Simonides of Keos, Lord, and I … I have come to bring you before the *ephors*!"

"We have ephors?" Dienekes muttered.

"Apparently so. Who are these ephors, Simonides of Keos, and what do they want with me?"

"As above, so below, Lord. The ephors are peers of Sparta, and what they want is your obedience. Will you answer their summons?"

Leonidas' brow furrowed. In the sunlit world of the living, the Spartan ephors, a council of five Spartiates elected annually to counter the power of the city's two kings, rarely summoned him – or any citizen of Lakedaemon, for that matter – in order to sing his praises to the heavens. They were quarrelsome, motivated by base politics and personal gain, and they had been a thorn in his living side since the death of his brother, Kleomenes, paved the way for his accession to the throne. *As above, so below?* Leonidas guessed as much.

"Will you answer their summons, Lord?"

"We will," Leonidas replied. He turned to Dienekes. "Assemble the Three Hundred. We must pay our respects to our ephors." Dienekes nodded and turned, bellowing the order to assemble. Instantly, a sense of urgency replaced the relative calm of the camp as the Spartiates donned burnished greaves and cuirasses, drew on their helmets and took up their spears. Though they lacked the signature scarlet cloaks of the Spartan soldier, the *lambda* scratched on their broad shields left little doubt as to their identity.

Simonides raised a hand, looking nervous, his voice all but lost to the sudden clamor arising behind the barricade. "L-lord? They called for you, alone."

"Alone? Were you Spartan, Simonides of Keos, then you'd know our laws hold that no king may travel unattended by his *hippeis*, his guard of honor. These…" Leonidas' proud gesture encompassed the three hundred warriors massing inside the gate, "…are mine."

*

In column by twos, Leonidas led his Spartans into the chasm-riddled country between their camp and that of the Argives, following a track that bore ever to the left as it snaked into the blasted highlands; with each step, the Spartan king saw reminders that they marched through a landscape shattered by eternal war. Pallid dust caked the corroded remnants of chariots and war-wagons, providing meager cerements for the bones of hapless soldiers and would-be conquerors alike. How many shades had arisen from the mortal grave to find new and infernal purpose as foot soldiers of Hades? How many nursed the same desire that thundered in Leonidas' own breast – to build and subjugate and grind the bones of his enemies under heel? And how many had these desires abrogated by a swift blade, a spear thrust, an arrow hissing from the brazen-black sky? Only Hades, lord of the underworld, knew such answers….

The Spartans marched to a lively tune skirling from a reed flute; they marched oblivious to the drifts of unburied bone, ignoring eidolons carved of rock and decorated with the skulls of the defeated. They glanced indifferently at trophy mounds surmounted by altars dedicated to a thousand different gods of war. The Three Hundred marched like jaded spectators who had seen every horror, every atrocity, every conceivable cruelty one man could inflict upon another.

"They fear nothing," Simonides remarked, glancing over his shoulder. The smaller man started at every shadow, averted his eyes from the most gruesome of the altars.

Leonidas followed his gaze. "What is there left to fear? We are, all of us, dead men in truth."

"'We count it death to falter, not to die,'" the smaller man quoted.

The Spartan king was silent for a moment. "Who were you, Simonides of Keos? Your name is familiar, yet you do not bear the aspect of a man of violence."

"I was a poet."

"Were you good?"

"Good enough to compose your epitaph, Lord." Simonides' face flushed with pride as he put his hand to his breast and spoke with lyrical flourish: "Go tell the Spartans, O stranger passing by, that here, obedient to their laws, we lie!"

Leonidas nodded. "Adequate. I gather our allies eventually drove the Mede from Hellas?"

"At Salamis a month after you fell, then the following year at Plataea," Simonides said. "Thermopylae was the war-cry of the Greeks." The poet looked askance at Leonidas. "There is a name you must commit to memory, Lord. That name is Ephialtes of Trachis."

"Who is he?"

"He is the man who betrayed you. The man who showed Xerxes a path around the Hot Gates. I have no doubt he, too, resides in Tartaros, should you wish to seek him out."

The Spartan king's eyes sharpened to points, like whetted knives. "My thanks, Simonides. I will remember the name of Ephialtes, you may count upon it."

They continued on in silence. Sandaled feet raised a pall of dust as the road ascended alongside a ragged gorge, its bottom given over to shadow. Thorn and black ivy clung to the side of the chasm. Leonidas felt a sense of familiarity, as though he'd seen this place before – even as he felt the unmistakable sensation of scrutiny.

"We're being watched," Leonidas said as Dienekes came abreast of him.

"I feel it, too." Dienekes indicated the gorge with a nod. "From down there."

"The *Ataphoi*," Simonides replied, shivering despite the stifling heat. "The shades of the unburied. Nigh upon animals, they are – and drawn to this place, though none know why. I shouldn't think they would dare attack a party of this magnitude. Still, it is fortunate we are near our destination."

"How near?"

"A *parasang*, perhaps. Maybe less."

Leonidas nodded. "Dienekes, pass the word. Simonides, have your slave blow a tune on his horn. Long and loud."

Simonides gestured to his salpinx-bearer, who filled his lungs and loosed a thunderous blast. Stones rattled down. Echo caught the voice of the salpinx and carried it deep into the gorge where the Ataphoi quailed and clapped hands to ears. And in answer, there came from on high the brazen roar of a trumpet.

Leonidas increased his pace; armor rattled as his Spartans did the same. The path upward became a flight of rough-hewn steps which carried them to the crest of a plateau. It was an acropolis, in a manner of speaking, treeless and wreathed in smoke. A circular temple dominated the plateau, its walls and columns pitted and stained black from countless attempts to burn it to the ground.

"Welcome to Caeadas, Lord," Simonides said with a breathless flourish.

Caeadas. The eerie hint of familiarity made sense, now. It resembled mortal Caeadas, in the heart of Mount Taygetus – Leonidas had been to that place many times as a living king; he had stood at the lip of the gorge and presided over the execution of criminals. There, too, was where Sparta disposed of the weak, the unfit, the deformed. How many babes had he left on the cold and unyielding rocks? How many had he left to the Fates?

Nor was Leonidas ignorant of the implication: if this site served a similar function, the ephors had summoned him to the place of judgment and of slaughter. His face settled into a grim mask as he shouldered past Simonides and made his way to the temple.

Knots of Greeks milled about the plateau. Some wore antique armor of heavy bronze, blood-streaked and dented, while others were clad in corselets of linen. Leonidas saw a profusion of helmets and crests: boars' tooth, Corinthian and Chalcidian; some like flat-brimmed kettles and others like Phrygian caps of hammered bronze. Men of other races and nations mingled among the Greeks, as well. The Spartan king glimpsed Persians with their curled beards, though clad in unfamiliar robes; he saw Nubians and Egyptians and pale men with ruddy complexions. And with each group stood a fellow clad after the same fashion as Simonides, in the manner of Athenian aristocracy – some read silently from rolled papyri while others conversed in low voices with the men around them, like advocates preparing their cases.

But even the most devoted among them stopped and stared at the sight of armed Spartans cresting the plateau. Whispers arose, and Leonidas heard his name spoken like a susurrant echo. He gestured Simonides to his side.

"These ephors, I take it they adjudicate claims and render binding judgments?"

"They do, Lord. They act under the auspices of she who is the Kore, to mitigate somewhat the violence of Tartaros; the aggrieved may come before them and know their cause will be heard and fairly judged. And she only chooses Spartans for this task – for who else can offer impartiality in matters of war?"

"The Kore chooses them?"

"With Lord Hades' blessing," Simonides replied. "When next she declares an Olympiad, all fighting in Tartaros must cease and she will select five Spartans to serve as her ephors until she calls for another Olympiad, and another truce."

"So they serve four years instead of one?"

Simonides waffled. "Perhaps it is four years, perhaps it is but one. Time has an odd quality here, Lord. A day might pass in the blink of an eye, or it may drag on for an eternity. It is easier to embrace the notion that an Olympiad is as long as it pleases the Kore and let that be the end of it."

Leonidas gave the poet a distracted nod as they neared the temple: it was a *tholos*, more a meeting house than a place of worship, and it looked as though Titans had dug its foundations and erected its walls. Half a hundred steps led up to the iron-studded doors, thrown wide open and guarded by a pair of obsidian statues – many-headed Kerberos, the Hound of Hades. They seemed to glare down at the Spartans as Leonidas set foot on the bottom course of stairs. He turned slightly.

"Dienekes, you're with me. The rest of you, stand ready. Lead the way, Simonides."

"We must wait –" the poet said.

"I think not." Leonidas ascended the steps. Before he reached the half-way mark, he heard a voice tinged with petulant anger echoing from inside the temple:

"Is that your final decision?"

"It is." The respondent sounded old, weary. "We do not seek to ally ourselves with you, Alexandros of Macedon. Instead, you should seek to ingratiate yourself with us! We are the ephors! We are the Chosen of Persephone, not you!"

"So be it, Lawgiver! But know this: I have extended my hand to you in friendship only to have it rebuffed! I will not extend it a second time!" Hob-nailed sandals clashed on tile.

"You arrogant whelp!" another voice bellowed.

"Arrogant? I conquered Persia without your kind, Spartan! I can conquer Tartaros just as easily!"

Leonidas was but steps from the head of the temple's stairs when a cluster of figures stormed out its doors. Six ruddy Macedonians – scarred fighters clad in black iron and linen – ringed a seventh: a golden-haired youth whose clean-shaven face was a mask of anger.

"Hidebound fools!" the youth said, switching from Doric Greek to the guttural argot of Macedon. "We dwell in a new land, where new rules are in play, and yet they prefer to sit on their backsides and bask in the dusty glory of forgotten Thermopylae!" The youth caught sight of Simonides, two imposing Spartans at his side. Tossing his hair back, shaking his mane like a young lion recovering its dignity, he offered Simonides a smile – though his eyes remained cold black motes of rage. "Well met, good poet of Keos! And you, friend Spartan!"

"It is counted an auspicious moment," Simonides replied, "when two kings meet under the banner of truce. King Alexandros of Macedon, I give you –"

"A Spartan," Leonidas interrupted, "for whom the glory of Thermopylae is neither dusty nor forgotten." His smile matched Alexandros' own, predatory and devoid of warmth.

The young Macedonian looked him up and down. "A Spartan and a king? You are Leonidas, then. You must forgive my ill choice of words. It's your peers, they … vex me."

"I understand."

Alexandros' eyebrow arched but he said nothing. After a moment, one of his Macedonian companions leaned closer to him, a spare and leathery fellow who wore a ferryman's coin on a thong about his neck. "Alexandros, we tarry too long."

"Of course, Nearchos." The young king stirred. "I would consider it a favor of the highest order if you and your men would come with us, Leonidas. And you as well, good Simonides. There is much I would talk with you about."

Simonides opened his mouth to answer, but Leonidas silenced him with a brusque motion, saying, "I have business with the ephors that cannot wait."

"I would insist, but I see that would be an exercise in futility with you." Alexandros sighed. "Pity. Another time, perhaps. I am honored to have met you, my brother king."

"And I, you." With a nod, Leonidas brushed past the Macedonians.

"That one's trouble," Simonides muttered, once he was sure Alexandros was out of ear-shot. "Even in life his arrogance was well known, or so I'm told. His mother claimed he was the son of Zeus and that was a notion he embraced, even if no one else did. And like a scion of the god, he went on to ally himself with the Thracians, conquer the Athenians and their allies, raze Thebes, devastate Asia Minor, shatter the Persians in two battles, and march into the very heart of India. He might have gone to the very ends of the earth had a jealous countryman not slipped poison into his wine."

"All well and good," Leonidas said, gaining the temple portico. Its pitted columns were like ancient tree-trunks. "But did he conquer Sparta?"

"No, he did not. Indeed, a scholar from a little village called Oxford told me that Alexandros, or perhaps his father, I do not recall – regardless, he told me one of them sent a message to your countrymen. 'If I enter Laconia,' so the message ran, 'I will raze Sparta to the ground.' Your peers sent back a single word in reply–"

"'If'," Dienekes interrupted. "The word was 'if.'"

"Yes. You've heard this story?"

But Dienekes shook his head.

Already monumentally ugly, the sudden frown twisting

Simonides' face lent him the aspect of a fearsome Gorgon. "Then how did you know?"

Dienekes and Leonidas exchanged knowing smiles. "We are Spartan, poet. What other answer could there be? But, enough. We will deal with this upstart Macedonian later. Come."

Simonides gnawed his lip, glancing from man to man as they marched past the brooding images of Kerberos and into the heart of the temple. The air inside was still, heavy with incense and the sour stench of fear. *Things* waited in the Stygian darkness; Leonidas saw nothing, but he heard the rustle of leathery wings, the scrabble of claws on polished marble, the faint hiss of infernal laughter. Perhaps they were the dreaded Erinys, waiting to deliver the judgment of the ephors; perhaps they were something else....

Ahead, hellish light seeped down from clerestory windows to illuminate a conclave of five men. Four of them sat uncomfortably on oversized seats carved of living rock, black basalt etched with silver runes and whorls; the fifth, a giant of a man clad in an antique cuirass, stood beside an empty seat.

"Mark my words!" the giant said, his voice a basso rumble. "That strutting little peacock will cause no end of trouble!"

"He is not our concern, Menelaos," replied the man in the center seat. Though frail through the shoulders and gray-bearded, he spoke with the power and conviction of a trained orator. "We are here to prosecute the Kore's will, not to become embroiled in petty politics."

"Petty, Lykourgos?" a third ephor said. He, too, had a beard more gray than black, with deep-set eyes that had seen too much of Hades' realm. "No. Menelaos is right – this Macedonian is dangerous. Dispatch the Erinys...."

"We have no cause, Agis!" Lykourgos said, ignoring the eager rustling of wings that erupted from the inky shadows. "No charges have been leveled; thus it is not within our writ to mete out judgment against Alexandros. We are not thugs, my friends!"

"Leave this Alexandros to me," Leonidas said, stepping into the circle of ruddy light.

The giant, Menelaos, whirled. "Hades' teeth! Who are you, wretched shade, to intrude upon the business of your betters?"

Leonidas met his gaze. "I do not see my betters standing

before me, Menelaos, once king of Sparta. I see only my peers."

"Your peers?" Menelaos took a menacing step toward Leonidas.

"Wait," Agis said. "You are Leonidas son of Anaxandridas, are you not?"

Menelaos stopped.

Leonidas nodded. "I am."

"Then," continued Agis, "you are my kinsman, though our bond is diluted as much by time as by death. As such, I tell you this: you risk much by barging in on matters that do not concern you."

"I have not 'barged' in on your proceedings, kinsman," Leonidas replied. He gestured to Simonides. "I was summoned to stand before the ephors. Thus, here I am."

Menelaos eased his bulk down onto his seat, glanced sidelong at Lykourgos.

"You are as arrogant as young Alexandros, Leonidas son of Anaxandridas," Lykourgos, called the Lawgiver, said after a moment. His eyes narrowed in disdain. "You think yourself a king in Tartaros when, in fact, you are nothing. You are a shade who tasted the nectar of glory in life! What of it? We all, every man here, have tasted the same nectar! In this world, it is those whose trust you keep who define your place. We *are* your betters, Leonidas, because it is the will of the Kore!"

Leonidas nodded in acquiescence. "Perhaps you are right, great Lykourgos. But if I am not as much a king in Tartaros as I was in the world above, why does this not register in the eyes of your companions, here?" Leonidas indicated the two silent ephors, who had been gazing upon him with something akin to religious ecstasy. Both men flinched and looked away.

Lykourgos frowned. "Brasidas and Lysandros are young, as the dead are reckoned. They were soldiers in life; neither ever felt the weight of the crown." The one called Brasidas started to speak, but Lykourgos shouted him down. "And they know when to keep their tongues between their teeth! You stand accused, Leonidas son of Anaxandridas!"

It was Leonidas' turn to flinch. "Accused? Accused of what, good Lykourgos? What is my so-called crime?"

"Impiety!" a voice bellowed from the shadows. Wings beat the still air and claws clashed on marble; a chorus of hisses nigh drowned out the clatter of chains as a gruesome apparition thrust himself into their midst. As one, Leonidas and Dienekes drew their swords and slung their shields forward. Simonides gave a bleat of terror and fell on his belly.

The figure laughed, a sound like nails scraping flint. At first, Leonidas thought it a man clad in blood-soaked rags. But, when the figure turned toward him he understood that what he took for cloth was actually ribbons of mangled flesh that hung from his lower limbs and belly. Pitted bronze manacles circled his wrists, and a veil of stringy black hair hid one eye from view. The other glowed with the light of madness. He pointed a black-nailed finger at Leonidas. "Impiety and murder are your crimes, dear brother!"

Leonidas lowered his sword. "Brother? Is that you, Kleomenes?"

"Kleomenes!" The figure tittered. "Poor, mad Kleomenes! Is that not what you called me, Leonidas? Poor, mad Kleomenes? Curse your abusive words! You may have had the power to utter them then, but I have the power to do you real harm now, dear brother! Dear, impious, murdering brother!"

"Calm yourself, Kleomenes," Agis said. "How do you answer these charges, Leonidas?"

"With scorn!" Leonidas sheathed his sword. "*This* is why you summoned me? To answer the ravings of a lunatic? I am saddened beyond words to see you in this sorry state, brother. Especially here. But you know as well as I that you died by your own hand! Did he tell you *that*, great Ephors? Did Kleomenes tell you how he came by those grisly wounds? He pilfered a helot's knife – one used to skin hares – and slashed himself from his ankles to his crotch!"

"Bah!" Kleomenes spat. "Your mouth opens and lies spew forth! You gave me the knife, Leonidas!"

"No, brother."

"Yes! You put it in my hand and watched as I made that first cut!"

"You were alone in your cell," Leonidas said. "Put there by our mortal ephors."

"No!" Kleomenes screamed. "You put me there, you bastard! You left me alone! Alone in the dark!"

"No, brother."

"Enough!" Menelaos' voice crashed like thunder. "Leonidas is right! I see no murder here, Lykourgos!"

"Nor do I," Agis said coldly. Brasidas and Lysandros, too, murmured their assent.

The lawgiver, his face a mask of solemnity, nodded. "We are agreed. The accusation of murder holds no weight, and the witness you have borne is false, Kleomenes. Willfully false! There must be a reckoning with the Erinys!"

Leonidas held up a hand. "Leniency, Ephors. I ask for mercy. Even in death, my brother is not right in his mind."

"Mercy." Kleomenes' shoulders sagged. "Mercy for poor, mad Kleomenes." Then, quick as a darting serpent, the blood-stained apparition lunged at Leonidas; it looked as though the brothers would embrace – until jags of light gleamed from the curved blade of a skinning knife streaking for Leonidas' throat. "Liar!" he howled.

Yet for all the madman's speed, Leonidas was quicker, still. He caught the wrist of Kleomenes' knife-hand, twisted it, and mercilessly drove the bronze-rolled edge of his shield into his brother's elbow.

Bone snapped. Kleomenes howled in pain as the knife clattered from his nerveless fingers.

Leonidas shoved him away.

The madman fell into a crouch, clutching the injured limb to his breast. He panted like a cornered animal, eyes darting as he sought an avenue of escape.

"That was necessary, brother," Leonidas said. "To keep you from hurting yourself further." He took a step toward Kleomenes…

…who screamed an incoherent curse and sprinted for the temple doors, barreling through Simonides. The poet fell heavily. The shadows exploded in rustling and clashing, hissing in rage. Menelaos and the other ephors leapt to their feet.

They might have given chase had Leonidas not stayed them with an upraised hand. "He is my responsibility. I will fetch him back so you may pass judgment on him. Even now, after this, I still ask for mercy. Do not set the Erinys on him!"

"We will see," Lykourgos said. "Bring him back and we will see."

Leonidas nodded. "Dienekes?"

The other veteran of Thermopylae, who had been helping Simonides to his feet, looked around at the temple doors and the silhouette of Kleomenes, who seemed to have paused on the temple's threshold and was hesitating.

Dienekes gauged distances. "I can catch him easily enough."

"Come, then."

But before either man could get off the mark, Agis called them up short. "Wait. Look. He returns of his own volition."

True enough: Kleomenes had stood there a moment more, limned by hellish light, then turned and staggered back in the direction of the ephors. He made an eerie mewling sound, like a wet sob. His broken arm hung slack; with his good hand he plucked at his throat.

"Kleomenes, my poor brother!" Leonidas walked toward him. "Let us be reconciled. Here, no doubt, we can find good uses for your madness."

Kleomenes sagged at the edge of the clerestory light filtering down from above. Leonidas reached him before he could topple and eased him to the tiled floor. The madman could not speak. Gouts of bright red blood cascaded from Kleomenes' mouth. Standing out a hand-span from his throat, Leonidas saw the ragged black fletching of an arrow.

And in that one galvanizing instant he forgot his dead brother. "Dienekes, outside!"

In tandem, the two Spartans bolted for the temple doors. The ephors followed suit, with Simonides and Lykourgos struggling to bring up the rear. The shadows around and above seethed with sound – a cacophony of shrieking, flapping, hissing, and scraping matched only by the howls and screams that bled in from outside.

The younger man reached the threshold first. "Zeus Savior," Dienekes muttered.

Beyond the temple doors, Leonidas beheld a scene of raw and bloody chaos. Caeadas was under attack. A horde of misshapen figures boiled over the distant edge of the plateau – grotesque caricatures of humanity, their filthy limbs askew or missing, their faces snarling and deformed. Some staggered on stumps of legs, others trotted on three, and still others ran on all fours like feral beasts. Leonidas saw an Athenian advocate savaged by a pair of thin, childlike creatures wielding daggers. A Cretan hero tried to intervene only to be split nigh asunder by an ogreish thing with an axe strapped to its sole arm. An instant later, a Nubian sent a bone-tipped spear straight into the ogre's gaping maw, then fell under a swarm of jackal-like figures. And at the edges of the fray, archers capered and loosed a hail of black-feathered shafts, their powerful bows sending the arrows arching over the heads of the combatants and into the ranks of those fleeing their advance.

"The *Ataphoi*!" Leonidas heard Simonides gasp. "Someone's armed them!"

An arrow shattered on the temple steps; another rang off Dienekes' shield – doubtless from the same contingent of archers who skewered Kleomenes.

Lykourgos' iron-shod staff of office sparked as he rapped it on the marble floor. "Close the doors! Let them waste their strength against those below!"

"No!" Leonidas replied, coldly. "If you be men of war, come with me!"

With that, the dead king of Sparta turned and stalked down the temple steps, Dienekes at his side. Brasidas, Lysandros, Menelaos, and Agis fanned out at his back, leaving Simonides and Lykourgos alone.

Poet stared at lawgiver.

Lykourgos tried to disguise his fear beneath a snarl of contempt: "Fools! Help me close the doors, Simonides."

Shaking his head, Simonides of Keos hurried to join Leonidas.

On the stairs they met a pair of Spartans coming to meet them – one was young and wounded, an arrow jutting from the small of his back; the other was older, sightless even in Hades, and he held his companion up and covered them both with the bowl of his shield.

"Eurytus," Leonidas said.

"We were coming to warn you when young Maron, here, took one in the spine." Blind Eurytus moved his shield slightly to catch another incoming arrow. It struck the bronze face like a mallet striking a bell, causing the Spartan to wince. Leonidas reckoned he could hear the wind rushing past each arrow's fletching.

Though unable to walk, Maron smiled. "I'll be all right, my king! I can still skewer the bastards!"

Leonidas nodded. "Rest, lad. There will be plenty of killing to do in a few moments. Simonides!" The poet hustled to his side. Leonidas clapped a hand on his shoulder. "Take charge of the wounded. Keep them safe. Eurytus, here, will help you." Simonides took the injured Spartan's arm and helped him sit as their blind comrade provided cover.

Leonidas turned his attention to the ephors, noting Lykourgos' absence. "Agis, kinsman, take the left flank. Noble Menelaos, you have the right. Brasidas, you and Lysandros are with me in the center." The ephors, the Chosen of Persephone, did Leonidas' bidding without complaint.

At the first hint of trouble, the Spartans had performed the task for which they had been bred, arraying themselves in a tight phalanx one hundred shields long and three deep. Now, they waited only for their king. Despite an enemy surging toward them, baying like wolves, Leonidas paused to speak to a few of his men; he strolled through their ranks as though they stood on a parade field, taking his Corinthian helmet from a squire even as he told a rude joke. Laughter rippled along the formation. The crest of Leonidas' helmet was bright scarlet—a splash of color amid the ash and grime of war.

His battle priest, stern-eyed Aristandros, waited at the center of the formation, clutching a kneeling captive by the hair. Here, they had no goats to sacrifice, no oxen to offer the gods. Here, they had only the shades of the dead. This one was a slave snatched at the last minute. Simonides' salpinx-bearer, Leonidas noted. No matter. He would serve their purpose.

Leonidas grasped an eight-foot long spear and thrust it aloft.

"Spartans!" he roared. All eyes turned toward him. "Lord Hades is our master, now! He has given us these dregs, these wretched *Ataphoi*, on which to whet our spears! They are not worthy of this honor, but Lord Hades' will must be done! There is no Glory, here! There is no Glory in the killing of such miserable creatures! There is only Mercy! Come, my Spartans! Come, my ferocious Three Hundred! Show our enemy the Mercy of the Spear! All of this for you, Lord Hades and for Lakedaemon!" With little effort, he drove the blade of his spear through the slave's body. Blood spattered the packed earth, hissing on naked rock. The omens were good.

"For Lord Hades! For Lakedaemon!" his men echoed. "And for Leonidas!"

"Advance!"

Pipers played a tune on their reed flutes as the hoplites stepped off in unison, spears upright, their strides precise and unbroken. Polished greaves and shield-faces flashed in the infernal light. Three hundred throats chanted the *paean*, a hymn to Hades:

"Theos Khthonios,

"Pitiless in heart,

"Dweller under the Earth..."

At stanza's end, Leonidas bellowed a command: "Spears!" And with that the bristling hedge of iron dropped from vertical to horizontal, creating a threshing machine of slaughter.

Now fifty yards' distant, the savage *Ataphoi* only increased their pace. They charged like a mindless mob, in knots and clusters that held no cohesion, moving as fast or as slow as their deformed limbs allowed. They did not spread out and try to envelop the Spartan line, but drove straight at their center, at the scarlet crest that marked Leonidas. Their archers drew and loosed with reckless abandon ... and to no avail.

The heavy bronze armor of the Spartans shrugged off this barbed rain of arrows. The Three Hundred marched on, implacable.

Behind them came the battle squires and helots, joined by the folk of different nations allied against the *Ataphoi*. From their ranks came a barrage of javelins, arrows, and sling stones that scythed into the unarmored mass of the enemy.

Howls of rage turned to agony; blood spewed as riddled bodies flopped to the ground under the rain of Spartan missiles, where the heels of their fellow *Ataphoi* kicked and trampled them into the dust.

A dozen yards separated them, now. Leonidas saw a festering mass of creatures, the cast-offs and detritus of a thousand years of natural selection. The things barreling toward him could never have survived in the sunlit world of the living: they were denizens of nightmare, seething with jealousy and hate.

Ten yards. Eight. Six….

Leonidas braced his shield, its rim scraping that of Dienekes' on his right. Aristandros was on his left. Knowing his brothers, his kinsmen, his friends stood in such close proximity filled Leonidas' heart with joy. He sang the paean:

Theos Khthonios!

Five yards, now. Four….

He singled out his first target: a naked, spitting thing with a misshapen head, sword clutched like a stick of driftwood in its gnarled fist. *No Glory, only Mercy.* Leonidas lined up his spear with the wretch's center of mass. A swift blow, through the spine…

Three yards. Two….

Seconds before impact, through the eye-slit of his Corinthian helmet, Leonidas watched the front ranks of *Ataphoi* convulse. Perhaps their dull brains felt the first tendrils of fear; perhaps the prospect of facing an unbroken wall of bronze suddenly daunted them. Whatever the reason, their steps faltered and their braying slacked off, replaced by a keening dirge of dread. But their close-packed ranks could not turn aside. Momentum drove them into the flesh-grinding teeth of the Spartan war machine.

They struck with the sound of a melon meeting an anvil, a wet crack that drowned out the screams and the song and echoed over the plateau of Caeadas. Leonidas' spear licked out, taking his first victim high, in the throat. Blood gushed from the hideous wound as the thing toppled backward….

Suddenly, Leonidas' field of vision became a wall of writhing flesh, reeking of sulphur and feces and rich red gore. Sheer numbers pressed in upon him….

A sword bites low and deep, slipping between bronze and leather to skewer his hip. He stumbles. The enemy surges forward. A misshapen arm catches him off balance; a second sword shatters on the brow of his Corinthian helmet. "Theos Khthonios!" he bellows; faces loom over him—cruel-eyed Ataphoi *with curled talons and blood-blasted fangs, lips peeled back in snarls of hate. They will pay dearly for this. Oh, yes! They will pay the butcher's bill, a hecatomb of blood and flesh for every Spartan, Lord Hades!*

He falls to his knees, hears a deep voice whisper his name: "Leonidas."

Time slows. He is at the Hot Gates, again. At hallowed Thermopylae. A tracery of clouds veil the face of the sun, creating bands of light and shadow across the stony face of Mount Kallidromos. He is not alone. A figure helps him arise. The Spartan sees a tall and perfectly formed being towering over him, his visage dark and brooding.

Lord Hades.

"Leonidas," the Lord of the Underworld says, in a voice pitched to such sweet perfection that the dead king of Sparta must fight back tears. "You are mine, now, and you have served me well. Go, and serve me still: henceforth you are my champion, the Chosen of Hades! Remember your oath!"

Time's flow resumes with a scream of rage.

Roaring, Leonidas surged upward. He flung creatures aside, bones snapping as his shield slammed into their faces, into their torsos. Though he bled from a wound in his hip, the dead king of Sparta was indomitable; his spear moved like a living thing, darting and biting. With each strike, another deformed shade lost its semblance of life. Blood slimed the stones, and steam rose from fresh pools of gore to wrap Leonidas in an infernal cloak.

The *Ataphoi* lines cracked against the bronze bulwark. They showed the Spartans their backs and fought their own kind in desperation. They fought to get away. They fought to return to the welcoming shadows of their dread gorge: they fought to live.

And, true to his word, Leonidas slaughtered them like cattle.

The day drew on, and when the king finally called for an end to the butchery only a lucky few *Ataphoi* remained to slink and scurry back over the rim of the plateau; he doubted they'd number enough to fill the seats of a small theater. Leonidas leaned on the cracked shaft of his spear – his hip throbbed, but the bleeding had stopped – and surveyed the carnage in his wake. It seemed as though the Temple of the Ephors rested on a sea of corpses.

Dagger-wielding helots rooted among the piles of stinking dead, dispatching those they found yet clinging to life. Others salvaged the allied wounded. Leonidas spotted Simonides picking his way toward him. The poet looked ghastly. Blood caked his hands and arms to the elbow, and he held a knife loosely by his side.

"Simonides of Keos! You survived."

The poet gazed in wonder at Leonidas, at the nimbus of hellish light seeming to wreathe him, and bowed. "Lord. We heard a rumor in the rear that you had fallen. I am pleased to see it was unfounded."

"I did fall," Leonidas replied. "But I arose again." He gestured to the field around them. "Thermopylae looked much like this, on the eve of the first day. How many of my Spartans have fallen?"

Simonides exhaled. "Thirty, lord."

"Thirty." Leonidas shook his head. He looked up, again, to see Dienekes approach. "Is it true, dear friend? We lost thirty brothers?"

Though blood-blasted and limping, Dienekes' eyes were alert. He nodded. "Mostly from the right. Alpheus, 'ere he died, told me that bastard Menelaos broke formation. Charged into the thick of them and left a hole in the front rank."

"That son of a Mycenaean whore! Where is he?"

Dienekes gestured up at the temple. "Near death. Agis had a few of the slaves cart him up there."

A dangerous light kindled in Leonidas' eyes. "Follow me. Both of you."

*

The trio threaded through the wrack of war, stopping now and again for Leonidas to speak in low tones with his brother Spartans. Though they exchanged smiles and jests, the malevolent gleam never left the king's eyes. His men apprehended danger. By the time they mounted the stairs to the temple Leonidas' cortege had grown.

He found the ephors in their accustomed place. Agis, Brasidas, and Lysandros sprawled wearily in their seats, still sticky with the blood of the slain. Pale and near death, Menelaos lay on a litter on the floor with Lykourgos attending to him. Near them, a pair of slaves held down a writhing captive: a naked *Ataphoi* glistening with sweat and blood, its hairless body deformed by a set of vestigial limbs sprouting from its back. Startlingly blue eyes pleaded with them to let it go.

"P-please ..." it croaked.

As Leonidas traversed the interior of the temple, the creatures lurking in the shadows grew silent. Their wings ceased to rustle; their claws were still. Their screeches faded as though gripped by fear.

"Ephors!" he said, his voice booming. "We have won a victory!"

Before any of the others could so much as greet Leonidas, Lykourgos shot to his feet. The old man rapped his staff against the floor. "Victory? What price this victory, Leonidas? One of our own lies stricken!"

Leonidas crossed to Menelaos' side and knelt. Swords and axes had dealt ferocious wounds to his torso, arms, and legs. It was a testament to his Homeric vitality that he still had enough essence to be counted amongst the living – or what passed for living – souls in war-torn Tartaros. The wounded man's eyes fluttered open; he saw Leonidas' blood-grimed face and smiled. "Rest easy," Leonidas said. He glanced at the captive *Ataphoi,* then at Agis, among the seated ephors. "Did that thing tell you who armed them?"

Agis looked askance at it. "It blames Kharon."

"Kharon?"

"F-ferryman," the creature sobbed. "Ferryman … c-came among us! G-gave us hateful knives! Told us … told us to rip and slay!"

"Liar!" Lykourgos barked. He struck the thing in the face with his iron-shod staff. Bone crunched; blood spurted from its nose and mouth. "I know Kharon! He would never stoop so low!"

The *Ataphoi* wailed. "F-ferryman!"

"If it speaks again, I will carve its lying tongue from its head!" Lykourgos spat.

"Get hold of yourself, Lawgiver." A grim smile twisted Leonidas' lips as he apprehended the truth: *a spare and leathery fellow who wore a ferryman's coin on a thong about his neck.* "I did not hear it accuse Kharon of any wrong-doing. In truth, I would wager this thing has never seen Kharon." Leonidas snapped his fingers. "Look at me! It was not the boatman of the Styx who gave you weapons, was it, wretch? Was it?"

The thing shook its deformed head.

Brasidas frowned. "Then who?"

Leonidas gave a mirthless chuckle. "Earlier, did you not see a tight-lipped rogue with an *obol,* the ferryman's coin, tied about his neck? It was Alexandros' man, Nearchos. Though in truth, I expect it was Alexandros himself who gave the order. The young whelp will make a worthy adversary."

"You have cause, now, Lykourgos," Agis said. "Call forth the Erinys!"

"No," Leonidas replied. "Alexandros is mine."

Lykourgos rounded on the Spartan king. "Impertinent fool! You think fighting a battle on our very doorstep gives *you* the right to counsel *us? We* are the Chosen of Persephone! *We,* alone, will render judgment on Alexandros of Macedon! Go! Take yourself away from here and await our summons, as it pleases us! There is still a charge of impiety hanging over your head! Go!"

But Leonidas did not move. He knelt there beside Menelaos, one hand stroking the fallen giant's sweat-slick brow. The air in the temple grew chill despite the infernal heat. "Simonides, you told me earlier that the Kore chooses only Spartans as her ephors. Correct?"

The poet of Keos shivered. "That is true, lord."

"There must be some mistake, then, for noble Menelaos is no Spartan born, is he Simonides? He is a son of Mycenae, is that not true? The mantle of kingship over Sparta does not a Spartan make."

"You are correct, lord."

Leonidas snatched a handful of Menelaos' damp hair and levered his head up. "And that's why thirty of my men have returned to the Darkness, to begin the journey anew! Because you are no Spartan, you Mycenaean swine!"

Despite his wounds, Menelaos struggled to rise; his lips peeled back in a bloody snarl as he spat at Leonidas. "D-dog!"

"Find me when you return, you miserable cuckold, and we will settle accounts like men!" With that, Leonidas ripped a broad-bladed dagger from Menelaos' own belt and plunged it into the Mycenaean's chest. Agis and the other ephors leapt to Menelaos' defense, only to be beaten back by spear-wielding Dienekes.

Leonidas twisted the blade.

Menelaos shuddered, his eyes rolling back in his head. To his credit, he uttered not a sound.

Into that gaping wound Leonidas thrust his hand; when he drew it back, slick with gore, it clutched Menelaos' still-beating heart.

Forgotten, the captive *Ataphoi* howled with mirth, its blue eyes aglow.

King Leonidas of Sparta staggered to his feet and slung that gobbet of muscle into the shadows, where things could be heard scrabbling over it, hissing and biting. He stared at Agis, Brasidas, and Lysandros. "I have no quarrel with you."

After a moment, Agis shook his head. "Nor we with you."

Lykourgos, though, strode forward in a towering rage, oblivious to the spear leveled at his breast. "You are judged, Leonidas son of Anaxandridas! In the name of Queen Persephone, I pronounce the Doom of the Erinys upon you! Arise, wrathful daughters of Ouranos! Arise and slay!"

Like a prophet of old, the lawgiver stood with his arms upraised and his eyes closed in divine ecstasy. Perhaps he expected the shadows to roil and flow over the offending Spartan, to hear his screams as the bronze claws of the Erinys tore the flesh from his bones. Perhaps he expected cries of mercy or of repentance as the bat-winged sisters swept down on Leonidas.

But what he got was silence.

Nothing stirred.

He opened his eyes and met the king of Sparta's gaze. There was no trace of mockery in his visage, only a grim sense of brooding majesty.

"I … I am the Chosen of Persephone! I judge you!"

"No," Leonidas said. He turned away, motioned for Dienekes and Simonides to leave the temple, for the slaves to haul the captive *Ataphoi* out of his sight. The three remaining ephors joined them, leaving Lykourgos alone.

"I am the Chosen of Persephone and I judge you, Leonidas!"

"No." The king of Sparta stopped; he turned back to face Lykourgos. "No, for I am the Chosen of Hades and I am your master! You are a coward, Lykourgos, called the Lawgiver, and I judge you unfit to wear the mantle of a Spartan! By *Theos Khthonios*, god of the underworld, the dread Lord Hades, I cast you into the shadows!"

“You are nothing! Nothing, do you hear?” Lykourgos rapped his staff on the marble floor. “Attend me, ephors! Denounce him!”

Leonidas merely shook his head. He resumed his path from the temple, and with his every step the umbra of hellish light surrounding Lykourgos shrank.

“I am the … the Chosen of Persephone!”

Leonidas crossed the threshold; behind him, the temple’s interior was plunged into darkness. Wings rustled. Brazen claws clashed on marble and tore flesh. And hissing voices rose in volume, drowning out Lykourgos’ screams….

Erra and the Seven

By

Chris Morris

Divinity of hell!
When devils will the blackest sins put on,
They do suggest at first with heavenly shows,
As I do now.

– William Shakespeare, *Othello*

When Lysicles awoke, the light hurt his eyes. So white and bright blazed this light, he could see nothing else. Tears were streaming down his face; he could feel them on his cheeks. He rubbed his face and his hand came away sticky. Around him he heard moaning and groaning. Then the moaning and groaning stopped; perhaps it was his.

He was lying on his back, this he knew for certain. He kept blinking, trying to clear his vision, struggling to see something beyond the blazing light. Then the moaning and groaning began again, guttural and wordless. His eyes hurt. His mouth hurt. His whole face hurt. His chest hurt. He touched his hand to his breast and felt a gaping wound. Then the light streamed even brighter.

Someone said, "Lysicles the Athenian. Put him with his kind, in Erebos," just before knowingness left him, scourged away by the bright white light until something huge and dark ate up all the brightness – until all that was left was pain and dark.

Erebos?

Then he wakes once again. His eyes, his mouth, his chest hurt. He is wounded. Now he can see blurred shapes, a crossroads. So is this Erebos on the shores of the Styx? He blinks and blinks again.

Is this Erebos, in the realm of Hades, amid the shadows between the world of the living and the world of the dead? Is this the crossroads where three roads meet: the road to Tartaros; the road to Asphodel; and the road to Elysion? If it is, souls are sent here to be judged and set on their deserved paths: to Tartaros, whence there is no return and no relief; to Asphodel's meadows, where stricken heroes wander who remember name and fame only by drinking blood; or to the fields of honor on the isle of Elysion, where bliss and loved ones wait.

But he remembers. Lysicles has already been judged, in New Hell: the fearsome Erra and his Seven, peerless champions, have eaten his damned eyes, his tongue, and his heart and sent him here to Hades, half blind, half dumb and too weak to stand, with a hole where his heart should be.

He remembers more. For many days he languished, healing from his wounds. How long? He doesn't know. His eyes came back (slowly, so slowly) and he could see ever more clearly the shadows of Erebos in which he now dwelt. His tongue came back, itching and burning, hard to control as it grew anew, until he could drink better and eat; then mumble, then mutter, then speak. His heart came back, thumping and thrumming in his chest, though his pulse still bumped and blood rushed in his ears whenever he tried to stand.

So he bided there, time uncounted, between the pool of Lethe, where common souls drink to erase all memory, and the pool of Mnemosyne, where initiates of the Mysteries drink their memories back into their heads. Sad souls came to tend him, blank-faced and shrouded.

Then someone brought him water from the pool of Memory.

"Drink this, brave Athenian," she said. Her gaze spun him breathless when she met his eyes.

Should he know her? Did he know her? She held out a bowl.

He drank, though it was hard with his tongue yet a stump. She resembled Hecate, goddess of the crossroads and magic, but why would mystic-eyed Hecate, far-darting genius of the underworld, take notice of Lysicles among all these dead – only one more burnt-out wraith of a mortal?

Still, he thinks it is she.

"Thank you, Blessed One," he mumbles with his stump of a tongue, carefully humble before this spirit of the dead who stoops to tend him.

And having drunk, Lysicles recollects himself completely, all that he had been, all that he had done while alive: he had kept to his oaths; he had kept his soul clean and pure, as Homer advised, and never let his heart be defiled by the taint of evil and venality. Never. Before his eyes flashes all that had happened to him in life, and why: how he had been tried in Athens and executed for the treason of rashness while his commanding general, Chares, went free.

When he looked up, the spirit with the bowl was gone. He was alone, sitting among those souls who staggered where Homer said the dead would go, "down the dank moldering paths and past Ocean's streams, past the White Rock and the Sun's Western Gates and past the Land of Dreams…."

Fury flooded him, bringing him strength. His heart pounded harder and he got to his knees, then to his feet, and stood wavering there. Nevertheless he stood: naked and ravaged but upright. He was a soul in Hades, not a war casualty, not a corpse. He had a second chance to win salvation and be reunited with his beloveds in Elysion. Forever.

Erra and the Seven had audited his appeal and sent him here. Lysicles would never forget Erra, the god of pestilence and mayhem, appraising him. He would never forget Erra's personified weapon, pitiless warrior with that molten gaze, who carved out his eyes, his tongue, his heart, killing him yet again. Nor would he ever forget the guilty looks of his counsels, Hammurabi and Draco, when sentence was passed. Or Alexander of Macedon, holding Lysicles while he was being mutilated, or old Aristotle, averting his face; or the new-dead soldier, Lawrence, muttering a prayer in Arabic and calling on a god that would not, or could not, help a Greek general having his eyes put out by one of Erra's seven *Sibitti*, terrifying sons of heaven and earth.

All that was his past. From it, he would make his future. If he passed whatever tests lay before him, he might return to the arms of his beloved wife, his sons, his *eromenoi.*

But first Lysicles will find Chares, rapacious betrayer, and exact his due. And then he will find Alexander of Macedon, and cut out the eyes and tongue and heart of his enemy. And then he will find Hammurabi and Draco and discuss this pound of flesh he'd paid to the auditors from Above. His counsels had failed in their roles as Lysicles' advocates: the Babylonian had done him no good, no matter how much Akkadian and Sumerian claptrap he understood; Draco was little better, full of himself and the iron taste of logic run amok. If those two lawmakers had succeeded, Lysicles would be with his loved ones now, not staggering around Erebos, trying to see, trying to speak, trying to heal.

Hell is different for each soul, he well knows. Few escape eternal torment. But here, in the brightest part of Hades' dim and shadowy day, he can glimpse redemption: the isle of Elysion beckons, green and gleaming on the horizon, close enough that it seems to Lysicles he could swim for it, strike out across the mouth of the Styx, across Ocean … when he was a little stronger. Between him and Elysion and his loved ones remains only the repair of his soul's flesh, and eluding or convincing those who tend the dead here in Erebos.

But first, he is hungry for revenge. Wrath consumes him. Somewhere in Hell, Chares and the others who have wronged him are hiding. Somewhere here, Chares waits, with his unbridled lusts and his dishonest heart. Somewhere….

*

Erra and the Seven, peerless champions, have brought pestilence and mayhem to the Ten Courts of Hell in Diyu laying low all ten Yama Kings who rule Diyu's endless dark mazes, spreading incessant torture and confusion as the Chinese gods prescribe. They have brought an unquenchable conflagration to Jahannam, where Allah sends the unfaithful to suffer their due, boiling in water and roasting in flames. They have visited upon bleak Helheim a deadly cold, spreading faster than Norsemen can run, freezing souls in their tracks as they flee. In each of these realms, the torture of the damned follows the mandate from Above: they suffer, they die; they are resurrected, only to suffer more and die again and be resurrected again. Wails of misery rise up to the heavens. Erra and his Seven are made glad.

It is good to be Erra, bringing punishment to the deserving. He and his seven Sibitti, terrifying weapons, sons of heaven and earth, are justly pleased. Hell's mandate is made fierce and shining like the sun, wherever they bring the righteous wrath of the heavens to the unrighteous.

All this time, red-winged Kur, lord of Ki-gal, and his Kigali boy have guided them unerringly from one region of the netherworld to the next. Wherever they have gone, Almighty Kur has kept his promise: Hell's every door has opened unto them; no underworld has escaped their withering glances, their fire, their ice, their torrents, their lightning, their yawning chasms, their pestilential breath. And all this time, Kur's *eromenos,* Eshi, watches wide-eyed but never says a word, while his black Kigali skin blooms red with angry blotches and he holds tight to his mentor's long-nailed hand, his spiky tail lashing, wings unfurled.

Now the fear of heaven pervades the manifold settlements of hell, and loosens the bowels of those rulers of underworlds become too pleasant, and haunts the nights of the too-complacent damned. All in hell quake in their places and in their beds.

So when they have finished their audit in the city of Pandemonium, when no stone remains unturned, no smile upon any face, Erra and the fearsome Seven are ready to quit the chastised city and return to Ki-gal for the night, satisfied, their bellies full of the flesh of tortured souls.

Then a tremor not of Erra's making shakes the ground. Snow begins to fall from the fiery vault overhead. Clouds of white snow and yellow snow and black snow and brown snow obscure the light from Above.

Erra's Seven draw their swords and crane their necks, seeking out a target, shaking back their cowls. These are his personified weapons, unrivaled and eager: battle alone brings life to them; they are grinning.

Out of the blowing snow comes a cold that rivals any cold that might issue from the swords of his Seven, a cold that could freeze a doomed soul to ice. And out of that cold comes a howling to curdle blood.

Aloft, a winged shadow soars, then dives from the snowy sky, whirling and churning and beating the air. Now feathered wings tuck tight. Down hurtles a huge and monstrous creature, with a tail and fangs and breath of fire. It is flanked by others of its kind, descending on its right and on its left: a dozen more winged serpents, falling fast. All these land on the snow beside the greatest of their number, whose eyes are huge and fierier than the eyes of the second of the Seven.

The Seven surround Erra and Kur and his Kigali boy in a circle, protective and threatening, their teeth bared, their swords sparkling and sparking and slitting the air, promising doom to whoever comes close.

The Kigali boy whispers, "Almighty Kur, what are they? They are like us but not like us…." Kur says, "Hush, Eshi. Be you still." And the Kigali boy wraps his tail around Kur's strong left arm.

Then the greatest of the feather-winged serpents gnashes its fangs and closes eyes that burn like stars in the night. Its huge wings bate.

Within the circle of the seven terrifying weapons from heaven, Kigali wings bate as well.

Snow swirls round the thirteen winged serpents with their flaming breath. When the blizzard clears, one feather-winged man and twelve winged serpents confront them. The man's arms are crossed, his face like doom.

"It's a cold day in hell, Erra, and here I am. What do you think you're doing here? We've asked no help from such as you."

Behind this first man, the other serpents now change form, into naked and wide-winged men, godlike but rent, with bloody wounds and blisters on their skin.

"Who are you, to question me, who have come from Above with my Seven on a mission from the elder gods?" Erra asked, though he knew full well who faced him – and hoped to face him down – on this snowy day in hell, on the plain between Pandemonium and Arali, where Irkalla, Babylonian goddess of the dead, rules her underworld.

"I am Satan, and your audits have so terrified the damned that they destroyed New Hell's Hall of Injustice, where I made my home. Now what have you to say? What compensation am I due?"

"Compensation? None. This inconvenience is your due. Be thankful it's not worse. My audit finds you full of blame; as a lord of hell, you're sorely lacking. If you are Satan, and these your pets among the fallen angels, then get thee back, all of you abominations, before I loose my weapons. As for your home: in six days, six hours, and six minutes from the moment of its destruction, you made that building rise anew – or so we heard – entombing all the tortured souls lamenting their lost brethren there. So I say again: get thee back, Satan, before we add you and yours to those trapped within the foundations of that diabolic hall, to reign from there forever. And I can do it: I am Erra, and you know I will make good my word."

It worked. The abominations gave back one step, then two: all but Satan, who held his ground. He reached down and made a snowball with his hands, and cupped it, and straightened up again. Now was Satan beautiful, as beautiful as a man can be, almost angelic with his white-feathered wings. And the snowball between his palms was white and black and yellow and brown and did not melt.

Erra's Seven stepped back as well, while the swords in their hands made arabesques in the chilly air.

The Kigali boy sneezed.

Satan turned his blazing gaze on the two Kigali: "You mix in this, you natives from the tribe of hell, you sons of Ki-gal? Why?"

"It is my honor to serve the higher heavens," said Kur. "We guide the auditors whither they goeth, from one hell to the next. Not simply your realm, but all realms here are being visited by auditors from Above. This, Satanic Majesty, you well know. So take up your displeasure not with me and mine, but with these, and the gods who sent them here – and sent you here."

Satan cast his icy-crusted snowball then, hard and fast, toward the circle of the Seven, toward the Almighty Kur and his Kigali boy. But the second of Erra's Seven sliced upward with his arcing sword and split the snowball in half. Then blue-white lightning crawled over the halves before they could hit the ground, melting them.

Satan raised a perfect eyebrow and said: "Keep out of my realm, Erra. And you Seven: be warned. *I* am supreme here in hell. I have the most souls of all. During only a single century on earth, one-hundred sixty million souls who died in new-dead wars have come to me. I have power rivaling all of heaven: my souls *believe* in damnation. How many souls believe in salvation anymore?"

Erra puffed himself up, discarding his aspect of a man, and

nearly scraped the snowy vault with his conical crown. And he said, "Enough souls to fill heaven with joy and celebration from end to end, despised one, and all of them deplore you. Get you back to your realm, and stay there, lest we decide that you and your horde of outcasts deserve more personal attention." *Oh, do defy me, lord of the latter-day hells. Give me cause to eat your eyes and eat your forked tongue and eat your blackened heart. Your stench repels me....*

"So say you, Erra. We shall see whose word reigns supreme." But Satan did not make himself great to meet Erra on the field of spirit battle. Rather he shriveled back into his serpentine form and flapped his feathered wings wordlessly, taking flight. And all his fallen angels rose and followed him into the snowy clouds above.

The snow clouds disappeared. The cold retreated. The fiery vault flared bright, then dimmed. Distant howls split the air, receding. Erra resumed his manly form and looked around.

The eyes of Erra's weapons were streaming tears as the Seven scanned overhead for treachery from Satan's retreating band of devils. Almighty Kur held his Kigali youth tightly under one wing.

"Sheathe your swords, Sibitti," said Erra. His weapons obeyed his command. "Turn loose your eromenos, Almighty Kur. The danger now is past."

Kur did not release the Kigali boy forthwith, but said, "Erra, we are here to serve. But Eshi has had a long day and seen many wonders, your glory not least of those. Will you return to Ki-gal with us now, you and your brave Sibitti, and leave the remaining nether regions unchastened till the morrow?"

"We shall, of course, Almighty Kur – but only because your Kigali boy is tired."

Kur had given Erra a graceful exit, and Erra was pleased to take it. Otherwise, he and the Seven might have felt the need to labor in the underworlds all night long – to prove to Satan that Erra and his weapons from on high were not afraid of any fallen angels, no matter how high in the heavens they once dwelt.

*

"I need to know something, godly Erra. Who judges *you?"* Eshi's voice is bold and strong.

Kur almost shudders, wishing Eshi had not spoken, then chides himself: Eshi is here to learn. So Kur says nothing to forefend what must come next, but continues walking among the Seven with Eshi close beside him, lashing his spiky tail.

"My judge is God alone."

"But *which* god? God of *what?*" Eshi's black wings rustle; he rubs his arms with his hands as they march along, two by two, toward the crossroads at Erebos. In front is Erra, god of pestilence and mayhem, with the first of his Seven by his side; then Kur and Eshi; then the second of the Sibitti and the rest of Erra's champions, on the dusty road to yet another judgment.

"God of what? God of all gods. God the highest." Erra's voice rumbles up from deep in his chest. The first of the Seven, walking beside Erra, looks around at Kur and his Kigali boy, catches Kur's eyes, and shakes his head.

Kur must intercede. Eshi has seen so much, so fast, he is taut as a bowstring. His downy black skin is blotched with red, aprickle with new quills sprouting – more every day. This youth's blood is quickening too fast.

"Quiet, Eshi. Enough. We fear neither gods nor men. We assist godly Erra, but we do not pry into the affairs of the damned and their keepers."

"But Almighty Kur, I need to understand what we're doing here and why –"

Kur can still glimpse the shimmer of Eshi's innocence out of the corner of his eye, but he knows it is fading. And not just because the second of the Sibitti hunts red-tails with Eshi every evening in the glow of the mountain's restive peak and gives him warm carcasses to rend and tear with his sharp white teeth. "No, Eshi," Kur says very softly, "you don't need to understand the affairs of men and gods. Whatever Erra and his Seven decree is what will be." He reaches for Eshi and once again takes the boy under his strong left wing. He can feel Eshi's body trembling: the war of child against adult is raging inside him. At this time, Eshi should be meditating, hunting, gaining surety about who and what he is; finding his place in Ki-gal, taking up the life that Kur has made for him. Not wandering among dead souls struggling against their fates like lizards in traps.

"But great Kur, you have taught me to question. You have

taught me this is how Kigali learn. Now I must learn about Hades and about Erebos: we will soon be there. Will I see Lysicles the Athenian? Erra sent him there. Will we see him again? Will we?"

Now Kur understands what Eshi wants to know: the plight of this single soul, Lysicles, the first whom Eshi had seen judged, has touched his black Kigali boy. Eshi had watched the second of the Seven cut out the soldier's eyes and tongue and heart.

"We will see him, Eshi, if Erra allows. And we will see that he has new eyes, a new tongue, a new heart. When a red-tail molts and loses its old tail, a new tail grows to take its place. Erra, will it be so?" Kur asks. "Will Eshi see the Athenian soldier, Lysicles, in Erebos – and see how your judgment plays out?"

"If it pleases you, Almighty Kur, we will try to arrange it. For your boy's sake. But these souls in Erebos have free will. It may not be easy to find one damned soldier among so many. His sentence stands. What he does now is up to him. We will see if he can be found. You have asked for nothing else, in all this time."

"We thank you, godly Erra," Kur replies, wishing that he did not need this favor, but knowing that he does. Erra was right: for the boy's sake; to quiet the uneasy heart that Kur can feel thumping against Eshi's ribs.

Now the second of the Seven breaks formation and strides up beside Kur. "Great Kur, if there's something I can do, just ask me. A weapon is only useful when it is wielded," and falls back to his place again.

The second of the Sibitti knows exactly who he is, and what his role is, and what his limits are: he is a weapon in a war he understands. Kur wishes that the second of the Seven understood less well: there was another war here, for Eshi's heart and Eshi's soul, that might go on for years.

Eshi has witnessed things that no child of Ki-gal could understand, and some things that Kur barely understands: the hatred of these gods and men for one another – and themselves; the battles in their hearts and in their souls over who and what they are, and where their trust belongs. Reckless, wild and dangerous, consumed only with destroying one another, they trust no one: they expect the worst and the worst comes unto them, every time.

Kigali have more faith. When Nature speaks, the children of

Ki-gal listen, and learn. It must be that Nature does not speak to gods and men, or that they have grown deaf to Nature's voice.

Full of questions, full of doubts, Eshi hadn't slept all night. Consequently, Kur had not slept. And now they trek into the realm of Hades, gods and weapons and Kigali altogether, to render yet another day of judgment on this ancient road to Erebos.

Eshi leans his head against Kur's chest as they walk along and says, "Almighty Kur, the second of the Sibitti will help us. He has never lied to me. Together, we can find the Athenian. It will be as you said: we will see how Erra's judgment plays out. And then will you tell me, after we see?"

Kur brought the boy closer, and bent his head close: "Tell you what, Eshi?"

"If this Erra and his Sibitti are good. Or not. If the second of the Seven is good, or not. If they belong in Ki-gal. If we should be helping them. Or not."

Kur shouldn't have been surprised, but he was: it had been so long since he was young. Eshi's blood was talking, hot whispers in his young head that were the whispers of a leader, coming to himself. Kur had never been so relieved: Eshi's sharp, clear mind had seen through all, to the truth. And to the hard questions whose answers no one knew.

So he said very quietly, bending even lower so his lips were close to Eshi's ear, "Eshi, we have given our word. How gods and men treat one another is not ours to judge. Nor should it be. You see the ugliness of vengeance. You smell the stench of it when they punish one another. When trust is gone. When hatred reigns. This is not our way. This is their way. And they are welcome to it. They do not ask us to change. We do not ask them to change. We will do as we have promised, and help those sent here from Above to fulfill their mandate. Kigali always keep their word. Always."

On the road to the realm of Hades, with Eshi safe under his wing, Kur felt proud. This boy, this precious youth who would steer Ki-gal's course someday, was learning more than words could say. Eshi was learning how to be a true Kigali: how to hold firm; how to find the proper path and keep to it. As for the questions no one could answer, those would remain unanswered until the great mountain that succored their tribe was no more.

*

"Laelaps? Can it be you, hound of Zeus?" Lysicles looked at the brown dog in the woods of Erebos and the hound looked at him, and bayed. "Here, boy." The soldier squatted down. The dog trotted over to Lysicles and sniffed his extended palm. "So, Zeus didn't turn you to stone after all." This could be no other hound: there were no unmagical dogs in Hell. Zeus had given Laelaps, a dog who always caught his quarry, to a woman whose husband used the hound to hunt the Teumessian fox, who could never be caught. Their fates fought, and neither hound nor fox returned from that hunt. "Better here than nowhere, pup. Will you help me? Track my enemies? Find my loved ones?" The lop-eared hound dog reached out and pawed Lysicles' chest.

After so much ill fortune, perhaps the Fates were being kind. Lysicles thought he spied a woman's shape between the light-dappled trees; then it was gone. He rubbed his tender eyes and looked again: no woman, just ash trees and the wine-dark sea and, in the distance, Elysion. His love was there. His life was there. Eternity was there.

And he was here, on the far shore at Erebos, where the Styx and Oceanus met, hoping for strength to swim across. At the water's edge, a boatman waited. Lysicles couldn't chance it: that ferry took too many to dooms he knew too well. He had a second chance now, at everything he'd thought he'd lost: he wouldn't trust his future to any hands but his own. Win or lose, the result would be of his own making.

Carefully, slowly, Lysicles rubbed Laelaps behind his ears, and scratched those ears until the hound's tongue lolled. If it wasn't Zeus's Laelaps, it was certainly a dog who hadn't bitten out his throat yet (though it could) or torn at his hamstrings (though it could) or run off into the woods or the brackish water (though it could). And he was lonely.

Then he heard wailing, behind him and not so far off, and buried his face in the dog's loose-skinned neck. *Not again.* Not here, in Erebos. But his blood chilled and his gut twisted and he knew what lay behind those cries: the terrible auditor and his weapons of destruction. Nothing less could raise such lamentation from the throats of the forgetful dead and the wistful dead of Erebos.

Laelaps bayed and bayed and bayed again, singing in chorus with the keening souls.

Then Erra and the Seven came for him. Lysicles stood up straight, and Laelaps was so tall he could put his hand on the hound's big head as he faced his tormentors.

Monsters walked with Erra and his Seven: a great red monster, with its bloody wings high and its quills raised all along its tail; a smaller, black-winged monster with eyes aglow and sharp white teeth. Lysicles could feel his heart race, frightened of being ripped from his chest again. But he stood his ground. He was still that much of a soldier.

On they came, mighty and fearsome, straight for him. The seven sons of heaven and earth were masterfully deployed around the pitiless Erra; the two monsters strode behind Erra, among his terrifying Seven. Any general who'd ever seen heroes fight would have killed to command such as these. The big red monster's eyes glowed like the moon; the smaller monster lashed its spiky tail and pointed at him, then screeched.

Lysicles recalled the glowing eyes that had watched him from the shadowed gallery in the Hall of Injustice where he'd stood trial.

He was naked and suddenly that mattered. He was cold and he was weak. He leaned against Laelaps and the hound bayed as if the world would end. Or as if the hound knew what happened the last time Lysicles faced this god of pestilence and mayhem and his bloodthirsty Sibitti.

Then a woman emerged from the shadowy grove of ash trees, calling, "Laelaps, good hound. Laelaps, here." She was as strong and tall as an oak, and mystic-eyed. He remembered her at once. She had brought him the water of Memory to drink. She was Hecate, goddess of the crossroads; today she wore her rayed crown.

She stepped between Lysicles and Erra's party and the hound ran to her, tail wagging, and sat, whimpering softly, brown eyes fixed on Lysicles. "Erra," she said. "My hound has found your quarry. Be swift, now, with this soul of mine who suffers here. He could have sought my comfort, but he didn't. He broods here. He recollects all – who you are and what you did and what he did. I will not hold him, or hold you from him. Or hold him for you." At that, the goddess and the whimpering hound were gone in a clap of thunder.

Please, O Blessed Hecate, don't let them take me. But the prayer in his heart came too late: a memory stirred, of lithe Hecate in a fragrant bed of myrtle, of her magic spells in the dark of night and the smell of a goddess. But he had been too consumed with rage to accept her offered comfort.... Absurdly, he mourned the loss of the hound, the company of the dog, the soft tongue upon his palm: Hecate's hound had tracked him down for these avengers, nothing more. Were they here to take yet another pound of his flesh?

Terror overwhelmed Lysicles, worse than in any battle gone awry he'd ever fought. Had Erra and his Seven and his two monsters come to eat his eyes again, his tongue again, his heart again? To take away his sweet hope of Elysion? The terrible Erra and his monsters and his seven personified weapons stared at him bleak-eyed, like men choosing a bull for slaughter.

He couldn't let that happen. His pride fell from him, and his anger dropped away, leaving only his loneliness and his hope of redemption.

Lysicles turned on his heel and ran. With strength he didn't know he had, with a determination he had always had, he sprinted: away from Erra and his Seven, away from the red monster and the black. Toward the shore and into the briny water.

His lungs burned. His eyes stung as he splashed into the tide where the river met the sea. He no longer cared if he ever found Chares, foul betrayer; he no longer cared to tear Alexander the Macedonian limb from limb; he no longer cared about his bumbling counsels, who had led him to this fate.

He didn't even care that he fled, as he had never fled in life, desperately, in cowardly rout, as no general ever should flee. Up to his waist, he plunged deeper into the water and stroked for Elysion with every bit of strength he possessed.

He swam. And swam on, deeper and deeper, leaving the shore of Erebos behind. He swam toward the gleaming light in the wine-dark sea, making for Elysion. He swam for salvation. He swam with his ravaged heart pounding and his blurry eyes stinging and with brackish water burning his tongue. It was a long swim. And if he could not make it, then at least his wife and his sons and his eromenoi would know that when he died again, he died trying to get to them.

*

"So, young Kigali, what do you think of your brave Athenian general now?" Erra asked as they watched the horizon until the soul of Lysicles disappeared from view.

"He *is* brave, godly Erra," the son of Ki-gal said. "He is full of love for his family. He wants to go home. Will he make it to the farther shore – see his wife again, his children, his friends?"

Erra saw the second of the Seven smile as all the Sibitti sheathed their swords. "What do you think, son of Ki-gal? Has he overcome his fury, his lust for vengeance, his rashness? He goes to his fate. As do we all."

The Kigali boy did not reply, only looked away toward far Elysion.

Making good on his word, Erra and his retinue traveled the length and breadth of Erebos all that day with the witch Hecate by his side and her hound beside her, spreading fear and misery among the innocent and guilty alike. But seldom in Erebos did they find injustice meted out unfairly; for Erebos does not lie in the depths of Hades' realm where venal souls abide, but only at the crossroads on its outskirts.

When the day was done, Hecate offered them a night in Erebos, a feast by the pool of Memory, and all pleasures from the realm of Hades. Erra declined: "We shall come back another time to visit Asphodel and its blood-drinking heroes, but not tomorrow. Now Duty calls my name."

So they took their leave under a roiling sky, but not to return to Ki-gal. Erra's heart was restless. Satan's threat still rankled: *We shall see whose word reigns supreme.*

"We will fly now, Sibitti, over Gehenna and to Lost Angeles." Erra would show Satan whose word reigned in the latter-day hells. "You, Kigali, take hold of the ropes that the second of my Seven will give you. Once we are in the air, fold your wings, for we'll spread out a hundred leagues and fly faster than Kigali can."

"If you do not hold fast to my ropes, you will be left behind," warned the second of Erra's Seven, pulling loops of bright blue lightning from the palms of his hands. "So take care, sons of Ki-gal, how you go. I will be with thee, watching over thee."

Almighty Kur and young Eshi grasped the glowing ropes and held on tight, their wings high and beating, and took flight with Erra and his Seven.

They all rose high, in concert, aloft on Erra's wind of retribution, and spread out through the air. Wherever their shadows fell, across a hundred leagues of Gehenna's putrid ground, blight bloomed before them and behind and on either side, striking crops and slaves and fruit and vine and city and town. Where the shadows of Erra and the Seven and the sons of Ki-gal fell over Christians and Israelites and Canaanites fighting on foot and with chariotry, the soil turned to quicksand and sucked the combatants down – all but their hell-spawned steeds, who ran away, neighing and snorting fire, to find new battles to join.

Over the deepest recesses of Sheol they flew, striking blind the souls below, bringing to the prideful and the learned dead a darkness that would not lift; setting fire to their books as they copied them.

Both the righteous and unrighteous flesh in Sheol, long removed from the light of god, now suffer Erra's havoc. Shadows of the passing auditors touch all the pedagogues of Sheol with forgetfulness: words, once spoken, are immediately forgot. Those proclaiming innocence and those bemoaning guilt are equally chastened.

From on high comes a just reward to those who'd lorded holiness and rectitude over lesser men, and filled peasants with shame, and castigated the ignorant, and made the common people pay to fund their studies. Politicians and poets and philosophers and physicians are struck deaf with the passing of Erra and his Seven and the Kigali: none can hear a word, not a single well-turned phrase nor clever argument; nor can they read or write or count or know any of mankind's hard-won wisdom ever again. These will always remember that once they had the keys of knowledge in their hands. But no more. The dead in Sheol's dank depths are brought low, every damned soul in its cities and its towns, in its streets and its assemblies, sunk into stupidity and hopelessness.

Onward flies the wrath from Above, into the latter-day hells of mankind's dark heart. On the wings of Erra and his Seven it comes, with the Kigali witnesses towed on ropes of flashing lightning that slit the sky.

Black shadows, beating wings, and torment fit for each benighted soul: they set afire every plain; they ignite every mountaintop for thousands of leagues, before and behind. Storm blows behind the wildfires, putting out the flames with raging torrents, flooding Purgatory and washing all artifice away. The earth cracks open here and there.

There is no forgiveness. There is no absolution for criminals who sin knowingly and cunningly and think they can merely ask for heavenly forbearance: this is hell in its horrible glory and all sinners here, no matter how adroit, will pay this day for every crime against the heavens.

Erra's wings bore him straight and strong, with his vengeful weapons beside him, until they reached Lost Angeles, swathed in its pall of vainglorious excess that turned the air stinking and yellow.

There they alighted on black-paved ground, between buildings high and long and gleaming with glass and sinners festooned with every sort of bauble: painted and perfumed and covered in silk and furs: men and women, clutching at each other lewdly, entwining and kissing and sucking on each other's bodies, copulating in the middle of the street. Erra waved his own mighty hand and the paint on each face puckered into running sores; silk turned wormy; furs came alive and sank toothy jaws into their wearers, tearing out throats and hearts before scampering up the blazing sky to heaven. Men ejaculated scorpions and spiders who ate their screaming partners from the inside out. Women selling sex sold torture now, and ground the members of their partners in gnashing teeth amid their nether parts.

Down Hellywood Boulevard did Erra and Seven drive their judgment: pointing here and there and everywhere; bringing first fire and ice and lightning, then pestilence and tempest and quake and disease. Erra raged on, with his terrifying weapons, carving up the very belly of this Satanic beast, Lost Angeles.

Whimpering sinners stumbled and ran. The Seven cut down soul after soul, broiled them, boiled them, shattered them where they fled, and opened the ground to receive the detritus. Meanwhile, behind them on either side, buildings tottered and toppled, showering glass and mortar and stone upon the fleeing hordes.

Then Erra heard sounds he'd never heard before: deep roaring; booming in the sky so that the vault above seemed to shake; deafening thunder from the middle of the air: the sound of Satan's forces, come to meet him in battle at last.

The seventh and the second of the Seven looked up and raised their arms. Huge metal darts swooped at them: some with souls inside, some not. Erra's two Sibitti spat lightning and incandescent plumes, and caught the flying machines and piloted contraptions hurtling down and dragged them from the air. These crashed amid the tenements and high-rising buildings with an awful banging noise.

Then the third of the seven looks at Erra and smiles his icy smile. Erra nods, and freezing cold quenches the fires where the metal birds and darts have crashed, and all the mechanisms of modern man's destruction fall away to glittering powder.

Satan, where art thou? Come face me.

But Satan does not come. Instead, a deep growl wells up: the tramp of marching men; the thrum of great wheels turning. Now come the tanks and the soldiers of the new dead, a vast army marching down the wide roads of Lost Angeles, crushing trees and people underfoot.

"Enough," Erra says aloud.

This one word frees the rest of his Seven, weapons beyond mortal comprehension: the fifth of the Seven spins himself into a whirlwind of bladed retribution, and goes among Satan's troops and death machines. Beside Erra, the first of the Seven opens chasms to the deepest underworld in the path of Satan's warriors and their tanks. The front ranks tumble into the abyss, victims of the unstoppable momentum of their own forces coming on behind them.

The fourth of the Seven blows his hurricane winds and deflects every projectile, every missile, every weapon aimed their way.

The sixth brings his torrents, to clean the streets; the third freezes armies in their tracks. Now the fourth calls forth a plague upon all the soldiers and all Hellywood's onlookers, voyeurs of death who hide among the rubble: those who could have run, but didn't, will learn their lessons too this day.

The torrents clean the streets of corpses; the chasms suck down all the wreckage and accouterments of war, and the city is silent: ravaged, ruined. No building stands. Sobbing and moaning and groaning fill the air with deserved songs.

Still, Satan has not come. So be it. With his word made good, Erra gathers his Seven to him, and the lord of Ki-gal and his boy.

"Make your ropes once more," Erra commands the second of his Seven. "We go to Ki-gal now, to rest from our labors. You fought well, all you weapons. And you Kigali, you have seen what sons of Ki-gal need to see: how the powers from on high treat those who resist the will of highest heaven."

Neither Kur nor his boy said a word: the Kigali youth had his wings wrapped tight round him like a cloak. His mentor stared around, speechless, at heaven's wrath.

The second shook out his ropes of blue lightning and the Kigali raised their wings high.

Then up into the air they went, Erra and his Seven and the two Kigali, with the Almighty Kur and Eshi holding tight to the ropes of lightning all the while.

*

Kur had never been happier to be back in Ki-gal, but Eshi was still troubled, lashing his tail, wings half raised. Kur wanted to take Eshi up the mountainside, let the boy soak his quill-pricked skin in the healing sulphur pools. Breathe the pungent steam, and let the mountain do its work while the feast-boards for the evening meal were being laid.

But the second of the Seven came for Eshi, as he always did, to take the boy hunting the red-tailed lizards who swooped and played in the green-gold clouds rolling down the mountain at the end of day.

The red-tails squawked overhead, fat and juicy, beating their wings, consumed with their lizardly games.

But tonight Eshi wouldn't go hunting with the beautiful son of heaven and earth: "I don't want to hunt now, Second. I need you to tell me some things and I want Kur to hear what you say." Eshi rubbed the back of one hand with the other, where his new quills itched.

"The three of us will sit together then, Eshi, and you can ask me what you want to know, if the Almighty Kur will indulge us." Of the seven Sibitti, this one was the kindest – or the smartest.

"Great Kur, can we? Do you have time? Will you sit with us?"

"Not here, Eshi," Kur said. "Come with me." Kur could see Erra and the other Sibitti, who had not yet repaired to their cavern, lingering close by.

Kur led his eromenos and the second of the Sibitti up and up the mountain's skirt, Eshi by his side with wings raised.

The three of them climbed high on the slope to sit by the steamy sulphur pools overlooking Ki-gal, magnificent in the gloaming. Kur said, "Now, Eshi, ask what you will. And you, second among the Sibitti, tell my boy what truth you know."

"What happens to you Seven when you are not terrifying mankind? Where do you go when you are not with Erra? Or are you always bringing pestilence and mayhem somewhere?"

The Sibitti cocked his head at Kur, then turned his beautiful face to Eshi. "They put us in a cupboard, prince of Ki-gal. Weapons must have targets – a purpose. When there are no targets, we have no life. There we wait, enclosed, away from the world, the sea, the sky. I hate being shut up. A Sibitti wants first to fight a worthy enemy and then to sleep in the open among honest creatures in a beautiful place such as Ki-gal." He waved his hand at the agora below, at the feast-boards, at the vault above. The tribe was gathering, soaring overhead, circling, riding the updrafts and the downdrafts, winging down to join the feast. "Ki-gal, of everywhere I have ever been, is the most magnificent. Free of all the foolishness of men. In harmony with nature. You are very blessed, you Kigali."

Kur was unmoved. This Sibitti still romanced his boy.

"What happens to Erra then?" Eshi pressed.

"He goes back to his godly seat in Emeslam and rules there until he is needed to bring his pestilence and mayhem once more. You have seen what we do, Eshi. We hide nothing. If Ki-gal ever were threatened, we Sibitti would gladly fight by your sides, if Erra would allow."

"Would you fight against us, if Erra said? If he commanded you?"

Kur's wings went up in surprise and he forced them down. Eshi's wings went higher and stayed high.

"Yes," said the second, son of heaven and earth. "If Erra so commanded. We would. We would have no choice."

"Then you are no friends to the Kigali. You are no friend to me."

"Eshi…" Kur touched Eshi's pinion. "He is honest with you, as friends are honest with one another." *Tread lightly, Eshi, with this peerless warrior.*

"I am only a weapon, Eshi. Not a man. Not a dead soul. Not a Kigali. I can be no more than what I am. But I am your friend. You can call me and I will aid you if the gods allow. Someday you will understand. You Kigali, you can be whatever you wish. I admire you."

Eshi said nothing. Wary, defiant, suspicious and hurt, he stared at the second of the Sibitti.

The second of the Seven rose to his feet. "I must go down. Erra and my brothers are looking this way. They will ask me what was said. I must tell them, Almighty Kur, what they want to know." This weapon was discomfited. His molten eyes held clouds like the sulphur billowing down from the mountain peak. Shrouded.

"I know," Kur told him.

"You have raised a great one, Almighty Kur. You can be proud."

"I am still raising him." Kur took Eshi under his left wing.

They watched in silence as the second of the Sibitti made his way down the slope to his fellows. All eight put their heads together and then looked upslope, where Kur sat with Eshi in the embers of the day.

"Almighty Kur?"

"Yes, Eshi."

"They are not good, these Sibitti."

"No, they are not. But they are not evil either. They are firm in their purpose. As are we."

"Do you trust him, this weapon?"

"I trust him to be a weapon. As I trust you to be full of questions. Now come with me into the sulphur pool: the waters will soothe your skin. And you can soothe my skin. It has been a long day for the 'prince' of Ki-gal."

"Prince? If I am a prince, then you are my king, great Kur, forever and ever."

Eshi threw himself upon Kur then, in a rush of legs and wings and arms, and grabbed Kur about the neck, and buried his head in Kur's breast.

They sat that way until Eshi's stiff body relaxed. Kur stroked Eshi's downy spine and his shivers eased. Eshi started to hum.

Then Kur got to his feet with Eshi in his arms and waded into the warmth of the sulphur pool. And it seemed to him then, holding young Eshi in his arms, that nothing could ever be more perfect than this night in Ki-gal under the smoldering vault above, with the tribe fluttering down to join the feast below.

CPSIA information can be obtained at www.ICGtesting.com
Printed in the USA
LVOW041848261012

304631LV00001B/195/P